Read

1.50

famille

LORD OF RAVENSLEY

LORD OF RAVENSLEY

CONSTANCE HEAVEN

COWARD, McCANN & GEOGHEGAN, INC.

NEW YORK

*Acknowledgement is due to Barrie & Jenkins for
permission to quote from* TRAVELLING HOME *by
Frances Cornford published by The Cresset Press
in 1948.*

This Cambridge country plain beneath the sky
Where I was born, and grew, and hoped to die . . .

Over the soft savannahs of the corn
Like ships the hot white butterflies are borne,
While clouds pass slowly on the flower-blue dome
Like spirits in a vast and peaceful home.

Over the Dyke I watch their shadows flow
As the Icenian watched them long ago.

                              Frances Cornford

Part One

OLIVER

1829

She took me to her elfin grot
   And there she wept, and sigh'd full sore,
And there I shut her wild wild eyes
   With kisses four.

And there she lulled me asleep
   And there I dream'd—Ah! woe betide!
The latest dream I ever dream'd
   On the cold hill's side.

John Keats

I

'Never take anything for granted. Fate or the Devil has a way of kicking you up the backside when you least expect it,' my grandfather used to say in his coarse way, not that it ever treated him so cavalierly and I never realized how right he was until one night in the summer of 1829.

On that night after weeks of torturing uncertainty I knew without any shadow of doubt that I had lost everything, the house I loved above all others, the rich black earth where my ancestors had tilled and sowed for generations, all my inheritance at one fell swoop. There was only one thing left to me and I clung to it with something like desperation. I looked down at Alyne lying in my arms.

'It won't make any difference to us,' I whispered urgently. 'It means waiting a little but I swear I'll not be beaten by any damnable trick of Fate or the Devil.'

She lay quiet for a moment and then deliberately moved away from me, sitting upright against the pillows.

'That's where you're wrong,' she said quite calmly. 'It makes all the difference in the world. I am not going to marry you, Oliver.'

I smiled because I didn't believe her. I thought she was jesting as she did often, teasing me, provoking a fight for the sheer delicious joy of making up afterwards. A faint shimmer of moonlight through the casement silvered the lovely curve of her breast. I stretched out a hand to her and she pushed me away.

'Don't,' she said. 'I mean what I say.'

'But you can't!' I exclaimed. 'If it had not been for father, we would have been married months ago. Now he is gone, what is to stop us?'

'Everything,' she said. She turned her head and I saw her eyes very large and clear and with the strange blankness that I knew so well when she chose to withdraw herself from me. 'He was wiser than he knew.'

'What are you talking about? It has always been you and me, always, from the beginning. We planned it . . .'

'You did. Not I.'

'Are you denying that you love me?'

'Oh love!' She made a gesture that seemed to include all the hours of love and rapture we had enjoyed together. 'It was Lord Aylsham of Ravensley whom I was going to marry . . .'

'My God, it's not possible!' Anger welled up in me. I gripped her by the arm, shaking her. 'It isn't true. You can't mean it.'

'It is quite true and I mean every word.'

She did not move or struggle. She lay quite passive in my trembling hands and for an instant I was possessed by violent rage and knew why men murder the thing they love and then it passed, leaving me deadly cold. I released her.

'Why?' I said. 'In Christ's name, why?'

She slipped from the bed pulling on her night robe. 'You've never understood, have you, Oliver? Why should you? You have fed on luxury since you were born, but I have had nothing, no name, no parents . . . what am I? Who am I? The waif, the changeling, the brat born out of the Fens . . .'

'You had love,' I said, stung to indignation. 'You were one of us . . .'

'Not really. Not love as other children know it,' she said with extreme bitterness. 'Charity for the most part and given grudgingly.'

'Not from my father, nor from me . . .'

'From everyone else, even your sister. Cherry is the Honourable Miss Aylsham and does not let me forget it, young as she is. I know what everyone says about me, but it didn't matter because one day I was going to be mistress of Ravensley and then it was they who would look fools, but now . . .'

'And what will you do now?' The words forced themselves out of me.

'I don't know yet, but there'll be a way,' and looking at her I knew she spoke the truth. The power she had, the magic that had enthralled me, she could use on other men and the knowledge was more than I could endure. In my pain I cried out to her.

'Have you never loved me?'

'Oh yes,' she said, 'often and often. We can have that still if you wish.'

'Never,' I said loudly, 'never, never! That's not all I have wanted and you know it.'

'Don't shout,' she said quietly. 'Do you want everyone in the household to hear you?'

'I don't care if they do. You're mine, you will always be mine . . .'

'No, Oliver, I belong to no one. You'll think better of it in the morning.'

'I won't. I shall never think better of it.' I was off the bed then and would have stopped her, but she had gone through the door and shut it in my face and to pursue her through the corridors of the sleeping house would have been unthinkable. I was left to my wretchedness and my despair.

I crossed to the window pushing the casement wide. Outside it was a warm June night and a faint light bathed the gardens with a ghostly pallor. Beyond the box hedges as far as the eye could reach stretched the Fens. Guests who came to the house said disparagingly that East Anglia was fit only to gallop across, racing at Newmarket or hunting the fox over field and heath. What did they know of the vastness, the sense of freedom, the myriad variations of cloud and sky, the mysteries of the hidden waterways and their reedy banks alive with flowers and wild fowl? I loved it passionately, every aspect of it, from the still breathless heat of June to the biting gusts and raw damp cold of November and it would be agony to leave it, but with Alyne I could have made a new life . . . The pain of rejection struck at me again and I brought my fist down bruisingly on the window ledge. I would not believe it. She was taunting me deliberately for some secret reason of her own and when I saw her again, she would come into my arms laughing at my folly. It is so easy to deceive yourself when the truth is too painful to be endured.

I fell in love with Alyne when I was fourteen years old which was strange for we had grown up as brother and sister, but after that everything between us became different. It was the beginning of happiness and frustration, of ecstasy and torment, though then I knew nothing of such things, only that it was as if my eyes were opened and I saw her for the first time and knew a wild joy.

What was there about her, what magic did she possess? I still don't understand completely but I remember the moment it happened exactly. It was my first holiday at home after I was sent to school. I had been out since dawn fishing with Jake in the waters of Greatheart Fen as we often did in the summer. I had moored the boat securely while Jake hurried off to his work in the fields and I was coming back along the bank ravenous with hunger. I had been lucky that morning and there were some fine fat bream in the basket slung over my shoulder. It was a lovely day, the song of larks high up in the sky overhead and the light shimmering over the illimitable expanse of the Fens, the meadow bright as a tapestry with scabious and milk parsley and the yellow of loosestrife. I came upon Alyne unexpectedly. She was sitting close to the water. She had woven a wreath of marsh flowers and her hair was so pale that the sun turned it into a fall of silver hanging straight to the waist. Her green cotton dress was wet and stained, her feet bare and muddy, and she was crooning softly to herself. There was an enchantment about her that I cannot explain. I stood still, my heart beating, a catch in my throat, too young to know what was happening to me but caught up in a wonder quite alien to my usual sturdy common sense. Years later I came across a poem that exactly described that moment:

> I met a lady in the meads,
>> Full beautiful—a fairy's child,
> Her hair was long, her foot was light,
>> And her eyes were wild . . .

and I realized its truth instantly. I would have done well to heed the warning in the rest of the poem but of course I didn't and anyway that was far in the future.

I was a boy still. I had no words to express the feelings that disturbed me. All I could think of saying was 'You shouldn't be sitting there. It's very damp and you'll take cold.'

She turned to look at me. Her eyes were bright hazel like the eyes of a bird, like the hawk Jake had captured one day and tried uselessly to tame.

'I like it here,' she said and turned back to the silver stream of water where the tall reeds sighed and rustled in the breeze. 'That's where I came from, that's my real home. I shall go back there one day.'

'Don't be silly. Ravensley is your home,' I said uncomfortably. Even at ten years old Alyne could be disconcertingly unlike other children. She could be a wonderfully imaginative playmate, ready with ingenious ideas to improve any game I could devise but sometimes she would simply shake her head, going off alone to her own secret places to which I was never admitted. Once when she was still very young, she was gone for a night and a day causing my father great anxiety. Everyone was out searching and it was one of the Fenmen who brought her back. She had unhitched my boat and gone floating down the river. Goodness knows where she might have ended up if he had not seen her when he was setting his eel traps.

'An' when I arst 'er where she thought she was goin',' he said, 'she looked at me queer-like and just shook 'er 'ead as if she were mazed. She'm a strange one, my lord, if you don't mind me sayin' so.' He gave her a sideways look and I saw him cross his fingers as protection against the evil one. They are very superstitious in our part of Cambridgeshire and still have a strong belief in the Devil and all his powers.

I said, 'Come on, Alyne, we'd better go back to breakfast. Nurse will be looking for you.'

She made a face as she pulled on her shoes and bundled together her wet stockings. 'She doesn't like me.'

'Yes, she does,' I said quickly. 'It's only that she worries over Cherry.'

My little sister's real name was Charity, but we always called her Cherry. She was eight and inclined to be delicate. Nurse, who adored her, was forever fussing over her coughs and sniffles.

We raced each other back to the house arriving laughing and out of breath. My father had just had his horse brought round. He was a big man with red-gold hair like mine. He grinned at me.

'You're back late, boy. Breakfast has been cleared an hour ago. Did you have any luck?'

'Five each for Jake and me. Fat ones.'

'Good. You're improving.' He bent to pinch Alyne's cheek. 'How's my girl this morning?' She stood quite still. She never liked to be touched. He gave her an awkward little push. 'You'd better be off to the schoolroom before Hattie catches you.'

Miss Harriet Bennet was the girls' governess whom I had long outgrown. Alyne turned and went into the house without a word. Father swung himself into the saddle. He looked down at me frowning.

'You'd better get yourself breakfast in the nursery, Oliver, or you'll go hungry,' he said and waved as he trotted down the drive. I took my basket of fish to Cook in the kitchen and then ran up the stairs.

Nurse still presided over the nursery and schoolroom and was loudly scolding Alyne about her stained dress and muddy feet as I came in. She stopped abruptly when she saw me.

'Now sit down for goodness' sake,' she said crossly, giving her a push, 'and you go and wash that nasty fishy smell off your hands, Master Oliver. Running about the fields at this hour of the morning and keeping me waiting, to say nothing of Miss Harriet. You're old enough to know better and I've got other things to do. I'm sure I don't know what your dear mother would have said if she were still alive.'

Alyne and I exchanged a secret smile and let her go on grumbling. Cherry raised a milky face and waved her porridge spoon to us. I felt quite extraordinarily happy.

I love every stick and stone of Ravensley and to me it has always been beautiful though I suppose by any real standards it is a shocking muddle of all kinds of architectural styles, torn down, added to and rebuilt ever since the Aylshams came into the property in the days of the first Plantagenet. Hundreds of years ago the Black Monks lived there and there is an old legend that when St Dunstan visited them, he was so shocked to see how riotously they lived with fine food and drink and the company of loose women that he turned them into eels and their descendants swim about in the Fens to this day. I used to stare fascinated at the squirming monsters in the eel traps and once shocked Isaac Starling by asking him which was the Abbot and if the pretty slim ones were the whores.

Nurse knew dozens of tales like that. She was Fen born and bred, the sister of Isaac Starling and Jake's Aunt Hannah. Starlings had lived on the marshes as long or longer than the Aylshams. She used to frighten the life out of me when I was very small, telling me about Black Shuck, the demon dog that haunts the Fens. Many a terrified traveller, she would say warningly, has heard him padding behind them, felt his icy breath on their neck and dare not turn for to see the red eyes and slavering jaws was to die within the year. I used to creep from my cot and stare out of the window at night. The screech of a marauding cat was the fearful howl of Black Shuck and I would shiver at the tiny points of light that sometimes bobbed up and down in the far distance, the Jacky Lanterns that led hapless wanderers astray until they were drowned in the bogs. According to her the great earthwork that ran north of Ravensley had been built by the Devil in the days when the land was inhabited by giants which I believed all the more firmly because I once dug up a huge thighbone. But father only laughed and said it was built by the Saxons against the Danes, the thighbone belonged to an ox and the Jacky Lanterns were marsh gases escaping from the miasma of the bogs. I preferred the legends.

The Aylshams are said to have Viking blood. The Danes came sailing up the creeks from the sea in their snake-headed long boats and burned the abbey to the ground. The blackened shell of the old tower still stands as proof of it. But one of them settled and married a local girl, a dark beauty descended from the Iceni whose Queen Boadicea had poisoned herself rather than fall into Roman hands. Thorkil, son of the Raven, driven insane with jealousy of his black-haired witch of a wife, had given the house its new name or so it was said. There is certainly a raven with cruel predatory beak carved into one of the old stone pillars. It was a daughter of the house who married an early Aylsham and brought us Ravensley as her dowry. There still survive two distinct strains in the family. We are tall and fair or slender and dark. You can see it in the picture gallery and oddly enough, it is always the dark ones who have behaved outrageously but prospered and the fair ones who have made fools of themselves. There was a Justin who was killed in a duel by a cuckolded husband, an Oliver who was drowned mysteriously in the Fens, an Edward who shot himself after gambling away practically all he possessed and my father . . . but more of that later.

My grandfather was huge and white-haired when I knew him but he had been a handsome golden-haired giant once. He ruled his tenants with a rod of iron. 'The Old Tiger' they called him behind his back but they respected him. He was ruthless, shrewd and cunning. He could be just if it suited his purpose and his women were said to be legion. There was many a red-gold head scattered through Ravensley and its neighbourhood though whether they were his bastards is anyone's guess. There must have been more than one Viking who turned from rape and murder and settled down to enjoy his plunder and grow his crops on the rich black earth.

My grandfather had two sons, Justin, and Robert who was my father. I could only just remember my Uncle Justin. I was rising four when he went away. I was too young to know rightly what happened and neither my father nor my mother would talk about it afterwards. There were rumours among the servants, half understood whispers when they didn't realize I was listening. There was a terrible quarrel with my grandfather and a man died but whether by accident or murder I was never sure. There was a lot of coming and going and a feeling of tension that even affected me in the nursery. Whatever it was, it was hushed up as happens so often in families. Then suddenly one day I was playing in the hall and I hid behind the chest because I could hear my grandfather's voice very loud and angry. I saw him fling open the door of the library. He looked enormous with his mane of white hair. He had hold of my uncle by the shoulder and he threw him through the front door so that he stumbled and only recovered himself halfway down the steps.

'Get out of my house and stay out,' he roared, 'and take your inheritance with you. Not another penny shall you get from me!' and he flung a leather purse after him. It split open and some of the gold coins spilled out and rolled down to the gravel. My uncle turned. He was thin and very dark and his face blazed with rage. I thought that he looked capable of anything, even murder. He stood there glaring and shaking, then he stooped to pick up the fallen money and I felt sure he would hurl it back but he didn't and in a queer way I was disappointed. My grandfather snorted contemptuously and went back into the library slamming the door after him.

It was then that I saw my mother. She came running down the great staircase and paused at the bottom.

'Justin,' she whispered, 'Justin . . .' She went slowly to the open door holding out her hand. 'You'll write . . . you'll let us know where you go . . . ?'

I was very young but my memory is clear, the scene etched itself into my childish mind though it had no meaning for me.

My uncle stood quite still, his eyes on my mother for what seemed a long time, then he said quietly, 'No, I won't write. Why should I? Go back to Robert. He's got what he always wanted now. Tell him to make the best of it,' and he went away down the steps and out of our lives.

My mother fell on her knees, her face in her hands and I thought she was weeping. I was terrified. It had never occurred to me that grown-up people could cry. I stayed there afraid to move until she had dragged herself to her feet and gone back up the stairs. Afterwards I found one of the golden guineas lodged in a crack under the stone urn and for some reason never showed it to anyone. I have it still.

There was a letter that came about a year later from India; not from my uncle but from some acquaintance of the family. My grandfather was failing then, but I believe it gave him pleasure. Then after he was dead, there came another from an official of the East India Company saying that my uncle had done very well for himself for a time. He had gone up country to open a new trading station, had contracted one of the fevers rife in that steamingly hot country and had died.

It meant nothing to me then. I had not liked my uncle very much. He had never had any time for a tiresome small nephew but sometimes when I looked at his portrait painted when he was seventeen and stared up at the lean arrogant face with the thin lips twisted into a faint sneer and the blue eyes that are the badge of all the Aylshams, it would bring my childish memories to life again. It was some years before I realized that my father was now Lord Aylsham of Ravensley and that I was his heir. One day when he died it would all be mine. It was then that my love of it grew, the house, the farms, the tenants, the great empty spaces of the Fens which my father had begun to drain, the black earth where the hemp, the wheat and the colseed ripened and where the cattle and sheep were pastured.

But my uncle was not dead. I knew that now. He was very much alive. For twenty years it seemed he had lived and prospered, yet made no attempt to contact the family who had cast him out until the news of his brother's death had somehow penetrated to the remote part of India where he lived. He had realized then that the title and everything that went with it was his and had been since my grandfather's death and he was coming back to claim it.

But why now? After so many years? He had every right, I knew that, but it did not make it any less painful for me.

My mind was in turmoil. It was useless to try and sleep. I belted my dressing gown around me, took up the candle and went down the stairs to the library. I took out the letter from Mr Gwilliam, the family solicitor, and read it again though I knew its contents by heart. After weeks of uncertainty the grim fact stared me in the face.

'There is no doubt at all, my dear Oliver, that the claimant who wrote to us from Calcutta is your uncle, Justin Aylsham. He has already arrived in England. I saw him some days ago and he has advised us that he will be at Ravensley on June 18th at latest . . .'

And that was tomorrow . . . tomorrow I would hand over to him all I possessed and walk out of the house a beggar, or almost a beggar. I had nothing but a small legacy that had come to me from my grandmother, the old farmhouse of Thatchers and the acres belonging to it which had been part of her dowry when she had married my grandfather, leased now to one of our tenant farmers.

I paced up and down the room obsessed by the problems that had chased through my mind all these past weeks. What manner of man was my uncle? I had only that distant childish memory. Had he a wife? Children? He had not seen fit to inform either Mr Gwilliam or myself and the question tantalized me. What would happen to Cherry? Would he look after his niece? And Alyne,

Alyne whom I had planned to marry in the autumn and make mistress of Ravensley . . . it was all over, all my hopes, all my dreams, vanished at one stroke. Why had she rejected me so utterly? I could not fathom her mind. I felt as if I had loved a stranger whose beautiful body entranced me and whose spirit eluded me. It was true what she had said. She had come to us out of the Fens.

I suppose it must have been about a year after my uncle left. Childish memories are apt to be vague about dates, but I remember it was October and very raw and cold with a thick white mist over the mere when Alyne came into our lives like Moses in the bulrushes which was one of the Bible stories my mother had read to me. Isaac Starling found the baby lying in an osier basket hidden amongst the sedge and reeds. She was wrapped in an old blanket and not knowing what to do for the best, he brought her up to the house. Huge eyes looked up at me beneath a fluff of hair pale as cream. I put out a cautious finger and the star-shaped hand closed around it tugging at it.

I said, 'Is she my new sister, Mamma?'

It was only a few months since Nurse Starling had told me I might have a baby sister soon and I had been very excited. But she had come and gone within a day and I had not even been allowed to see her so now it seemed quite natural that this baby lying so quietly in the stained blanket was another brought by the stork which I saw occasionally standing motionless on one leg in the shallows.

'She could be, Oliver, she could be,' said my mother slowly.

My father was frowning. 'Some poor betrayed girl has abandoned the child. I will have enquiries made.'

My mother knelt down and gently touched the baby's cheek, 'She is very young. She will need care. Shall we keep her with us, Robert?'

My father hesitated before he nodded. 'Very well. Let Nurse take the child for the time being. Afterwards we shall see.'

They must have settled it between them and it took some weeks. Then a decision was taken. One Sunday the baby was christened Alyne and came to join me in the nursery. Hannah Starling disliked her from the very start.

'You oughtn't to do it, my lady,' she said to my mother on the day we came back from the church. 'You don't know where she comes from. She could be a gypsy's child, born of some bad-living slut from God knows where. The kitchen is the place for her. It's not right her growing up with Master Oliver.'

'Nonsense,' said my mother putting the baby in the cot that used to be mine. 'What does it matter where she came from or who her parents were? She is herself and Oliver is sturdy enough to take care of himself, aren't you?' and she tousled my mop of fair hair.

I adored my mother and was proud to be thought grown up and responsible. I took my elder brother status very seriously. Nurse went on muttering to herself what she dared not say aloud.

'Such a heathenish name, not fit for a Christian,' she said darkly. 'Isaac ought to have known better than to bring her to the house. A tinker's brat more than likely or even worse. A changeling, that's what she is, spawn of the devil . . .'

'What do you mean, Mrs Starling?' whispered Annie, the under maid fearfully.

'You know well enough what I mean, Annie Pearce. This is witch country, always has been, and there have been some I could tell you of even in my time.' She looked round at me and I pretended to be absorbed in my brickbuilding. 'There was Abbie Preston up by Gibbet's Close. When she died, they buried her in the middle of the road as far from Christian folk as they could and they do say you can still feel the heat of her body burning in hellfire when you pass over the spot.'

' 'Tis true, 'tis always dry just there,' said Annie shivering pleasurably. 'And do you think little Alyne was born of one of those then, Mrs Starling?'

Nurse sat up primly and tossed her head. 'Who am I to say one thing or the other but I know what I know. Did you ever see a baby so quiet and them big eyes of hers? 'Tisn't natural Lord Aylsham adopting her, making her one of the family like he has. 'Tisn't decent.' They put their heads together, nodding and whispering so that I heard nothing more.

I thought Alyne looked more like the child of an angel in my picture book but then when she was two years old, something happened that revived all Nurse's worst forebodings. My sister Cherry was born and my mother nearly died. She was never really the same after that. She was often sick and sometimes I would go running into her room and find her weeping. But she loved me, I always knew that, and to me she was someone very dear and precious. Cherry was three years old when the doctor recommended a warmer climate so my father took her to Italy. They were there for nearly two years and she never came back.

It was my first grief made even worse because my father never spoke of her death. I took it badly and for a long time I turned my back on Cherry. It threw me more and more with Alyne, particularly as Nurse was always so much harder on her than she was on my sister and me. But children get over things in their own way and when I was eleven the Fentons came to live at Copthorne. We had always been very isolated at Ravensley except for the tenants and the villagers. Our nearest neighbours were Sir Peter Berkeley and his sickly son over at Barkham. But Copthorne was only a mile away. The vegetable garden ran alongside one of our paddocks and my pony once broke through and nibbled all the tops of the young lettuces. Miss Jessamine Cavendish chased him out herself with an umbrella. The sharp-tongued old lady (she was not above forty but at that time she seemed old to us) frightened the life out of Jake and me when we raided her orchard for plums but when her sister came to live at Copthorne and brought her two children with her, everything changed.

My father was a shy man and not given much to entertaining since my mother died but he took an instant liking to Mrs Fenton. Her husband was a Colonel in the Dragoons and away with the army fighting Napoleon. I had an idea that they were not well off. At any rate my father discovered that Susan Fenton had a great love of horses and was a brilliant rider so he offered her the choice of his stable.

The first time the children took tea with us was a disaster. Alyne and I thought Clarissa horribly conceited because she never stopped boasting about her hero of a father and Harry, who was only seven, stuffed himself with Cook's rich cakes and was led away by Nurse to be sick. But after that we became inseparable, Jake and me with Clarissa and Alyne while Harry and Cherry, the little ones, tagged behind.

Clarissa already rode well and was as fond of horses as her mother so it formed quite a bond between us. It was the one thing that Alyne and I didn't share. Strangely enough she was afraid of them and would never ride if she could help it. My old white pony who was the gentlest creature alive once bit her and Nurse said nastily, 'Some animals have more sense than humans!' Alyne would be jealous and sulk when Clarissa and I rode together and I used to laugh at her about it.

Those summers we spent together were a golden time when we were entirely happy and quite oblivious of what was happening outside our little world. And now they were gone and Alyne too, Alyne who had been the centre around which I had built all my plans for the future.

There were stirrings in the house. The servants were up already and would be wondering what I was doing in the library so early in the morning. I crossed to the window and pulled back the curtains. Dawn had begun to break and above the Fens the racing clouds were already tinged with pink and gold.

I had an overpowering need to escape, to get away from the fevers and frets of the night if only for a few hours. I would saddle Rowan and ride out over Greatheart. I had done it before when in trouble. That vast untouched wilderness that had seen so many rebels come and go had a way of bringing calm, of reducing problems to their right proportion. I replaced Mr Gwilliam's letter in the desk and went upstairs to dress.

2

I met Jake on my way to the stables. He was bringing a basket of vegetables up to the kitchens and he stopped me on the path. He was as tall as I, his hair dark brown, his face very tanned from being out in all weathers.

'When does your uncle come?' he asked.

'This afternoon.'

'It is going to mean changes, a great many changes. Your father was a good man, a just man.'

'So is my uncle for all I know,' I said shortly.

'There are some who think different. I mind what my father used to say and others too when old Lord Aylsham sent him away.'

'That was twenty years ago.'

'Aye, but they've long memories hereabouts and these are hard times. They've been looking to you, Oliver, now that your father is gone.'

'There's nothing I can do about it.' I knew all that he implied and I shied away from the responsibility he would have heaped on my shoulders. I said abruptly, 'I am thinking of leaving here as soon as I have handed everything over to him. It will be best.'

He shot me a quick glance and then shrugged his shoulders. 'Mebbe you're right. I feel like that sometimes. If it weren't for Mam and the little 'uns I'd go with you. To get away, see a bit o' the world, find out how other folk like us live, it 'ud be a grand thing but no one can do as he wants, not in this damned old life.'

I knew only too well what he meant, but not even to Jake could I explain about Alyne. He had never really liked her for one thing and in any case he had been a rebel at heart ever since they hanged his father. He had never forgotten that terrible day and neither had I. He had forced himself to watch and because I was his friend I stood beside him though sickness rose up in my throat and it was all I could do to swallow it down.

I thought about Isaac Starling as I went on down to the river through the dew-soaked grass. That morning I had a feeling that I was saying goodbye to all my childhood. Jake's father was one of the kindest men I have ever known. Starlings have worked for Aylshams as far back as anyone can remember and though Isaac had little book learning of any kind, he had the wisdom of the countryman who lives close to the earth and has a warm innate sympathy with all living creatures human or otherwise. Jake has it too but in a different way. He wants passionately to change things and has always had a desire to learn, a hunger for knowledge far greater than mine. When he was still very young, he worked as gardener's boy to Miss Cavendish and she taught him to read and write. After that there was no holding him. He used to borrow my books and somehow slog through them asking me to explain things that not even my tutor had taught me and how he did it surrounded by five brothers and sisters in their tiny cottage was a miracle. I always remember the first time I went there because it came as a startling revelation of a way of life of which I had never dreamed in my sheltered luxurious existence at Ravensley.

It was after my mother died that my father began to teach me to shoot and gave me a gun. It had been made specially small and light by the famous Joseph Manton of London. When I showed it to Jake he touched it with reverence.

'Would you let me fire it, just once?' he said looking up at me with longing eyes.

'I might,' I replied grandly.

In point of fact I had been strictly forbidden to touch it without my father's permission but I couldn't resist the temptation to show off. One morning very early I stole into the gunroom and took it from the rack, meeting Jake outside and going off to the marshes with him. Why we didn't murder one another I can't imagine since we were both of us raw beginners and took it in turns to bang away at everything. At last more by luck than judgement I shot a snipe. We sent Belle, my spaniel bitch, after it, but she was no more a gun dog than I was a marksman, and in trying to retrieve it myself, I fell into one of the treacherous bogs that are such a hazard on the Fens. If it had not been for Jake I should have sunk without trace and it was a terrifying experience but he managed to haul me out by clinging with one hand to the thick sedge until slowly inch by inch he dragged me from the sucking mud and even saved the gun. I was covered with stinking green slime from head to foot and must have looked a sorry sight shivering in the icy wind that seemed to come straight from the wintry sea. My teeth were chattering with cold and fright so Jake, not knowing what to do, took me to his home.

The Starlings lived in a stone-walled cottage with one room downstairs and two tiny attics above. The walls were brown with smoke and the floor was beaten earth. It seemed unbearably crowded to me with the big wooden table and rough heavy furniture carpentered by Isaac himself. A tousled mongrel growled threateningly at Belle and a ginger cat watched with baleful yellow eyes from a basket of kittens on the rag rug. There was a thick heavy smell of food, animals and people.

Mrs Starling stripped the filthy clothes off me, clucking in dismay, and then washed me down with warm water in front of the smouldering peat fire before the solemn-eyed gaze of Jake's little brothers and sisters down to the baby in the wooden cradle. She rubbed me with a coarse towel until I glowed. Afterwards, warm and snug in Jake's best shirt and breeches, I ate hot bread and milk and a slice of fat bacon cut from the flitch hanging from the ceiling, toasted at the fire and put between two slices of thick rye bread and never enjoyed anything more. Jake came in, clean and rosy-cheeked from a dousing under the pump in the yard and was given a mug of boiling hot onion water flavoured with nutmeg as an infallible remedy against catching cold. I took a sip of it, grimacing and burning my tongue, as we watched Isaac clean lovingly every part of the precious gun.

'It's a rare fine piece and worth a mint o' money, Master Oliver,' he said, admiring the walnut barrel inlaid with silver. 'A man and his family could live a year or more on quarter the price o' that,' and for the first time it struck me how unfair it was that something given to a child almost as a plaything could mean a matter of life to so many others. But there was little envy or spite in Isaac Starling, only a feeling for the sufferings of others, a passionate desire to see justice done. He took me back to Ravensley, smuggling me into the house so that except for Nurse's scolding I escaped punishment; and this was the man they were to hang as a brutal murderer. Was it any wonder that it lit a spark of rebellion in Jake's heart that never died?

At the stables Rowan pushed her nose against me affectionately and I put my arm round her neck, my face pressed against her soft cheek. She had been bred at Ravensley and I was proud of her. I had thought once that I would like to enter her in one of the races at Newmarket or Spalding where I could ride her myself. My father had never been a racing man and he smiled at my ambition.

'So long as you don't make a habit of it, my boy,' he said warningly. 'Aylshams have been haunted by two vices, gambling and women,' and I had laughed and swore that neither would ever bedevil me. What fools we are when we are young, so overconfident, so recklessly sure of ourselves.

When she was saddled, I took the path through the woods to the river. My father had broadened and deepened it and sometimes I came here to swim. The early morning mist had vanished. The sky was like pearl and the air scented with meadowsweet. The wide stretch of water and fen gave me a feeling of liberation. Then I saw her. Alyne must have come down before me. She was barefoot, standing among the reeds and yellow loosestrife. The light breeze flattened the thin cambric of her shift against the slender body. She was Ondine, she was Aphrodite born out of the foam of the sea, and I caught my breath because that was how I had seen her one morning last summer. It was the day after I had quarrelled bitterly with my father when I told him I wanted to marry Alyne. He had laughed incredulously at first and then when I persisted, he grew angry.

'Marry Alyne? The idea is preposterous, boy. Why you've grown up together. She is like your own sister.'

'What difference does that make? I love her and she loves me.'

'Rubbish. This is some ridiculous boy and girl affair.'

'I'm not a boy. I'm nearly twenty-four.'

'Then you should know better. I brought her up because I promised your mother but I never intended to marry her to my son. It's out of the question. I will not hear of it. You can put the idea out of your mind, Oliver, once and for all,' and he brought his hand flat down on the desk with an angry gesture quite unlike my gentle father who so rarely lost his temper.

I had said nothing to Alyne that night but when I went out early the next morning, she was there down by the river. It had taken me by surprise. No other girl I knew would have ever done such a thing but then she had always been different from others, it was part of her fascination, part of her magic. I had stood there, watching the slender white body slip into the cool green water before I threw off my clothes and plunged in after her. She gave a small shriek as I came up behind her and would have escaped me. Then we were laughing and splashing one another like children. We had come out of the water together. She ran for the towel she had left on the bank and I caught her in my arms. She stumbled and we fell on to the mossy grass turf. She turned her face away when I would have kissed her.

'No, Oliver, you must let me go. Someone might see us.'

'What do I care? I love you.'

She twisted under me and I saw the flash in the wide hazel eyes. 'Your father does not wish us to marry, does he, Oliver. I knew last night. I think I've always known.'

'He will. Give him time and he will grow used to it.'

I kissed her open mouth in a wild flurry of passion that would not be denied. I had not intended it or planned it but it seemed the most natural thing in the world that we should come together. Her body melted into mine and it was pain and rapture and glory. We had loved one another since but never with quite the same estasy. Maybe we should not have yielded to our passion, but I never felt any sense of shame and neither did she. I loved her with all my heart and the night my father died when I was overwhelmed with grief for him, she came to me putting her arms around me, her mouth on mine, gentle yet demanding, because now nothing could destroy our happiness.

I stood there remembering . . . remembering that last night she had gone away from me, cool as water, denying our love, our promises to one another as if they had never been because I could not make her mistress of Ravensley, I could not give her riches and fine clothes, and the taste of her rejection was bitter in my mouth.

I was tempted to go to her, seize her in my arms, throw her down on the bank, make her realize once and for all that I was not to be trifled with. Then she had vanished, diving into the river, swimming effortlessly, and I knew that violence would achieve nothing. In that mood she would escape me with that strange quality that dragged at my senses and yet held me in its spell. There would be another time. I would not let her go from me so easily.

I galloped Rowan across Greatheart till both of us were sweating and it was long past noon when I returned, riding more easily, some of the fever purged from my blood, ready to face what lay before me.

My uncle arrived at about four o'clock in the mellow sunshine of that June afternoon. I heard the carriage come up the drive but something stubborn inside me prevented my going to the porch to greet him. I waited until Annie Pearce, risen now to the status of housekeeper, opened the door of the library.

'Lord Aylsham is here,' she said stumbling nervously over the title. Then she was thrust aside and my uncle stood there.

'Thank you, Annie, that will do,' I said quietly.

She closed the door behind her and for an instant, seeing him facing me, tall and thin with the same arrogant tilt to his head, I was a small boy again crouched behind the chest in the hall and shivering with fright as on that morning so long ago. Then he took a step forward and I saw how much he had changed. There were lines on the lean face, sallow from the years of tropical sun, and the dark hair was turning grey though he could not have been more than fifty.

He said with a faint smile, 'So this is Oliver. The last time I saw you, you were a baby still wetting your diapers.'

There was a touch of mockery and I resented it. 'Not quite, Uncle, I was four years old after all. Did you have a good journey? How are you after all these years?' I held out my hand and he took it, his grasp cool and firm.

'Has it given you a shock to know I'm still in the land of the living?'

'We have had time to recover from it,' I said dryly. 'Will you take something? Tea . . . a glass of wine?'

'Later, later.' His eyes roved around the walls lined with books. 'The old place hasn't altered much. I remember this room. This was where your grandfather flogged me into learning my letters.

You've not made many changes but then Robert was always conservative. Are you like him?'

'In some ways, I suppose, not all. There has scarcely been enough time for changes,' I began stiffly.

'No, of course not,' but he was not really listening to me. He had crossed to the hearth looking up at the portrait of my mother, painted when she was still very young in a white ball gown with a few crimson roses held in her hands. 'That lawyer of yours told me that Rosamund was dead. When was it?'

'A long time ago now. Five years after my sister was born.'

'I remember that she was pregnant when I went away.'

'The baby died at birth. Cherry was born two years later . . . and then there is Alyne.'

He turned round quickly. 'Alyne? Who the devil is that?'

'Didn't Mr Gwilliam mention her? She was an orphan. My father adopted her.'

'Adopted, eh?' Then his face broke into a grin. 'One of Robert's little adventures come home to roost. Your mother won't have liked that.'

'No,' I said with some heat. 'No, you're quite wrong. That was never my father's way.'

'All right, all right. No need to grow so hot about a jest. Alyne . . .' his eyes narrowed, 'an unusual name.'

'I think it was my father's choice.'

'I see.'

I couldn't read the expression on his face but suddenly a number of things clicked into place, my mother's tears when he left, my father's silence, whispers among the servants, looks and hints that had meant nothing to the small boy I was then. The words came blurting out before I could stop them.

'Were you in love with my mother?'

'What an extraordinary question!'

'Were you? Is that why grandfather was so angry?'

'One of the reasons perhaps. Your mother was very beautiful.' He smiled maddeningly and let himself drop into the armchair. 'That's old history now.'

What was old history? The fact that he and my mother had been lovers? Not my beloved mother. I would not believe it. He was deliberately taunting me and anger surged up in me.

He waved his hand airily. 'Don't stand there glowering at me. Sit down, boy, tell me about yourself.'

'There is nothing to tell. Mr Gwilliam will have informed you about the estate. All the records are here. You can see them when you wish.'

He was sprawled at his ease in the leather chair. 'I see you are like Robert after all. He was always an excellent book-keeper.'

His cool manner as if it was he bestowing a favour galled me unbearably, but I held myself back. 'I have done my best, but these are difficult times for owners of land.'

'So I gather,' he replied indifferently. 'There were long faces in London. Anyone would think the guillotine was round the next corner. By the way there was a fellow outside who came to take the horses and looked daggers at me. Who is he?'

'That would be Jake . . . Jake Starling.'

'Starling, Starling?' he repeated thoughtfully. 'I remember an Isaac Starling, damned radical he was too. Your grandfather once clouted him right across this room for some piece of insolence and Robert took his part.'

'Isaac Starling was one of the best men we ever had,' I said warmly. 'Father had a high opinion of him.'

'Did he indeed? What happened to him?'

'He was hanged in the riots of 1816,' I said reluctantly.

'That's one trouble-maker the less,' but for some reason I couldn't fathom, I thought he looked relieved. He glanced up at me. 'And this fellow Jake is one of the same breed, I have no doubt, more than ready to stick a knife into me. I know the type, never satisfied, always wanting more than they have. In India I slept with my pistol under my pillow.'

'That will not be necessary here.'

'I hope not.' He leaned forward, his fingers drumming on the arms of the chair. 'Tell me, Oliver, I'm curious. How did your father die? Robert was a year or so younger than I after all and he'd had an easy enough life, God knows. Gwilliam hinted at something and then shut up like a clam when I questioned him.'

'The doctor called it congestion of the lungs.'

'But what caused the congestion? That's the point, isn't it?' he said shrewdly.

'It was one night last December. He was riding home across the

Fens from a meeting he had attended in Ely but he never arrived. We thought he had stayed the night in the town but in the morning we found his horse in the stableyard, trembling and splashed with mud and slush. We went out in search of him.'

'He couldn't have been drunk,' remarked my uncle dryly, 'that was never Robert's custom if I remember rightly.'

'When we found him, it was already midday. He was lying half in and half out of the bog water and still largely unconscious from a blow on the head.'

'Had he been thrown?'

'I don't know. He could have been.'

'The village numskulls went around saying Black Shuck was after him, I suppose.'

'Some of them . . .'

'And what do you think?'

I hesitated. I had discussed this with Jake a hundred times without finding an answer. Men had been set upon and robbed before now, but my father had been loved. The only time I ever remembered encountering a violent hostility had been when Isaac was hanged and the boy who had been responsible for that had been safely in Botany Bay these ten years. I said slowly, 'He never fully recovered consciousness and he could remember little of what had happened to him. Nothing had been stolen and he was carrying quite a considerable amount of money on him.'

'There is always someone who bears a grudge against those better off than themselves,' said my uncle grimly, getting to his feet, 'and Robert was ever foolhardy. I shall take it as a warning and go armed when I ride alone.'

'You must do as you wish. It was not my father's habit. Would you like to meet the girls now? Or will you go to your room first? We sup at seven.'

'That's soon enough,' he said. 'There's plenty we shall have to decide.' He turned on his way to the door. 'Tell that serving woman of yours to bring me some coffee, hot and black. I suppose they can manage that in the kitchen. By the way, where have you put me?'

'Grandfather's room has been prepared.'

He smiled sardonically. 'Damned ironic that. Enough to make

the old man turn in his grave. You must be wishing me in there with him, young Oliver. Come on, take that sullen look off your face, boy. That's the way the world goes, down one minute, up the next. I survived and I daresay you will.'

When he had gone, I poured myself a glass of brandy. I felt I needed it and I sipped it slowly trying to sort out my impressions. There was something elusive about him. I had a strong feeling that the casual offhand indifferent manner was a mask and the man behind it was quite different from what he seemed. I was standing with the glass still in my hand when Annie poked her head round the door.

'May I speak to you, Mr Oliver?'

'Yes, of course. Come in, Annie, what is it?'

'You didn't ought to be drinkin' that, not at this time o' the day,' she said disapprovingly, stepping inside the door and closing it carefully behind her.

'Nonsense, Annie. I'm not a child now, you know.'

She pursed her lips. 'Your uncle has brought a servant with him.'

'Well, what's remarkable about that?'

'He's black, Mr Oliver!'

'Black?' I repeated, amused at the outrage in her voice.

'Well, dark brown anyways . . . and a heathen.'

'Now how do you know that?'

'He wears a rag tied round his head and says his name is Ram something or other. Who else but a heathen would have a name like that and what am I going to do with him in my kitchen?'

'Treat him just the same as if he were white,' I said. 'He's an Indian, that rag round his head is called a turban and he's probably just as good a Christian as you are.'

She gave me a scornful look. 'I don't know what things are coming to. Lizzie is scared out of her wits already and as for the others . . . I wish he'd stayed in his own nasty country and Mr Justin too,' she said darkly, 'coming out of his grave like that and upsetting us all,' and she went off before I could say anything more.

Just then my uncle's Indian servant seemed the least of my worries.

Cherry was first in the drawing room when I came down to supper. She looked very pretty with pink ribbons in her curly dark hair and threaded through her white muslin gown. She came running up to me, putting her arm through mine.

'Oh Oliver, have you seen him already? I only caught a glimpse from the window as he got out of the carriage. Isn't it dreadful having a stranger here in the place of dear Papa?'

'You'll grow used to it.'

'I won't. I shall hate him, I know I shall. Darling Oliver, when you go away, take me with you.'

'How do you know I'm going away?'

'Jake told me.'

'He had no right,' I said annoyed. 'I told him in confidence. Nothing is settled yet.'

'Jake tells me everything.'

'Now listen to me, Puss, I've told you before. You're not to run off to Jake at every tiff and turn.'

'Why not? We have always been friends.'

'That was when you were a child. You're nearly seventeen now, a grown-up young lady.'

'Oh don't be stuffy, Oliver. Why must you go away? Why can't things go on just as they have always done even if Uncle Justin is here?'

'Because they can't,' I said shortly. 'Now don't fret, Cherry. Everything is going to be all right. Where is Alyne?'

'Still dressing. She said it was very important that she should make a good impression. I don't see why. He is not her uncle. Oliver, she says you are not to be married in September after all. Why?'

'There are reasons and for heaven's sake don't say anything about that now,' I said hurriedly, 'I think I hear him coming.'

Against my will I had to admit that my uncle had an air of distinction. Without being exactly handsome he carried himself well and his black evening coat was elegantly cut. There was no touch of the provincial about him and my clothes made by the tailor in Cambridge seemed suddenly ill-fitting and countrified.

He paused in the doorway smiling. 'Is this my niece or is it the other one?'

'I am Cherry,' said my sister shyly.

He took her hand and drew her to him, kissing her cheek. 'I'm delighted to meet you, my dear. You will be able to play elder sister to your cousin. Jethro will be coming from India soon.'

'Jethro!' I exclaimed. 'We had not expected . . .'

'That I had a son? Didn't they tell you? Jethro is ten. Sorry to put your nose out of joint, Oliver.'

'Will your wife be coming with him?'

'I have no wife.'

He had taken us by surprise and if I had needed any other incentive to make me leave, it was here now facing me in the unknown boy who would take my place. Perhaps always at the back of my mind there had lurked a hope that I would still be my uncle's heir and now that had gone with the rest. I was just about to ask when the child would be arriving when a slight sound made us all turn. Alyne stood just inside the door.

She said, 'I am to tell you that supper is ready.'

She had always known instinctively how to make an appearance and she looked so ravishing in the simple sea-green muslin that my heart thudded quickly and then stilled chokingly because all that beauty was no longer for me.

'Well,' said my uncle with open admiration, 'so this is my other niece.'

'I am Alyne, Lord Aylsham,' she said coolly. 'I hope you are well.'

'All the better for seeing you, my dear.' Gallantly he took her hand and kissed her fingers, then looked from her to Cherry. 'The fair and the dark, the two sides of the coin of beauty. I am indeed fortunate. Come, shall we go to supper?'

He took them, one on each arm, going before me into the dining room and leaving me to follow as best I could.

Hattie was waiting for us at the supper table. Miss Bennet was a mousy little woman growing old but she was no fool and she was well bred. When her headstrong charges outgrew her, my father had asked her to stay on as companion and chaperon to the two motherless girls.

My uncle talked brilliantly while we ate. He fascinated us with descriptions of the maharajahs whose palaces he had visited on business, the silks and jewels and perfumes, the gardens scented with exotic flowers, the cheetahs used for hunting, gold masks on their cat faces until they were released to go after their prey swift as lightning, the tigers he had shot from the backs of elephants, the temples where strange and frightening Gods were worshipped. How much was fact and how much fiction I had no idea, but I saw Cherry's eyes grow round with wonder, Alyne listened avidly and even Miss Bennet was enthralled.

His Indian servant, slim and dark, whose name I discovered was Ram Lall, stood behind his chair. It was difficult to tell from the smooth-skinned impassive brown face, but I reckoned him to be not much younger than my uncle. The black eyes were watchful and I wondered how he would get on with our slow stubborn Fen people who hated strangers as much as they detested change. I had an uneasy suspicion that to some of them he would appear in the guise of a familiar, a dark spirit at my uncle's bidding. Well, I reminded myself, that would no longer be my concern.

'We must entertain a little when I am settled in,' remarked my uncle casually, folding his napkin. 'How are we off for neighbours, Oliver?'

'We are rather isolated out here at Ravensley. There is Sir Peter Berkeley and his son over at Barkham . . .'

'Hugh is always sick,' interrupted Cherry, 'and he's afraid to dance because it brings on his asthma.'

'We shall have to remedy that, won't we?' said my uncle smiling at her. 'Young ladies are still looking for husbands, I presume?'

'I'm not,' said Cherry defiantly, 'not if they're like Hugh Berkeley.'

'He is a very pleasant young man and very attentive to you. You shouldn't speak of him like that, my dear,' said Hattie reprovingly.

'Oh you always defend him because he brings you sweetmeats,' said Cherry irrepressibly. 'So there you are, Uncle, you needn't worry about me and Alyne is engaged to Oliver . . .' then she clapped her hand over her mouth and gave me a quick crestfallen look.

'Is that so?' remarked my uncle.

'No, of course it isn't,' said Alyne keeping her eyes on her plate. 'It was a childish affair that meant nothing.'

'What do you say, Oliver?'

Traitor, traitor to our love, cried my heart. Aloud I said coldly,

'It is Alyne's decision,' and had an idea that my uncle had shrewdly summed up the situation and found it amusing. But he said no more and Hattie rose with a rustle of her stiff black bombazine skirts.

'Tea is served in the drawing room, Lord Aylsham,' she said quietly. 'Come along, girls,' and they followed her out of the dining room leaving us to our wine.

My uncle dismissed Ram Lall with a wave of his hand and bent forward to pick up the decanter of port. He filled his glass and looked across at me questioningly. I shook my head.

'Perhaps you're right. I'm a brandy man myself. Robert was always sober as a judge.' He made it sound like a reproach but I said nothing and he leaned back in his chair, savouring the wine before he went on. 'And what about you, Oliver? What the devil am I going to do about you?'

'You need not concern yourself with me. As soon as it is convenient I shall go away.'

'Indeed.' He raised his eyebrows. 'I hope you don't feel I am driving you out.'

'That has nothing to do with it.'

He took out a cigar case and lit the long black cheroot from the candles on the table. He looked down at the glowing tip smiling to himself. 'Crossed in love, eh?'

'No,' I said angrily, 'nothing of the sort. You don't want to believe everything Cherry says. She is still little more than a child.'

'I see.' He raised his eyes, studying my face. 'Does it rile you so much to watch me in your father's place?'

'Is that important? I prefer to go.'

'Very well. Have you any money?'

'Enough.'

'Brave boast! My experience is that there never is enough. Well, it will certainly make things easier. I shan't have the neighbourhood making comparisons between the gallant young heir and the black sheep who has come back out of nowhere to dispossess him.'

The irony was not lost on me. I said, 'You can jest about it if you wish.'

'I'm not jesting, believe me, I know what will be said, but

enough of that. There is, however, one further point. I gather from Gwilliam that a certain part of the estate still belongs to you.'

'Yes. A small farm of a hundred acres. It is leased to one of our tenants, to Will Burton in fact.'

'Hardly large enough to show much profit, my dear boy. Supposing I buy it from you.'

For a moment I was tempted. I could take the money and go away, abroad perhaps, start a new life somewhere else and then I knew it was impossible. Maybe it was foolish but I wanted to keep a stake here in the Fens. I did not want to cut myself loose entirely.

I said, 'No. I would prefer not to sell.'

He shrugged his shoulders. 'As you please. I think you may be sorry.'

'That's my affair.' He was smiling to himself as he idly tapped the ash from his cigar and I was suddenly curious. I leaned forward. 'Tell me, Uncle, why did you come back?'

'Ah why? An interesting question.'

'If you were doing well in India, why didn't you stay there? You could still have claimed the title and the estate and we could have sent you the rents as they came in.'

'Leaving you still little king at Ravensley. That's what you would have liked, isn't it? Hasn't it ever occurred to you that I too have a feeling for this place? That I *wanted* to come back. It was my home once. I'm an Aylsham too, remember.' He ground out the cigar with a violent gesture. 'I had been thrown out, disinherited, cast off like a beggar with only a few guineas in my pocket. Those first few years were hell, unspeakable hell, something pampered youngsters like you can't even imagine.'

There was a suppressed savagery in his voice that startled me for a moment, then he laughed, a harsh bitter sound and went on in his usual sardonic way. 'I used to dream of it, ridiculous, isn't it? Dream of coming back and forcing the old man to apologize. As if the old tiger ever would! But now he's dead and Robert is dead and I am here, very much alive. Ravensley is mine and I'm going to make the best of it. Nothing and no one is going to stop me. As for you, Oliver, you are free to stay or go.'

For an instant there was a thread to sympathy between us but then I thought of Alyne. 'I shall go,' I said.

'As you wish.' He got up, pushing back his chair. 'We'd better move to the drawing room or that sour-faced spinster will think we're drinking ourselves under the table. By the way what can be done about the cook? Damned tasteless food she dishes up. Do you think she'd allow Ram to teach her how to make a curry?'

'I doubt it. They don't like novelties here.'

'Is that so? Then they will have to learn, won't they?'

It was not a pleasant evening. Cherry was shy, Hattie worked assiduously at her tapestry frame and my uncle and I were stiff with one another. Once Alyne went to the harpsichord. In the glow of the candles, her pale hair was like an aureole of light round the small shapely head. I wanted her so agonizingly that it was like a physical pain. Then I saw my uncle. He lay back in his chair and in his eyes as he watched her there was the same avid look I had seen in other men and it chilled me.

When she rose from the instrument, he smiled and thanked her, then glanced around at us.

'Speaking for myself it has been an exhausting day. I shall say goodnight. Perhaps tomorrow, Oliver, before you turn your back on us, you would spare me a little of your time,' he said dryly.

'If you wish.'

When he had gone I tried to catch Alyne's eye but she avoided me.

'I'm tired too,' she said. 'I think I shall go up. Are you coming, Cherry?'

'In a minute.'

The bedroom candlesticks were on the hall table. I picked one up and handed it to Alyne. Our fingers touched and for an instant our eyes clung together but in hers there was no promise, no warmth. Then she took it from me and went quickly up the stairs.

Cherry said, 'I'm sorry I said what I did. It slipped out somehow.'

'It doesn't matter.'

'Are you very unhappy about it?'

'Don't ask so many questions, Puss.'

'I love you.' She reached up to kiss me and I gave her a hug. 'He's nicer than I thought. I might even get to like him in time,' she murmured into my neck.

'Good. Now go to bed, Cherry.'

'You're not going away yet?'

'Very soon.'

'I wish you weren't.'

'Go on, Pussie.' I gave her a little push. 'Goodnight.'

'Goodnight.'

I watched her run up the stairs and felt a pang of guilt because I had thought so little of her when I planned to leave. She was so young. I hoped my uncle would be kind to her.

I went back into the drawing room and poured myself some brandy. I paced up and down waiting until the house had fallen silent. Then I extinguished the candles and went quietly up the stairs and along the corridor. The evening coming after the long frustrating day had been too much. I could not rest. I had to talk to her now while my spirit chafed and my heart was hot with anger. I looked quickly round me before I lifted the latch.

The door was locked. I don't know how long I stood there fighting a crazy impulse to hammer on it, break it down, anything rather than accept tamely what she had done to me. If it had been possible I would have gone out of the house that night, left the usurper to flaunt himself in the place that was mine, but I couldn't. A sense of responsibility nagged at me. There was Jake, there were others, helpless people who had depended on my father and now looked to me.

Damn her, I said to myself, damn her for her faithlessness!

> She found me roots of relish sweet,
> And honey wild and manna-dew,
> And sure in language strange she said
> 'I love thee true'

That poor wretch of a poet had coughed his life away in Rome so they said but by God he knew . . . he knew too well how women could make you suffer.

3

I sensed a queer hostility towards my uncle even on that first day when I rode around the estate with him. Nothing was actually said and my uncle's manner was often genial enough but there were silences and sullen looks particularly among the older men. It had begun at the house with Annie Pearce and Hannah Starling.

Nurse was old now and spent a good deal of her time in a small room in the attics darning and patching the household linen. It was isolated and yet it was a hive of gossip. She always knew before anyone exactly what was going on in house and village. I used to wonder how she managed it.

She expected me to look in on her occasionally and the morning after my uncle arrived, she kept me back when I tried to get away.

'I don't like it, Mr Oliver,' she said, 'I remember him all those years back, a dark strange boy he always was. Cursed like all the black Aylshams and so I said often and often.'

'Now that's foolish, Nurse,' I began and she interrupted me.

'What does a boy like you know about such things? The Old Tiger, your grandfather, he knew. He saw the devil in him from the start and he were right. He cast him out for what he did.'

'What did he do, Nurse?' I asked, humouring her.

'Bygones is bygones and you'll never get me to speak against the family,' she said stubbornly, 'not if I were to be torn to pieces for it, but I know what I know and there's blood on his hands and death, and that's something you can't never wash away no matter how much you try. I saw it coming again when your father died like he did . . .'

'My uncle had nothing to do with father's death.'

'How do you know that?' she retorted. 'Out there in that heathen country there's no telling . . . he's brought trouble back with him . . . him and that black devil who follows him like a shadow . . .'

'Nonsense,' I said impatiently.

'And now you're going away. 'Tisn't right, 'tisn't natural.'

'Well, that's how it is. It's happened and we have to put up with it.'

'There'll be a reckoning you mark my words.'

I didn't want to hear any more of her gloomy forebodings. At any moment she would start talking about Alyne. 'I really must be off,' I said and made for the door but she plucked at my sleeve.

'Mr Oliver, afore you go, there's summat I'd like you to do for me.'

'What is it?'

'I wish you'd have a word with Jake.'

'Jake? Whatever for?'

'I don't like what he's doing. He gets himself into bad company.'

'Jake does! I don't believe it.'

'He takes care of the little 'uns, I'll say that for him,' she said grudgingly, 'but what's he want with going into Ely regular once a week, getting mixed up with those who ought to know better. Talking about their rights and speaking out against them they work for. You know what that leads to, same as me. Didn't they hang poor Isaac for what he never done?'

'That was a long time ago,' I said gently. 'Nothing like that is going to happen again. Jake wants to improve himself, that's all.'

'For what, that's what I asks meself. 'Tisn't proper the way he goes on. 'Tisn't no use him trying to ape the gentleman for he'll never succeed however hard he tries and it won't do him a mite of good. There's a place for the likes of him just as there is for you and you tell him so, Mr Oliver. He ought to be wed and settling down by now. He won't listen to his Mam nor to me but mebbe he'll take it from you.'

'Very well, I'll speak to him,' I said, simply to satisfy her and with no intention of doing anything of the kind. We had been friends far too long and had shared too much. Jake worked hard and apart from that he could do as he wished without any interference from me. But I wished she had not reminded me of Isaac. It brought back too vividly what had happened over ten years ago and could so easily start up again.

All this last year there had been unrest, not only in East Anglia but all over the country. The poor harvest, pitifully low wages and high taxation had brought starvation and ruin. I had wanted to raise our farm labourers' money but Sir Peter Berkeley had warned me against it.

'Give them a penny more and they will be asking for the moon,' he said when he came to my father's funeral. 'There is revolution in the air, my boy, you know that well enough and we landowners have got to stand together or they'll rob us of everything we have. Do you want to see heads roll as they did in France? Isn't your father's death warning enough?'

I thought he exaggerated but felt too uncertain of myself to make sweeping changes. Well, now it would be my uncle's responsibility not mine. I went down the stairs and out to the courtyard. The horses were ready saddled but my uncle had not yet come down. I paced up and down impatiently, waiting for him. At the end of the flower garden Jake was kneeling on the edge of the turf planting out seedlings along the border. He had always had a skill with growing things and after Isaac's death, my father had given him work in the gardens and with that and what he earned digging and hoeing for Miss Cavendish at Copthorne, he had been the main support of his mother and little brothers and sisters.

That year after Waterloo had meant the end of childhood for both of us. I was nearly twelve, a year younger than Jake, and it was a terrible time for England though she had won the war against Napoleon. I used to hear my father talking gloomily of the National Debt, the high taxation, the sudden fall in prices now that war contracts had ended. The harvest of 1816 was the worst ever known. It never stopped raining, the potatoes rotted in the ground, there was no fodder for the winter and animals and men faced starvation. Once a band of labourers went marching through Ravensley with a banner reading 'Bread or Blood' and they burned one of our ricks and destroyed a barn.

All that winter there was fearful talk of revolution and a troop of soldiers was stationed nearby to keep order. There was a night in November when I woke to hear shouting outside. From the window I could see the red of fire spreading all across the dark sky and my father was down in the courtyard with some of our men. There had been an attack on Sir Peter Berkeley's house at Barkham. They started off peaceably enough begging for some of the corn he had stored in his granaries to save their wives and children

from starvation but when he refused pointblank, they grew angry.
Some of the hotheads began to break down the doors. He sent for
the soldiers. Clubs and rakes are not much avail against guns and
bayonets but maddened by hunger they had fought savagely and
Sir Peter's bailiff was wounded so severely that he died before
morning. Isaac Starling was arrested for his murder.

I didn't believe it and neither did Jake. Isaac Starling had never
been a violent man but he had been taken up gun in hand and the
magistrates were determined to make an example and stamp out
revolt before it spread to other parts of the country. Isaac was to
hang with five others and more than thirty were to be transported.

I had stood beside Jake watching the grisly preparations for
death and felt my stomach turn over sickeningly when the upright
figure in the ragged shirt was brought out. I kept remembering
how he had made me a fishing line and taught me to catch eels
with a glaive as all the Fenmen do and how tenderly the blunt
fingers had mended the wing of a damaged bird I had found.
Something was born in me that day, a revulsion against tyranny, a
feeling that something must be wrong with a law that allowed a
man to die for what he had not done. It was to take a long time
before it bore fruit but there were many days and nights before I
could forget the writhing figure at the end of a rope.

The crowd had been so dense we could not force our way out
immediately and it was then that the men who were to be transported were marched past us and pushed into the carts that would
carry them to the docks. Ragged and thin, loaded with chains, they
were a pitiful sight. Only one of them was defiant, a boy of fifteen
or sixteen perhaps, his fair hair tousled and filthy, his bloody shirt
half torn from his back. He fought the soldiers every step of the
way. The families of the condemned men were trying to reach
them, crying out and holding up babies and children for a last look
at father or brother so that the procession halted immediately in
front of me. The boy flung up his head and stared directly at me. I
met his eyes, bright blue under the grimy matted hair. Then quite
suddenly he leaned forward and spat full in my face. He was
jerked away so roughly that he stumbled and one of the soldiers
kicked him to his feet. I stared after him, sickened and horrified.
Why me? What had I ever done to him?

It had haunted me for a long time and then in the way things do the memory faded until last December when we had found my father half drowned with that purple bruise on his forehead that could have been caused by a fall and could have been struck by a vengeful hand. But revenge for what? My father had pleaded for mercy and had been overruled.

I thought of it now standing on the edge of the lawn and looking across the shrubbery to the limitless horizon of the Fens. It was almost unheard of for a man to serve his seven years in the penal colony and then contrive to earn enough to pay his passage home. And yet stranger things have happened and Greatheart was the home of wild and savage creatures, human as well as animal . . . a hand was clapped on my shoulder and my uncle's voice sounded gratingly in my ears.

'Dreaming, Oliver? That's not the way to get anywhere, my dear boy. Work, initiative, energy . . . that is what is needed and we have a good deal to get through if you are to take wing and be off . . .'

He turned to the horses without waiting for my answer and I followed him silently down the drive. We spent the morning with the tenant farmers. My uncle could be charming when he chose but there was no real warmth, only a cool aloof manner that kept me and everyone else at a distance.

Will Burton who leases one of our largest farms kept forgetting and addressing me as 'my lord' and I saw how it irritated my uncle.

After a little he said icily, 'I'd be grateful, my dear fellow, if you would remember that I am Lord Aylsham and not my nephew.'

The farmer's brick-red face turned a dull purple. 'I'm sure I'm very sorry, my lord, it's just that it seemed natural-like . . .'

'Quite so, but times have changed. Make sure you don't forget in future who is master of Ravensley.'

Will Burton gave me a quick glance but I said nothing and I saw his mouth tighten and the frank cheerful manner replaced by a sharp wariness.

In the late afternoon our circular tour brought us to Thatchers. The old farmhouse is on the edge of the Fen and my uncle looked it over disparagingly.

'So that is your inheritance. What do you think to do? Live in it?'

The taunt in his voice irritated me. 'There are worse places. When my father's old farm bailiff lived there, we were in and out of it all day long.'

'You are too attached to the past, Oliver.'

Beyond Thatchers on the edge of Ravensley land, there were a couple of cottages which my father had renovated shortly before his death and I could see Mrs Starling hanging out sheets in the garden with Jenny, the second daughter, helping her. Her eldest was already in service with Miss Cavendish at Copthorne. The two younger boys, Seth and Ben, must have been out working in the fields.

My uncle frowned. 'Who are these people?'

I answered reluctantly. 'Their name is Starling.'

He gave me a sharp glance. 'The widow of the man who was hanged? Is that whom you mean?'

'Yes.'

'They had a relative, I believe, a cousin or such who lived over at Westley.'

I looked at him in surprise. 'I never heard of it.'

'Your friend Jake obviously does not tell you everything.' He waved a hand carelessly. 'It is of no importance. They live rent free, I presume.'

'Father had no immediate use for the cottage so he let them move in,' I said defensively. 'There were a number of children younger than Jake and they were wretchedly poor.'

'What is parish relief for if not for people of that kind?' retorted my uncle. 'Your father was a soft-hearted fool,' and he spurred his horse forward without acknowledging Mrs Starling's nervous curtsey. Jenny smiled shyly up at me and I waved to them both before I caught him up.

The track took us further into the Fens. Father had begun to drain the land here. When I was a child I used to think the tall windmills looked like giants, gaunt and black, guarding the Fens. The great sails moved slowly in the sluggish wind, turning the scoop wheel with the huge paddles that lifted the water from the peat bogs into the high-banked dykes leaving the earth spongy and black, ready for planting. We rode on beside the sluice until we came in sight of the wide stretch of Greatheart. This wild and lovely place was where Jake and I had come so often, the dawn turning the sky pearly pink and only the chattering of the reed warblers or flights of widgeon coming in from the north with a rush of wings disturbing the stillness. In winter when the wild geese flew overhead with their haunting cry we skated for miles on the frozen mere. Here I had come with Alyne barely a month ago, our punt nosing through the water lilies, lying close in each other's arms and all around us the delicious heady scent of meadowsweet. Oh God, how could I bear to go away and leave it?

My uncle's jarring voice broke in on me. 'How many acres of this waste do we own, Oliver?'

'I don't know exactly. It is on the estate plans. Greatheart alone is something like four to five thousand acres.'

'And no damned use to anyone but poachers, wildfowlers and vagrants! Did your father think of having it drained?'

'No, never.'

'Why the devil not?'

It was difficult to answer. There were so many reasons. Partly I think because he loved Greatheart as I did. 'There would have been exceptionally strong opposition and he did not want to cause unnecessary hardship,' I said at last.

My uncle snorted. 'There is always opposition to any improvement. Most men are fools. They don't know when they are well off. It's the price you have to pay.' He was staring around him. 'It could be made profitable. I picked up some information while I was in London. The use of these new steam engines instead of windmills could make all the difference.'

'They do not always succeed. A few years back the banks broke under the weight of the winter tides and there were floods.'

'You have to sacrifice something in the cause of progress.'

'But not lives surely. Besides you cannot take everything from the Fenmen. They have lived here for generations. For a great many of them the wildfowl, the fish, the eels provide their only living.'

'And so they profit at our expense.'

'It's a desperately hard existence,' I said ironically. 'And if they do earn a wage, seven shillings a week does not go far if they can't take a little of their food from the Fens.'

'The money is certain, isn't it, and regular. There's too much sympathy wasted on people like that.' My uncle swung round in his saddle to look at me. 'Are you another of these damned radicals, boy? Or just a stick-in-the-mud like your father who dare not make a move for fear of the consequences?'

'My father was not like that and neither am I,' I said, stung by the scorn in his voice. 'He made a great many improvements but men and women were more important to him than the money he could make out of them. I think I'm as forward looking as anyone but I know these people and their problems. I have grown up with them.'

'Trouble-makers like your friend Jake Starling, I suppose? It is always a mistake to become too familiar with servants. God knows I learned that in India to my cost.'

Anger flared up in me. 'India is not England and there is nothing wrong with Jake.'

He stared at me for a moment then the thin lips curved in a faint sneer. 'That is what you think. You're too trusting, Oliver. Well, we shall see who is right.'

He turned his horse and trotted back along the track leaving me to follow. I was aware of the antagonism between us that I had tried to avoid but if that was going to be his attitude then he was not going to get very far, not here, but he was right in one way. Perhaps my feelings were confused. Perhaps it is a mistake to see two sides of a question. Maybe it was purely sentimental but I hated the thought of Greatheart being torn apart, its beauty destroyed and with it the sense of freedom, the feeling of liberation. For centuries men had taken refuge there from tyranny, from injustice, from cruelty. Some of them had been my boyhood heroes. Damn it! I was thinking like a romantic idiot, I told myself savagely, putting Rowan to the gallop to catch him up.

One thing did comfort me. If my uncle thought to install steam engines for draining, then the estate finances would never stand it. My father had once gone into costs and even the smallest installation would be priced at more than five thousand pounds and with very doubtful results. Ravensley was rich enough but not in ready cash. Our wealth lay in the produce of the lands and the sheep and cattle pastured there. We had never lived like our grand neighbours with their fine houses, their carriages and lavish entertaining. Unless my uncle had brought home a small fortune from

India, he would have to think again. I didn't know then how strong his determination was when he was challenged.

As we came up the track to Ravensley I caught sight of Miss Cavendish waving to me from her white gate so I let him go ahead up the elm-shaded drive.

'Your uncle has arrived, I see,' she said in her abrupt way as I halted. 'How do you like him?'

'I am not sure,' I said guardedly. 'He seems friendly enough.'

She looked up at me, her eyes bright under the huge flat straw hat she wore when she was gardening. 'Is that why you are running away?'

'How do you know?'

'Word gets around.'

'I am not running away.'

'Sounds uncommonly like it to me.'

'It's not easy,' I replied stiffly, 'to watch someone else in father's place.'

'Nor in your own, eh?' Her face softened a little. 'I understand. I even sympathize.'

'Miss Cavendish, did you know him in the old days before he went away?'

'Ah,' she said, 'I was young then. Yes, I knew him. He was clever, fascinating and quite ruthless. That's why he made such a foolish mistake.' What mistake, I wondered, but she went on before I could ask. 'You've taken a hard knock, Oliver. What do you intend to do?'

'God knows. I've not been trained to anything useful,' I said ruefully, 'and I'm no scholar, or else I might have turned schoolmaster. I'd thought of the army but there are no wars. Emigrate perhaps, take ship for Canada and begin a new life. They say they need farmers out there.'

'Rubbish,' she said. 'Isn't England good enough for you? You'll come back here, you know. The Fens never let a man go and you're as much a Fen Tiger as any of them.'

I laughed. The Fenman's bitter and stubborn courage had earned him that nickname long ago. 'Maybe I am,' I said, 'but I'm going to London all the same. I feel a need for change.'

'And a need to escape, eh?' and I wondered if she had guessed about Alyne. She was a shrewd old lady in many ways. 'Go and call on Clarissa while you are there. She is lonely, poor girl.'

'Clarissa lonely? In London?'

'Cities can be the loneliest places on earth. Can't stand 'em myself. London is full of dust, dirt and smoke. Always makes me feel I can't get my breath. Give her my love. Tell her she owes me a visit.'

'Perhaps I will.'

She nodded to me as I lifted my hat and rode away. It was odd that she should mention Clarissa. It must be all of five years since I had seen her. The Fentons had not come back to Copthorne after that cold windy day in October when I was home for the weekend from Cambridge and the hunt met at Ravensley for the last time. Clarissa had been very excited and happy as we waited in the courtyard.

She said, 'Isn't Alyne coming with us?'

'She doesn't care to ride and she hates the thought of killing anything.'

'Oh I don't think about the fox at all. It's the horses and the country and the fun of it that I love,' and she laughed up at me.

I turned to wave to Alyne but she had disappeared from the steps and only Cherry was there, deeply disappointed because father said she was too young to ride with us.

It was a grand day with the grass crisp with early frost and the air fresh and intoxicating as wine until the terrible moment when we reached the dyke. I still don't know exactly what happened. I heard Colonel Fenton who was a daring horseman shout a challenge to his wife. She urged her horse to jump and for some reason he stopped dead on the muddy brink sending her over his head. She was half in and half out of the mud, trampled by the others before they could stop themselves. I remembered how I had held Clarissa in my arms hiding her face against me so that she should not see them lift the slight twisted body of her mother on to the improvised stretcher. I took her home to Copthorne because her father was nearly out of his wits with grief and it was late when I got back to Ravensley. Everyone was very upset. Cherry was white-faced and crying. After I had comforted her as best I could I went in search of Alyne. I found her at last in a corner of the old schoolroom. It was cold there and already dark. She was crouched on the floor by the window. I knelt beside her and felt her tremble when I put my arms around her.

'What is the matter, Alyne? Whatever are you doing here?'

'Clarissa . . .' she swallowed. 'I heard what they said about Clarissa. She is dead, isn't she?'

'It was not Clarissa,' I said gently. 'It was her mother who was killed.'

She stared at me, her eyes wide. 'But Clarissa was riding Blackie . . . I saw her . . .'

'No, she wasn't. They changed horses just before we rode off. Mrs Fenton thought him too powerful for Clarissa.'

Her hand flew to her mouth and then she flung herself against me. 'I didn't know . . . I didn't know . . .'

It had been a shock for all of us and it was only natural that she should be distressed. I soothed and comforted her and when she lifted her face all wet with tears, I kissed her for the first time as a man kisses a woman and she clung to me. We kissed again and again and in the cold and the dark I was a boy of eighteen no longer but a man passionately in love and despite the tragedy of the day I was intensely happy.

I thrust the memory away from me angrily as I dismounted at the stables. All day I felt I had been seeing the last of the Fens and I delayed deliberately, unsaddling the mare and rubbing her down myself before I went out into the warm dusk and walked slowly up to the house.

I made my farewells at supper that night and left very early the following morning without speaking again to anyone. I was to ride Rowan to Ely and take the stagecoach from there, sending her back with one of the grooms. Annie would pack the rest of my baggage and send it to London by carrier.

There was a mist over the Fens, clinging to the trees in long thin strands as I went up the drive, but birds were crying overhead and it would be a lovely day. At the lodge where the gate opens into the road a dark figure slipped out from among the trees and I saw it was Alyne huddled in a long cloak against the chill of the early morning.

I reined in. 'Are you going to open the gate for me?'

She put a hand on my bridle. 'You didn't come and say good-bye to me last night.'

'Did you expect it? I thought all that was finished between us two days ago.'

She came nearer and slid her hand up my thigh. 'Why must you go?'

'You should be able to answer that for yourself.'

I dismounted, brushing past her to open the gate and she came after me.

'I shall miss you.'

'I wish I could believe that.'

I turned to look at her and all my resolutions fled away with the wind. I caught her roughly in my arms, the scented cloud of her hair was damp with mist.

'Come with me, Alyne. We'll be married tomorrow. I'll sell Thatchers to my uncle and we'll go away, anywhere, abroad if you like and let the rest of the world go hang.'

I slid my hands around the slender body under the cloak and kissed her wildly, passionately. 'You must come with me, Alyne, you must. I cannot go on living without you.'

I felt her body yield and was ready to laugh in triumph, then she struggled against me, pushing me away.

'And what should we live on?'

'I'll find a way. We'd be together and that's what matters.'

'No, Oliver, no.'

'Then why the devil are you here?' I held her at arms' length feeling her tense in my grip. 'Was it simply to taunt me?'

'No, no . . .'

'Why then?'

'I don't know. I wanted to see you again.'

'My God, is that all?' I watched for a moment the lovely face that had such power to turn my blood to water and now seemed a beautiful mask concealing only emptiness.

'You can't have your cake and eat it,' I said roughly.

I thrust her away from me, flung myself into the saddle and rode hell for leather down the road, not trusting myself even to look back.

I had seen the last of Alyne and of Ravensley, I told myself savagely, but Fate or the Devil, whichever you please to call it, has a way of making fools even of the best of us and so it was to be with me.

Part Two

CLARISSA

1830

I loved, I love you, for this love have lost
   State, station, Heaven, Mankind's, my own esteem,
And yet can not regret what it hath cost,
   So dear is still the memory of that dream.

Lord Byron

I

It seems strange now that the night in April 1830 that was to alter my whole life was only two days after the evening when I met Oliver Aylsham again after so many years. The two events would appear to have no connection and yet one led to the other though I did not realize it until afterwards.

I knew Oliver was in London because Harry told me. He came home one evening during the autumn full of it. He had met him at a cock-fight which was one of the sports he and his set indulged in. Ever since Harry had obtained his commission in the Dragoons and had been taken up by Bulwer Rutland he had changed. I suppose it was only to be expected. My brother was nineteen and quite naturally at the age when he wanted to be as hard riding, hard swearing and hard living as the young bloods with whom he associated every day. Only he hadn't the wealth behind him that most of them had and the extravagant life they led, their crazy escapades, the gambling, the huge sums won and lost, quite frankly terrified me.

I was surprised, I must confess, that Oliver should be mixed up with such a wild set. It did not seem like him somehow and so I told Harry.

'I'd never have believed it myself, Sis, if I hadn't seen him. Oliver was always so steady and reliable. Remember how we used to look up to him at Copthorne? And there he was a slap-up swell and throwing his blunt around free as water; yet everyone says he's living on credit and will come a fearful cropper if he doesn't watch out. Hasn't a penny to bless himself with since that uncle of his turned up from God knows where and disinherited him. Deuced bad luck I call it. Probably wants to cut a dash before he goes to pot!'

Harry prided himself on using all the up-to-date lingo of the crowd he went around with.

I thought Oliver might call on us, but he didn't and neither did he attend any of the concerts, routs and balls held during the season though his name cropped up now and again usually accompanied by raised eyebrows and a shake of the head among the dowagers. The penniless nephew of Lord Aylsham was not a particularly good bargain. Then one evening in January Harry came home earlier than usual and put his head round my bedroom door as he does now and again. He is a boy still though he believes himself to be so grown up.

'You awake, Clary?'

I put down my book. 'Yes of course. Come in. Did you have a good evening?'

'Pretty fair.' He plumped himself down on the bed rubbing his hands. 'By jingo, it's cold. It's snowing again outside. Got something to tell you dashed interesting, Sis. I believe old Oliver has been crossed in love.'

'What! Oh don't be silly. What on earth makes you say a thing like that?'

'Well, we were at Crockfords tonight and . . .'

'Oh Harry, I do wish you wouldn't go there. You know how high the stakes are.' Crockfords was the most fashionable of all the gaming houses patronized almost exclusively by the *haut ton*. 'Aren't father's debts enough to put up with?'

'Don't be such a spoilsport, Clary. I don't play . . . or not much. I haven't got the ready. I went with the Bull and he's got money to burn, you know that.'

I did indeed. Bulwer Rutland, rich as Croesus, known as the Bull among his sporting cronies. I suspected cynically it was as much for his prowess in bed as for his fame in the boxing ring though I would never have dared to say so. It would have been far too indelicate . . . Bulwer Rutland who kept asking me to marry him and wouldn't take no for an answer.

'Yes, I know Captain Rutland,' I said tartly. 'Go on.'

'Well, Oliver was at the Hazard table playing very high and losing every time. Honestly it gave me the shivers. I thought he looked pretty sick but by God he's a good plucked 'un. He never turned a hair but stuck it out and then, damme, the luck changed as it can sometimes and it came rolling in with them all crowding around watching. He was stuffing it into his pockets when the Bull said something about being lucky at cards and unlucky in love. Oliver looked daggers at him but the Bull went on. "Met your uncle today, Aylsham. Came to see my father on a matter of business. Had a damned pretty filly with him, dressed to kill . . . now what did he call her? It was something queer . . ."

' "Would it be Alyne?" says Oliver frowning.

' "Aye, that's it. By Jupiter, she was a stunner and knew what to do with it too. You should have seen the way she looked at me . . ."

'I thought for an instant that Oliver would knock him down but he didn't, just said in that icy way of his, "Alyne happens to be my adopted sister. I'd thank you to keep your dirty tongue to yourself," and off he went, leaving the Bull staring and everyone else grinning. He don't often get such a set-down.'

'Well, I don't think much to that,' I said dryly. 'I don't blame anyone for resenting Captain Rutland's witticisms.'

'Ah but you didn't see the way Oliver looked, old girl. Tight round the mouth and mad as a snake. Oh well,' he yawned prodigiously. 'I'm off to bed. 'Night, Clary.' He pecked my cheek and left me alone.

I remembered Alyne from the old days at Copthorne. Even as a child she had been lovely as a dream, not that we were ever close. She had a way of keeping you at a distance but I used to envy her because while my hair stuck out stiff as a brush, hers hung soft and silky to below her waist. But she had grown up as Oliver's sister. He could not be in love with her. Harry must have got it all wrong.

Later that month when I asked him casually if he had seen any more of Oliver, he said he'd gone off to Paris.

'Didn't want to meet up with his uncle probably. Can't say I blame him. It's a damnable situation.'

I wondered about him once or twice and then we went to the ball at Devonshire House and amazingly he was there. I hadn't wanted to go at all but father insisted. He had dragged me to every social event that season in a desperate attempt to get me married and off his hands. He was furious with me because I had refused Bulwer Rutland's offer and kept hoping I would change my mind. The fact that I was happy to stay as I was rather than marry a man I detested never seemed to strike him.

Oliver must have arrived late because I didn't see him until just before the supper interval when I had escaped into an anteroom. I had been obliged to waltz with Bulwer much against my will. I hated the way he held me, the touch of his gloved hand on my back, his face far too close to mine, his breath on my cheek, the compliments he poured into my ear. I got away from him on the plea of a torn flounce on the hem of my gown.

In the little room off the ballroom I looked at my flushed face in the gold framed mirror above the fireplace, pinning up a curl that had come loose and wishing I could go home.

'You're too stand-offish, Clarissa,' my father had said once, 'you look at men as if you despise them. That's no way to catch a husband.'

He didn't understand—how should he, being a man?—that it is the only defence you have when you are being hawked around the marriage market. A girl without a dowry and with no particular looks is at a serious disadvantage and I did have my pride. Then the door opened and I turned round quickly, afraid it might be Bulwer but it was Oliver shutting the door behind him and leaning back against it.

I knew him instantly. He had not changed all that much from the boy of eighteen except that he had filled out a little. He was still tall, broad-shouldered and slim-hipped, his fair hair had darkened to harvest gold but his eyes were the same dark blue. He stared at me for a moment and then broke into a smile.

'By Jove, it *is* Clarissa, isn't it? Clarissa Fenton? I'm Oliver Aylsham.'

'Yes, I know.'

'Are you escaping too?'

'Something like that.'

He came across to me taking my hand and kissing it. 'I owe you an apology.'

'Whatever for?'

'I've been very remiss. I promised Miss Cavendish that I would call on you months ago and I have not done so.'

'No doubt you have been occupied.'

'Not with anything worthwhile. She said I was to give you her love and tell you that you owe her a visit.'

'Dear Aunt Jess. It is such a long time since I've been there but it's not easy. Father doesn't care to go back to Copthorne.'

'Understandably after what happened. Come and sit down. Tell me about yourself.'

'I ought to go back to the ballroom.'

'Not for a few minutes surely.'

'Very well.'

I let him draw me to the sofa and for a moment we said nothing. He was leaning back, his eyes on my face. Then he said suddenly, 'I'd never have believed it. You've turned into a raving beauty.'

I laughed outright then. 'Well, that's frank anyway.'

'Oh Lord, I'm a clumsy fool. You must forgive me but I was never any good at pretty talk like those out there.' He waved his hand to the ballroom.

'I think it makes a welcome change.'

'It doesn't make for popularity.'

'Do you mind?'

'Not particularly.' He was silent for a moment looking down at his hands. He has nice hands, not plump, smooth and scented like Bulwer's but brown and muscular. Strong hands that can make things. 'Do you know about me, Clarissa?'

'I know your uncle has returned. It must have been a great shock.'

'It was and I took it badly. I walked out and left him to it. Ever since I have been making a pretty fool of myself trying to be something I'm not, trying to make up my mind what to do with my life and failing dismally. The truth is, Clarissa, that I'm a countryman born and bred,' he went on ruefully. 'I miss Ravensley. I miss the Fens quite horribly. Does that sound ridiculous?' He turned to me suddenly. 'Advise me, Clarissa, tell me what I should do.'

I was startled. 'How can I?'

'You know us all and yet you are outside, you can be impartial.' He paused for a second, smiling at me. 'Do you remember when you hid in my boat because you wanted to come duck shooting with Jake and me?'

'Yes, I do . . . and how angry you were when I fell in the water . . . you spanked me . . .'

'You had freckles on your nose then.'

'I still do if I'm not careful and sit in the sun too much.' I put a
hand to my face blushing a little as I remembered how he had
turned up my petticoats and slapped my bottom before wrapping
his coat round me and taking me home.

'There you are, you see, we are very old friends. The truth is
that my uncle wrote to me some time ago, in January in fact, when
he was in London and I refused to see him. There has been a great
deal of trouble with the tenants and with the villagers. He has been
away so long and now he is pushing them too hard. They resent
him. He wants me to go back and manage the estate for him.
Should I go or should I let them all go hang?'

He was looking directly at me and yet I felt it was not really my
opinion he sought so much as fighting out the problem inside himself.

'What about Cherry?' I said, 'and Alyne? What do they feel
about it?'

He looked away from me. 'Cherry is still very much of a child
but she *is* my sister . . . I don't like to think of her there alone.
Then there are the Starlings . . . so many people depended on father . . . I wish to hell I didn't feel responsible for them.'

'But you do,' I said, 'so doesn't that settle it? You'll have to go
back even if it is only for a time. You'll never live with yourself if
you don't.'

'I wonder.' He sighed and then grinned at me and for an instant
I caught a glimpse of the boy I used to admire so much. 'You're a
tonic, Clarissa, bracing as a dip in the ice-cold river.'

'What a very uncomfortable thing to be,' I said laughing again.

'There I go, saying the wrong thing. Alyne told me that once.'
Then he stopped short, pushing impatiently at the lock of hair that
was apt to fall across his forehead. 'I shouldn't be burdening you
with my worries at all. Come and dance instead.'

He drew me to my feet and for a moment we stood close together hand in hand. He smiled down at me. 'It feels good to be
with you, Clarissa, like going back to the old days.'

Then the door opened and Bulwer came in. He was a
magnificent figure in the scarlet and gold of his regimentals and he
looked from me to Oliver with a frown.

'I've been hunting for you everywhere, Clarissa. It's the last
quadrille before supper and I think you are promised to me.'

He was not my fiancé and he had no rights over me but I hesitated, much as I would have liked to turn my back on him and dance with Oliver. I knew Bulwer so well. He was not drunk but had taken enough to make him aggressive and I had no wish to provoke a quarrel.

I said, 'I'm sorry. I had forgotten. Time goes by so quickly and Mr Aylsham and I are old acquaintances. I believe you already know one another.'

'Yes, indeed.' Oliver nodded to Bulwer and released my hand. 'It has been delightful meeting you again, Miss Fenton. Please give my regards to your father.' He bowed and went swiftly from the room.

I took Bulwer's arm and as we went through the door he said irritably, 'What the devil do you mean by hiding yourself away with that fellow?'

His peremptory tone annoyed me. 'We have known each other since we were children and I really don't see that it is any concern of yours.'

'Everything about you concerns me, Clarissa. You know how I feel about you.'

'I've already given you my answer, Captain Rutland. Must I keep on repeating it?'

His grip on my arm tightened. 'You're going to marry me, you know, I always get what I want.'

'Not this time,' I said and then we were in the ballroom and had moved to our places in the dance.

I knew he was angry with me, not because he truly cared but because it piqued his vanity that any woman should refuse him. Luckily Harry came to join us at supper so that I was spared Bulwer's more intimate attentions but I could not see Oliver anywhere. He must have already left.

Two days later a basket was delivered crammed with primroses, damp and earthy, smelling of spring woods. The card with them said simply 'Thank you'. I buried my face in them and wondered if Oliver had gone back to Ravensley. I had no idea that I had unwittingly started something that was to have momentous consequences for both of us.

I was alone that evening. Father and Harry were both out so I supped alone and went up to bed rather earlier than usual. My bedroom was on the first floor of our house in Soho Square. For some time now aristocratic society had begun to move westward to Piccadilly and St James's Street but father who lived mainly on his wits and what he could win at the gambling tables had never been able to afford to move from the tall narrow house that he had inherited from my mother.

I looked from the window before I drew the curtains. A faint glow came from the lamp on its bracket by the front door. It was very quiet. The last carriage had long since rattled over the cobbles leaving the square to the night prowlers who crept out of their rookeries in St Giles and Seven Dials. It was always dangerous to be out walking at night. One of our maidservants, coming back late from meeting her sweetheart, had been beaten up for the few pence in her pocket and the cheap cotton scarf round her neck and it had been known for rich young men who had drunk too much to be lured into a dark alley and robbed of purse, rings and watch before in their fuddled state they knew what was happening to them.

It was a warm spring evening so I raised the window a trifle before getting into bed. I lay awake for a long time thinking of Oliver and the old days at Copthorne. I had loved Aunt Jess's old rambling house with its cosy panelled rooms, the shabby furniture, the faded rugs on the polished wooden floors, the dogs all over the place and the horses in the stables at Ravensley which Lord Aylsham had let us ride whenever we wished. We had lived there all the time while father was fighting in the Peninsular and when he came home after Waterloo, one of Wellington's young heroes, handsome and gallant as Harry was now, there had seemed no cloud in the sky until that hateful day when mother was killed.

I drowsed into sleep at last and dreamed of Copthorne, something I had not done for years. Oliver was in my dream and it was I he loved and not Alyne which was ridiculous since he had never showed me anything more than the most ordinary friendship. But you cannot control your thoughts in sleep as you do in your waking moments. In the day I would have been deeply ashamed of such indulgence and thrust all such fantasies away from me but in my dreams his arms were round me, his mouth moving against mine so that a warm glow ran through me and I was gloriously unutterably happy.

I have no idea what time it was when I awoke. For a breathless moment I was still wrapped in my dream before it turned into ugly reality. Then I was alive to the horror of a man's mouth clamped down on mine, a strong smell of brandy, arms that gripped me crushing my breasts against him, a hard masculine body invading mine. Despite my terror I acted with an instinctive defence. I brought up my knee with a bruising force so that my attacker taken by surprise let out a yelp of pain and rolled sideways. I struggled madly, kicking myself free. I opened my mouth to cry out, the invader clapped his hand over it and I sank my teeth into it with all my strength. He snatched it back with an oath and I screamed.

'Keep your mouth shut, for Christ's sake!' he muttered scrambling off the bed and sending my night table crashing to the floor. In the faint light I could see nothing but a tall bulky shape. He retreated to the window cursing under his breath but before he could make his escape, the door was flung open and father stood on the threshold, a candle in one hand, his pistol in the other.

'What the devil is going on?' he demanded furiously. My nightgown had been ripped from neck to hem. I was crouched at the end of the bed huddled under the sheet and he said sternly, 'What is the meaning of this disgraceful scene, Clarissa?'

The injustice hit me painfully. I was trembling from shock and reaction. I pointed a shaking finger. 'I woke up and that wretch was here . . . he was trying to . . . trying to . . .'

Then I stopped appalled because father had raised the candle and for the first time I saw the face of my ravisher. It was Bulwer Rutland. Anger swept through me that he should dare to break into my room like this. The very fact that it should be he, the man whom I had refused over and over again to marry seemed to make it ten times worse. Beyond father I could see the servants crowding into the doorway, the sly grin of Betsy, the housekeeper, Patience, the parlour maid, Crabbe, father's valet, even Peg, the kitchen maid, her mouth open, her eyes starting from her head. I felt the colour rush up into my face. Shame and outrage overwhelmed me.

I said, 'Make them all go away, Papa, please . . . please . . .'

'Yes, of course, my dear.' He waved his hand angrily. 'Send the servants back to bed, Crabbe, and be quick about it. As for you, sir,' he turned to Bulwer, 'you will come with me at once. I want an explanation of this outrageous conduct and it had better be a good one.'

It was a sorry figure in shirt and unbuttoned breeches who shuffled across the carpet in stockinged feet and if I had not been so distressed I might have smiled at his baffled rage at appearing in such a ludicrous light. This could have been no part of his intentions whatever they were.

Crabbe was shepherding the servants out into the passage when Harry burst through them, his hair tousled and his dressing gown pulled on anyhow over his nightshirt.

'What in God's name is happening? I heard Sis screaming her head off. I thought the house was burning down!' Then his eye fell on Captain Rutland and his face darkened. 'What the hell are you doing in my sister's bedroom, you damned bounder? For two pins I'd call you out for it.'

'Do what you cursed well please,' growled Bulwer more and more discomfited.

'You'll do nothing of the sort,' snapped my father. 'Go back to bed, Harry, and keep your mouth shut. Do you want the whole square to know that your sister was found with a man in her bedroom? This is my affair and I'll settle it. Clarissa has had a bad shock. She needs rest and quiet. You'd better bring your mistress a hot drink, Betsy. It will soothe her nerves. As for the rest of you, get back to your beds and forget what you've just seen. Do you understand?'

The servants went reluctantly with backward looks, whispering and giggling. A fine piece of gossip for them to talk over in the kitchen, I thought bitterly. Father came to me, putting the table to rights and lighting my candle from his own.

'It's all over now, my dear, and no harm done, I trust. You've nothing more to worry about.' I was badly in need of comfort and reassurance and I caught at his hand. He patted my shoulder awkwardly. 'There, there, my child, don't fret. I shall handle this, you will see. Now try and get some sleep.' He looked across at the young man still standing uneasily between him and Harry. 'You'll come with me, Captain Rutland.' He thrust him out of the room before him closing the door behind them.

Harry hesitated and then came and sat on the side of the bed. 'Are you sure you're all right, Clary? He didn't . . .'

'No, no . . . I'm all right.' Then disgust overcame me. I buried my face in my hands. 'Oh Harry, it was horrible, horrible.'

'What a confounded coil! Can't imagine what came over the Bull. Never dreamed he'd really do such a thing.'

I stared at my brother, a dreadful suspicion darting suddenly through my mind. I sat up against the pillows pulling the sheet up to my chin. 'Harry, you don't mean that you actually *knew* . . . that he talked about it . . .'

My brother stirred uncomfortably. 'There was something . . . it was just a joke, Clary, a bit of nonsense . . . you know what men are . . . we'd all had a glass too much . . .'

'Oh how could you! Your own sister! I could have been raped and you did nothing to prevent it. It's disgusting, it's vile . . .'

'I never believed it, honestly I didn't. I'd have knocked his head off if I had . . . it was Oliver who started it . . .'

'Oliver?' I exclaimed.

'It was after the ball at Devonshire House. It was so damned dull we went on to supper at Mott's . . .' then he stopped, looking a little shamefaced.

'It's all right. I know about that,' I said dryly. Mott's was a very fashionable supper room which I suspected was little more than a high class and expensive brothel, something of which I would never even have heard if it had not been for father and Harry.

'The Bull was a trifle high flown, you know what I mean, and he began talking about all women being the same under the skin, re- fusing a man's honest offer only because they wanted to be pressed . . .'

'Meaning me, I suppose?' I said ironically. 'He can't endure to think he is not irresistible to every woman he meets.'

'Your name wasn't actually mentioned,' mumbled Harry so awkwardly that I could guess at how much more had been said that didn't bear repeating.

'Well, go on, what happened?'

'Oliver took him up on it and the Bull gave him a nasty look and said he'd bet him or any man fifty pounds to a penny that he was right, that women wanted only one thing and he damn well had a mind to prove it. Oliver said he never made bets that in- volved a woman's honour and went off. Honestly I thought that was the end of it and that the Bull would have forgotten every word of it the next day. You know, Clary, to be fair, he was fearfully cut up when you refused him.'

'He does not want me,' I said scornfully. 'He wants what father can do for him. We may be poor as church mice but we are invited to Court and the Duke of Devonshire calls us cousin even if it has never done us a scrap of good.'

'Well, you can't blame the Bull for that and he has got the cash, old girl,' said Harry lightly, 'bags and bags of it even if Papa Rutland was only a grocer and we *are* devilish hard up.'

'Money, money, everything always comes back to money,' I said passionately. 'I won't be sold, not for your sake, nor for Papa's . . .'

'No, of course not,' Harry patted my hand soothingly. 'Nobody's asking you to do any such thing, but all the same Rutland's not a bad sort, Clary, you shouldn't be too hasty. You're so clever, you could twist him round your little finger if you wanted to.'

'Oh go to bed, Harry,' I said wearily, despairing of making him understand how the very thought of Bulwer touching me made my flesh crawl. 'Don't worry about me.'

'It's given you an unpleasant turn. You'll feel differently in the morning.' Harry grinned. 'I wager father will be reading him a fine lecture. I wouldn't be in his shoes for all the tea in China.' He leaned over to kiss my cheek and then stood up. 'Goodnight, Sis.'

'Goodnight, Harry.'

At the door he met Betsy coming in with a glass of milk on a tray and bestowed his charming smile on her. 'You take care of Miss Clarissa now,' he said.

'I will that, Master Harry, don't you fret,' said the young woman with a pert look. She brought the milk to the table. 'I thought it might help you to sleep, Miss,' she went on smoothly. She crossed to the window shutting and bolting it before rearranging the curtains. 'Fancy that Captain Rutland climbing up like that and finding the window open too. You ought to be more careful, Miss. Why he might have fallen and broken his neck. He must be mad with love for you trying a trick like that.'

'I don't want to talk about it,' I said coldly. I could hear the avid curiosity in Betsy's voice. It would spread like wildfire through every kitchen and drawing room in the square and beyond . . . the cool aloof Clarissa Fenton was just like all the rest, inviting a man to her bedroom and then putting on an act of outrage when she was found out. Anger flooded through me that Bulwer Rutland should have exposed me to such detestable scandal.

Betsy was fussing around the bed, tucking in the blankets and smoothing the coverlet. She was a plump young woman who had only been with us for a year and I disliked and distrusted her.

I said, 'Thank you for bringing the milk. You can go back to bed now.'

'Wouldn't you like me to stay with you, Miss?'

'No, thank you. I shall be quite all right now.'

'Very well. If you are sure that's all you want.' Her curiosity unsatisfied, Betsy flounced out of the room closing the door behind her.

I watched her go then scrambled out of the bed and went to the washstand. I poured ice-cold water into the basin and stripped off my torn nightgown. Shuddering I sponged my face and neck and breast as if to wipe away every vestige of the hot male touch. I dropped the towel and stared at myself in the pier glass. The candlelight flickered over long legs, rounded hips and slim waist. 'A raving beauty' Oliver had said and I wished it were true and then blushed remembering my dream and the strong caressing hands. I wondered what it was about me that always seemed to attract the wrong kind of man. It was not because Bulwer was the son of a tradesman that I despised him. I had rather liked old Joshua Rutland when I met him. There was something honest and unpretentious about him. He had told me once with simple pride that before he bought the grand house in Arlington Street and sent his only son to Harrow, he had lived over his warehouse in Cheapside, rising at five in the morning to wash himself under the pump at the corner of Bread Street and working till midnight in his counting house. It was the coarseness, the vulgarity, the greedy grasping after wealth and privilege that disgusted me, what father called 'the yellow streak' in one of his rare moments of rebellion against the society in which he moved. Even Harry had become tainted with it. So many of the young men were the same . . . reckless, heartless and showy. Harry once told me with glee how Bulwer driving home in his phaeton after a midnight revel smashed every window of the high street with his whip terrifying the humble townsfolk and when one of their comrades protested, he threw him into the horsepond. There were times when I longed to escape but how could I with father to think of and no money. I shivered taking a fresh nightgown from the bowfronted chest of drawers and pulling it over my head.

Back in bed I sipped the hot milk, too disturbed to sleep. If only mother had lived, everything might have been different. It was over five years since she had died. If I closed my eyes, I could see it all again, the Ravensley pack of hounds streaming across the flat fields of the Fens, the riders in their pink coats, a slight mist and the sun breaking through to touch the trees with gold, the dykes and the galloping horses . . . and then suddenly, unbelievably, tragedy.

I still felt guilty about it. If only we had not changed horses . . . if I had been riding Blackie I would never have dared to jump the water, I would have gone through the gate . . . if only father had not shouted that challenge . . . so many ifs . . . I don't think I shall ever forget the sight of mother in her fashionable riding habit slimed with mud, half in and half out of the water, father's stricken face and Oliver's arms around me desperately trying to comfort.

When it was all over, when mother lay buried in Ravensley churchyard, we had never gone back to Copthorne. Aunt Jess lived on there caring for the house and farm and cultivating her beloved garden. Jessamine Cavendish was mother's elder sister. She was tall, angular and plain and her tongue could be sharp. She had strongly disapproved of father, the handsome reckless soldier who had married her dearly loved sister. But all the same she came up to London with us and stayed on determinedly until I was nineteen. Miss Cavendish, second cousin of the Duke of Devonshire, was a formidable figure with her beaky nose and complexion unfashionably tanned by the sun, her outmoded brocaded gowns and air of great distinction. They might laugh at her behind her back but never to her face, not when the great Duke of Wellington came to take tea with her, roared with laughter at her caustic remarks and danced with me at my coming-out ball. She did what she called her duty by launching me into society, then had a blazing row with my father over Harry's future.

'For God's sake, put the boy into something sensible. Breed him to the law or the church. What do we want with soldiers now that the Corsican monster is safely in his grave at St Helena,' she snorted when Harry was promised a cadetship in father's old regiment as soon as he should be of suitable age.

'It's no use, my dear,' she said to me later that same evening. 'I can't get on with Tom Fenton and that's a fact. We just don't see eye to eye so we're better apart. I could wish your mother had never married him, but there it is.'

'He grieves for her still,' I pleaded.

'Maybe but that don't prevent him drinking, gambling . . . and worse,' she said darkly, then patted me on the shoulder. 'There, there, Clary, I know how you feel and he is your father after all.'

'I shall be very lonely without you, Aunt Jess.'

'Nonsense, you're a sensible girl, you know what's what. I've done my best for you, now it's up to you. Find yourself a good husband. I shall always be at Copthorne if you need me.'

I was deeply fond of Aunt Jess and well aware of the kindness beneath the brusque manner but I had never gone back to Copthorne. I had my pride and always there had been something to prevent it. But often and often while father went on in his rackety spendthrift way I had wondered what had happened to the children with whom I had played during those summers long ago.

I sighed. A sensible girl, Aunt Jess had called me, and I don't think I was greatly given to self pity but after she had gone and with father becoming increasingly unstable and Harry so young and rash, it had not been easy. Sometimes I wondered if it would have been better if father had married again but with all his vagaries he had loved his Susan and refused to put another in her place though I knew there were other women and this last year had been certain that Betsy sometimes shared his bed. I shut my eyes to it. The only thing I regretted was the wasted prodigal living that had dissipated his own fortune and mother's inheritance. Sometimes I would have been hard put to it to pay the monthly grocery bill if it had not been for the tiny income that came to me from my grandfather's will and that not even father could touch.

Unwillingly my thoughts came back to Bulwer and his outrageous assault. Even now I could scarcely believe it had happened. It was nine months since Harry had first introduced him at the regimental ball. He had pressed his attentions even then though I had been as cool as I dared and father had encouraged him to visit. He had dined with us, accompanied us to Drury Lane, yawning openly all through the play, invited me to drive with him, sent me flowers and sought every opportunity to ingratiate himself. I had refused his offer of marriage with indignation and father had been angry with me.

'For the Lord's sake, Clarissa,' he had said, 'you're twenty-two. Do you want to end up a dried-up old maid like poor Jess?'

'I'd far rather be like Aunt Jess than married to a man I dislike.'

'What is it you're waiting for, a knight in shining armour?' he said ironically. 'They only exist in cheap novels from the circulating library. Men are men, my dear, with faults as well as virtues. You're old enough to realize that, God knows.'

And it is you who have taught me, I might have retorted, but instead I said quietly, 'I'm sorry to displease you, Papa, but my mind is made up.'

His face had softened momentarily. 'You're a good girl, Clarissa. All these years since Susan died . . .' he turned away abruptly, his voice hardening. 'Luckily for you, Rutland refuses to take no for an answer. Think it over, my dear. It could be important for you, for all of us.'

That had been only a few weeks ago and I had been deliberately cold to Bulwer ever since, refusing to see him when he called and returning his gifts of flowers and sweetmeats. Was this the result, this brutal attack compromising me in the eyes of society? Well, if he thought that he could force me into marrying him, then he was greatly mistaken. I would fight for my freedom whatever the cost. I had begun to feel drowsy at last. I blew out the candle and tried to sleep, only to dream and wake again shaking, struggling against invisible terror. I was glad when morning came.

2

I was already up and partly dressed when Patience came knocking at the door and asking if she should bring me tea or chocolate.

'Neither, I'm coming down,' I said. 'Is my father up, Patience?'

'Yes, Miss, at breakfast with Master Harry. He did say he'd like a word with you as soon as you were dressed.' She hesitated, eyes alive with curiosity. 'Such a shocking night as it must have been for you. Fancy waking up and finding a stranger in your bed . . . well, almost a stranger . . . such a handsome gentleman too!' She shivered pleasurably. 'Are you sure you feel quite well this morning, Miss?'

'I am perfectly well. Tell the Colonel I shall be with him directly.'

'Very well, Miss.'

In the mirror my face looked pale and there were faint shadows under my eyes. I looked at myself with dissatisfaction as I hooked the neck of my striped morning gown and brushed my thick brown hair into ringlets. Then I went downstairs to the morning room. Harry was at the sideboard helping himself to a second plateful of cold beef. He looked up as I came in.

'Down already, Sis. Shall I bring you something?'

'No, thank you, I'm not hungry. Where is Papa? I thought he was breakfasting with you.'

'Betsy took his coffee into the study.' He turned round, plate in hand, grinning at me. 'I gather there was something of a to-do last night. Some devilish rogue decamped with the Bull's boots and his tunic out in the square. He could hardly go back to Arlington Street in his stockings, especially as it had come on to rain, so father borrowed a pair of mine which are a size too small. By God, you should have seen Rutland's face, black as the devil, as he hobbled down the steps in father's second best cloak.'

'It wouldn't really distress me if he had to walk home in his bare feet,' I said feelingly, 'and you can tell him so next time you see him, Harry.'

'Oh I say, that's a bit hard on the old fellow,' said Harry with his mouth full. 'It was dashed bad luck to lose his boots, made by Hoby too in St James's Street which is more than I can afford.'

'Not nearly as hard as he deserves,' I retorted crisply and went out, crossing the hall to knock at the door of father's room.

Colonel Tom Fenton was standing at the window, coffee cup in hand. The long velvet dressing gown hung open over shirt and fashionable fawn pantaloons. He was not yet fifty but the tall elegant figure had begun to thicken, there were grey streaks in the brown hair and deep lines running from nose to mouth. For perhaps the first time I looked at him not with the uncritical eyes of a child but clearly and impartially, noting what the years had done to him. A weak man who had allowed grief and disappointment to carry him into a way of life that had debauched and corrupted him. The horrible suspicion that had lain at the back of my mind all night leaped into sudden life but all I said was, 'Patience told me you wanted to see me, Papa.'

He turned round. 'Clary, my dear, I had not expected you to be down so early. How do you feel this morning?'

'Quite well.'

'Good, good. Come and sit down. Would you like coffee? I'll ring for a fresh pot.'

'No, thank you, Papa.'

He poured himself another cup and eyed me over the rim of it. 'We must talk over this most unfortunate business of last night if you don't feel too upset.'

'I am not in the least upset, Papa, only very angry.'

He shot me a glance and seated himself behind his littered desk. 'I know, my dear, but we must be sensible about it. I spoke severely, very severely indeed to Captain Rutland last night and he is deeply apologetic. He asked me most particularly to tell you this.' He paused but I said nothing and he went on. 'You must realize that in some ways, my dear, you have brought this on yourself by refusing to listen to him, by acting so coldly and returning his gifts. You have driven him to desperation.'

'Is that what he told you, Papa?'

'He knows he has behaved badly, but he had this mad notion of breaking into your room and pleading with you. There is no excuse and I was very angry with him of course, but I have been in love myself . . .'

'He was not pleading with me, Papa, far from it, he was . . .'

'Oh you're mistaken, my dear, I'm sure,' he went on hurriedly. 'It is quite natural. You woke in fright and misunderstood his intentions. You gave him no chance to explain. You cried out too soon.'

My anger and indignation boiled over. 'What should I have done? Let him rape me and cry out afterwards?'

'Clarissa, that is a shocking thing to say. He is truly sorry. He is prepared to make amends. He will marry you whenever you wish and his offer is generous, very generous indeed.'

'How kind!' I said ironically. 'I suppose I should go down on my knees and be grateful to him for bandying my name among his disgusting friends, for destroying my reputation and making me a byword throughout London society.'

'Oh nonsense, my dear, you are exaggerating. I don't deny there will be talk. You know what servants are as well as I do, but it will mean nothing when your engagement is announced and he can give you everything you could possibly wish for, a fine house, clothes, carriages, horses, all your mother wanted for you and I've been unable to provide . . .'

'How much are you selling me for, Papa?'

'Clarissa! Is that the way to speak to me when I want only your happiness? Do you think I would allow anything to touch my daughter's honour?'

But despite the outrage, the bluster, I saw how his eyes shifted and knew there was some truth in my accusation. He had guessed what Bulwer intended to do and had done nothing, seeing it as a way of forcing me into a marriage I detested and the thought sickened me.

'I won't do it, Papa, I won't. I am not going to marry him.'

'But you must, Clarissa, indeed you must. There is no other way out. Do you think any decent man will offer for you after this?' There was a note of desperation in his voice that puzzled me.

'I know there will be a scandal, but I don't care. I'll live it down.'

He got to his feet and walked away from me. He said in a muffled tone, 'It is worse than that.'

'Worse? In what way?'

He went on with his back to me. 'You know how it has been these last few years. Never enough money to live as we should and there has been Harry to think of. He is your brother after all. When Rutland first came to me asking for your hand, it seemed a godsend and his father was so pleased . . .'

'So you and Joshua Rutland planned my marriage between you.'

'No, no, it was not at all like that. I told him it depended on your consent . . . but it is a great match for you . . .'

'How much was the bribe, Papa?'

'Not a bribe, Clarissa, how can you say such a thing? Just a loan to pay a debt . . .'

'Which you need not return if I marry his son, is that it? Oh how could you, Papa, how could you agree to such a thing?'

'I had to, Clarissa, I swear I had no choice. It was a debt of honour . . . to fail would have meant disgrace, prison, the finish of our life here, the end for Harry in the regiment. I never dreamed that you wouldn't see it as I did. He has so much to give you . . .'

I hated the abject pleading on father's face. How low had he sunk that he should descend to bargaining over his daughter's future, but this was my whole life and I could not sacrifice it, even to save him, I couldn't . . . I knotted my hands together in an agony of indecision and knew he watched me. I had always done his bidding and he could be kind and loving when things went his way.

He said persuasively, 'Think it over, Clary. I am sure you will see that I am right. We are due at Bedford House tonight and Bulwer will be there. It will be so easy for you. One smile and he will be at your feet.'

I looked up at him. How could he be so insensitive, so unfeeling? I could see the gloating eyes, hear the whispers. I knew exactly what they would all be saying. I had seen it happen to other girls, heard the sneers, the laughter, the cruel jests, and I could not bear it.

'I shall not go.'

'You will, Clarissa. In this I will be obeyed.'

'You cannot force me.'

'I can and I will. You will go with me tonight as we intended. You will tell Captain Rutland that you accept his offer and I shall send an announcement of your engagement to *The Times* in the morning.'

'And if I refuse?'

'Then you will compel me to disown you. I shall let it be known that your conduct has been such that I can no longer tolerate you in my household.'

I did not think he meant it for a second, but he must be desperate indeed to make such a threat. I didn't answer because the resolution had already hardened in my own mind. I knew what I was going to do.

I got up and moved to the door. He looked after me, his voice softening a little. 'Don't be angry with me, Clarissa. It is you I am thinking of after all.'

I paused, turning back to face him. 'Have you ever thought of me, Papa? Have you ever thought of anyone but yourself? Did you think of Mama when you challenged her to jump that dyke?'

I saw the hurt on his face and went swiftly before my resolution should weaken. I would go now, go to Aunt Jess at Copthorne. It would need planning but I had to escape even if it was only for the time being and if he followed me as he well might, then Miss Cavendish would be more than a match for him.

I went back to my room. The bed had already been made and I began to put together the clothes I would need. The moment father left the house I must be ready to go. Luckily the small basket trunk I had used on our last trip to Brighton had not been placed upstairs in the attics but was stored in a cupboard at the end of the passage. There was no one about so I fetched it myself dragging it along the landing as quietly as I could. I started to pack, my hands trembling, my heart thumping. The slamming of the front door sent me hurrying to the window. Father had paused on the steps, elegant as ever, with his lemon-coloured gloves, his hat at a rakish angle, his cane under his arm, and I felt guilty because I loved him dearly in spite of everything and I did not want to see him ruined. Then the memory of the cold-hearted way he had planned my future hardened my heart. He had always got himself out of trouble before, he could do it again.

I had never travelled alone by stage but I had a recollection of

Harry telling me once that the Cambridge coach set out from the Bull Inn at Aldgate. It was barely ten o'clock. If I left at once, I might be in time. I rang for Patience and told her to call Tim the bootboy to carry down my trunk and then fetch a hackney carriage.

She looked at me with surprise. 'But the master said you would be going out tonight, Miss, and I have been pressing your gown.'

'Never mind that. The Colonel thinks it best I go into the country for a little. Now don't argue, Patience, just do as I say.'

Tim shouldered my trunk and took it downstairs while I changed into my travelling dress, gathered cloak, bonnet, gloves, and all the money I had which was not a great deal. I would have to hire a postchaise at Cambridge to take me to Copthorne and that would be expensive. I raided the housekeeping box. The butcher's bill would have to go unpaid for another month.

When the carriage came I was waiting. It smelled frowsily of dirt and horse dung and stale straw, but I didn't care. Crabbe watched me disapprovingly from the steps and Peg stared up from the area, broom in hand. Other eyes were no doubt peering from behind curtained windows as we circled the square. I could imagine what they were whispering . . . 'Have you heard? A man in her room! The shame of it . . . the disgrace!' Let them scandalize as much as they pleased. Better that than being married to Bulwer Rutland for the rest of my life.

The journey was entirely uneventful except for the discomfort to be expected when travelling in a public conveyance. I had to wait till past noon but by a lucky chance I obtained a seat inside since a passenger who had booked did not turn up at the last moment but I was wedged against an enormously fat man who overflowed in every direction and finally went to sleep on my shoulder. Opposite sat a lady with a small dog on her lap which yapped itself into hysteria and then was sick. Her maid was carrying a large box whose sharp corners dug into me at every jolt. But these were trifles. I had a day's start before father realized that I had gone and once at Copthorne I would be safe.

It was dark when the coach went thundering into Cambridge with the guard sounding a merry blast on his long tin horn. The fat man woke up with a start asking where we were and I eased my cramped limbs thankfully.

It was raining heavily when we alighted and the courtyard of the Hoop Inn in Bridge Street was full of puddles. I picked my way gingerly through them and was disconcerted to find myself the only female in the taproom, the other ladies having been carried off by friends who had come to meet them.

Innkeepers are snobs to a man and reserve their courtesies for wealthy customers travelling in their own carriages. The landlord looked me up and down and said curtly there was no postchaise available to carry me to Copthorne that night. I hesitated about engaging a room alone in a busy tavern. Already the room was filling up with boisterous young men from the Colleges. Bold roving eyes examined me curiously. I was stiff, tired and very thirsty. I ordered some tea and toast and withdrew to a quiet corner, pulling my bonnet forward and trying to look as inconspicuous as possible. When the tapster put the tea in front of me, he gave me a nudge and a knowing wink, waving a dirty hand to the end of the table.

'The gentleman sitting there is going your way, Miss. Perhaps he might give you a lift.'

I didn't think I had the courage to accost a stranger and make such an impertinent request that might well be misinterpreted, but while I poured my tea, I did give him a furtive glance. He was between forty-five and fifty, not handsome but of striking appearance, with a lean pale face and a thin line of dark moustache. With him was a small boy about ten or eleven, very slim with hair black and glossy as a crow's wing and a dark olive skin. In front of them had been placed heaped platefuls of a rich meat pie which the man was attacking vigorously while the child sat mute, fork in hand, staring at it unhappily.

The father, if it was the father, said irritably, 'Eat your food, for God's sake, boy. You've taken nothing all day. Do you want to make yourself ill?'

The child shook his head dumbly and his companion looked at him with exasperation.

'Now what is it? Can't you do as you're told for once or do you want another touch of the whip?'

The boy had huge dark eyes fringed with long thick lashes and as I watched they slowly filled with tears that rolled silently down his cheeks and seemed only to make his guardian more angry.

'Now don't start blubbering again. Haven't we had enough of that during the last few days?'

It was nothing to do with me and yet I couldn't help a stir of pity. I remembered how bitterly Harry had wept when mother died and how impatient father had been when the long carriage journey to London made him travel-sick.

I leaned forward. 'Excuse me, sir, but perhaps your little boy finds the food too rich and heavy. It might be better to try him with a slice of toast and some tea.'

A pair of blue eyes startling in the sallow face were turned on me freezingly, then he said abruptly, 'Did you hear what the lady said, Jethro? Is that pap more to your fancy?'

The child seemed too frightened to reply so I quickly put a finger of toast on my plate and placed it in front of him.

'Try and eat a little,' I said coaxingly. 'You'll feel better if you do.'

'Will I?' The boy looked at me doubtfully before he began to nibble at the toast.

'There now, doesn't it taste good?'

His father said, 'It's very good of you. I'll order more.'

'Please don't trouble. I have had sufficient. But perhaps we could have another cup.'

When it came, I poured the tea and Jethro began to sip it, afterwards eating with more relish.

His father watched him, frowning before he said, 'The boy's nurse has fallen sick and left him on my hands.'

Without the slightest notion of how to care for a delicate sensitive child, I thought to myself. I smiled at the boy and put more toast on the plate.

The man tapped his fingers impatiently on the table. 'I was afraid he'd make himself ill and I must go on to Ravensley tonight.'

'Then you must be Lord Aylsham,' I exclaimed.

'Yes, I am,' he sounded surprised. 'Justin Aylsham. Have we met?'

'No, but I am acquainted with your nephew. I saw him in London a few days ago.'

'Indeed.'

So this was Oliver's uncle. I examined him with renewed interest. Nothing had been said about a son. I found myself wondering about the boy's mother.

'I am Clarissa Fenton. I'm on my way to stay with my aunt. She is Miss Cavendish and lives at Copthorne.'

'Copthorne?' he repeated. 'That's only a mile or so from Ravensley.'

'Yes, and the landlord informs me there is no conveyance available,' I said ruefully. 'I am afraid I shall have to spend the night here.'

He gave a quick glance around and then turned back to me with a ghost of a smile. 'Scarcely suitable if I may say so, Miss Fenton. Your aunt and I have some slight acquaintance. If it will be of assistance, I can offer you a seat in my carriage.'

I accepted gratefully, quite sure that it was simply because he welcomed any help with the boy and thanking heaven for a travel-sick child.

It was past nine o'clock and Lord Aylsham was anxious to be on his way. He hurried us out to the inn yard where the carriage was waiting with the fresh horses already in the shafts. A slim dark shape materialized out of the shadows and I realized that Justin Aylsham must have brought his Indian servant with him. At a word from his master he silently put my trunk into the boot and then mounted the box beside the coachman. I was handed into the carriage, Jethro was lifted in beside me, my benefactor took the seat opposite and we set off.

He did not engage in conversation and I was glad of it. It seemed a very long time since I had set out from Soho Square that morning. My head ached and I was only too happy to lean back against the cushions and close my eyes. The child was so slight that every jolt of the carriage almost jerked him off the seat and so I put my arm around him. At first he resisted, trying to sit bolt upright but after a while fatigue overcame him and he drowsed against my shoulder.

It was a dark night and little could be seen through the windows but presently gusts of wind lashing the rain against the glass told me that we were already on the narrow causeway that crosses the Fens to Ravensley. I must have dozed off because the next thing I knew the carriage had pulled up so abruptly that I was flung almost into Lord Aylsham's lap.

'What the devil!' he exclaimed as I muttered an apology and scrambled back on to the seat.

'What is it? Why have we stopped?' he shouted and when there was no reply, fumbled impatiently with the door handle, opened the door and jumped out.

Jethro dazed with sleep was clinging to my hand. 'What's the matter? Where has Papa gone?'

'It's all right. Don't be frightened.'

Curiosity overcame alarm. I wanted to see for myself. I climbed down from the carriage with difficulty and then wished I hadn't been so rash. A wild wind caught at my bonnet blowing the rain into my face and water was flowing freely across the narrow track from the stream that ran alongside. It soaked into my boots.

The coachman was standing beside Lord Aylsham pointing fearfully forward with his whip. 'There, my lord, there, look, d'ye see? There's summat in the road.'

'Then move it, man. It's a fallen tree probably.'

'No, 'tisn't that. It's summat unnatural. The horses took fright. They wouldn't go on nohow.'

'Oh for heaven's sake!'

My eyes had grown accustomed to the dark and I could just make out the black shape that lay across the road. One of the horses whinnied and jerked against the harness. Lord Aylsham strode forward and the shape rose slowly to its feet. Beside me the Indian drew a sharp breath and the coachman crossed himself fervently. They infected me with their superstitious fear and I shivered in the wind and rain. Then in the faint light of the carriage lamps, the black shaggy monster turned itself into a man wearing a coat of some rough kind of fur; a dark streak of mud or blood ran all down one side of the white face but the extraordinary thing was that for an instant I could have sworn it was Oliver staring wildly from one to the other of us. In that moment of time none of us moved, then the man uttered a hoarse snarl and hurled himself at Lord Aylsham. The coachman stood as if paralysed but the Indian did not hesitate. He flung himself into the struggle and all three were locked together swaying backwards and forwards. Then Lord Aylsham was thrown to the ground, the Indian reeled back and their attacker went plunging across the road, splashed through the stream and disappeared into the blackness of the Fens.

I ran to help Lord Aylsham but his servant was before me, assisting him to his feet. Mud plastered his caped coat. I picked up his hat and handed it to him.

'Are you hurt, my lord?'

'No more than a bruise or two.' He stretched himself painfully. 'There's your Black Shuck for you,' he said angrily to the coachman. 'Some damned poacher! Fortunately he had no weapon. Now get back on to the box, you too, Ram, and let's be on our way.'

It had all happened so quickly, I felt confused. I said, 'Are you sure you're all right?'

'You should have stayed in the carriage, Miss Fenton,' he said frowning. He took my arm to help me in and Jethro grabbed at his hand.

'What happened, Papa? What was it?'

'A lot of fuss over nothing. Now don't start crying. I'm not dead and neither is Miss Fenton. Come along now. At this rate we will be fortunate to be home by midnight.'

Once we were seated the carriage jolted forward again and he sat, silent and brooding so that I didn't dare to question him. I wondered if he too had been struck by that extraordinary likeness or if I had only imagined it in the agitation of the moment.

When at last we reached Copthorne, the whole house was in darkness. Lord Aylsham said reluctantly, 'Miss Cavendish would appear to have retired to bed. Would you like me to wait until the door is opened?'

'No. It is kind of you but there is really no need. I have taken you enough out of your way already and I am most grateful.'

While the Indian carried my box to the porch, Jethro looked down at me shyly. 'Shall I see you again?'

I smiled. 'Perhaps . . . if your Papa has no objection.'

'None whatever,' he said politely. 'I'm sure my niece will be pleased to call on you and your aunt.'

It was not until the carriage had driven away leaving me alone that the true enormity of what I had done struck at me and I wondered what on earth Aunt Jess was going to say to a muddy, bedraggled, penniless niece arriving on her doorstep at almost midnight. Then I resolutely tugged at the bell. Nothing happened so I tugged at it again. Immediately there was a wild outburst of barking. Then a window shot up and my aunt's head appeared surmounted by a muslin nightcap.

'Go away whoever you are and come back in the morning,' she said. 'I don't open doors in the middle of the night.'

'But it's me, Aunt Jess, it's Clarissa,' I called out just as the barking rose to a crescendo.

'What's that? Who? I can't hear a word.'

'Clarissa,' I yelled. 'Clarissa Fenton.'

The window immediately slammed shut. But by this time the whole household was astir. Presently I could hear the door being unbolted and it was opened by aunt's ancient manservant. A frenzy of dogs came flying along the passage and leaped up at me, barking madly. My aunt appeared at the top of the staircase in her red flannel dressing gown, a candlestick in her hand.

'Down Prickle,' she said commandingly, 'down Warwick, down James.'

The dogs slunk back as she sailed majestically down the stairs. 'What is it, child? What has happened? Is your father sick? Is the king dead?'

It was all so dear, so familiar, so comforting. 'Not yet,' I said between tears and laughter, 'and nobody's sick but you did say I owed you a visit.'

'So I did and better late than never. Come in, my dear, don't stand there in that wind catching your death.'

My aunt asked no questions, that was not her way. Time enough for that in the morning, she said. 'Come into the kitchen, Clary. It is cosier there. I'll get you a hot drink while Prue takes a warming pan to your bed.'

She stirred up the fire and in no time at all I was happily sipping hot chocolate and eating biscuits, watched with eager eyes by the three dogs sitting on the rug in front of the fire.

'Lord Aylsham gave me a lift from Cambridge otherwise I'd never have got here at all,' I said breaking an arrowroot into three and giving the dogs a piece each.

'So Justin is back from London, is he? Then look out for fireworks.'

'What do you mean by that, Aunt Jess?'

'Oliver has returned just as I knew he would. It would seem he is to act as his uncle's steward.'

'And they won't get on together. Is that what you mean?'

She shrugged her shoulders. 'Well, what do you think?'

'Then why did Lord Aylsham ask him to come back?'

'Ever since Oliver went away last summer, there's not a man here who will do a stroke of work for Justin Aylsham. They don't say no, they just find they have other things to do. Our Fen Tigers can be as stubborn and obstinate as a set of mules,' said Aunt Jess, wildly mixing her metaphors, 'and he's mad as a monkey over it.'

'I wonder if he knows that Oliver has returned,' I said thoughtfully.

'Why, child, what makes you say that?'

I was about to tell her about that odd encounter on the road and then stopped. It was quite absurd. It could not possibly have been Oliver though, God knows, he had reason enough to dislike his uncle and yet somehow I did not want to talk about it.

'It was just that he didn't mention it, but then we did not speak very much at all.'

'Well, it's none of our business,' said my aunt cheerfully. 'Come to bed, my dear, and we'll have a good talk in the morning.'

I followed her up the stairs. For the moment it was enough to know I was here, safe, loved and made welcome.

3

Aunt Jess said thoughtfully, 'I don't like the sound of this Captain Rutland and he has certainly behaved abominably, but in a worldly sense it might be to your advantage to marry him, Clarissa.'

'Oh no!' I exclaimed horrified. 'You can't mean it. How can I possibly marry a man I don't love?'

'A great many girls do and I don't know as it turns out any the worse for them in the end,' she replied dryly, putting down a piece of toast for Prickle who had been patiently waiting beside her all during our breakfast. 'Is it just because you dislike the young man, with some reason I may say, or have you set your heart on some-one else?'

'It's not that at all,' I said rather too quickly. 'Oh Aunt Jess, you are not going to make me go back?'

'No, my dear. I think you need a good long stay in the country, time to get your breath which you can't ever do in London. You are far too thin and you look peaky to me and so I shall write to your father.'

'Bless you!' I jumped up and gave her a hug. 'I knew you'd see it my way.'

'Did you indeed? There'll be no balls and late nights down here,' she said warningly, 'and you'll have to do your share of the housekeeping.'

'I don't mind that at all,' I said happily and set about helping to clear the breakfast dishes. Aunt Jess had only two indoor servants besides John; Prue who had been with her since she was a girl and Patty Starling who was only fifteen and had come to work in the kitchen.

The letter was written but before it could be despatched, my father had arrived and in a fine rage. It was two mornings later and I had been out walking with Prickle. The little bitch was a love-child, an abandoned puppy found by Jake one morning partially buried in the rubbish heap and immediately christened Prickle by my aunt because her coat had been stuck thick with burrs where she had been struggling to free herself. She looked rather like a small black woolly rug with two pricked ears and a pair of bright eyes behind a fringe of silky hair.

I heard father's voice as I came into the hall, loud and hectoring, which wasn't really like him at all and only proved he was ill at ease. I paused guiltily to listen.

'She has behaved disgracefully and I shall insist on her coming back with me immediately. I have every right. Clarissa is my daughter after all and I would prefer you not to encourage her in her disobedience.'

'She may be your daughter but she is also twenty-two and has a mind of her own. She is very like Susan. Something you never seem to have recognized,' said Aunt Jess quietly. 'Now stop shouting, Tom Fenton. It doesn't impress me in the least and I refuse to be bullied. If Clarissa wishes to stay here, then stay she shall, whatever you say and I'll not have her forced into a marriage because you've made a fool of yourself again at the gaming tables.'

'Now don't start on that, Jess. I'm not a saint, nor have I ever pretended to be . . .'

'More's the pity.'

'Oh to hell with all this! Damn it, where is the girl?'

It was no use. I had to go in and face him so I plucked up courage and opened the door. Father was standing with his back to the fire, frowning and irritably flicking his boots with his riding crop, and because I had escaped, I couldn't help remembering how much I used to love him.

I went straight up to him and kissed his cheek. 'Good morning, Papa. I am very happy to see you.'

'The devil you are! I don't know how you have the impertinence to say such a thing after the dance you've led me,' he growled, 'walking out on us, leaving everything in an uproar and the servants all at sixes and sevens. Poor Harry was devilishly upset about it.'

'I'm sorry but you left me no alternative. I had to go . . .'

'Leaving me to attend that damned ball alone and a fine fool I looked. What in God's name did you expect me to say to Rutland?'

'As a matter of interest what *did* you say to him?' asked Aunt Jess curiously.

'What could I say except that his outrageous conduct had sent the girl into a *crise des nerfs* and the doctor had recommended country air as the only cure. He didn't believe me of course and neither did anyone else. The scandal that is going about is nobody's business. It really is unendurable that I should have to suffer it!' He was working himself into a rage again and Aunt Jess looked at him coldly over her spectacles.

'From what I gather you richly deserve it,' she said crisply. 'However it gives Clarissa a reprieve and scandal never killed anyone yet. Will you stay and eat with us, Tom?'

'I suppose I might as well now I'm here,' he said, ungraciously.

'Very well. I will tell Prue to set another place,' and she went off to the kitchen leaving us alone.

Father dropped into a chair by the fire and though he might go on grumbling, I knew the battle was won for the time being at any rate. He looked up at me broodingly. 'You've ruined your chances, you know that, don't you, Clary?'

'Perhaps. I don't think I mind all that much.'

'Well, you should.'

'Papa,' I hesitated and then knelt beside him. 'Papa, what has happened . . . about the money you owe to Mr Rutland?'

'Oh that. God knows. I'll manage somehow. There are always the Jews.'

'But you are so much in debt already. There is my money . . . the legacy from grandfather. I know it isn't much but if it will help . . .'

He touched my cheek. 'No, child. I'm not quite the rogue your Aunt Jess would have you believe. I'll not rob you of that. It's not enough anyway. Old Joshua is not a bad sort and you might come round to marrying his cub yet.'

'I won't, you know.'

'Well, we shall see.'

He rode away after we had eaten and even showed a little tenderness when we said goodbye. He leaned from his horse to pinch my cheek. 'I shall miss you, Clary, and so will Harry. Don't stay away too long.'

'Take care of yourself, Papa,' I called after him as I watched him trot down the path. Poor father. It was weakness with him rather than villainy and there was something endearing and a little pathetic about the jaunty manner with which he had accepted the inevitable. I couldn't help feeling anxious about him and yet at the same time thankful that I was free of his world for a few months. So that is the end of Bulwer Rutland, I thought to myself as I went back to the house, and did not know how wrong I was.

I did not see Oliver until I had been more than a fortnight with Aunt Jess. I busied myself helping her in the house and garden and was surprised to find how content I was with such a simple existence. The stress of the winter had tired me more than I believed possible. Then one morning when I was on my knees weeding the rose bed, Prickle started to bark and I looked up to see Jake coming along the path with a fashionably dressed young girl.

Jake I had seen already. He did all kinds of odd jobs for Aunt Jess and I thought what a fine young man he had grown into from the tow-headed lad I remembered. He and Oliver had been inseparable then and I used to yearn to be a boy with them. How long ago it seemed. I got to my feet as they came up.

Jake said, 'Good morning, Miss Fenton. I ran into Miss Aylsham at the gate. She was coming to call on you.'

He had a quiet unassuming manner but I was always conscious of a steady pride and self respect that distinguished him from the rest of his family and indeed from most of the farm hands. He shouldered the axe he was carrying and went off to the orchard where he was cutting down one of the old apple trees.

Cherry looked after him. She was flushed and if it had not been so unlikely, I would have thought she had been quarrelling with the young man.

'I could kill Uncle Justin for dismissing Jake like he has,' she burst out suddenly. 'It's so unfair when he did nothing, absolutely nothing.'

'Has Jake been dismissed? I didn't know.'

'He'd never say anything. He's much too proud but it's so unjust. Whatever is he going to do?'

'Surely that is his affair,' I said, a little amused at her childish vehemence.

It seemed to pull her up. She turned to me breaking into a smile. She had a piquant face, not exactly pretty but charming with a tip-tilted nose, the Aylsham blue eyes and dark curls escaping from under her bonnet.

'Oh dear, you must think me so strange talking like that,' she said frankly, 'only it does make me so mad.' Then she held out her hand. 'I'm Cherry and you are Clarissa of course. It seems such an age since we met. I was still quite a little girl and I used to think you so grand and grown up. I did mean to come before. Jethro has talked about you quite a lot since uncle brought him back from London.'

'Has he settled down? I thought him rather an unhappy little boy.'

'I think so,' she said carelessly. 'I don't see him much. He is in Hattie's charge for the time being.'

I asked her to come in and when Prue had brought us cakes and coffee, I said, 'You must be very glad to have your brother back at Ravensley.'

'Yes, of course. I missed Oliver terribly, only he's not at the house with us. He is living at Thatchers.'

'Thatchers?'

'It belongs to Oliver, the house and the farm. It's where Mr Robbins used to live when he managed the estate for Papa and Oliver says that since that is his position now, he'd rather stay there and not with the family. It's so stupid because it's not at all comfortable and he hasn't anyone to look after him and I think it's all because of Alyne . . .' Then she stopped. 'Oh goodness, I shouldn't really have said that. It makes him so cross, but I expect you know about it already. He and Alyne were to have been married but that was finished when Uncle Justin came back.'

'Were they engaged?'

'Not exactly because Papa was against it, but after he died, we all knew what Oliver intended.'

'Why was it broken off?'

She shrugged her shoulders. 'Because Oliver hasn't any money,

I suppose. Alyne doesn't talk about it. Nothing has gone right this past year.'

I thought of that dark silent unapproachable man. 'Is it because of your uncle? Is he unkind?'

'No, not really. It's just that . . . he's apart from us somehow. He is not a bit like Papa. He doesn't belong . . . oh I can't explain. Nurse says he is like someone who has died and come back to life but that's silly, isn't it?'

'Yes, it is, very silly.'

'You will come and see us, won't you, Clarissa? Come often. It's lonely at Ravensley sometimes. It's been such a long winter. We were snowed up for months and months and didn't see anyone.'

'Of course I will, but now that spring is here, you will have a great number of visitors, I'm sure.'

'Will your brother be coming? Harry and I used to have such fun together when we were little.'

She sounded so wistful that I smiled. 'I expect so but he is in the regiment now, you know. He can't do exactly what he likes.'

When she had gone, I went back to my bower bed. So Harry had been right after all. Oliver was in love with Alyne. I wondered if it was he who had broken it off between them. I dug savagely at a particularly tough weed and told myself not to be so foolish. It was high time childish dreams about Oliver were banished once and for all. It was quite absurd and I had always known it. But all the same my resolution did not prevent me from being curious about Thatchers. I remembered the old farmhouse. It was only about a couple of miles from Copthorne on the edge of the Fen. Aunt Jess only kept one pony to pull the trap and he was old and fat so I couldn't ride but there was nothing to prevent me walking. A few mornings later I pulled on my thickest boots and set out. Prickle came bounding out of the house after me and Aunt Jess who was planting out some young seedlings with her skirts carefully pinned up above the flannel petticoats, looked up at me from under her mushroom hat.

'Prickle is a faithless little bitch. She seems to have adopted you, Clarissa. Where are you going this morning?'

'I thought I might walk as far as the Fen. We used to go there so often when we were children.'

'Well, take care. There were floods earlier this year and it's still very wet. Don't fall in a bog.'

'I won't.'

How strange that I who scarcely walked anywhere in London except for a turn or two in the parks should now be willing to tramp for so long and not feel at all weary. When I stood at the edge of the Fen and looked across the narrow waterways, the banks already starred with spring flowers, I felt all the old enchantment. It was there still, the thick sedge, the green spears of the reed mace, the constant sound of birds, the strange thrilling unforgettable river smell.

Thatchers was so old, it seemed to grow out of the earth. Moss and ivy swarmed over the stone walls and the deeply eaved roof was covered with the brown thatch cut from the sedge of the Fen that gave the house its name.

It looked quite deserted so I walked round to the back and was surprised to see a small gig waiting with a glossy pony in the shafts. On that side of the house deep windows almost reached the ground and one was open to the gentle May sunshine. Then I paused because there was the sound of voices and though I couldn't distinguish what was being said, it was quite obvious that someone was angry. Out of sheer curiosity I drew close enough to peer through the nearest casement. I could see Oliver quite clearly, the other had his back to me but I was almost sure the tall spare figure was Justin Aylsham. I caught the tail end of what he was saying.

'. . . I think I'm the best judge of the people I employ, Oliver. However you are my nephew and I am prepared to be generous but I do want cooperation in return. Joshua Rutland will be visiting here soon and I shall expect you to be present. Your knowledge of the Fens will be invaluable and I want him convinced. Do you understand me?'

It was the last thing I had expected and I stood petrified. Whatever could that old tea merchant want with Justin Aylsham?

Then a voice behind me said sweetly, 'Why are you spying on them, Clarissa?'

Startled I turned round and saw Alyne leaning against the wheel of the gig swinging her bonnet by its green ribbons and smiling at me.

'I heard that you were staying with Miss Cavendish,' she went on. 'Have you come looking for Oliver?'

Somehow she had put me at a disadvantage. 'I was out walking . . .'

'And decided you'd call . . . didn't Cherry tell you that he is living here now?'

Oh God, she was beautiful! Far more so than when she was a child. It wasn't fair. Nobody had the right to possess such grace and loveliness even in the simplest dress. She had always had a rare quality of stillness and now, just standing there with a tiny smile playing around her mouth, she contrived to make me feel awkward and ill at ease. Then Prickle created a diversion by flying across the yard in pursuit of one of the cats, the tension broke and the men came out of the house.

Lord Aylsham did not notice me. He swung himself up into the gig and took the reins. 'Come, Alyne,' he said brusquely.

She followed him and then hesitated looking at Oliver. 'Aren't you going to help me?'

'Yes, yes, of course,' he said hurriedly. He put his arm round her waist and lifted her into the high seat and the look on his face told me everything I didn't already know.

The gig clattered out of the yard and I would have slipped away unnoticed if Oliver had not turned and seen me.

'Why, Clarissa,' he said in surprise. 'Whatever are you doing here? Why didn't you come in?'

'I didn't want to interrupt.'

'I might have been glad of it,' he said wryly. 'Cherry told me you had come and I've been meaning to call and haven't. I seem to be always apologizing, don't I?'

'It doesn't matter.'

'Come in.'

I followed him into the main room of the farmhouse. It was very large and sparsely furnished, with rough-cast white-washed walls and beams of black bog oak. A peat fire smouldered on the wide deep hearth, but the whole place had a dusty uncared-for look.

'I am afraid I can't offer you any refreshment. As you see I live rather barely.'

'Don't you have anyone to look after you?'

'Not yet, but I am thinking of asking Mrs Starling to come in and do the housekeeping.'

I remembered what Cherry had said. 'I hear that Jake has been sent away from Ravensley.'

'Yes.'

'Is that what the argument was about?'

'So you heard?'

'Not really . . .'

'I thought it unjust and so I told my uncle. The bad winter has caused serious distress in the neighbourhood. There is a great deal of unemployment and I don't know what the Starlings will do without Jake's money coming in.'

'Is that why you're going to ask his mother to come here?'

'At least it will be a roof over their heads. My father allowed them to stay in one of the cottages rent-free but Uncle Justin had them evicted while I was away and when Jake protested, and surely he had some right, he was dismissed for insolence.'

He spoke with a restrained anger and I looked up at him standing with his back to the fire liking the fierce indignation on behalf of his friend, and thinking irrelevantly how attractive he looked and how well his country clothes became him.

He turned to the fire kicking the peat apart so that it glowed red before he said thoughtfully, 'I have only been back here a couple of weeks and already I am wondering if I was wise to take your advice after all, Clarissa. My uncle and I don't see eye to eye, I'm afraid. I think I may do more harm than good.'

'I don't believe that. This is where you belong.'

'Perhaps.' Then he looked down at me, smiling. 'I forget my manners as usual. I should be congratulating you on your engagement to Captain Rutland.'

'But I'm not engaged.'

He raised his eyebrows. 'Everyone in town was talking of it as a foregone conclusion.'

'That's because he hates to think anyone can refuse him,' I said bitterly. 'I am not marrying him,' and I wondered how much else he had heard and had the delicacy not to mention.

'I suppose I should say I am sorry, but I'm not,' he said frankly. 'I don't like him.'

I longed to ask why old Joshua was coming to Ravensley but did not care to reveal that I had been eavesdropping.

I said, 'I ought to go. Aunt Jess will be wondering what has become of me.'

'Are you walking? Shall I accompany you?'

'No, it's not at all necessary and you must have other things to do.'

He glanced at the pile of account books on the table and grimaced. 'My uncle likes to sneer at book-keeping but someone has to do the work and there's a year's confusion to clear up.'

As we went out of the house together, he said, 'I know Miss Cavendish doesn't keep a stable but I am sure my uncle would be very pleased to loan a horse if you would care for it.'

'Oh I should . . . very much.'

'I will speak to him. I know Cherry would be delighted if you would ride with her occasionally. I am afraid she is very lonely at times.'

'I hope to go up to the house soon.'

'Good.' He took my hand and after a moment kissed it lightly. 'It feels right to have you back at Ravensley, Clarissa, like the old days.'

Only it was not like the old days, I thought sadly. We were children then, single-hearted, happy, without a thought for the future. Now there were so many other pressures and problems and none of us was the same. I looked back once and he waved to me before returning to Thatchers. Then I called Prickle and walked quickly away up the track.

4

They say that old houses have a soul of their own and that when you enter them you can feel it, friendly or hostile, as the case may be, but I don't think it lies in the bricks and stone but comes simply from the men and women who live there. Ravensley, like Copthorne, had remained in my memory as a place where we were always happy despite its age, the gallery of family portraits and its long history which had been violent enough and I believe it had stemmed from Oliver's father. He had been a quiet and gentle man but he had inner strength and one was aware of his influence, a feeling of serenity, a certainty that despite trouble and griefs, the world and his particular part of it, the Fenland which he loved, was a good place in which to live. But now all that was changed. I could not put my finger on it but there was an uneasiness, an edge of tension. I felt it in Cherry's discontent, in the attitude of the servants, even in the dogs banished now to the stables, and though it may sound fanciful to say so, I felt it emanated from that tall, dark, restless man, the silent Indian who followed his master like a shadow and the homesick little boy largely ignored by his father, bewildered and lonely in the great house where everyone down to the maids in the kitchen treated him as an unwelcome intruder.

I had become quite a frequent visitor whenever Aunt Jess could spare me, partly at Cherry's pressing invitation, partly because Miss Harriet who was growing old and frail found teaching the boy sometimes too much for her and one morning when she was laid up with a heavy cold enlisted my help. I was reluctant in case it might seem like presumption but Lord Aylsham coming into the schoolroom a day or so later and finding Jethro and I bent over some books together, thanked me gravely.

'It is most kind of you, Miss Fenton, to take an interest in the boy. I intend sending him to school in the autumn but in the meantime it has not been easy for me to find a suitable tutor.'

'I enjoy it and indeed it is no burden,' and I spoke the truth. I had often given Harry lessons when he was a child and Jethro was a naturally good child, perhaps too quiet and well behaved. I would have preferred to see more spirit.

I said a little hesitantly, 'Isn't he rather young to send away to school?'

'My son has to learn to be an English gentleman, isn't that so, Jethro?'

'Yes, Papa.'

He drew away from the hand on his shoulder and I had an uneasy feeling that the boy was afraid of his father and not without cause. A few mornings later I happened to be there when Lizzie was changing the child's shirt. I saw the long red weal on his neck and asked him how it had come there.

'Papa was angry with me.'

I met Lizzie's eyes above the boy's head and she nodded significantly. Afterwards she said quietly, 'It were a couple of days back, Miss. Jethro don't care for milk and when he wouldn't take his breakfast porridge, his father gave him a touch of the whip.'

'Oh no,' I exclaimed horrified, 'for so little a thing.'

'Tweren't the food, Miss, don't think that. He don't care what the boy eats so long as he don't fall sick, but he don't like to be disobeyed.'

It seemed an unnecessary harshness and so because I was sorry for the child, I continued to help Hattie and never once confessed to myself that part of my pleasure in going so often to Ravensley was the opportunity it gave me of seeing Oliver as he came and went though it was little more than a few words in passing.

One morning in late May after a couple of days of incessant rain which had kept us all indoors, I volunteered to take Jethro walking in the park. Oliver who had been working in the estate room emerged yawning and complaining of feeling stifled so I invited him to come with us. At the last minute just as we set out, Alyne came running down the steps to join the party.

It was a blustery day, cold for the time of the year, with a sharp wind. We walked briskly as far as the abbey ruins. They are not very extensive, a ruined arch at one end of what must have been the nave of the church, a fragment of wall with a flight of steps running up to a lancet window and a stone slab that might once have been part of the high altar. This part of the Ravensley grounds was on the edge of the Fens. Beyond the ruins, buried in the rank grass, lay crumbling tombstones of long-dead monks. It was an eerie place with the wind whispering incessantly in the tall reeds and the haunting cry of birds far overhead.

I said, 'What a bleak and dismal spot this must have been when the first monks came to settle here.'

'There is an ancient legend that it was a hermit who led them to this place,' said Oliver lightly, 'and when he lay sleepless at night in his hut of wattle and straw, he was beset by strange creatures crawling out of the mists and bogs of the Fens, monsters with enormous heads, long necks, fierce red eyes, teeth like horses and spitting fire out of their slavering mouths . . .'

'Oh don't! You'll terrify Jethro,' I said. 'The poor man must have been suffering from a marsh fever.'

'Very probably,' said Oliver smiling. 'I remember it was one of Nurse's favourite threats when I'd done something wrong. The monsters would creep out from Greatheart and come after me.' He put his hand on the stone slab. 'When the Danes came, they murdered the Abbot here on his own altar and I used to have horrible nightmares of them coming to split my head in two.'

A cloud had blotted out the watery sun and somewhere out on the Fens an animal, a polecat perhaps, screeched in the stillness. I could see the desperate scene in my mind's eye, the tall men in their horned helmets, the terrified monks, the blood, the devouring flames, and I shivered. 'It's a cruel and savage place.'

'Only if you are afraid of it,' said Alyne suddenly. She was in one of her strange contrary moods. 'After all the Danes were conquered in their turn. One of them might have been Oliver's ancestors, Thorkil son of the Raven and he was murdered by his wife.'

'Is that true?'

'So the legend says,' said Oliver. 'She poisoned him with henbane because he threatened to kill her lover.'

'Not nice people,' said Alyne. She had gone up the steps and stood framed in the pointed window. The hood of her cloak had fallen back and the wind tore the pins from her hair so that it streamed around her, pale and lovely, like the halo of some medieval saint.

Oliver was gazing up at her in a way that stabbed me with sudden pain. Then he said abruptly, 'Come down from there. It's dangerous. The stone is crumbling.'

She laughed provocatively and held out her hands. 'Come and fetch me.'

Then while he hesitated, she ran lightly down the steps and straight into his arms. He held her for an instant, his cheek close to hers, and then set her on her feet. He said quietly, 'You shouldn't do that. You could have broken a leg if you had fallen.'

Jethro who had been clinging tightly to my hand suddenly huddled against me, burying his face in my cloak. 'I don't like it here,' he whispered. 'It frightens me.'

Oliver who had never seemed to take much notice of the child put his hand on his shoulder gently. 'What are you afraid of, Jethro?'

'This is a bad place. There are Djinns here.'

'What are Djinns?'

'Wicked spirits, demons, my ayah used to tell me about them.'

'That was in India. Djinns don't live here.'

'Are you sure?' said Alyne with a sideways look at him.

'Of course I'm sure. I've yet to meet a Djinn in an English village.'

'We have devils though, witches too and ghosts,' she was kicking moodily at one of the black crumbling stones. 'A great many people died here savagely. Haven't you heard them when you wake up at night, Jethro, muttering and moaning in the reeds?'

'Don't talk about such things,' I said angrily, aware that she was deliberately teasing the child.

Jethro was looking from her to Oliver. 'I wish my Mamma was here.'

'Do you miss her so much?' I asked gently.

'Yes, I do.' His lips trembled. 'It's so lonely.'

I stole a glance at Oliver and saw how he stared down at the boy. Then he smiled and ruffled his dark hair. 'Come along now, Jethro, that's no way to go on. Shall I tell you something? I've thought of just the right thing so that you won't be lonely any more.'

'What?'

'You'll see.'

All the way back he laughed and joked with the boy and when I saw how happily the child responded to him, I was glad. It was not until some days later when I happened to be riding past Thatchers that I saw Jethro playing with Ben, the youngest Starling child. I knew then what Oliver had done and only hoped that it would not lead to trouble with Lord Aylsham.

All during that summer I thought how strange it was that Alyne seemed the only one unaffected by the fraught atmosphere of the house. She sailed through it serene, untouched. When guests came, and it was surprising how the gentry had accepted Justin Aylsham, in some subtle way that was never obvious, it was she who was the daughter of the house and I knew there were times when Cherry resented it. I was puzzled by her attitude towards Lord Aylsham. She was deferential, obedient, but never called him uncle and she spoke to him as an equal. Occasionally when I spent the evening there and she played the harpsichord or sang to us, I would see his eyes fixed on her and wondered what he was thinking. Oliver only came rarely in the evenings and when Cherry complained about seeing so little of her brother, her uncle said dryly, 'My dear, Oliver has amusements more to his liking in Cambridge.'

'What do you mean? What amusements?'

He shrugged his shoulders. 'Surely you don't need me to elaborate.'

I knew what he implied and wished I didn't. There were gaming rooms there and women too. Living with father and Harry had taught me a great deal about men's needs and their pleasures.

So the weeks passed, the pale green wheat ripened and grew varnished and brown as polished wood, the barley tassels trembled rustling like shot silk in the breeze and we came to harvest. The hard winter seemed forgotten though I knew Aunt Jess worried about some of the poorer cottagers and sent me to distribute baskets of eggs and vegetables or cast-off clothing to those most in need. It made me realize as I had never done in London how desperately close to starvation they lived. I was ashamed of myself for fretting over trifles and would go back to Copthorne hot with indignation.

'Sentimentalizing over them does no good,' said Aunt Jess caustically. 'That's the way things are and unless the law changes, there's little we can do.'

She was right but it did give me a sympathy with someone like Jake who was trying so hard to lift himself out of the ruck of the downtrodden.

To my great relief I heard no more of Joshua Rutland. Perhaps whatever business Oliver's uncle had hoped to transact with him had come to nothing. I fervently hoped so. A brief note had come from Harry telling me nothing of importance except what I already knew and which he put with brotherly bluntness.

'Half society are calling the Bull a scoundrel and the other half have bedded you with him and sent you off to the country for a reason you can guess . . . not the best of them, Clary, so don't worry overmuch about it. I miss you, Sis, it's not the same here without you and the servants are playing merry hell. When are you coming back?'

So that was what they were thinking about me. In no time at all I would be brought to bed with Bulwer Rutland's bastard. I was angry and thankful that I didn't have to face him down here where they knew nothing. A postscript scribbled on a corner of the folded sheet caught my eye. 'Father has not been so well.' I knew a flicker of anxiety and tried to ignore it. I didn't want to go back to Soho Square, to the noise and clatter of London streets, to the marriage market of ballroom and drawing room where, innocent or not, I would be made to feel the burden of a tarnished reputation.

Will Burton rented the largest of the Ravensley farms and the harvest supper, the Horkey as it was called, was to be held in his barns. All the last days of August they were busy in the fields. The agonies of winter were forgotten. There was work for everyone, Jake along with them.

Once I saw Oliver with his coat off, his shirt open to the waist, working beside his friend. We had been on easy terms of friendship during the summer. Sometimes he came riding with Cherry and me. Alyne still hated horses. One day he came by Copthorne when I was in the garden and invited me to go with him across Greatheart. We laughed together at ridiculous childish memories. We waved greetings to the wildfowlers who lived far out on the Fens so isolated they might almost have been in some other country. He knew them all and I think they liked and respected him for his father's sake. We passed windmills churning out the brown peat-stained waters in a creamy flood and presently in the great expanse of the undrained Fen we came to what was virtually an island in the midst of a network of waterways. The track had become no more than a sodden grassy drove and as we splashed across a shallow ditch, I saw a couple of men standing at the low door of a thatched hut rising up like a huge sedge-covered lump overshadowed by a straggling clump of willow. They were small, dark, leathery-skinned and in their shapeless jerkins and long boots they might have been their Iceni ancestors who had fought so long and savagely against the Roman legions under their brazen eagles.

They called something to Oliver in so broad a dialect I couldn't understand a word and he grinned.

'Wait for me here, Clarissa,' he said and slid from the saddle. He disappeared into the hut with the two men. I looked after him curiously. Linnets and goldfinches twittered and sang in osier cages outside the hut. There were nets, eel traps and baskets piled together and a thin thread of smoke drifted up from the brown hump and curled into the still air.

I was holding Oliver's bridle. The horses stamped and pulled aside to munch at the rich grass and a punt came slowly down the stream and went gliding past. The sun touched with gold the bare head of the young man paddling it and he turned to look at me as he went by. I caught my breath because I could have sworn I was looking at Oliver though his clothes were rough and his hair wild. I could not be sure and yet it seemed to me the face I had seen once before on that dark night in April. Then there was a burst of laughter, the two men came out of the hut, clapping Oliver on the back. One of them was grinning with a flash of white teeth in the tanned face, a couple of cock pheasants swinging from his hand. He handed them up to Oliver as he hoisted himself into the saddle.

'They'll make a rare tasty supper for Jake and his Mam,' he said, 'but mind now, Mister, we never poached none. They ran into our nets and wrung their necks o' thesselves, ain't that so, Nampy?'

'Aye, stoopid great lumps!' said his comrade and they exchanged winks, highly pleased with themselves.

'Who on earth are they?' I asked as we trotted away.

'Moggy Norman and Nampy Sutton, two of the greatest rogues unhung and I greatly fear these pheasants came from Sir Peter Berkeley's new coverts,' said Oliver wryly. 'They're good fellows at heart all the same. They eat rough, sleep rough and fight rough but they'd not let a comrade down whatever the cost.' His mouth tightened: 'If my uncle knew they hunted over his land, he'd have them run off and transported. It worries me sometimes, Clarissa. If trouble comes, it's men like that who will be at the heart of it.'

'Is trouble coming?'

'I don't know but I remember what happened when I was a boy. I remember the riots when they hanged Isaac Starling and sometimes I think I can sense it in the very air we breathe, the smell of hunger and discontent.'

I thought of the man I had just seen going by in the punt and long since lost to view, but it seemed silly to say 'There's someone living on the Fen who looks just like you.' Instead I said, 'Are there men who hide out here, outcasts, hunted men, even criminals?'

'Lord yes, numbers of them. It's been a place of refuge ever since Hereward the Wake defied William the Conqueror. It would take an army brigade to search these Fens and then they'd not succeed in rounding them up.'

When we returned to Copthorne, he held up one of the pheasants. 'Would Miss Cavendish like one of these?'

'No. I'm sure the Starlings can do with both of them . . . and you.'

He laughed. 'Poached game always tastes the sweetest. It's been a good day, Clarissa, thank you for coming with me.' He waved as he rode away.

He liked me well enough, I knew that, but all the same there was an ache inside me. Never in all the time we had spent together had he once looked at me as he did at Alyne.

It had always been the custom for those in the great house to take part in the harvest supper, usually leaving discreetly before the merriment became too boisterous. When we were children, we had come riding back from the fields on top of the wagon. I remember how envious I had been when Alyne had been crowned with flowers and allowed to carry the precious corn dolly roughly shaped from the last corn to be reaped which would be carefully preserved in the farmhouse till next year to ensure the continuance of the harvest.

We were all there in the great barn when the last cart came rolling down the lane with Jake riding triumphantly on the golden sheaves.

The reapers had appointed him Harvest Lord, King of the Festival, and I had a strong conviction that it was done deliberately to prove their independence and show Justin Aylsham how much they resented his arbitrary dismissal of one of their own. I thought how handsome he looked, his face bronzed and his hair bleached by long days in the sun, his white linen shirt freshly washed and ironed, a red neckerchief round his brown throat. We sat at the top of the table with Farmer Burton and his wife. Lord Aylsham had an air of bored indulgence. Alyne sat beside him, lovely and withdrawn, but Aunt Jess in her flowered gown was enjoying herself vastly and Cherry was wildly excited.

The table was heaped with more food than many of them had seen for months and they did ample justice to the boiled hams, joints of beef, home-made pickles and fruit pies, the immense creamy cheese, fresh baked bread and great jugs of ale. A good many of them would be drunk before the night was over. After we had eaten and before the dancing began, they sang the traditional harvest song.

Jake began it, his strong untutored voice rising above the din and hushing it:

'I'll sing the one O'

Another took it up:

'What means the one O?'

Then the whole company in chorus:

'When the One is left alone
No more can it be seen O . . .'

I leaned across to ask Oliver what it meant.

'The Trinity, I suppose,' he said. 'All these old rhymes had religious significance once but it's so ancient, nobody now remembers what it means.'

And so it went on through the verses, question and answer:

> 'Twelve's the twelve Apostles, O!
> 'Leven's the 'leven Evangelists,
> Ten's the Ten Commandments,
> Nine's the gamble rangers . . .'

Cherry was listening entranced, her eyes on Jake.

> 'Eight is the bright walkers,
> Seven's the seven stars in the sky,
> Six is the provokers,
> Five's the thimble in the bowl . . .'

I saw Justin Aylsham's hand steal out and close over Alyne's. She did not move but a slow blush ran up into her pale cheeks. Oliver moved restlessly and the sunburnt hand on the table clenched and unclenched. The singers came to a triumphant conclusion:

> 'Four's the Gospel makers,
> Three, three's the rare, O!
> Two two's the lily white boys
> That clothed all in green O
> And when the One is left alone
> No more can it be seen O.'

It might be religious but it was pagan too, a wild rejoicing that the harvest was gathered and was good which meant food all winter through for those who had so little.

We stayed a while longer to watch the dancing. Oliver said, 'Would you like to join in, Clarissa?'

'I don't know if I can.'

'It's easy, a country measure and they like it if we do.'

In other years, I thought with a touch of bitterness, it must have been Alyne's hand he had taken and now deliberately he turned his back on her.

'Go on, my dear,' said Aunt Jess cheerfully. 'It's nothing but a jig. I'd join in myself if I were ten years younger.'

So we jigged away in and out of the barn and it was hot and dusty and great fun until suddenly I saw that Cherry was dancing with Jake and though there should have been no harm in it, I felt a stab of apprehension. Oliver didn't appear to have noticed and neither did his uncle. I was glad when the fiddler stopped playing to mop his brow and swallow thirstily a tankard of ale.

'Time we went,' said Lord Aylsham curtly, getting to his feet.

Farmer Burton, red and perspiring, shook hands heartily and ushered us out. I took Aunt Jess's arm and we walked together towards the gate where the gig waited with the horses. At the side of the track where the big chestnut drooped its boughs, half hidden but still visible, were Cherry and Jake in each other's arms.

Lord Aylsham uttered a stifled sound and strode towards them. He seized Cherry by the shoulder and swung her away so that she stumbled and nearly fell.

'What in God's name do you think you are doing?'

'We were kissing,' she said defiantly. 'There's no harm in it. It's all part of the game.'

'You're not a village slut, you are my niece and an Aylsham, so behave like one. As for you,' he turned on Jake with a fury all the more telling because he did not raise his voice, 'I have had enough of your insolence. If you so much as lay a finger on her or even speak to her again, I'll have you run out of the village and the county. I'll make damned sure you never work again.'

'No.' Oliver had stepped forward. 'You can't do that. He is not going to suffer for a piece of folly that's as much Cherry's fault as his. She's thoughtless, a child still . . .'

'I'm not a child,' protested Cherry.

'Be quiet, Puss, leave this to me.'

'This is my affair, not yours,' said his uncle icily. 'I am Cherry's guardian and I decide what is best for her.'

'Are you going to whip me as you whip Jethro?' said Cherry shrilly.

There was a frozen shocked silence then he said coldly, 'I shall do whatever I consider necessary to punish you and put a stop to

such vulgar behaviour,' and he would have walked on if Jake had
not prevented him.

'One moment, my lord. I apologize to Miss Cherry. It is my
fault. I shouldn't have let her forget herself with someone like me,
but you'll not touch her, do you hear me?' I saw Justin Aylsham's
eyes flash and he would have spoken but Jake went on. 'You can
do what you like to me, but I'll have you remember that I'm a
man and I have my pride, I'm not a worm to be crushed under
your feet and if I choose to speak with her again, then I shall do
so and nothing you can do will stop me.'

It was unheard-of madness for a young man in Jake's position
to speak as he did and yet my heart warmed to the boy who had
the courage to stand up for his rights as a human being. Then to
my horror Lord Aylsham raised the riding crop in his hand and
struck him twice across the face so swiftly that no one could have
stopped him. Jake did not move. He stood quite still with the
weals scarlet across his cheek.

'That was a devilish thing to do!' Oliver moved between them,
but his uncle thrust him aside. He walked on without another
word, flung himself into the saddle and rode away.

The fiddler was still sawing away at his instrument and some of
the dancers stopped to stare. Jake turned and went quickly up the
track. I saw Mrs Starling, white-faced, her hand at her mouth, and
Jenny clinging to her arm with frightened eyes.

Cherry had begun to cry. Oliver patted her shoulder awkwardly.
'It's all right, Puss, don't upset yourself.'

'Oh why is he so cruel, so unjust . . . ?'

'You shouldn't have done it, Cherry. Don't you see? It's you
who have been unfair to Jake.'

'Why, why? I didn't mean to harm him . . .'

Oliver gave me an appealing look. 'Look after her. I'm going to
Jake.'

I put my arm round Cherry and drew her along with me, trying
to soothe and comfort her.

Alyne said disgustedly, 'Oh for goodness' sake pull yourself together, Cherry. Everyone is looking at you.'

'I don't care . . .'

'Well, you should. If you wanted to kiss him, why didn't you go
somewhere where you couldn't be seen?'

'I'm not like you. I'm not ashamed of what I do,' sobbed Cherry.

'Oh stop it! Stop it, both of you!' I said angrily. 'You'll only make it worse.'

I guided Cherry to the gig and helped her into it. Alyne followed and just as I was wondering whether to go with them, Oliver came back. He climbed up and took the reins.

'I'll drive them back to Ravensley,' he said.

'Don't worry about us,' said Aunt Jess quickly. 'Clary and I are not afraid of a little walk.'

'If you're quite sure . . .'

'Of course I'm sure. Now off you go and take care of your sister. She is very distressed.'

It was a good mile to Copthorne and we plodded along the dusty road, hot, footsore and disturbed. It was not yet dark but the sweet September evening was spoiled by the ugly little scene we had just witnessed. We had gone about half the distance when Aunt Jess stopped suddenly.

'There's going to be trouble there,' she said. 'That child is in love with Jake Starling and it won't do.'

'Oh no,' I protested, 'not really in love. It's just that she has known him so long.'

'That's reason enough. He's extremely attractive and she doesn't see enough young men. It's Oliver's fault. He is so taken up with resenting his uncle and mooning after Alyne that he never remembers that his little sister has become a young woman.'

'He's very fond of her.'

'Of course he is, just as he is fond of his dog or his horse and that's the end of it,' said Aunt Jess wrathfully, 'and it's not sufficient. Write and ask Harry to come down, Clary.'

'What on earth has Harry got to do with it?'

'It will give her a chance to make comparisons. The only other young man who has looked at her with admiration is Hugh Berkeley and he, poor boy, is a mere shadow compared with Jake.'

I couldn't see Harry fitting into life at Ravensley and I thought Aunt Jess exaggerated. Then before I could do anything about it, circumstances had made it unnecessary.

5

The Michaelmas ball at Ravensley, said Aunt Jess, was the first really grand occasion at the great house since Justin Aylsham had returned from India.

'He's beginning to feel his feet,' she went on dryly, frowning down at the card of invitation in her hand. 'The county were inclined to look askance at first. Some of them remembered that he left under a cloud even if it was twenty years ago and they never knew the precise details, but now they'll come flocking as much out of curiosity as anything else.'

'Are we to go?'

'Of course we are. I wouldn't miss it for the world. I want to see their faces. It will be good for Cherry too. The child is living in a backwater. It's a great pity that Justin didn't bring a wife home with him who could have given her a London season.'

'What about Alyne?'

'Alyne has always been able to look after herself,' she said cryptically.

I wondered if Aunt Jess still believed in the value of a London season where husbands were to be picked up by the dozen. It wasn't so easy if you were fastidious or possessed an independent spirit as I knew to my cost.

I had not seen much of Cherry or Alyne since the harvest supper. Aunt Jess had suffered a severe chill due to working out in the garden in all weathers. Much to her annoyance the doctor had confined her to bed where she fretted and fussed and was short-tempered with Prue as well as me. She was missing Jake and the odd jobs he had so willingly undertaken for her. When I questioned Patty as to where he was, she looked mysterious and said her brother had gone off to Ely in search of better paid work than farm labouring. In some ways I was thankful.

On the night of the ball I looked critically in the mirror. 'You've put on weight,' said Aunt Jess approvingly. 'You've got distinction, Clarissa, and that's more than most of the rabbity girls nowadays.' It seemed poor enough compensation when I thought of Alyne's ravishing beauty. My dress was of lilac gauze trimmed with purple velvet ribbon and I wore a cluster of parma violets in my hair and at my waist. It was not new and I only hoped it did not look too old-fashioned. Fortunately the day was fine since we had no carriage and had to make do with the pony cart driven by John. There was a sweet nutty smell and a warm glow of autumn had touched the tall elms as we trotted the mile or so to Ravensley muffled in cloaks and scarves to the eyes.

It was a long time since I had seen the old house look so splendid. The dust covers had been whipped off and the gilt furniture though a little faded was still handsome. There must have been thirty couples or more in the large drawing room and tables had been set out for cards in the parlour on the opposite side of the hall.

Cherry was receiving the guests beside her uncle but it was to Alyne the men's eyes were turned; Alyne, slender and exquisite as a lily in her pale yellow gown dusted with gold stars. She wore no jewel, no ornament of any kind, only a cluster of yellow roses in the shining hair. Beside her Cherry looked no more than a gawky schoolgirl in white muslin and I felt sorry for the child. She caught at my hand as I came up with Aunt Jess.

'Stay with me, Clarissa.'

'But Cherry, I shouldn't . . .'

'Please, just for a little.'

I stood behind her, nodding to those few people I knew. I greeted Sir Peter Berkeley and his son. Hugh had a kind sensible face but I could see at a glance how the flaxen hair, the stooped figure with the hollow chest paled beside Jake who was so strong and vital, despite Hugh's handsome coat and sweet smile. He was eager to remain with Cherry but she had already turned impatiently away. Then beyond them I glimpsed a tall bulky figure in scarlet and black beside another squat and baldheaded, grossly overdressed with a flashing diamond pin in his stock, and my blood turned to ice. I would have escaped but it was impossible. They were almost upon us. They were already speaking to Cherry.

Trembling a little I held out my hand. 'Good evening, Captain Rutland.'

He walked straight past me as if I didn't exist. It was such a deliberate insult that for the moment I could not move or speak. Maybe not so many people noticed as I thought though somewhere near me there was a faint titter and I felt the hot colour come up into my face. I muttered something to Cherry and walked quickly away aware of curious eyes boring into my back. The musicians had begun to play, the floor seemed to stretch endlessly and I wished that somehow I could become invisible. Then a hand was placed on my arm, a hoarse breathy voice said, 'Not so fast, young lady. I want a word with you.'

Joshua Rutland was trotting at my side and it only seemed to make it worse. I stared straight ahead refusing to reply and he went on.

'He shouldn't have done that, you know, cutting you dead. Ain't quite the proper thing, but the boy was upset when you jilted him.'

'I did not jilt him, Mr Rutland.'

'Well, you wouldn't marry him, would you, comes to the same thing, running off, leaving him high and dry. What's wrong with him, eh?'

'Everything,' I said bitterly.

But oddly enough he was not offended. 'Well, that's straight from the shoulder anyway. Not that I agree with you, mind, but I prefer plain speaking myself. You know where you stand.'

'Mr Rutland,' I said firmly, 'I must go back to my aunt. She will be looking for me.'

'Now that ain't true, Missy,' he said wagging a stubby finger at me. 'She'll be thinking you're enjoying yourself with one or other of these young sparks.'

'Well, I'm not, am I?'

'True enough. You're having to make do with old Josh,' and he gave a hoarse chuckle. 'Didn't much want to come meself and that's the honest truth. Not my style, feel like a codfish swimming about in a glass bowl.' He looked around him with a kind of contempt. 'Not that I couldn't buy most of them up three times over.'

'That may be,' I said in exasperation, 'but money isn't everything and I don't see what it has got to do with me.'

'Don't you go despising money, Missy,' he said, shrewd little eyes looking into mine. 'Your Papa don't and that's a fact.'

I was immediately alarmed. 'What about my father?'

'Don't you worry. I'm not pressing him, not yet, though I could, you know, I could have him in Newgate tomorrow.'

I stopped aghast. 'You'd not commit him to prison?'

'Nay, nay, it don't matter to me, not that much. What I'm asking meself is this. Why does my Lord Aylsham with his fine gentlemanly airs want me to give him a loan, eh? Want it so badly that he even invites poor old Joshua Rutland who used to shovel tea into his own sacks to come down here when he's entertaining his grand friends. Why? Answer me that.'

'Where did you meet him?' I asked curiously.

'We did some business together when he was in India,' he said cautiously. 'A question of tea and he wasn't so high and mighty then by a long chalk, couldn't afford to be.'

'If it's anything to do with the estate,' I said firmly, 'it is not I to whom you should be talking but his nephew Oliver Aylsham.'

'Aye, he did mention him, and what kind of young man is he, eh? Crafty as a monkey like his uncle?'

'No, he's not,' I replied indignantly. 'He is honest and he will deal fairly with you.'

'Will he? I'm glad to hear it. Like him, do you, young lady? And where can I meet him?'

I suddenly remembered that I hadn't seen Oliver since I had arrived. 'He must be here somewhere,' I said and then gratefully caught sight of Aunt Jess. 'Excuse me. My aunt is wanting me.'

Stubbornly he remained beside me so I was obliged to introduce them. Aunt Jess in her voluminous gown of crimson brocade with a muslin cap surmounted by ostrich plumes towered above him.

'I've heard a great deal about you, Mr Rutland, and your son,' she said pointedly.

'Pleased to meet you, ma'am,' he bent awkwardly over her hand. 'Your niece is a fine girl.'

'I'm glad you think so, sir, because that happens to be my opinion.' Aunt Jess could be remarkably crushing when she tried.

Mr Rutland shuffled his feet, bowed, mumbled something and moved away at last.

'So that's the man who might have been your father-in-law,' she remarked. 'Vulgar of course and dressed up like a tailor's dummy, but a shrewd old party I should say.'

'I'd rather marry him than his son,' I said feeling a little light-headed with relief.

'He'd be no worse than Lord Haversham over there, my dear, who drinks like a fish and expects his wife to entertain his latest fancy whenever he feels like indulging himself.'

'Oh Aunt Jess, can that be true?'

'Don't giggle, girl, it's missish. Of course it's true. Lady Haversham told me so herself. Is *the* young man here?'

'Yes.'

She shot me a keen glance. 'Ah well, off you go, enjoy yourself, child. I'm too old for these junketings. Peter Berkeley has invited me to join him in a game of whist. It'll have to be a penny a point. I've no money to waste.'

I went with her to the cardroom. After I'd seen her settled with Sir Peter and two more of her particular cronies, I came back into the hall and saw the little cluster of young women whispering to-gether behind the banked flowers. I guessed they spoke of me and I didn't want to listen and yet could not help myself.

'Did you notice?' said one of them. 'He walked straight past her.'

'Brazen I call it, coming here at all when she knew he would be present.'

'What really happened?' That was Alyne's voice.

'Don't you know? Of course you're so out of the way down here. I don't know how you exist. They were to have been en-gaged. Mama said it was quite certain. Then her father found her in bed with a man . . .'

'Clarissa? Surely not.'

'It's true, I assure you. Mama's maid had it from the Colonel's Betsy. Her kind are always the worst.'

'Who was it?'

There was a whisper and a smothered giggle. 'It was hushed up of course but they do say her father took a whip to her before he sent her away.'

'Poor Captain Rutland . . .'

I felt sick. So that was the tale he had taken care to put about . . . and he would be believed. Men always are. It is only the woman whose good name is ruined. I had always known what would be said about me and had told myself I didn't care, but to hear the spiteful lies with my own ears . . . the injustice of it struck at me painfully. Despite myself I felt hot tears spring to my eyes. I turned away blindly and bumped into someone who apologized brusquely, and then held me at arms' length.

'What is it, Clarissa?' said Oliver. 'What has happened?'

'Nothing.' I made a valiant attempt to steady the shake in my voice. 'Nothing at all,' but I knew at once that he too must have heard every word.

'Aren't you enjoying the ball?'

'Not very much.'

'Neither am I. I nearly didn't come at all. Shall we escape for a few minutes?'

'Where can we go?'

'Out on the terrace. Will you be cold?'

I shook my head and he guided me through the hall. Outside the air was fresh and I took a deep breath.

'You're not crying, are you?'

'No,' I said tremulously.

'I believe you are.'

A pale light slanted through the long windows and the music came only faintly. He had his arm lightly round my waist. He bent his head and kissed me on the lips.

I drew away. I was raw and hurt still and bitterness welled up. 'You wouldn't have done that if you hadn't heard what they have been saying about me.'

'I don't listen to gossip,' he said dryly. 'What have they been saying?'

'It doesn't matter.'

'I just thought we both needed a little consolation.'

I glanced up at him, the set jaw and the grim line to his mouth. 'Why you and why tonight particularly? Is it Alyne?'

He looked away from me. 'How long have you known?'

'Ever since I have been at Copthorne.'

'Cherry, I suppose.'

'No.'

'Is it so obvious?'

'To me, it is.'

'Damnation! I thought better of myself,' he said wryly, 'and you, Clarissa? Since we're in confessing mood. Why the tears?' But I couldn't answer him and he went on gently. 'Not those malicious young women surely?'

'Not entirely. It's just that I had not expected to meet Captain Rutland here . . . it was distressing.'

'Why?' he frowned. 'What has he done?'

'You'd better ask the others.'

He looked puzzled and then grinned. 'Would you like me to go and call him out for insulting one of our guests? It would give me great pleasure.'

'Don't be absurd. Joshua Rutland is here too,' I said, remembering suddenly. 'He is looking for you.'

'Is he, by Jove? Well, he hasn't far to look.' He turned his back on the garden and took both my hands in his. 'We are being very foolish, you know. This is a ball and we are supposed to be enjoying ourselves. I have an idea, Clarissa. We'll dance and we'll pretend we adore one another. That will give them something to talk about.'

'It will indeed,' I said trying to match the lightness of his tone.

'Do you mind?'

I shook my head returning his smile. He didn't realize what he was asking of me. Why, I thought to myself as we went back to the ballroom, why on earth was I such a fool as to feel like this about a man who cared nothing for me, who was in fact besotted with another woman a hundred times more beautiful and desirable than myself, a man whom I suspected of using me for no other purpose than to try and make her jealous?

The evening dragged on. Oliver was with me a great deal of the time which gave me a bitter sweet happiness. I danced with this young man and that. I laughed, I chatted. I drank lemonade and ate ices and wished passionately that I was somewhere else. Captain Rutland was having a great success. He was the only red coat there and the girls fluttered around him. Once I saw how his eyes lingered on Alyne and I wondered what she really felt about

Oliver. She was the most secretive girl I had ever met and never gave anything away.

Then they were playing a waltz, that daring dance that had been all the rage in London but was still considered not quite respectable in this country place. Oliver came across to me again. I was tired now and I closed my eyes letting myself drift into an impossible dream until suddenly I realized what he was saying.

'I've been talking to Joshua Rutland. What do you know of him, Clarissa?'

'Not much except that he is very rich.'

'And a remarkably canny old bird I should have thought. Do you know what I believe? My uncle is going to mortgage Ravensley to him and use the money to drain Greatheart and all the land surrounding it.'

I stared up at him. 'Would that be such a bad thing?'

'You don't understand, Clarissa. It could destroy everything father tried to build up here, the goodwill, the trust and affection between him and his tenants, everything Ravensley has ever stood for. My uncle wants power and he wants money and he doesn't care who he tramples on to achieve it. But he is not going to find it so easy. I shall fight him, Clarissa, I shall fight him every step of the way.'

His arm tightened round me and I trembled at the savage determination in his tone. There seemed something irreconcilable between him and Justin Aylsham that nothing would ever bridge.

The dance was over and I felt I could take no more. I said, 'I think I had better go and find Aunt Jess. It is late and she may be wanting to leave.'

He took my arm and we moved towards the cardroom together when there was a sudden disturbance at the other end of the room. Sir Peter Berkeley appeared at the door looking agitated and beckoned to Justin Aylsham.

Oliver said, 'Excuse me, Clarissa. I had better go. Something seems to be wrong.'

He crossed to the door and after a moment's hesitation I followed after him.

In the hall Sir Peter was saying quietly, 'I don't want to cause a disturbance, but two of my keepers have come over from Barkham. They've nabbed one of the rascals who had been regularly poaching my coverts. They recognized him as a young man who has worked at Ravensley, Aylsham, so they thought it best to bring him over here.'

'Who is he?' asked Oliver quickly.

'A gang of those damned rogues has been getting away with my pheasants for weeks,' went on Sir Peter wrathfully. 'Time and again my men have almost had them and then they got away, slippery as eels. But this time one of them was not so lucky. He caught his foot in a trap and it floored him. The ringleader I shouldn't wonder, name of Jake Starling.'

I heard Oliver draw a sharp breath. 'Where is he?' he said.

'They've got him outside. Roughed him up a bit, I'm afraid, but he fought like a demon. Thought I ought to have a word with your uncle about it.'

By that time Lord Aylsham had joined them. Together they moved to the front door. On the steps two men were holding Jake by the arms. He was a pitiable sight, his shirt ripped, blood on his chest and oozing from a cut on his forehead. The marks of Justin Aylsham's whip still showed lividly on his cheek.

I was suddenly aware that Cherry had come up beside me. 'What is it? What has happened?' Then she caught her breath as she saw Jake and would have started forward if I had not held her back.

'Don't,' I said, 'it will only make it worse for him.' I felt her tremble and put my arm round her waist to steady her.

'Well, my man,' said Sir Peter loudly, 'so they've caught you at last. What have you got to say for yourself?'

'Nothing except that I was not poaching your game,' said Jake lifting his head proudly.

'Oh come now. What were you doing then? Taking a stroll through my woods, is that it?'

'And if I was . . . is that a crime? There is a right of way.'

'Don't you take that tone with me, young man,' threatened Sir Peter. 'It will do you no good.'

'It's the truth. Ask your keepers. I carried no gun, I had no game in my pockets . . .'

'That's right, sir,' interrupted one of the men who held him. 'It's my belief he threw it to his mates before they got away and left this fellow to take the rap.'

'More than likely. That's thieves' honour for you,' said Sir Peter contemptuously. 'What do you say, Justin?'

'He is no servant of mine,' he replied tonelessly. 'I had occasion to dismiss him some time ago and he has been causing me trouble ever since. So far as I am concerned, he deserves all he gets.'

'D'you hear that, my fine fellow. You'll come up before me on the bench and you'll be lucky if you don't hang.'

Oliver had stood helplessly, aware that to interfere would be worse than useless at this stage. Now I saw him go down the steps to Jake.

'Try not to worry. I'll do all I can.'

'Don't let it concern you, Mr Oliver. You'll only harm yourself. They'll have their way whatever you do . . . only . . . break it to Mam for me, will you?'

The men jerked him away so roughly that he tripped and fell. They kicked him to his feet and I saw how painfully he limped as they went down the drive.

Oliver came back up the steps and Cherry caught at his arm. 'You'll save him, won't you?' she whispered. 'You'll not let them hang him.'

He put his hand on hers for a moment. 'Don't cry, Puss, for God's sake, don't cry.' Then he put her from him and went into the hall and I knew by the look on his face that he had very little hope of being able to free his friend.

'He's got to do something,' said Cherry wildly, 'he's got to. Jake's innocent, I know he is. It's just that uncle hates him. He always has and now he hopes they'll murder him . . .'

'Stop it,' I said, 'stop it this minute and pull yourself together. Go back inside and pretend nothing has happened. Do you want everyone to talk about you? It won't help him and it won't help you.'

My harshness shocked her into silence. She looked at me reproachfully but after a moment she dabbed at her eyes and even managed a watery smile at Hugh Berkeley who had come to the door asking what had happened and if there was anything he could do.

'You can take care of Cherry,' I said. 'She is a little upset.'

I delivered her over to his charge finding it strange that the musicians should still be playing and the dancing continuing so gaily as if a man's life did not hang in the balance for the sake of a few paltry pheasants.

6

Jake was brought up before the court over which Lord Haversham presided with Sir Peter Berkeley and his fellow magistrates and condemned not to hang but to be transported to Botany Bay for seven years.

Aunt Jess was deeply distressed when Patty brought the news. 'So far as his mother and his family are concerned, they might as well have sentenced him to death,' she said heavily. 'That poor woman will never see her son again.'

Oliver had done what he could. He had stood up in the court and testified to the previous good character of the accused, speaking out so vehemently on his behalf that he was severely reprimanded for sympathizing with a trouble-maker and a rebel against authority.

'I might have been on trial myself,' he said angrily when I ran into him at Ravensley the next day. ' "Remember you are an Aylsham," said Lord Haversham . . . what does that old rake know of the people here? He only comes once or twice a year for the shooting. "I *am* remembering, my lord," I told him, "and if my father were still alive, this would never have happened." But I might have been speaking into the wind for all the good it did. Uncle Justin's testimony had damned him from the start.'

Later that morning when I was sitting with Miss Harriet and Jethro, Cherry came bursting into the schoolroom, flushed and upset.

'Have you heard what they have done to Jake? How could they be so wicked?'

Hattie said quietly, 'I know, my dear, and I am sorry for the poor young man. It's terrible but it is the law and there is nothing we can do about it.'

'Then the law should be changed,' exclaimed Cherry passionately, 'and there *is* something I can do. I shall go to Ely. I shall visit him in the gaol.'

'They will not permit it,' I said quickly, 'and it will do no good.'

'At least I can tell him it is not we who have done this to him,' she said wildly. 'I can take him food and clothes and money . . .'

'You will do nothing of the kind.' Lord Aylsham had come in so quietly that none of us had heard him. His fingers closed round Cherry's wrist and he swung her to face him. 'I thought I'd put a stop to it but now I see I'm mistaken. What is wrong with you that you have to run after this wretched young man like a bitch on heat? Is he your lover that you are so hot for him?'

Cherry stared at him, her eyes wide and terrified. 'I don't understand you,' she whispered.

He pulled her close to him. 'I think you do and I'll not have it, do you hear, I will not have it.'

His face frightened me. It was white and strained, the lips drawn back from the teeth. I half rose from my chair but before I could say or do anything, Alyne was there. She put a hand on his arm.

'Don't do that, Justin,' she said quietly. 'Let her go.'

He shivered at her touch and then released his hold. For an instant he did not move, then he said harshly, 'You will not see or communicate in any way with this young man. Do you understand me, Cherry?'

'Yes.'

'Have I your promise?' And when she was silent, he took a step towards her. 'Answer me, damn you!'

'Yes,' she whispered. 'I promise.'

'Very well.' He turned on his heel and went out of the room.

Alyne said irritably, 'Why do you provoke him, Cherry? Surely you know your uncle by now.'

'I know that he likes you and detests me because I am his brother's daughter. That's really what it is, isn't it?'

'Don't be silly,' said Alyne quietly and went out closing the door after her.

Jethro looked from Cherry to me. 'Why was Papa so angry? What has Cherry done?'

'Now, don't fret, child,' said Miss Harriet. 'Your Papa has a great deal to worry him one way and another. Now come along, we must go on with our lesson.'

She spoke quite calmly but I saw how the old hand trembled as it turned the page and it gave me a glimpse into what life was like at Ravensley with this difficult unpredictable man.

Cherry was rubbing her wrist. She said nothing but I knew from the obstinate look on her face that she had no intention of keeping her promise and so it proved. I tried hard to dissuade her but she had made up her mind.

'At least speak to Oliver first,' I said.

'He will only try to prevent me and I'm not going to let him. No one is going to stop me.' Then she gave me a pleading look. 'You wouldn't come with me, Clarissa, would you?'

I agreed in the end simply because if I hadn't done so, she was headstrong enough to go alone and that would have been unthinkable. I felt a traitor but I did try to speak to Oliver about it first. I went up to Thatchers only to find that he was away for a couple of days and Mrs Starling didn't know when he would return.

'I am going to try and see Jake if I can,' I told her. 'Is there anything you would like me to take to him?'

'Oh Miss Fenton, sometimes I feel I shall run mad when I think of what they have done to my boy, sending him to that terrible place so far away from us all. I've washed and ironed his things, shirts and such like. There isn't much. He weren't a boy to spend on hisself.'

'I'll take them,' I said.

She gave me the little bundle, touching it lovingly with her work-worn hands. 'You'll give him our love, Miss. Tell him we'll try and be there, all of us, to say goodbye on the day they take him away.'

'I am sorry . . . we all are.'

'I know, Miss. Mr Oliver too . . . I mind so well when they were boys together . . .' her voice choked on a sob. 'Mr Justin, Lord Aylsham as he is now, he hated Isaac all those years back when he were a young man. I never knew for why and when he come back and Isaac is dead and gone, then it seemed that he had it in for poor Jake. It don't seem right. He's been a good boy all these years. You tell him, Miss, we and the little 'uns, we'll not forget.'

Her patience, the long-suffering of the peasant under injustice, made me angry. I wanted her to fight against it. I wanted to fight myself but there was nothing any of us could do, only it made me all the more determined to go to Ely though I had no idea whether we would succeed in our mission.

I drove the gig myself with Cherry sitting silent beside me, the basket of food and clothes on her lap. A warm October sun lit the fields and hedgerows to a fiery glow of scarlet, gold and russet. It was not a day to be visiting a prison. I had never done such a thing before and the reality was far worse than anything I had ever imagined. The gaol was under the jurisdiction of the Bishop of Ely and not so far from his palace beside the Cathedral whose lantern tower was the glory of the Fens. I wondered if he had ever realized what a hideous place the prison was.

At first they would not admit us since we had no signed pass from the Keeper but then I suppose our dress, our manner and the gold I put into their hands impressed them. They muttered to one another. Their dirty fingers turned the basket inside out, examining everything in case we had concealed a file or weapon. Cherry would have protested when they took some of the food for themselves but I held her back.

'Don't make them angry,' I whispered, 'if you do, they'll not let us in at all.'

They eyed us up and down, sniggering, and I tried not to listen to their lewd jests while I repacked the basket. Then one of them led us down a passage, the floor running with muddy slime, and unlocked a door. The sickly stench that poured out was almost overpowering.

'In you go. Five minutes only,' he said and slammed the door behind us.

There were several men crowded together in the tiny room with only one small window high up in the wall. They stared at us with dull apathetic eyes. Then one of them lurched to his feet and made a grab at the basket. Cherry shrank back against me. I was beginning to realize that we should never have come when a filthy tattered figure shuffled through the straw thrusting the other men aside and standing between us and them, shielding us from their gaze. It was hard to recognize Jake, unshaven, his shirt in rags, his ankles raw and bleeding from the iron shackles, and yet there was still some quality about him, a courage, a dignity, not the dreadful apathy and despair on the faces of the others.

'You shouldn't have come, Miss Cherry, nor you, Miss. This place is not for the likes of you.'

'We've brought you some clothes and food,' I put the basket in his hands, 'and money too. It may help for the journey.' I looked quickly round and slipped the little leather bag into his hand so that the others wouldn't see.

'It's good of you. Mr Oliver has been kind too.' But though he spoke to me, his eyes were on Cherry and hers on him. Oh God, I thought to myself, it is true. Something has sprung to life between these two that is strong enough to fight against obstacles and conventions, and yet it is all so crazy, so hopeless.

'Your mother, Jake,' I said softly, 'she sends her love.'

'Poor Mam,' he said. 'Thank you for coming. I shan't forget ever. Now please go. Don't stay in this vile place.'

He was holding Cherry's hand as if he could not bear to let it go.

'Oh Jake,' she murmured, 'dear Jake.' Then suddenly she reached up and kissed his cheek. One of the men guffawed obscenely and I pulled her away.

'Come, Cherry. Jake is right. We should not stay.'

The turnkey was at the door unlocking it. We stumbled through and down the stinking passage. Outside in the street I drew a deep breath of the clean air. Cherry was leaning against the wall, looking white and sick.

'I didn't know, Clarissa. I never dreamed prison was like that. Will it be as terrible in Botany Bay?'

'No,' I said, 'no, I'm sure it won't. Jake is strong and clever. He will find good work . . . with a farmer perhaps.' I had only the vaguest idea of what happened to convicted prisoners but I had to comfort her somehow. She was quiet all the way home and I thought she is growing up. She has learned how harsh and unjust life can be for some and it is not an easy lesson. Before returning I had insisted on Cherry and I visiting the linen draper and the confectioner, to serve as an excuse for our expedition into the town. We were displaying the ribbons and laces to Miss Harriet and Jethro was excitedly opening the box of sugared almonds we had bought for him when Justin Aylsham walked into the room.

Cherry looked up apprehensively but there was no need. He was pleasant and charming as he could be on occasions.

'You've been buying fripperies, I see. Did you have an enjoyable day?'

'Yes,' I said quickly. 'We did all we set out to do, didn't we, Cherry?'

'Look, Papa,' said Jethro holding up the pink striped box of sweetmeats. 'Look what Clarissa brought for me.'

'She spoils you,' said his father. 'Now don't eat too many and make yourself sick.' For a moment the smile vanished. 'You've kept your promise, I hope, Cherry.'

'Yes, Uncle,' she said loudly, looking him straight in the face. 'Yes, Uncle, of course I have.'

'Good,' he said.

I was aware of the tension and I think Hattie guessed but she said nothing. I got up picking up my cloak and bonnet. 'I must go. Aunt Jess will be wondering what has become of me.'

I kissed Cherry and made my escape thankfully with an uncertain feeling that we had escaped disaster by a mere hairsbreadth.

It was astonishing that no word of our escapade reached Justin Aylsham. There was some advantage in being so isolated from the town and with so few visitors. One afternoon a few weeks later I set out to walk up to Thatchers. The weather had turned cold for early November and I walked briskly. Ben had suffered a bout of bronchitis and Aunt Jess had a cupboard full of remedies for just such emergencies. I offered to carry a bottle of liniment to rub on the boy's chest and a soothing syrup distilled from coltsfoot and mixed with honey for his cough.

Ever since Jake's arrest disquieting rumours had filtered through to us from all over the country. Riots of farm workers had broken out in Kent and Surrey and were spreading to Hampshire and Dorset. King George had died in June and his brother William, the pineapple-headed Duke of York with his bluff sailor manners whom I had met once at a court ball, had come to the throne and with him there came a change in government. The Tories had been defeated in the October elections by the Whigs, and there were some who looked for more radical reforms. But across the Channel there had been revolution. In Paris there was fighting in the streets once again. Fat old Charles X had been forced to seek refuge in England and the new French King, Louis Philippe, was the son of the man who had voted for the death of his cousin Louis XVI and had himself died under the guillotine.

'London is a melting pot of rumours,' father had written, 'and the government are shaking in their shoes. They are so scared that the disaffection may spread to England that anyone breathing the word reform is clapped into gaol. They are like ostriches burying their heads in the sand and refusing to acknowledge the wind that is blowing through Europe.'

It was unlike Papa to concern himself with politics so the situation must have become serious indeed, but down here in this remote place twists and turns of king and government meant little to the country people. What they feared was more immediate. If the winter was as hard as the last had been, then what they faced was cold, unemployment, starvation. I wondered what Justin Aylsham would do if the gangs came to Ravensley, burning ricks, smashing the threshing machines that had driven so many of them out of work, demanding higher wages and breaking open the granaries where the landowners and the farmers had stored their corn. Then I put the thought from me. I was concerning myself with something that might never happen.

At Thatchers, Mrs Starling was deeply grateful. 'I've been trying to keep the boy warm and Mr Oliver has been so good. He said I must have extra milk and eggs, but Ben frets after his brother. They took Jake away yesterday, Miss, and he begged to come with us to say goodbye. I didn't want him to go but he cried fit to break your heart. It were a long cold trip even in the carrier's cart and he were coughing worse than ever when we come back.'

Before I left she put a hand on my arm with a nervous glance towards the living room. 'I wish you'd go in and have a word with Mr Oliver, Miss. I'm that worried about him.'

'Why? Is he sick?'

'No, not sick,' she said doubtfully, 'though he looked right poorly when he come in late last night. Said he'd had a fall from his horse and Rowan were covered with mud and slush . . . but I don't know. If it hadn't been Mr Oliver, I'd have said he'd been fighting,' she went on apologetically.

'Fighting?'

'Aye. He asked for hot water and he were stripped to his

breeches when I took it in to him but he wouldn't let me do nothing for him. Then Miss Alyne came this morning with a message
from Lord Aylsham, she said, and he hasn't been out since.
Wouldn't touch his food though I cooked something special. He's
just sitting there with the brandy at his elbow and that's not like
him. He don't drink much, not like some of the other gentlemen.'

When I went into the room, Oliver was at the table in his shirt
sleeves, his coat flung untidily across the chair, the untouched food
pushed aside and the brandy decanter beside him two parts empty.
It was growing dark already and only the firelight lit the room.

I said cheerfully, 'Mrs Starling is very anxious about you. You
haven't eaten her good dinner and she fears you're sickening for
the marsh fever.'

'Nonsense, I'm just not hungry, that's all.'

'Brandy is no substitute for a square meal.'

'Don't preach at me, Clarissa.'

He got to his feet and limped to the fire coming back with a
taper and lighting the candles on the table. I saw then how pale he
was. There was a livid bruise all down one side of his face and he
straightened himself painfully. He gave me a half smile.

'It's all right. I'm not yet drunk if that's what you're thinking.
What are you doing here, Clarissa?'

'Aunt Jess sent some liniment and cough medicine for Ben. Mrs
Starling said you'd had a fall from your horse.'

'Yes, I did.'

'How?'

He shrugged his shoulders and moved to the fire, leaning his
hand on the mantel and staring down into the dull red glow of the
peat. I hesitated and then crossed to him.

'What is wrong, Oliver? There is something, isn't there?'

'Yes, I suppose there is. I'm a damned fool to let it trouble me
when I've known it for weeks. It's just that idiotically you still go
on hoping that you're wrong.'

'Wrong about what?'

'You should know, Clarissa, you're often enough at Ravensley.
Alyne is going to marry Uncle Justin.'

'What! I don't believe it.'

'It's true enough. She was gracious enough to come here and tell
me herself . . . this morning. I think she rather enjoyed it.'

'But why? She can't be in love with him.'

'Love!' he laughed sourly. 'There was a time when she loved me or so I believed.' He walked restlessly away, staring through the window at the darkening day with his back to me. 'He wants her all right. I knew that from the first night he came here, only I never dreamed . . . Alyne and my uncle . . . Christ! It sickens me even to think of it.'

'But he is so much older . . .'

'What does that matter? She is selling herself for all the things he can give her and I can't.'

It still seemed to me unbelievable. Alyne was no older than I and Justin must be fifty at the very least.

'He is a widower . . .'

'Is he? Is he, Clarissa?' Oliver swung round to face me. 'I have sometimes wondered whom he left behind in India.'

'You mean . . . but that would make Jethro . . .'

'A bastard . . . a bastard to inherit the Aylsham name. Uncle Justin's revenge on the brother whose wife he wanted, who took from him what he thought of as his.'

He spoke with such savagery that I was afraid. 'But it wasn't your father's fault or yours.'

'What has that got to do with it? Perhaps he thinks to breed new sons . . . Alyne's sons . . .'

'You can't be sure.'

'No, I can't be sure and it's not Jethro's fault,' he said wearily. 'He's unhappy enough, poor little devil. How he hates it here.'

I could think of no way to comfort him. I moved a little closer. 'I wish there was something I could do.'

But he was not listening to me. He said broodingly, 'He thinks he has me beaten and that gives him pleasure. He thinks because I came back at his bidding that he can have me dancing like a puppet while he pulls the strings, but he's wrong. I can't prevent him taking Alyne from me but he shan't wreck Ravensley. He doesn't know the Fens or the people here as I do. They're slow but they're stubborn and they are fighters to a man . . . and if need be, I will join with them . . .'

'What do you mean?'

'You'll see. Two hundred years ago when the Dutchman Cornelius Vermuyden came to drain the Fens, they fought him every step of the way because they believed that he was destroying their livelihood. I've no wish to see that happen again and I'm not against progress, but it's got to be progress for all, not the kind that puts riches in one man's pocket and robs others of the very right to exist.'

I had never heard him speak out so vehemently and I thought then how like he was to his father. I remembered him well and though I was only a girl then, I was aware of the steely strength beneath the gentleness, the inner integrity that pushed into a corner would not yield and I was glad. If I'd done nothing else, I had roused Oliver from the apathy and despair into which Alyne's rejection had thrust him. It was then that there came a thunderous knocking at the door.

'Who the devil is that?' he exclaimed.

Mrs Starling came in, looking agitated. 'There's a gentleman, sir, asking to speak with you.'

'A gentleman? Did he give his name?'

'A Captain Rutland, sir.'

I started and Oliver gave me a quick glance. 'Would you rather not meet him?'

'It doesn't matter.'

'Very well.' He picked up his coat from the chair. 'Show him in,' but the Captain was already in the room, his sergeant stationing himself at the door.

'Thank you, Mrs Starling,' said Oliver calmly. 'Good evening, Captain. We have not met since my uncle's ball. You are acquainted with Miss Fenton, I believe.'

Bulwer's eyes swept round the room and then rested on me for a second. He gave me the faintest of bows. 'Good evening, Clarissa.'

Oliver motioned to the brandy. 'Will you take a glass? It is a cold night.'

'Thank you, no. I am here on duty.'

I could not possibly imagine what Captain Rutland could be doing in this part of the country and Oliver raised his eyebrows questioningly.

'Duty at this hour?'

'I and my men with the local militia were detailed to escort a gang of prisoners, and a cursed unpleasant job it was too.'

Oliver smiled. 'Not quite the same as guard duty at the palace.'

Bulwer stiffened, sensing the irony. 'I understand that one of these wretches, a certain Jake Starling, is known to you.'

'Yes, he is. His mother is my housekeeper.'

'I'll be brief. He was being conveyed with other prisoners to London for embarkation to Botany Bay. On the heath outside Newmarket we were ambushed and this same Jake Starling escaped.'

'You don't say! How very unfortunate for you, Captain,' said Oliver dryly. 'I deplore it, of course, but I don't really see what it has to do with me.'

'Two of the local militia are ready to swear that one of those who attacked us was you, Mr Aylsham.'

'I? Oh come now, that is absurd. Why should I risk my life in such a ridiculous venture?'

'I understand you spoke up on behalf of the prisoner before he was sentenced and you are very well known in these parts.'

'This is nonsense,' I said coming forward. 'Mr Aylsham would never do anything against the law.'

'You think not, Clarissa? I didn't know you were so intimately acquainted with him.'

The implication was obvious and Oliver interrupted him. 'This is all beside the point. Surely any recognition would have been extremely problematical. It was already dark.'

'How do you know the time of day?' said Bulwer quickly.

'Oh come, I was well aware at what hour the escort were setting out since Mrs Starling begged the day off to see the last of her son and damned inconvenient it was for me too.'

There was a tiny sneering smile on Bulwer's lips. 'I presume you could supply an alibi if necessary.'

Oliver shrugged his shoulders carelessly. 'Probably. I am out and about the Fens most of the day but I daresay if I was pressed, I could find someone to vouch for me. There is another trifling fact, Captain. You are a stranger here. You would be hardly likely to know that my grandfather had the unfortunate habit of siring sons all through the Fens. The family likeness has a habit of cropping up now and again.'

I don't think Bulwer was convinced but Oliver was an Aylsham and a gentleman even if he was living in a half furnished farmhouse and he dare not use his usual bullying tactics. He said abruptly, 'Have I your permission to question the prisoner's mother?'

'Certainly, if you think it will do any good,' said Oliver smoothly. 'But if you imagine Jake has taken refuge here then I can assure you, you are mistaken, and I do beg you to be gentle with her. I have had enough of weeping and wailing to last me for a lifetime.'

Captain Rutland gave another quick glance around him. 'I apologize for disturbing your tête à tête,' he said unpleasantly. 'Goodnight, Mr Aylsham . . . Clarissa.'

'Damned bounder!' exclaimed Oliver as the door closed behind him.

'Never mind about him,' I whispered. 'You were there, weren't you? You planned the escape.'

'Ssh!' Oliver moved silently to the door, opened it a crack and then came back, smiling and rubbing his hands.

'What do you think?'

'Oh Oliver! How could you be so rash! Did you know that Captain Rutland was to be in charge of the escort?'

'No. It was too dark to distinguish faces. I admit I was surprised to see Dragoons as well as the militia. It must mean that the government is giving way to panic and seeing red-hot revolution everywhere.'

'What will Jake do? Where will he go?'

'Never you mind. Best you know nothing, Clarissa.'

But I did know. Out on the Fens, in the middle of Greatheart with Moggy Norman and Nampy Sutton, the home of rebels and hunted men for centuries.

'Did you think I was going to let Jake sweat out seven years and longer in that hellish country? Never! It's the first step, Clarissa. Let Uncle Justin take warning.'

In sheer exuberance he swept me up against him and kissed me full on the lips so that I was suddenly dizzy. When Bulwer had touched me I had felt only disgust and revulsion, but this was different. I let myself yield, his grip tightened, and it suddenly became momentous, passionate, real. Then he thrust me away from him.

'Go, Clarissa, please go,' he said thickly.

'Oliver . . .' I was shaking. I knew that he did not love me. I knew that at that moment, lonely and unhappy, swinging from despair to feverish exultation, he desperately wanted someone, anyone to share it with him and I was there within reach. In that moment of madness I would have given him all he asked and cared nothing for the consequences. But Oliver had walked away. With his back to me, he said stiffly, 'It's late. You should go back to Copthorne. I'll tell one of the boys to go with you with a lantern.'

It was a douche of cold water and I was ashamed, horribly ashamed of the response that had flamed within me at his touch. It would be so easy to stay but afterwards he would hate me as I would hate myself.

'It's all right. I don't need anyone with me.'

I pulled my cloak around me and almost ran out of the house. Outside it was darker than I had expected and frost had crisped the mud of the track. I hurried up the lane stumbling over the ruts and when I heard the horses behind me, I shrank back against the hedge. I had no wish to be seen by Captain Rutland or his sergeant. When they had passed, I walked more soberly, my hood pulled forward over my face, my mind so full of Jake's escape and Oliver's part in it that I did not pause to wonder at the strange coincidence that had brought Bulwer Rutland back into my life when I thought to be free of him for ever.

7

'I don't usually agree with Tom Fenton but your father is right for once,' said Aunt Jess grimly to me one morning when Patty came running in with a horrific story of one of Farmer Burton's ricks having been burned to ashes by a mob of ruffians during the night. 'We are a lot of ostriches burying our heads in the sand. Discontent is contagious as the plague, once it starts there is no holding it.'

She was right too. For a couple of weeks after Jake's escape nothing happened. Life in the village seemed to be going on in its usual quiet sleepy way, then suddenly without warning we were in the thick of it.

It was baking day at Copthorne. We had just finished an early luncheon when Prue came flying in, her hair escaping wildly from under her cap, her arms covered with flour and dough to the elbows.

'Come quickly, Miss, quickly,' she said breathlessly. 'They've got poor John and they'll beat the life out of him if you don't stop them.'

'Who will? What are you talking about, Prue? Pull yourself together.'

'They've gone mad, Miss, I swear they have . . . Jack Cobb, Bill Maggs, all of 'em. They're trying to break into the storehouse.'

'Are they indeed?'

Aunt Jess threw a shawl over her head as she ran out of the house and I followed her. A little knot of men were gathered outside the barn where our winter wheat was stored. I could just see John's white hair blowing madly in the wind. He was spread-eagled across the door hanging on to the lock like dear life and valiantly defending his mistress's property.

Aunt Jess said sternly, 'What is all this? What is going on? Don't just stand there, Jack Cobb, let me through.'

I knew most of them by sight. I'd often enough taken blankets and food to their wives and children. Some of them shifted their feet shamefacedly as she took up a stand beside John, outfacing them, brave as a lion.

'Come along now,' she said, 'speak up, one of you. What is it you want?' She looked from one to the other and then singled out a big shock-headed fellow who had occasionally done a day's digging at Copthorne. 'You there, Bill Maggs, why aren't you getting on with your work instead of encouraging a lot of idle rascals to break into my barn?'

'There bain't no work, Missus, you know that and we got to eat same as other folk,' he mumbled sullenly.

'We aren't meanin' no harm to you nor the young lady neither,' spoke up another voice more boldly. 'But we need that there corn . . . we need it bad for bread to put into our children's mouths and there ain't a penny left to buy so much as a crumb . . .'

'If you worked harder and didn't pour your wages down your throat all summer, you'd have something put by for bad times,' said Aunt Jess crisply.

An angry chorus answered her and they moved in closer. I was frightened. I could sense the menace. They had a wild desperate look. One false move on our part and their half bullying, half timid mood could turn ugly. I edged nearer to Aunt Jess, but she stood there, firm as a rock, quite unafraid.

She said quietly, 'Clarissa, go and ask Prue and Patty to bring out the bread they have been baking this morning.'

'All of it?'

'All of it,' she replied firmly.

I went reluctantly and felt the men's eyes following me as I ran back to the house. When we returned with the baskets filled with loaves, Aunt Jess said, 'Share and share alike. No one shall say I keep more than my due. That's my baking for the week. Clarissa, keep one and help Prue hand out the rest.'

We distributed the warm loaves into the eager outstretched hands. Some of them grabbed at the bread but the majority muttered half audible thanks.

'Now,' said Aunt Jess, 'go home, the lot of you, and behave yourselves. I shan't say anything about this folly and nor will you if you have any sense which I sometimes doubt. The law's the law and if you go breaking into barns and robbing your betters, then you will pay the price and you know what that can be just as well as I do. Be off with you and make sure your wives and children get a bite of that bread.'

They shuffled away and old John looked after them angrily. 'They ought to be ashamed,' he muttered, 'comin' here and robbin' you after what you've done for the likes of them. Danged lot of thieving rogues, that's what they be.'

'No, they're not,' said Aunt Jess, a little wearily now it was all over. 'They're simple ignorant folk half out of their wits with terror of what the winter will bring them. I greatly fear this is only the beginning. We shall see worse before the month is out. You mark my words.'

Oliver said the same when he called later in the day to enquire after our safety. 'I heard there had been trouble and I came as soon as I could. Has there been any damage?'

'None to speak of except to John's dignity,' said Aunt Jess dryly. 'It was just foolishness on their part. I don't think they will come here again.'

'I hope not for your sake but it's not the end of it,' said Oliver sombrely. 'It's like a festering boil and when it erupts, there's going to be violence. I should advise you to stay quietly at home and don't venture into Ely whatever you do. There's an ugly mood abroad and it's not pleasant to be caught up in a riot.'

Aunt Jess had been more shaken than she cared to admit so I left her resting and walked down the path with Oliver to where he had hitched Rowan at the gate. He stood for a moment with his hand on her bridle.

'You know, Clarissa, I've sometimes felt that this has been simmering below the surface for years and that was why father tried to guard against it. The boys who watched Isaac Starling hang and those others with him are men now and they have never forgotten.'

'Do you mean Jake? Is he at the back of this?'

'I have not seen him,' but he avoided my eyes and I knew he lied.

'But you know where he is . . .'

'Perhaps.' He swung himself into the saddle and then looked down at me. 'Jake would not willingly harm anyone but he is on the side of justice as I am. The worst of this kind of thing is that it gets out of hand and even small grievances assume gigantic proportions. It is a wonderful opportunity to pay off old scores.'

'Are you thinking of your uncle?'

'Yes, I am. They resented his coming and he has been harsh in his dealings. He has become a living example of all they hate and fear most. I've warned him but he laughs at me.'

'What do you think will happen?'

He shrugged his shoulders. 'Your guess is as good as mine. Take care of yourself, Clarissa,' and he trotted away into the gloom of the winter afternoon.

It was a strange time and perhaps the worst part of it was not so much what actually happened but the frightening rumours that reached us of mobs gathering and marching, of travellers attacked and murdered, houses broken into and robbed and market places running with blood when the military tried to restore order. Aunt Jess discounted most of them as wild exaggerations but Prue and Patty were in a state of constant terror and night after night when I went to draw the curtains, I saw the red glow of fire in the dark sky and it added to the nervous tension that gripped us all.

Menacing letters began to appear mysteriously on breakfast tables so that even household servants were suspected of sympathizing with the rioters. Farmer Burton received one threatening to smash his threshing machine and one morning when I was up at Ravensley, Sir Peter Berkeley arrived in a furious passion.

'D'ye see this, Aylsham?' he exploded when he was hardly inside the house. 'Who the devil is this fellow who calls himself Captain Swing? I am being beset by a gang of murdering smugglers, poachers and rascals promising to burn Barkham to the ground if I don't give them what they demand. I'll see them damned in hell first.'

'You're not the only one. You should do as I do, throw them in the fire, my dear fellow,' said Justin Aylsham contemptuously. 'Rabble, that's all they are, presuming to dictate to their betters. I've appealed to the military. A company of Dragoons is to be stationed at Ravensley and Captain Rutland will be staying in the house. If they come here, then they'll receive a warm welcome, I promise you. I had trouble like this in India. The thing to do is to stand firm. Show the slightest weakness and you are lost.'

He disappeared into the library with Sir Peter and I picked up the letter that had been tossed on the settle in the hall.

'Sir,' I read,
'Your name is down amongst the Black Hearts in the Black Book, and this is to advise you to take heed and make your will. It is the third time of warning and if you don't do as we demand, we will burn down your barns and you in them.
Signed on behalf of us all,
Swing.'

It was printed but neatly written and not mispelled. 'Has Lord Aylsham received letters like this?' I asked Alyne.
'Yes. He destroys them. He refuses to be intimidated.'
'Aren't you afraid?'
'What can they do against us?' and I wondered at the arrogance in her tone. It seemed strange to me that Alyne, the waif, the child from the Fens, should have so little sympathy or feeling for the dispossessed, but then I never rightly understood her.

It was typical of Justin Aylsham that he should show his defiance of the threats by refusing to cancel the small celebration he had planned to mark his engagement to Alyne. Aunt Jess was suffering from a heavy cold and declined to go so John drove me to Ravensley alone and with the heaviest foreboding because of something that I had discovered the day before.

I had been in the habit of exercising Rowan for Oliver on those days when he was occupied elsewhere and that afternoon I took her back to the stables, delivered her over to Ben Starling and went into the house to have a word with his mother. She was in the living room and seemed unusually awkward and ill at ease when I asked if she had received any news of Jake.

'Never a word, Miss, but then he wouldn't write. He'd not wish to bring any harm on me or his brothers and sisters.' She opened the window to shake out her duster and the breeze blew a handful of papers off Oliver's desk to the floor. I stooped to pick them up and then stood aghast staring down at what I held in my hand.

There were some half a dozen of them, all clean and unfolded, threatening notes, each of them signed 'Swing'. Who had written them? Jake or Oliver himself? Surely he would not be so rash. But he might well be permitting Jake to use pen and paper, even hiding him in the house. Whatever it was, it was criminally reckless to leave the evidence lying here on the desk where anyone might see it when already the most harmless of people were being arrested merely on suspicion. I hesitated and then thrust them out of sight at the back of the desk closing it down.

Ravensley was brilliantly lit and the dozen or so guests had come from near and far despite the dangers of travelling. I think perhaps they were glad of any diversion in this uneasy time. I was taking off my cloak in one of the upstairs rooms when Alyne came in with Cherry. There was an unusual flush of colour in her cheeks that made me wonder if something had upset her.

She came to me at once, kissing me lightly. 'I'm so glad you were able to be here, Clarissa. I hope Miss Cavendish is not really sick.'

'It's only a chill. Things have been worrying lately. She sends her love and hopes you will be very happy.'

'Of course she is happy,' broke in Cherry with a touch of spite. 'She's got what she's always wanted, haven't you, Alyne?'

'I don't know what you mean.' Alyne crossed to the mirror and adjusted the flowers in the coils of pale silky hair. 'I am very fond of Justin.'

'Fond, fond!' repeated Cherry scornfully. 'You don't marry a man because you're fond of him.'

'You're too young. You don't know what you're talking about,' Alyne was maddeningly calm.

'That's what you're always saying but I do. I know more than you think,' said Cherry rebelliously. 'You were in love with Oliver and when you knew he wasn't going to inherit Ravensley, you jilted him. I think that is vile.'

'You're being very silly,' said Alyne, 'and anyway it is long past now and Oliver is quite happy. You ask Clarissa. She'll tell you I'm right.'

I sensed a faint hostility in her voice but before I could reply Cherry had swung round, two bright spots of colour flaming in her face.

'He's not happy, he's miserable,' she said tempestuously. 'He was your lover, wasn't he, and if you had your way, he still would be even if you are going to marry Uncle Justin . . .'

I suppose in my secret heart I had already guessed the truth but to hear it spoken so openly was still a shock.

Alyne suddenly flared into anger. She seized Cherry by the wrist, her eyes blazing. 'Stop it, do you hear, stop repeating those stupid lies.'

'I won't stop and they are not lies. If I didn't think it would hurt Oliver, I'd tell Uncle Justin what I know!'

'Tell him,' said Alyne, her temper cooling to ice, 'tell him and see what he says. He'll laugh at you for the liar you are.' She turned to go and then paused looking back over her shoulder and there was a deadly threat in the quiet, silky voice. 'If you say one word, I'll make you pay for it. I'll tell him about you and Jake . . . you'd not like that, would you?'

'There's nothing to tell that he doesn't know already,' exclaimed Cherry defiantly, but her lips trembled and as Alyne went out of the room, she dropped on the bed beating one small fist on the pillow in a frenzy. 'I hate her, Clarissa, I hate her. She spoils everything.'

I sat beside her, putting my arm round her shoulders. 'Cherry, you've not been seeing Jake, have you?'

'I would if I could but how can I? I don't know where he is,' she said stormily. 'Oh Clarissa, I'm so unhappy. I wish I were dead.'

'Of course you don't. You're just being foolish.'

'When they are married, I shall go away. I shall go and live with Oliver at Thatchers.'

'If you do, you'll only get your brother into trouble. Uncle Justin is your guardian. Now dry your eyes and come downstairs. It won't help to look as if you've been crying.'

It was not a good start to the evening but far worse was to come before the day ended.

We sat down to eat and if there was some talk of the disturbances there was a good deal of gaiety and laughter too. We drank a toast to the happy pair. Oliver sat opposite me. He said little but he did not drink when the glasses were raised and I saw how often his eyes strayed to Alyne. I wondered what he was thinking and how much truth there was in what Cherry had said.

When Miss Harriet rose, we all did, following after her to the drawing room and leaving the gentlemen to their wine. The tea tray was brought in and Alyne began to pour out with Cherry sullenly assisting her. I was conscious of a feeling of uneasiness that I could not shake off. I withdrew to the window seat. It was the sudden glare of light through the half-closed curtains that first attracted my attention. I turned to look out. It was a dark night and for a moment I could only distinguish strange moving circles of light. Then I realized they were torches of burning pitch. Involuntarily I let out a cry of alarm. The others came crowding behind me. I pushed open the window so that now we could see the dark shapes that milled backwards and forwards on the terrace luridly lit by the flaring torches.

'What are they doing out there? Who are they? What do they want?' exclaimed one or other of the ladies in fright.

'I'll go and tell Oliver,' said Cherry. She ran from the room and I went with her, but by this time the servants had already spread the alarm. In the hall Lord Aylsham was giving orders to Ram Lall.

'Go now,' he said, 'warn Captain Rutland. Tell him to bring his Dragoons here as quickly as possible.'

'No,' exclaimed Oliver. 'We can deal with this ourselves. Bring in the soldiers and there will be murder done.'

'This is my house,' said his uncle coldly, 'and I shall defend it in my own fashion. Go by the back way, Ram and hurry.' The Indian left swiftly in his usual silent manner. Some of the ladies had come to the top of the stairs while their husbands were gathered in the hall, angry and apprehensive. They were all talking at once when Sir Peter Berkeley suddenly held up his hand.

'Listen! What are they saying out there?'

Then we heard it, a deep monotonous chant, 'We want Lord Aylsham! We want Lord Aylsham!' It had a power that was frightening in its intensity.

Oliver made a move. 'I'll go out to them.'

'No,' his uncle held him back. 'Do you think I am frightened of a bunch of village yokels?' He turned to Alyne. 'Go back to the ladies, my dear, tell them there is nothing to be afraid of.'

She stared at him. 'Take care, Justin,' she said and then went slowly up the stairs.

He had courage, I'll say that for him. He walked to the door, flung it wide and stood on the steps facing them.

'Here I am. What is it you want from me?'

It came in a confused roar from many voices. 'An answer to our just demands . . . two and sixpence for every man per day and a promise that we'll not be turned from our homes . . . bread for our children . . . it's little enough . . .'

'I'll not be threatened,' he said contemptuously. 'Come to me in the proper way and I'll give consideration to your plea.'

There was a fierceness in their shouting now. 'We've heard that before too often . . . where has it got us?' They surged forward menacingly to the foot of the steps and the flickering light picked out an angry face here and there.

Oliver was standing beside his uncle, his voice rose strongly. 'Listen to me. Go home now. If you don't, it may well be worse for you. Believe me, I speak the truth. Leave it to me. I promise to see that you get justice.'

'We've no quarrel with you, Mr Oliver. We know you. It's your uncle, Lord Aylsham's promise we want and by the living God, we intend to have it.'

I could not be certain but I was almost sure that it was Jake I heard speaking from the very heart of the mob that seemed to grow larger every minute moving up and down the stones of the terrace. Then suddenly there came another voice, deep and powerful.

'God damn you to hell, Justin Aylsham, for a bloody murderer!'

One of the lighted torches came flying over the heads of the crowd and fell at his feet sizzling and spluttering in a thick acrid stench of pitch. It seemed to inflame the crowd. They pressed forward and one of them hurled a stone. It whistled between Oliver and his uncle missing Alyne by inches before it shattered a mirror on the wall. She gave a small muffled shriek.

There was a moment of shocked silence and in it I heard the sharp word of command and saw the red coats of the soldiers. Within minutes the terrace had turned into a battlefield as the Dragoons thrust their way through, shouting to the men to disperse and hitting out at them roughly with their rifle butts. There must have been women among them because I heard screams.

Some of the men began to move off but others driven to a raging anger were fighting back viciously.

Justin Aylsham watched for an instant, then turned his back and moved towards Sir Peter and the other men, but Oliver still stood there.

Sickened by the brutality, I whispered, 'Why do they stay? Why don't they go?'

'They're starving and hopeless. What have they to lose?' he said bitterly.

Then suddenly there was commotion behind us. Jethro in night-shirt and dressing gown came racing down the stairs. As he passed us he screamed, 'Ben is out there. I saw him. They're hurting him.'

He must have been watching from an upper window. Miss Har-riet was on the landing clinging to the banister rail and crying out helplessly, 'Stop him, stop him!'

I moved to go after him but Oliver pushed me back. 'Can't you see? They're using bayonets.'

He ran down the steps and thrust his way into the struggling heaving mass. There were still a few torches burning and the light flickered eerily over white faces smeared with dark blood. There were fewer now. A good many of the men must have slipped away. Some who had been struck to the ground were staggering to their feet and limping down the path while others lay ominously still. The soldiers had rounded up a dozen or so herding them bru-tally together. Bulwer Rutland came up the steps.

'It's all over, Lord Aylsham. We've taught them a lesson they'll not forget in a hurry and we've taken a fine batch of prisoners.'

He stopped as Oliver pushed past him with Jethro in his arms. The child hung limp and white-faced, blood running freely from a great gash on his forehead. Behind him limped Ben, his clothes ripped, his face streaked with dirt and tears.

'He did it for me, he did it for me,' he was sobbing out over and over again.

Justin Aylsham stood quite still staring down at his son. 'What was the boy doing out there?' he said in a hoarse whisper.

'He saw his friend being attacked by the soldiers and he went to help him.'

'Friend? What friend?' Then his eye fell on Ben. 'My son and that . . . that filth!' Ben shrank from the rage on his face and I put my arm round him.

Alyne said in a queer cracked voice, 'Is he . . . is he . . . ?'

'No, he's not dead.' Oliver put the child down on the settle that stood along one side of the hall. 'You'd better fetch Annie Pearce. She'll know what to do.'

Then he straightened up and faced his uncle. 'Your son has more pity than you have. I warned you, didn't I? I warned you that there would be a reckoning to pay for this.'

'That's what you wanted,' snarled Justin Aylsham, his voice low but perfectly audible to everyone standing in the hall. 'It's what you were counting on.'

'I'm not like you. I don't play with people's lives.'

But his uncle did not seem to have heard him. He went on as if he had not spoken. 'Don't think I don't know. It's you I have to thank for this tonight, you and that damned rascal Jake Starling. Where is he? Where have you hidden him? It's what you hoped for, isn't it? Both of you. To see me dead and my boy with me, but I'll have him hanged for it this time and you too . . .'

The two men were face to face and the hatred seemed to crackle between them. I saw Sir Peter take a step forward while the others watched greedily.

Then Oliver said quietly, 'You must be out of your mind. I've no idea where Jake is. Far away from here if he has any sense. You had better look to your son.' He turned to the door. 'Come along, Ben. I'll take you home.'

Alyne had come back with Annie Pearce. They were bending over Jethro. I ran up the stairs pushing my way through the ex- cited chattering women and collected my cloak. I came down quickly and hurried after Oliver. He was crossing the garden to- wards the stables when I caught up with him. He turned as I put a hand on his arm.

'What are you doing out here, Clarissa? Isn't John driving you home?'

'It's not far to walk across the fields. I had to speak to you.'
'Why?'

I looked at Ben and he put a hand on the boy's shoulder. 'Go on and start to saddle Rowan for me.'

'Oliver,' I said urgently as the child ran ahead, 'is Jake this Captain Swing?'

'You surely don't believe that. There is no Captain Swing.'

'But the letters . . . I saw them on your desk at Thatchers.'

He stared straight ahead before he said coldly, 'The contents of my desk are private. I'd be glad if you would remember that.'

His tone chilled me but I persisted. 'I'm sorry. I wasn't prying but I did see them. Do they suspect you?'

'Why should they? I have done nothing, only tried to restrain them. If it had not been for me, my uncle could well have been murdered as my father was murdered.'

'There is someone who hates him, isn't there? Someone who looks like you.'

He put a hand on my shoulder. 'Keep out of this, Clarissa. You've no need to worry about me or any of us. Our troubles are not your concern.'

'But I want to help . . .'

'I don't need help from you or anyone. Shall I see you back to Copthorne?'

I drew away from him. 'It's not necessary. It's not so far across the paddock and I'm not afraid.'

'Goodnight then.'

I longed to say more but how could I in face of his cool rejection? He went on to the stables and I watched him for a moment before going down the path that we had used so often and so happily as children running between the two houses. Aunt Jess was in bed when I reached Copthorne but the lamp still burned in the living room. I turned it out and went wearily up the stairs. She called to me as I went along the passage and I put my head round her door.

'Come in, my dear. Is everything all right? Prue said she saw a great number of men on the road and she thought they were going up to Ravensley. I have been worried about you. Has there been trouble?'

'Some . . . but it is all over now.'

She gripped my hand. 'Are you sure?'

'Yes, quite sure.' I kissed her cheek.

'Goodnight, my dear.'

'Goodnight, Aunt Jess.'

After what had happened I thought I would lie awake all night
but I didn't. Prue had put a hot brick in the bed and I was so tired
that I fell asleep almost at once. I woke to see light streaming in as
Patty drew back the curtains.

I yawned. 'What time is it?'

'Nearly eleven, Miss. The mistress said to let you sleep on.
You'd know soon enough.'

'Know what?'

Patty came to the bed twisting a corner of her apron. 'There's
terrible news, Miss.'

I sat up, the events of the previous night flooding back and grip-
ping me with anxiety. 'What do you mean? Is it Jake?'

She shook her head. 'Not Jake. It's Mr Oliver.'

'Oliver?'

'They are saying that Lord Aylsham has been murdered, Miss,
and Mr Oliver has been taken up for it.'

8

Rumour exaggerated as it so often does. Lord Aylsham was not dead, but he had been badly hurt and his condition was critical. During the day we heard some details of what had happened. After Oliver and I had left Ravensley, the soldiers had marched their prisoners away but Bulwer Rutland had remained with two of his men on guard. At some time during the night one of them had seen the glow of fire on the edge of the estate bordering on the Fen. Lord Aylsham was roused and had insisted on going with them to investigate. It was an old disused granary and it was obvious that it had been set alight as an act of defiance and revenge. The fire was not serious and they had beaten it out, but in the dark and confusion someone had set upon Justin Aylsham bludgeoning him to the ground. Bulwer and his men had come to his defence, but his assailant had slipped through their hands and fled across the fields into the safety of the Fen where they dare not follow him but not before they had seen his face. They were prepared to swear on oath that it was Oliver, the man whom only a few hours before they had watched boldly outfacing his uncle on the steps of the house.

'I don't believe it,' I said when old John came to the end of his story. 'It can't be true. It's ridiculous. Oliver would never do such a thing, never.'

'What did he say when they went to Thatchers to arrest him?' asked Aunt Jess.

'Scarce uttered a word, Miss, except to swear he knew nought about it and had not been out of the house all night.'

'Can't Mrs Starling bear witness to that?'

'It seems she never heard him come in. The only witness is the boy. They crept in quietly because Ben was scared of what his Mam would have to say to him when she had forbidden him to leave the house. But he did let out that after Mr Oliver had seen him to his bed, he had gone out again.'

I could hazard a guess as to where he might have gone but I dare not admit what I knew about Jake.

'Very well, John, that will do,' said Aunt Jess. 'Let us know at once if you hear anything further.'

'Aye, Miss. I will that.'

I stared at her across the table when John had closed the door. 'What will happen to him?'

'He will be charged at the magistrates' court in Ely and if the charge is substantiated, he will come up for trial at the assizes. If his uncle dies . . . or even if he recovers . . .'

'He will hang,' I caught my breath, 'hang or at the best be transported.' I thought of that terrible prison and the horror of the transport ships. It couldn't be true, it couldn't happen to Oliver. 'There must be something we can do, Aunt Jess.'

'Did he quarrel with his uncle last night, Clarissa? You had better tell me everything.'

'It was not really a quarrel, but Oliver was very angry because Lord Aylsham had called in the soldiers . . . and then Jethro was hurt . . . there were bitter words between them, and Sir Peter and the other guests were there, they must have heard what was said.'

'It will go against him,' said Aunt Jess heavily. 'They like Oliver and they don't care overmuch for his uncle, but at times like these, men think of their own skins and are not disposed to be merciful to anyone who endangers them.'

That was not all, I knew that. There was Jake. There were those letters. Oliver had always shown far too openly where his sympathies lay.

In the afternoon John brought the news that all the prisoners including Oliver would be brought up before the court at Ely on the following day. They were wasting no time. Fear of revolution could make even kind-hearted men determined to teach rebels a sharp lesson.

I said, 'Aunt Jess, I want to be there. May I take the trap?'

'You will only distress yourself, my dear. What good will it do?'

'I don't know, but I must go,' I said obstinately.

She looked at me shrewdly. 'In that case, if you are determined, then I shall go with you.'

'No, dear Aunt Jess.' I put my hand on hers. 'It will be a long tiring day when you have not been well. It's just that . . . I don't know . . . but I may be able to do something.'

'I don't like the thought of you going alone. John must drive you there and wait to bring you back. You will take care, Clarissa. Sometimes I fear that a little of your father's reckless spirit lives in you. Promise me that you will do nothing foolish.'

'I won't,' I promised.

I had never been in a court before and this was not the assizes so there was no pageantry. The magistrate, a cold stern man, was a stranger to me as were his colleagues with the exception of Sir Peter Berkeley. The first part of the proceedings dragged on tediously. One after the other the men who had been arrested that night were charged and led away. They looked lost and bewildered, the fight all gone out of them, so that now there was only hopelessness and despair. When I glanced around the court, there was no pity anywhere on the well-fed, complacent faces, only a fear that any mercy shown to the law-breakers might damage their own pockets.

Then Oliver was brought in and interest quickened. An Aylsham suspected of murdering his uncle did not happen every day in the week. A ripple of excitement ran around the spectators which rose to a crescendo when Alyne came in on Bulwer Rutland's arm and then was quickly silenced by the clerk of the court.

Oliver looked pale but quite composed and he answered the questions put to him calmly. He had taken Ben home to Thatchers and smuggled the boy to his bed to avoid punishment.

'Did you then go to bed yourself, Mr Aylsham?'

'No, I went out again.'

There was an audible gasp among the listeners. 'You admit you went out? For what purpose?'

'There was no purpose. It had been a disturbing evening and I was restless. I knew I would be unable to sleep.'

'Did you go back to Ravensley perhaps, to enquire after Lord Aylsham's son who, I understand, had been injured in the riot?'

'No.'

'Then where did you go?'

'Nowhere in particular. I simply walked for an hour or so and then returned.'

'And went to bed?'

'Yes.'

'You did not continue your walk as far as the granary that was set on fire, seize the opportunity to strike your uncle to the ground and then return to your own house?'

'No, I did not.'

'You will hear, Mr Aylsham, and it grieves me to say this, that this is precisely what you did do. We have evidence from reputable witnesses, including an officer of the King's Dragoons who fortunately prevented you from committing the murder you intended. By the grace of God, Lord Aylsham still lives and we can only pray that he will in time make a full recovery.'

So then it began, the series of sworn statements, each one more alarming than the other. It was all brought out into the open, the quarrel, the hostility between Oliver and his uncle, even the fact that only a short time before he had spoken out in defence of Jake.

'It has been suggested, if never proved, that you took some part in this criminal's escape. What have you to say to that?'

'I thought his sentence unjust and I said so at the time.'

There was a murmur all through the court and Sir Peter Berkeley looked up with a frown.

'Do you presume to question the integrity of His Majesty's officers of the law?'

'In this instance I consider the judgment mistaken.'

'You are a very bold young man,' remarked the magistrate dryly. 'There is also another matter. When you were arrested, Mr Aylsham, certain papers were impounded from your desk . . .'

'They had no right . . .' interrupted Oliver quickly and angrily.

'If you are innocent, you have nothing to fear,' said the magistrate sternly. 'Amongst these were found certain letters . . .' Then the question came swift and sharp. 'Are you this notorious Captain Swing, Mr Aylsham?'

Oliver laughed, a harsh bitter sound. 'So-called Swing letters have been received all over the south of England. Do you think I ride by night like a witch on a broomstick?'

There was a roar of laughter from the public benches and the magistrate said angrily, 'If there are any more interruptions, I will have this court cleared.' Then he turned to Oliver again.

'How do you account for these letters being found in your possession?'

'I act as Lord Aylsham's steward. They had been brought to me by some of our tenant farmers.'

'That's right enough,' called Will Burton, standing up in the body of the court. 'Three of the danged things I've had myself and I took 'em up to Thatchers . . .'

'Silence!' thundered the magistrate. 'When we require your evidence, we'll ask for it.' He paused until the chatter had subsided before he went on gravely. 'The name of Aylsham has long been respected in Cambridgeshire. I knew your father and it would distress me to be forced to send you for trial. But the charge has been brought against you and the facts remain. Not only has there been strong enmity between you and Lord Aylsham because you felt, quite unjustifiably, that he had stolen your inheritance from you, but the lady whom you hoped to marry has rejected you for your uncle. Isn't that so, Mr Aylsham?'

Oliver looked at Alyne sitting beside Bulwer Rutland. 'I suggest you ask her,' he said.

I sat there with my heart pounding wildly while the preposterous notion that had leaped into my mind hovered before me, crazy but tempting. I could save him if I only had the courage. I could see the danger he was in and all kinds of thoughts went scurrying through my mind—Bulwer's rape, the vile scandal that had circulated about me, father saying 'You've ruined your chances, Clarissa,' the plain fact that if Oliver was to die whatever he had done, then I did not know how I would go on living. It was like a madness that possessed me. Suddenly, almost without any volition of my own, I was standing up, my voice sounding queer and strained in my own ears.

'I can tell you where Mr Aylsham was that night.'

The magistrate's eyes turned to me examining me coolly and impersonally before he spoke. 'Who are you, Madam?'

'I am Clarissa Fenton, niece to Miss Jessamine Cavendish of Copthorne.'

Aunt Jess's name still carried weight. He turned and conferred with Sir Peter. I was playing desperately on the frail hope that, despite everything, Oliver was a gentleman like themselves and they were not anxious to condemn one of their own kind.

He frowned. 'You had better take the stand, Miss Fenton, and then tell us what you know.'

My knees were shaking, but I took the Bible in my right hand and swore to tell the truth and nothing but the truth knowing it to be a deliberate lie and that if it was discovered, I could go to prison for perjury.

'Now perhaps you will be kind enough to inform the court where Mr Aylsham was at this critical time.'

'He was with me.'

To say there was a sensation throughout the listeners would have been an understatement. I saw the shock on Oliver's face. I met Alyne's eyes and read disbelief and shivered at the contemptuous twist on Bulwer Rutland's lips. I felt sick and yet at the same time in complete control of myself.

Oliver's reaction was swift. 'Don't listen to her. It is not true.'

The magistrate was looking directly at me. 'You hear what Mr Aylsham says. He denies that he was with you. What is your answer to that, Miss Fenton?'

'He is chivalrous and wishes to spare me, but I cannot see him suffer on my account when he is innocent.'

There was an absolute silence before he said, 'Do you realize what you are implying?'

'Yes.'

'Very well. I think you had better tell us exactly what happened.'

The very fact that I was lying helped to carry conviction. They took my hesitation for shame and though that was real enough, they did not realize how desperately I was seeking to give my story the stamp of truth.

'When Mr Aylsham says he left the house, it was because he came to meet me as we had arranged. I then returned with him.'

'How long did you remain?'

Frantically I tried to remember when the assault had taken place. 'Until the morning.'

'Were you in the habit of making these nocturnal visits?' asked the magistrate ironically.

'Do I have to answer that?'

I dare not look at Oliver. I kept my eyes lowered. I could see my hands shaking and tried hard to keep them still, praying that I wouldn't faint.

'Does Miss Cavendish know that you and Mr Aylsham spent the night together?' went on the magistrate dryly.

'No,' I whispered.

'I see.' He conferred with his colleagues for a moment and then turned back to me. 'Well, Miss Fenton, I think the young man owes you a considerable debt of gratitude for your courageous admission. I only hope he knows how to repay it. You may stand down.'

I had done it. Surely they could not hold him after this. I don't know how I got out of the courtroom. The eyes fixed on me, the whispers, the hateful looks—it was worse, far worse than anything I had ever endured in my life. Somehow I got through the door and outside almost fell into old John's arms. I had forgotten that he would have seen and heard everything and I dare not think of what Aunt Jess would say.

He had his arm around my waist. 'Steady now, Miss, you look ready to drop. You didn't ought to have done it, not for no man.'

He supported me to the inn and tried to persuade me to take a glass of wine but I wanted only to go home. The frost was still crisp on the roads and the sun was a great fiery ball sinking behind the black skeletons of the trees as we drove back to Copthorne.

When we arrived and John was helping me down from the trap, I said urgently, 'Say nothing to my aunt, John, please. I would prefer to tell her myself.'

'Never a word, Miss, never a word. Don't you fret now.'

But when I was confronted with Aunt Jess, when she had exclaimed at my wan looks, sent Prue for tea and toast and asked eagerly for news, I found myself totally unable to tell her what I had done.

'The evidence was inconclusive,' I said lamely. 'There was not sufficient to hold him. I think he will be released.'

'Thank God there is some justice left in England,' she said fervently.

I still felt shaken and my head ached so violently that as soon as I could escape, I went up to my room to lie down. It was much later in the evening when Prue came knocking at the door.

'Your aunt sent me, Miss. Mr Oliver is asking to speak with you very particular.'

So he had been freed. The wave of relief was followed by apprehension. I did not know how to face him and I delayed deliberately, peering into the mirror, combing my hair, tidying my dress, before I went down the stairs.

Aunt Jess was in the drawing room with Oliver when I went in. 'Here she is,' she said cheerfully. 'Clarissa looked so poorly when she returned that I sent her up to rest. How do you feel now, my dear?'

'Quite well thank you, Aunt Jess.'

'Good, good.' She glanced from me to Oliver and I wondered what he had said to her. 'I'll have Prue bring in a glass of wine. I've just been telling Oliver how thankful I am that everything has ended so happily for him.'

She bustled out of the room and for a moment there was silence between us. Oliver was standing half turned towards the fire. The warm glow lit his face and the dark gold of his hair. He said abruptly, 'There were certain formalities. It all took time. I came as soon as I could.' Then he swung round towards me. 'Why did you do it, Clarissa, in God's name, why?'

I sat down by the table because my knees were trembling. I said helplessly, 'I had to do something and it was all I could think of.'

'But of all things . . . Christ, if you had seen their faces!' he said violently. 'If you had heard the sniggering, the dirty jests . . . !' He hits his clenched fist against the carved wood of the mantel. 'You shamed me as well as yourself.'

I don't know what I had expected but it was certainly not this. Indignation welled up in me. I struggled to my feet. 'Would you rather be hanged for something you didn't do?'

'A thousand times rather than you should destroy yourself on my account.' He pushed back the hair that fell across his forehead. 'Why are you so sure that I didn't try to kill him? I hated him enough that night, God knows.'

'Did you?'

'No, damn it, but it could have been any one of those poor devils . . .'

'Were you afraid that it might have been Jake?'

'He would never do that.'

'Who is he then, this man who looks like you?'

'There is no one. At night in the dark it is easy to make mistakes and Rutland does not like me . . . in any case, none of that is important. Oh God, Clarissa, do you think I don't realize what I owe to you, my life, my future, every damned thing, that's the devil of it . . . you've made me feel . . .' He took a turn across the room and came back to face me. 'I have come here tonight to ask you to marry me.'

I stared at him. I had acted instinctively without any thought of the consequences. Now suddenly I was faced with them. I said slowly, 'There is no need . . .'

'There is every need. Don't you understand, Clarissa, what you have done?' he went on with mounting anger. 'Our names will be linked together on every tongue. In all honour what else can I do?'

'Thank you,' I said ironically, 'but you really don't have to sacrifice yourself on my account. I know well enough how you feel.'

He looked taken aback. After an instant he said, 'Don't you care for me at all?'

'I think it is I who should ask you that question.'

'Damn it, Clarissa,' he said, seizing me by the shoulder, 'you can't get out of it like that. I'll not be made to look a fool and a scoundrel, I'll not endure it.'

'You'll not endure it!' I shook myself free and suddenly the tension between us could only find relief in a wild anger.

He said, 'I'll not be made a laughing stock like Bulwer Rutland.'

'How dare you say that to me! How dare you!'

'To hell with him! Will you marry me or won't you?'

'No, never, never!' I spat at him passionately. 'I won't marry a man besotted with another woman.'

'Isn't that why you said what you did?'

So that was what he believed . . . that I had been trying to trap him. I was trembling with rage. It urged me to say what I did not really think. 'Was it Alyne whom you went out to meet that night and would not betray? How many times had you met her before?'

'No, it wasn't. What do you take me for? She is to marry my uncle.'

'But she doesn't love him. She loves you, isn't that the truth?'

'No, it's not. I only wish it was.'

We were glaring at one another and suddenly I was so wretched, I could not bear it a moment longer. I said, 'I think you had better go. There is nothing more we can say to each other.'

He looked so desperately tired that my heart turned over, but I was exhausted too and bitterly unhappy.

He said more gently, 'Clarissa, I did not mean it to be like this.'

'It doesn't matter. Please go, please.'

'Very well, if that's what you wish. I'll come back when you are in a more reasonable mood.'

I think that made me more angry than anything. 'I'm perfectly reasonable. Come if you like but I shall not be here.'

He stood still for a moment and then took up hat and gloves and went out of the house without another word.

I was still standing, fighting back the tears, when Aunt Jess came in with a tray of wine and looked around her in surprise.

'Has he gone already? I thought to ask him to stay and sup with us.'

It was so ordinary, so matter of fact, after the strain and the emotion that I began to laugh helplessly and she put down the tray and came across to me.

'Stop it, Clarissa, stop it, do you hear?'

But I could not stop. 'If you only knew, Aunt Jess, if you only knew!'

'Knew what?' She was shaking me. 'Why did he come?'

'He asked me to marry him.'

'And you refused him? Why, Clarissa, why?' She was holding me by the shoulders as I still swayed between laughter and tears.

'He thought he owed it to me . . . because . . . because it was I who saved him from hanging.'

'Saved him? For goodness' sake, child, what are you talking about?'

I struggled for self control. 'There was so much against him and he could not prove where he was that night so I told them . . . I told them . . . that he spent the night with me.'

She looked at me for what seemed a long time before she said, 'I might have guessed you'd do something like that. You should have let me go with you. You've a wilful streak just like your mother when she ruined her life by running off with Tom Fenton. You're in love with him, aren't you?'

'I don't know, Aunt Jess, I don't know,' and then the tension broke in a storm of weeping and she drew me close to her.

'There, there, my dear, it's not the end of the world. He will come back.'

'No,' I said, my face muffled against her. 'He doesn't care for me. It's Alyne he loves and if his uncle dies, I think she'll go back to him and he'll be glad of it. I want to go away, Aunt Jess, help me to go away . . . back to father.'

Her arms tightened around me. 'We'll see, Clarissa, we'll see.'

But I did go, just as soon as I could, and when Oliver called the next morning I was packing and refused to see him. From my window I watched him unhitch Rowan and ride away. Copthorne which had been my refuge, my dream for so long, had become a purgatory I wanted only to leave.

Aunt Jess tried to persuade me but my mind was made up. At the last moment when John was helping me up into the trap, she came out of the house with Prickle in her arms.

'Take her,' she said. 'She'll only fret after you.'

'But I can't. She's yours and you're so fond of her . . .'

'I've got Warwick and James. She'll remind you of Copthorne.'

'She'll miss the Fens in Soho Square,' I said, but the warm snuggling body, the rough little tongue that licked my face, did give me some small comfort.

It was a long cold journey and as the stagecoach jolted over the snowy roads, I tried not to think of what I had done. How was I ever to explain to Papa? It sounded insane, I knew that. 'And why,' I could hear him saying, 'why, for God's sake, refuse his offer? He owes it to you. He should be down on his knees pleading with you' but that was just it. I wanted him . . . Oh heaven, how much I wanted him! But not on those terms. I sat quite still under the covert glances of the other passengers, swallowing my tears, and bracing myself to face a future bleaker than I had ever imagined.

Part Three

ALYNE

1831

Dwell in the dreams of wish and vain desire,
Pursue the faith that flies and seeks to new,
Run after hopes that mock thee with retire,
And look for love where liking never grew.

Sir Walter Ralegh

I

I was sitting beside Justin's bed. The lamp had been turned low but the fire burned brightly and the room was stiflingly warm. There was a heavy smell of drugs and liniments and sickness. It was a week since he had been struck down and though I knew I had to play my part in the nursing, the confinement was beginning to tell so that sometimes I felt I was being suffocated. I longed to go out, race in the garden, breathe fresh cold air, anything to escape the oppression and feel myself free. I was stiff and cramped from the long vigil but it would be some time yet before Annie Pearce came to relieve me.

Justin stirred restlessly and the Indian on the other side of his bed moved into the circle of lamplight. I saw the lean brown face and the gleam in the black eyes. He was never far from his master's side, especially now. I knew he disliked me as much as I disliked him. I think I was even a little afraid which was strange because I could never remember feeling afraid of anyone except . . . but that was another matter. That was something I was trying hard to put out of my mind.

Justin's hand was plucking at the coverlet. He was murmuring something and I leaned forward to listen.

'I can't see,' he muttered, 'why can't I see?'

'Don't worry.' I touched his cheek gently. 'Your head was hurt and the doctors think it best to keep your eyes bandaged a little longer.'

'I am not . . . I am not . . . blind?'

'No, no. You mustn't try to talk. You have to keep very quiet.'

'Is that Alyne?'

'Yes.'

When they brought him in that night, he had been unconscious for four days and this was almost the first time he had spoken coherently. So he was not going to die after all. He would recover and we would be married. There was relief in the thought and something else too, something that I did not dare to analyse.

'There was a fire,' he was murmuring. 'I remember a fire . . .'

'Yes, there was, but don't think about it now.'

I nodded to the Indian. He lifted Justin's head and I held the cup to his lips.

'Drink this. It will help you to sleep.'

He swallowed the draught obediently and lay back against the pillows. His hand moved gropingly towards me.

'You'll not go away?'

'No.'

I sat there with his hand in mine until his regular breathing told me that he slept again, more easily now, and then I quietly withdrew my hold and stood up. I crossed to the window pulling back the curtains. Outside the gardens lay very still, sleeping under the blanket of snow. It was strange to remember that in another fortnight it would be Christmas; not that there would be any festivity this year.

I came back to the bed and knew that Ram Lall watched me. He always watched me, moving about the house with his silent cat-like tread, spying on me. The devil's shadow, old Nurse Starling called him, which was fanciful but sometimes I think I believed it. When we were married, I would persuade Justin to dismiss him, send him back to India where he belonged . . . he and Jethro with him, though I knew that was impossible. Whatever Justin felt about his Indian servant, he would never part with his son. I was thankful when Annie knocked and came in.

'I've brought your thick shawl, Miss. It's turned fair biting tonight. There'll be more snow before morning, I'm thinking.'

'Is Miss Cherry in bed?'

'An hour since and I've taken brandy to that Captain Rutland in the library.' There was a note of strong disapproval in her voice which made me smile. Annie, like all the villagers, has no love for the military. 'How long is he going to stay with us, Miss Alyne?'

'Only another day or so . . . until the formalities for the trial are over in Ely.'

'Thank the Lord for small mercies, that's what I say! Now you get off to your bed, Miss. I've put hot milk in your room.'

'Thank you, Annie.'

She was more respectful now that I was going to marry Justin, all the servants were, except Nurse Starling. She would willingly have seen me burned at the stake, I'd always known that, but the others were not fools. I was no longer the waif, the changeling child, the nameless penniless nobody, but the future Lady Aylsham, mistress of Ravensley. They were aware that Justin listened to me and they had no wish to be shown the door. It amused me a little but I liked it too. I have always got my own way in the end.

Outside the door I paused. I was bone weary but I didn't want to go to bed, not just yet. I wrapped the thick woollen shawl closely around me and ran down the stairs past the library to the front door. It was locked and bolted but in a moment I had it open and stepped on to the porch. I looked out on a magical world, white and sparkling under a pale moon, the trees etched in silver against a dark sky. I took a deep breath of the sharp frosted air. Beyond the gardens fading into the misty silvery distance lay the Fens, part of me as I was part of them. Whatever happened, however much I longed to go away from Ravensley, and Justin had promised that he would take me to Paris, perhaps even to India one day, I knew I would have to come back. It was like the cord between mother and child, it would tug at me for ever. Perhaps it was the best part of me, something I had shared with Oliver from the beginning . . . poor Oliver . . . I'd not treated him well, but he had never had the slightest idea of the kind of person I really was. He put me on some impossible pedestal whereas I had always had my feet firmly on the ground . . .

An arm came round my waist and moved upward to my breast and Bulwer lifted the weight of my hair and kissed the nape of my neck. His touch seemed to burn into my flesh and I trembled with that terrible aching desire that seemed to rise from the very centre of my being and turned me sick and faint. I tried to free myself.

'You shouldn't do that, Captain Rutland.'

'Why not? You love it just as much as I do. Come in, my sweet, you'll freeze in this bitter air.'

He drew me in, closed and bolted the door and then turned to face me. He had discarded his uniform for a dark red brocaded dressing gown. He was tall, strong and handsome, but it was not that, it was something else, some vital spark that flamed between us, that turned my blood to water. I didn't love him, but I wanted him . . . God, how I wanted him! My flesh craved for his passionately and he knew it. I was afraid, desperately afraid, not of him but of myself.

He was smiling at me. 'Why do you fight me, Alyne? You know you'll come to me in the end.'

'No. I'm not listening to you, Captain Rutland.'

'Captain, Captain,' he mocked. 'Little fool. We're far beyond that.' He stretched out a hand and touched mine. 'Why not tonight? Why not now? We're alone in the house with a dying man.'

'He is not dying. He is recovering and I'm going to marry him.'

I wrenched my hand away and went swiftly up the stairs. Behind me I heard him laughing softly and I fled down the passage into my room, closing the door and leaning against it as exhausted as though I had run a race. I had brought it on myself. I had meant to test my power and I had succeeded only too well. Now I was caught in a trap of my own making.

It was at the ball when Bulwer came with his father and Justin asked me to be especially charming to them because he was hoping to involve old Joshua Rutland in one of his schemes to make Ravensley richer than it had ever been. I realized what kind of man Bulwer was from the beginning. He was hard like me and quite ruthless with those who stood in his way. He knew what he wanted and he set out to get it. I suppose that is what attracted me at first. It was so different from Oliver who lets himself be swayed by feelings of compassion and generosity that get him nowhere, like all that fuss he made over the Starlings which did him no good with Justin. Jake was always very capable of looking after himself and always had been since we were children, but Oliver had this absurd devotion to him.

Bulwer had wanted Clarissa because though her father is a penniless rake, he still has the highest connections and it maddened him because she resisted him. I never believed a word of that story about her inviting a man to her room. Bulwer must have tried some bit of villainy and still nursed anger against her because he failed. I thought she was a fool to refuse him. With his money she could have made a fine splash in London society, but then Clarissa was crazy about Oliver. Anyone could see that except Oliver himself. I shall never forget the shock on his face when she stood up in court and swore they were lovers. I rather admired her for it. I don't think I would have had the courage, but then I've never really been in love, not yet. I wondered what he said to her afterwards. It was two days since then and though he has sent to enquire after his uncle, he has not come to Ravensley and Justin knows nothing yet of what actually happened that night. If Clarissa thought to trap him, she is wrong. Oliver is mine still. Sometimes it gives me a comforting feeling, like having a safe refuge to which you can always come back when you set out on a dangerous venture.

When Bulwer insulted Clarissa at the ball and I saw the hurt and chagrin on her face, it was like being given a challenge. I wanted to show her how easy it was for me to bring a man to heel and I succeeded and gloried in it at first. I did not realize until afterwards what I had done to myself.

I have always known I had the power. I suppose there are some who would laugh at me, call it coincidence or self-delusion, but I feel it within myself like a force thrilling through me, that belongs to me alone and yet is not of my own making. If I will something to happen with all the strength of my being, then I know with certainty that it will happen. I was eleven when I knew about it first. One day in the summer when I met Martha Lee. That was not her real name. I knew that by her teasing smile and the sly look in her eyes when she told me and I never saw her again after that one time and yet in a way she changed my whole life.

Even as a child I liked to go off on my own into the Fens. It was the wild secret places that drew me like a magnet, places that not even Oliver knew about and I would have to go, escaping Nurse and Hattie and more often than not risking punishment for it when I came back to Ravensley.

It was a bright sunny day when I unhitched the boat. Cherry was in bed with a chill and Oliver was away at school. It was never difficult to hoodwink Hattie and it was easy to paddle the skiff through the waterways. We had done it so often and I knew them intimately. But this time, seduced by the mellow sunshine, by the elusive cry of the curlews, by the winding river, every bend luring me onwards, I went further than I had ever done before into the mystery of Greatheart through the whispering reeds and banks thick with loosestrife, purple willow herb and creamy cow's parsley. Deep in the heart of the Fens there are islands, pockets of land where willow and buckthorn grow in dense knotted clumps. When the sky clouded over and it began to rain, I looked about me for shelter and it was then that I saw the crumbling reed-thatched hut half hidden among the trees. I glided onto the bank, moored the boat to one of the willow branches and climbed up the path. There was smoke curling from a hole in the roof but I was not afraid. Most of the Fenmen, however rough and surly, will share their fire with a stranger. What I saw as I came up the track was so unexpected that I paused to stare.

The door was open and peat smouldered on the hearth. In front of it seated on a low stool was a woman, dark blue skirts spread around her, a yellow shawl over her shoulders, black hair gathered up in a loose knot. Beside her lay a dog absolutely still, head on paws. In front of her crouched a long sleek brown creature, its whiskered face lifted to hers, watching the outstretched hand while she crooned to it in a soft lilting voice. I had never seen an otter so close before nor one so tame. They are wild shy creatures glimpsed only as dark shadows slipping through the reeds with their high whistling cry. As I watched fascinated, it half rose, taking the fish from the thin fingers in its front paws and nibbling at it.

It was the dog who gave me away. He raised his head and growled. The otter was gone in an instant and the woman looked up and saw me. She stared for a full half minute before she spoke. She had a deep rich voice.

'Come in, no point in getting soaked to the skin. The fire is free to all lost creatures.'

'I am not lost.'

I moved slowly forward though there was nothing frightening about her. She had a strong-featured bony face, handsome in a way. I knelt by the fire stretching out my hands to its glow.

'Have you come far?'

'From Ravensley.'

'Are you hungry?' She pushed a wooden platter of griddle cakes towards me. 'Eat and drink if you wish.'

I took one of the cakes and sipped from the earthenware mug on the hearthstone. It had a curious taste, powerful and very sweet.

'It is mead,' she said. 'I make it myself from wild honey. What do they call you, child?'

'Alyne.'

'I knew an Alyne once but she lies buried in Westley church-yard. Where do you live?'

'At Ravensley. All this land belongs to Lord Aylsham.'

'Robert Aylsham?'

'Yes.'

'Is he your father?'

'Why do you ask?'

'Never mind. Do you think I am trespassing?'

'I don't know. A lot of people live on Greatheart. Who are you?'

'Those who seek my help call me Martha Lee.'

I wondered then if she was a Wise Woman, one of those whom the peasants go to for remedies in sickness but she did not look at all like Mother Babbitt who lived outside Ravensley and was shunned by the villagers unless their cattle were stricken with disease or their babies dying of spotted fever. The hut was very clean and bare. There was no rancid smell of animals or reek of herbs brewing on the fire and she did not speak in the rough East Anglian dialect.

'How do you live?' I asked curiously.

She shrugged her shoulders. 'I manage. I sing or tell fortunes and when I weary of it, I go home.'

'Where is your home?'

She smiled enigmatically, but did not answer. And then something curious happened. The otter came back. He edged across the floor on his belly to within a few inches of me and then stopped, the round head cocked, looking up at me with eyes like wet brown stones.

'Speak to him,' whispered the woman.

'What shall I say?'

'Anything but gently, otherwise you will scare him.'

So I murmured something and the otter came closer until he could thrust his sleek head under my hand. I felt it warm and vibrant with life and then the dog stirred and he was off again in a trice.

'I have never seen him do that with anyone but me. You have the power,' said the woman.

'What power?'

'To summon anyone to you, animal . . . or human.'

'I don't know what you mean.' I thought she was making fun of me and I sat up, half resentful, half fascinated. 'Oliver laughs at me because the horses don't like me.'

'Horses are kittle creatures, shy and nervous of what they don't understand. If you know the right words, you can do what you like with them.'

Now I knew she was teasing. 'There is no such thing.'

She smiled. 'Who told you so?' She leaned towards me and repeated half a dozen words in a language that I had never heard before. 'Repeat that to yourself and any horse, no matter what it be, will remain stock still and not move again until you liberate it with a word of release.'

'I don't believe you.'

She sat up. 'Try it sometime and you will see. Repeat them after me.'

Her eyes held me and I mouthed the strange words until I had them by heart. 'What do they mean?'

'Who knows? Maybe it is Celtic, maybe even older from a time nobody now remembers.' She took hold of my wrist and her eyes that were sometimes green and sometimes yellow as a cat seemed to bore into me as if to my very soul and suddenly I was afraid. I tried to pull away.

'I must go.'

'Wait, child,' she whispered, 'listen to me. The power . . . it can bring happiness and sorrow. I've only known one other who had it and to her it brought death so be warned, Alyne of Ravensley. Use it carefully.'

'Are you a witch?' I asked fearfully.

'Witch, witch!' she laughed mockingly. 'A word only. In the old days they'd have burned us, you and I, my pretty Alyne, because men are blinded and kill what they do not understand. Are you afraid of me?'

'No,' I said defiantly. 'Why should I be?'

'Brave words!' she reached up a hand and touched my hair and then my cheek with her long bony fingers. 'You would make the world your kingdom and the men in it your slaves, isn't that so?'

I didn't understand her and I jerked myself free. Her voice came after me as I escaped to the door.

'Come and see me again.'

'Will you still be here?'

'Perhaps . . . perhaps not.'

But when I did go back a few weeks later, she was gone. The fire was only ashes and the hut was swept clean and empty. Afterwards I tried to find it again and couldn't. The Fen waterways in high summer all look alike and I never spoke to Oliver or anyone else of that day.

I told myself she was crazy, a madwoman who talked nonsense to a credulous child, and yet I cherished it deep within myself. I, who had nothing, now possessed something unique, a gift given to few. It gave me strength, it gave me confidence. The petty barbs of the servants, Nurse's tantrums, Cherry's spite, Annie Pearce's sly digs, meant nothing any longer because I was free of them.

Perhaps they were right and somewhere I did have witch blood in me. I used to long and long to know who my mother was and where I came from . . . I used to dream that one day she would come out of the past to claim me and then as the years went by, the yearning faded. I was myself and that was all that mattered. I mentioned the horse spell once to Nurse Starling and she seized me by the shoulders staring into my face.

'Where did you hear that spoken of, child?'

'I don't know . . . somewhere.' I wriggled myself free. 'Is it true?'

'True, true, what's true?' she muttered. 'There are some folks still . . . but don't you go talking about such things, d'you hear me? 'Tisn't for such as you to meddle with.'

She used to frighten us with so many silly old tales . . . we laughed at most of them . . . but that did intrigue me. I only used it once and it still makes me sick to remember it. I tried over and over again to tell myself that what happened on the day of the hunt was not my fault, it was pure chance, but the doubt remained.

We watched the riders from the steps. Cherry was a child still and she was dancing up and down with excitement.

She said, 'Doesn't Clarissa look lovely? How well she rides. You can see how Oliver admires her. I think he is in love with her, don't you, Alyne? And Papa does too.'

'No,' I said savagely, 'no, it is not true.'

But it could be. That was the damnable part of it. They did make a handsome pair and I could see how Oliver's father beamed on them. That day Clarissa seemed to have everything I lacked, birth and grace, a beautiful mother and a handsome hero of a father, and suddenly I was madly furiously jealous. I was choked with it. I went away upstairs into the old schoolroom, standing there, my eyes closed, until the wild rage ebbed and I could breathe again. When I looked from the window, they had all ridden away. Faintly from the distance came the huntsman's horn and I stood there, my forehead pressed against the cold glass, and thought of Clarissa on her fine black horse while the words that Martha Lee had taught me came back and I repeated them softly to myself. She prided herself so much on her brilliant riding and I wanted to humiliate her. I swear to God that was all I wanted, but it was Clarissa's mother who died . . . of course it was not I who caused Blackie to balk at the dyke throwing her to her death. How could it be? Such things don't happen and yet I felt like a murderess as I crouched shivering on the schoolroom floor until Oliver came and there was solace and comfort in his kisses.

I had wanted Oliver and now he was mine. Lord Aylsham would have forbidden our marriage though he was a kind man and had been good to me. I did not wish him dead, but when he was struck down in the Fens, I knew that fate was on my side. I would have been a good wife to Oliver, but how did I know what was going to happen? We made great plans together but my dreams did not include living in poverty at Thatchers with a man who cared more for a few half-starved villagers than he did of building a fortune and making a great name for himself and me.

I suppose there are some who would call me selfish, a scheming heartless bitch, thinking only of myself, but what else could I do? His father's will left everything to Oliver. For a few months we were wonderfully happy until Justin came back from the dead. I did not set out to capture him. How could I . . . a man of the world twice my age? But I had to look out for myself and we were so isolated at Ravensley. We met so few people and what did I

have to sell except my looks? I know I have beauty. I'd be a fool
not to be aware of the desire in men's eyes when they look at me,
even Sir Peter Berkeley, even that sickly son of his who believes
himself to be in love with Cherry, even strangers whose glances
follow me when we go to worship in Ely Cathedral.

So I played my cards carefully. The first time I met Justin's eyes
in the drawing room, I read admiration in them and afterwards it
was easy. I had no thought of marriage then, only of winning his
interest. Cherry was his niece, he had a duty to her, but he owed
nothing to me. I let him talk; men always find pleasure in speaking
of themselves, and I listened when he told me of India, that far-off
dark country with its riches and its disease-ridden poverty, its
baked cracked earth and its exotic flowers, its powerful and frightening Gods, Siva, destroyer and creator, ascetic and sensualist, and
Kali Devi, most fearful of all, the only Goddess among the eight
terrible ones, defenders of the faith, who wears a necklace of
severed heads and ornaments of writhing snakes. I think they
meant more to him than the Christian God of love and compassion
and in some queer way I understood his fascination and shared it.

He was a strange man, dry, ironic, master of himself but with
sudden violent rages that swept through him like a storm and left
him shaking. I saw it once when he whipped Jethro. The boy had
been forbidden to play with Ben Starling and Jethro, who was so
timid, such a weakling in every other way, defied his father, refusing to give up his beloved companion. I saw the whip descend
again and again. I think he might have half killed him if I had not
clung to his arm. He stopped then, staring at me as if he had
woken out of a trance. He thrust me aside and went out of the
room leaving the child sobbing on the floor. I knelt beside him and
tried to lift him, but he pushed me away so I called Annie Pearce
and bade her care for him.

I remembered then the dark tale that Justin had killed not once
but twice . . . perhaps that explained his hatred of the Starlings.
Perhaps it all stemmed from far back in that time before his father
drove him from Ravensley.

He did not try to seduce me. He never even touched me until
the day of the harvest supper when there was all that fuss about
Cherry and Jake. After we arrived back at the house, Cherry ran
off to her room. She is like Oliver. She has this romantic attach-

ment to Jake and thinks it brave and noble to flaunt it in the face of her uncle. It's so stupid. He is handsome enough but how could she ever be allowed to marry a farm labourer, even though he has had more education than most, but she has never had any common sense.

Justin called me into the library as I prepared to follow her up the stairs.

'Is she very distressed?'

'She'll get over it.'

'It's indecent. How could I possibly allow such a thing? She had to be stopped.'

He was striding up and down the room. Then suddenly he paused and turned round to face me, still with that darkness in his face.

'What was there between you and Oliver?'

The question took me by surprise, but I answered truthfully. 'He wanted to marry me.'

'And you?'

'I was fond of him. We grew up together.'

He smiled crookedly. 'But not fond enough to fancy living on a pittance, is that it?'

'I think you're being unfair.'

'Very possibly.' He was staring at me. 'Oliver is soft, like his father, a man of ideals and stubborn loyalties, a romantic. I don't think you're like that and neither am I. What would you say if I were to ask you to marry me?'

I gasped. It was so unexpected. 'I have never thought of such a thing.'

'Haven't you?' he smiled cynically. 'Well, think of it now. I am twice your age, I know that, but I can give you everything you want.'

It was dazzling and yet I drew back. 'I don't know . . .'

And suddenly he was angry. He reached out and pulled me to him, his face close to mine. 'You must know. You must feel it as I do. A recognition . . . it happened that first evening I came here . . . like the stab of a sword. In India they have a name for it . . . reincarnation . . . a memory of some other life . . .' he was shaking as he held me at arms' length, his eyes searching my face.

'That's all rubbish of course, but I am not so old but I can still breed sons for Ravensley.'

'You have a son,' I said chilled.

'Yes, there is Jethro.' There was a faint contempt in his voice and yet I knew he was fond of the boy in his own way. Then he drew me to him. His kiss was fierce, possessive, demanding and yet without warmth. It aroused nothing in me, neither desire nor disgust. Involuntarily I glanced at the figure of the God he had brought with him from India, Siva, destroyer and creator. Then he held me away from him. 'Well, what do you say? Yes or no?'

'You must give me time.'

'Take all the time you want.' Then he released me and was again his usual dry self. 'There's just one thing. I'm expecting Joshua Rutland and his son to visit us soon. Make them welcome. It is important to me.'

'Yes, of course, whatever you wish.'

So I did as he asked and wished to God that I had let well alone. How could I marry Justin now, feeling as I did? What would I say if Bulwer asked me to be his wife? Was that what I wanted? Perhaps . . . but I knew only too surely that was not his intention . . . I might just as well ask for the moon.

2

After that night Justin improved rapidly. Two days later he was sitting up in bed, part of the bandages removed, demanding food and proving himself a difficult irascible patient. On the third day Bulwer Rutland left and I was thankful to see him go. It gave me breathing space. I was free of the terrible feeling of being torn in two. If he never returned, perhaps I could forget him and the torment that obsessed me. Then when he went to say goodbye, Justin invited him to come back at Christmas.

'That is if you will not find us too dull,' he added apologetically. 'I am afraid we shall not be entertaining a great deal of company, but if the weather holds, there should be some excellent skating.'

'Skating?' repeated Bulwer with raised eyebrows.

'We're famous for it in this part of the country. When the meres freeze you can skate up to twenty miles and the Fenmen race against each other. They come from miles around and the bets laid are quite prodigious. When I was a boy, it was one of the highlights of the winter season and it still is, isn't that so, Alyne?'

'Yes,' I said. 'Last winter was not so cold and the ice did not hold, but it will be different this year.'

'Oliver is something of a champion, I understand.'

'He was,' I said, a little reluctantly, unwilling to remember those winters when we were still children, the excitement, the thrills, the wonderful year when Oliver came of age and the future had seemed so simple and rosy.

'Was he indeed?' said Bulwer. 'It sounds tempting. I've taken quite a liking to rural pastimes in the last few weeks.' His eyes turned to me and I moved away quickly lest Justin should see the flush that rose in my cheeks.

'Bring your father with you if Mr Rutland cares to come.'

'I will ask him, my lord, if you're quite sure it will not be too much for you and your household in the circumstances.'

'Nonsense. There are one or two matters I should be glad of an opportunity to discuss with him and the girls will make you very welcome.'

'I am sure Cherry will be delighted at the prospect of your company, Captain Rutland,' I said a little maliciously.

'In that case, I shall naturally do my best to be here,' he countered pleasantly.

He shook hands with Justin and followed me down the stairs. In the hall his hand was on my shoulder, his breath on my cheek when Oliver came out of the library.

'I beg your pardon,' he said. 'I wanted to know if I can see my uncle. Is he well enough?'

I moved quickly away aware that he must have noticed the familiarity. 'He is very much better. I'll come up with you. Captain Rutland is just leaving.'

'So I see.'

Bulwer took my hand and kissed it. 'Thank you for your generous hospitality,' he said smoothly. 'I hope my next visit will be a more peaceful occasion.' He nodded briefly to Oliver and went out to his waiting horse. I turned to the stairs.

Oliver said, 'I thought his business here was concluded.'

'So it is but Justin has invited him to spend Christmas with us. Don't tire your uncle too much. He is still very weak.'

'What I have to say won't take long.'

It was ridiculous that we were so formal with each other. Justin was propped up against his pillows as Oliver followed me into his room. He grinned devilishly.

'So you tried to kill me, nephew. How unlucky for you that you did not succeed.'

'Is that what they have told you?'

'I have heard how you slipped your neck out of the noose. You must have more charm than I gave you credit for, Oliver, to persuade a cool young lady like Clarissa Fenton to swear away her reputation for your sake. Or was it true, eh? Come on, boy, don't stand there glowering at me. I'm no arbiter of morals. You can amuse yourself with as many young women as you please . . .'

'Of course it was not true,' interrupted Oliver violently.

'Indeed. Then perhaps you really did club me on top of the head after all.'

'No, I did not,' said Oliver goaded beyond endurance by Justin's mockery, 'and don't pretend you believe it. What I said in that damned court was the exact truth, but I'm beginning to wish I had possessed the courage of whoever did attempt it. You richly deserved it.'

Justin was watching him with a maddening smile on his lean face. 'So now we know. Puts you in a devil of a fix though, doesn't it. What are you going to do about the girl? Marry her?'

'I didn't come here to discuss my personal affairs.'

'Turned you down, has she? She's got pluck that young woman as well as good sense.'

'Are you going to stop baiting me and listen to what I have to say?' said Oliver and I saw he controlled himself with difficulty. 'I came to tell you what has been decided throughout the county.'

'Go on. I am listening.'

'Briefly, a proposal has been put forward that the men's wages should be raised by one shilling to eight shillings a week. I presume that you will want me to agree to the rise on your behalf.'

'By all means if it will keep the fools quiet and bring them back to work. When everything is under control again, we can cut it off easily enough.'

'No,' said Oliver, 'not if I can help it. There has been too much suffering already, too much blood shed for the sake of a beggarly shilling and by God, I intend to make sure that they keep it.'

'Well, we shall see, won't we? The rioters knew what they were doing and were well aware of the consequences. I've told you before. You waste your sympathy.'

'There are two opinions on that point.'

I knew Oliver would go on and on if I didn't stop him. He could never see that there was no sense in arguing when Justin had made up his mind. I said quietly, 'I think you've been here long enough. The doctor was insistent that your uncle should have plenty of rest.'

'Very well. I don't want to tire him.' Oliver paused before he said, 'You don't need to concern yourself while you are sick. I will take care that everything needful is done.'

'Very good of you, boy,' said Justin dryly. 'And convey my good wishes to Miss Clarissa Fenton.'

'She is no longer here. She has gone back to London.'

'Walked out on you, has she? Bad luck!' and I heard Justin chuckling to himself as we went out of the room.

At the top of the stairs, Oliver stopped. 'What about the boy? Has he recovered?'

'Jethro? I don't know. I suppose so.'

'My God, Alyne, don't you ever think of anyone but yourself?'

'That's not fair,' I said stung by his reproach. 'Justin has been very sick. Annie Pearce and I have had to sit up with him night and day. Cherry is no good at all when it comes to sickness.'

He looked slightly ashamed. 'Yes, of course . . . oh damn it, I'm sorry. I didn't mean to be churlish. I might as well see him while I am here. Ben has been asking after him.'

In the schoolroom Jethro was in the big armchair, looking very white and thin, with a rug over his knees while Cherry sat on a low stool in front of him, a games board between them.

I stayed in the doorway while Oliver crossed to the boy. 'Well, my wounded hero,' he said cheerfully, 'how are you? All healed up?'

'I had to have four stitches and I've had a fever,' said Jethro importantly. 'But I'm better now. Cherry has been playing draughts with me and I won.'

'Splendid, that's the spirit.'

'Somebody has to trouble about the child,' said Cherry with a look at me. She scrambled to her feet and put the board aside. 'We'll play another game later on.'

Oliver smiled at his sister and dropped on to the stool. 'Ben sends his love, Jethro.'

'Could he come up and see me?' asked the boy wistfully.

'Well, I don't think your Papa would like that, but when you're better, Cherry shall bring you to my house and you can play with him there.'

'Can I?' The boy's eyes were shining and he fumbled in the pocket of his dressing gown. He brought out something that gleamed gold in the firelight. 'I've got a present for him. I was going to keep it for Christmas, but I'd like him to have it now.'

'Where did you get this?' There was a queer note in Oliver's voice that made me curious. I crossed to look over his shoulder. He was staring down at a small oval of gold and when he turned it over, I saw that the other side was cornelian beautifully carved in

an intricate design. It had a rare charm and might have been a seal
or a man's fob or even a pendant to hang on a chain.

'My Mama gave it to me,' said Jethro. 'She said I was to keep it
safe and give it to someone I like and I do like Ben very much.'

'When did your Mama give it to you?'

'When I was nine. It was just before she fell ill. She had a fever
like mine, only she died, and Papa went away to England afterwards with Ram Lall and I was left all alone except for my ayah.
It was horrid.'

The boy's lips trembled and Oliver put his arm round the thin
body and pulled him close to him.

'I know but that's all over now and when the spring comes, I'll
take you fishing on the Fens. We'll find where the wild swans nest
and hunt for martens and otters as I used to do when I was your
age. Would you like that?'

'Will you teach me to shoot?'

'We shall have to ask your Papa about that.'

'Can Ben come too?'

'Yes, of course Ben can come,' said Oliver smiling at him.

It was strange, but I felt a curious pang as I watched them, a
spasm of regret, a feeling that I had deliberately tossed aside
something valuable, a warmth, a generosity, a kindliness of spirit
. . . then I put it out of my mind as a weakness in which I could
not afford to indulge.

Oliver was saying, 'I think you should keep what your Mama
gave you, Jethro. It is too valuable for Ben.'

'But I want to give it to him.'

'He wouldn't know what to do with it, but I know what he
would like . . . a pair of skates of his own, skates of lovely
gleaming steel.'

'Oh yes,' Jethro clapped his hands. 'He told me about the skating. Will you get them for him?'

'I will and you shall give them to him yourself. As for this,' he
held out his hand with the gold bauble. 'Will you lend it to me for
a little while? I'll take care of it and you shall have it back, I
promise, whenever you wish.'

'All right,' said the boy looking up at Oliver trustingly. 'And
you'll not forget about the skates?'

'I won't forget. And now I must go. Get well soon.'

Cherry followed us to the door. 'What is it that Jethro gave you?' she whispered.

'Nothing important. I just think it is a pity if he should lose such a valuable memento of his mother.'

'Is that all?'

'What else should there be?'

I knew there was more to it than that but if Oliver chose to keep silent, then nothing would induce him to speak.

As we went downstairs, I said, 'Is it wise to encourage this friendship with Ben Starling?'

'What is wise? The boy is lonely. He needs a companion.'

'You know how Justin feels about the Starlings.'

'Then he must learn to feel differently. I shall do what I think is right and he can go hang.' Then he paused and looked down at me. 'I am sorry. I keep forgetting that you are going to marry him.'

'Do you hate me for it?'

'Hate . . . love . . . they are only words. How can I hate you? You are in my blood, you know that, don't you? And it pleases you.'

Then his arms went round me and I was leaning my head against him. It was a long time, more than a year, since he had touched me. There was no excitement any longer, none of the choking desire that Bulwer aroused or the queer tug that linked me with Justin, only a feeling of peace, of safety. Why couldn't I be content with that?

Then Oliver muttered thickly, 'It's no use, Alyne. We can't go back, not now. I wish to God we could.'

He put me away from him and went quickly down the steps towards the stables where he had left his horse.

It snowed all through the week before Christmas and it was bitterly cold, but it stopped on the day Bulwer came with his father and the garden sparkled under a brilliant sun as their carriage crackled and slithered over the icy ruts. We were not entirely alone over the holiday. One or two of our neighbours called with greetings and Sir Peter Berkeley rode over with Hugh, but otherwise we were very quiet. Oliver came once only and refused to share the Christmas dinner though Cherry begged him to stay.

'I'm not in festive mood,' he said dryly. 'I should be a skeleton at the feast. I prefer to eat alone.'

'Do as you please,' said his uncle. 'I wish you joy of it.'

He had given me a necklace of amethysts set in gold and I saw Oliver's eyes on it and on my new gown of green velvet bound and trimmed with lilac taffeta before he went out of the house.

Justin was up and about again, but still had to be careful, husbanding his strength, so our evenings were quiet with a little music and singing. Joshua and his son sat down to cards with Justin and old Miss Cavendish who had come up from Copthorne and enjoyed a mild gamble. I asked after Clarissa and she answered me guardedly. Her father was sick, she said, and she would not be coming back to Copthorne for some time.

Bulwer rode in the mornings and took a gun out on to the Fens and though we made no move towards one another, the tension was there like a harpstring stretched to breaking point. Did he feel it as I did? It had never happened to me before. Was it love or obsession? A fever, a frenzy in the blood, like a sickness? And would it go, if once, just once, I let it have its way? I did not know and I was thankful when old Joshua said business would call him back to London in the New Year.

But first there was the skating. The mere and waterways had frozen so thick and solid that the villagers had marked out their course for the last day of the old year. It was a lovely morning despite the intense cold. The sun was like a huge red ball with the black windmills standing out stark against the wintry sky and the clumps of trees, rare enough on the Fens, like dark sentinels in the icy purity of the snow. The Fenmen had come in great numbers from nearby villages, crowding on to the ice in their thick doublebreasted coats, their otterskin caps and leather breeches, gartered at the knee with dried eelskins.

'They wear them as a guard against rheumatism,' I told Bulwer, 'just as they carry a molesfoot in their pockets to ward off the evil eye. They were very superstitious still.'

'And what do they wear to protect themselves against palehaired witches who promise much and give nothing?' he said softly.

I drew away from him. 'I'm cold. I'm going to buy some of the hot chestnuts.'

Cherry was standing by Mother Babbitt whose nuts were roasting on the top of an old Dutch oven. Bulwer bought a handful. We tossed them between us, burning our fingers through our gloves as we cracked and ate them. There was a box on wheels, drawn by two dogs, selling gin and hot water in tin mugs. We shared one, sipping from the same cup and the spirit ran through me like fire.

Justin had the servants bring a chair down to the bank with a couple of fur rugs to keep out the cold. Most of the Fenmen still wore the 'bone runners', the sheep leg bones polished and secured by a leather strip round the ankles, but I saw Ben proudly showing off his steel skates with an excited Jethro hovering round him and I warned the boy to keep him out of his father's sight.

'Where's Oliver?' he demanded. 'He promised to take me skating with him.'

I had missed Oliver too. It was not like him to be absent on a day when the villagers were out to enjoy themselves. 'I have no idea,' I said. 'Now do be sensible, Jethro. We don't want any trouble today.'

The bitterness and strife of only a month ago seemed forgotten. The Fenmen were not exactly friendly and many familiar faces were missing, but this was their particular sport in which they took great pride and they tolerated our presence. Some of them, the 'Tigers' as they call them, skated like the wind and could cover a mile in less than four minutes. The competition in the races was fierce and perversely it pleased me that Bulwer, who had been prepared to scoff, was taken aback when again and again he lost his wagers. I sensed his irritation. He was not a man to relish being beaten at anything and so later in the day when Oliver suddenly appeared with Jethro in tow, he was restlessly wanting to prove himself as good or better than any man there.

He said, 'What about you and I racing against one another, Aylsham?'

'I was not intending to stay,' said Oliver shortly. 'I have other things to do. I came only because I had promised the boy.'

'Oh come now,' said Justin, 'is there any need to spoil the sport? Captain Rutland is our guest after all. I'll give a prize . . . twenty guineas to the winner.'

'And I'll double it,' said old Joshua Rutland, who had been stumping around in his thick boots and fur-lined coat, thoroughly enjoying himself and, I suspect, indulging freely in the wine and brandy brought down by the servants with the soup and hot pies for our picnic luncheon.

Oliver shrugged his shoulders. 'If you wish, but I warn you I'm out of practice.'

I knew what the result would be. Oliver had skated since a child, as we all had. Bulwer was outclassed from the first. The course was a three-mile stretch there and back, making six miles with a difficult turn at the halfway post, and Oliver won it easily, gliding back in just under thirty minutes, cool and unruffled. The villagers were cheering madly. He had always been popular with them and more than ever now. I saw the dark fury on Bulwer's face when he came in minutes afterwards, his coat stained by a fall at the turning point.

His father made it worse. 'You should take more exercise, lad,' he said, thumping his discomfited son on the back. 'Young Noll had you beat properly. But I'm not a man to go back on my word.' He pulled the leather purse from his pocket and laboriously counted out the forty guineas, adding them to the twenty from Justin. 'Take it, boy. It'll maybe do you a mite of good. Buy Miss Clarissa a fairing for the New Year.'

Oliver took the money and looked down at it for an instant. The men, women and children of the village had drawn to one side watching avidly. He glanced at his uncle and then strode over to them.

'Here you are, lads,' he said. 'An unexpected bounty from the Gods. Make the most of it.' He tossed the shower of gold coins among them. There was a mad scramble amid laughter and cheers. I saw Ben Starling go into them like a little animal burrowing under legs and emerging triumphant with one of the guineas.

Oliver watched for a moment and then turned back to Mr Rutland. 'Thank you, sir, for the opportunity to give pleasure to those who have little enough.' Then he sketched a salute to him and his uncle and skated across the ice and into the faint mist that had begun to creep out of the Fens.

'Damn the fellow!' exclaimed Joshua Rutland. 'I'd not expected to see my hard-earned cash go that way. From all I hear, he could do with it.'

'It's a way he has,' said Justin dryly. 'A gesture that means nothing. One of these days he'll be forced to count the cost. It's growing cold. Shall we go back to the house? Come, Alyne.'

There was an angry look in Bulwer's eyes and he seized me by the wrist as I turned to follow.

'Not yet,' he whispered savagely. 'Are we never to have a moment alone together?'

'Not now,' I protested. 'I must go in. They'll be wondering where I am.'

'Later. You're coming with me first.'

He propelled me across the ice so that I had no choice but to skate with him. We went up the mere, his arm round my waist, with the short winter's day already darkening around us. Soon we had left everything behind. We were alone in a silent waste with only the reedy banks, the distant isolated trees and the sinking sun turning the sky blood red and casting a rosy shadow across the grey ice.

'We should go back,' I said. 'It will be quite dark soon.'

'To hell with that!' He pulled me towards the bank where a huge willow trailed its branches down to the frozen water. Then I was in his arms and he was kissing me with a force and a passion that drove everything else out of my head.

God knows what might have happened out there on the ice in the hush of the December day if another couple had not suddenly appeared round a bend of the waterway.

'Stop, please, let me go, we shall be seen,' I breathed.

'Damn them!' Then he looked up and I saw his face change. 'By Jupiter,' he exclaimed, 'it's that cursed rascal who gave me the slip. I've suspected all along that he had hidden himself somewhere in this neighbourhood.'

I could see them now myself. Jake and Cherry were skating slowly, hand in hand. There was no mistaking her scarlet coat and white fur hood.

'I'll have him if I die for it!' went on Bulwer. 'There's five hundred pounds reward for every one of those rogues.'

'No,' I said revolted. 'Let him go. It's blood money.'

'Do you think I care a tinker's curse for the reward? It's what he did to me. My men ambushed, one of them all but murdered, a reprimand for negligence and that fellow Oliver Aylsham laughing behind my back!'

His angry frustration surprised me. I had no particular love for Jake, but he had been part of my childhood, part of the past life at Ravensley, and I'd not see him taken without a chance of escape so I struggled with Bulwer, but he was stronger than I. He thrust me aside and started forward, but near the bank the ice was deeply ribbed and rutted. His skates caught, he spun round and fell heavily, his leg doubled under him. He fought to rise and then fell back with a groan.

'What is it? What has happened?' I knelt beside him.

'My leg . . . oh God, my leg!'

The others had woken from their absorption in each other. They skated towards us. I doubted if they had recognized us hidden under the shade of the willow, but now Cherry stopped, her hand on Jake's arm. She was obviously urging him to go quickly before he was recognized, but he shook his head and came on.

'He's hurt,' I heard him say. 'We'd better see what we can do.' He bent over Bulwer. 'What is wrong? Do you think you can stand?'

'I doubt it. I believe my leg is broken.'

'Help me, Alyne. You too, Cherry. We'll get him to the bank.'

Together we half pulled, half carried Bulwer to the shore and propped him up against the tree.

Jake stood up. 'I had better fetch help. We need a stretcher.'

'No,' said Cherry. 'Not you. I'll go.'

Bulwer's face was twisted with the pain, but he pulled himself up with an effort. 'You are a convicted felon, my man. If I were to do my duty, I should report you.'

'Do what you like, Captain,' said Jake calmly. 'I doubt if all His Majesty's Dragoons searching the Fens for a week would find me.'

'Don't be so sure. We can do a great deal with dogs and what about those who helped you? Oliver Aylsham, wasn't it, and that pretty little filly who is so almighty fond of you.'

I saw Jake's mouth tighten. If Bulwer had been on his feet, I thought, he would have knocked him down.

'You can prove nothing against them so don't waste your breath.'

Suddenly I was weary of it all. I said, 'Go, Jake, go now. I'm grateful for your help, but Cherry will come back soon. I'll stay with him. He'll not give you away or anyone else, I promise you.'

Jake looked from Bulwer to me, then he went quickly, fading almost immediately into the darkness and mystery of the Fens.

The shock and pain were beginning to have their effect. Bulwer shivered as he leaned back against the tree. I tried to ease his position a little and he caught at my hand.

'You shouldn't make promises you can't keep, my girl. I am a soldier. I have a duty to perform.'

'Not this surely. What does it matter? No one will know.'

'A typical woman's answer! It does matter.' He pulled me nearer to him, looking into my face. 'I never thought you cared so much.'

'I don't, but it's all over and done with. Why bring it all back?' Suddenly I knew it was not Jake so much, or Cherry, but Oliver I cared about. This would hurt him beyond everything and I had done him enough harm already. I said, 'If you do anything to injure Jake, I'll never forgive you.'

He smiled. 'I wonder . . . what will you give me if I keep silent?'

'What have I to give?'

'I think you know.'

We were staring at one another and in that moment everything changed. I can't explain, but there was a queer look on his face as if he had come up against something in himself he had never recognized. He moved restlessly and clenched his teeth against the wave of agony from his injured leg.

'Hell and damnation! I'm not bargaining. I never intended to do anything anyway, only frighten him. Let the poor devil go free. It must be hellish enough to live as he does, hunted from pillar to post.'

He closed his eyes. He had gone very white and I thought he might faint. I gripped his hand hard and then I saw Cherry coming out of the growing darkness and there were men with her carrying lanterns and bringing an improvised stretcher with blankets. They lifted Bulwer on to it wrapping him warmly and started back across the ice.

'One of the servants has ridden off for Dr Thorney,' said Cherry as we followed after them. 'Where is Jake?'

'He has gone.'

'Will Captain Rutland . . . ?'

'No, he won't,' I said quickly.

'Are you sure?'

'Quite sure. How long have you known about Jake, Cherry?'

'Not long. It was just before Christmas. I went down to Thatchers to speak to Oliver about something and he was there . . . in the kitchen with his mother.'

'And Oliver has known all the time?'

'Yes.'

'It's madness. Hasn't he been in enough danger? Why does he do these things?'

'If you are fond of someone, you don't think of risks,' said Cherry simply.

We were whispering together like conspirators. I wondered if I would ever love anyone enough to act as they had done. 'For heaven's sake, be careful,' I said. 'If your uncle were to find out . . .'

'He won't. You needn't be afraid for me, Alyne.'

I had always thought of Cherry as a child, foolish and impulsive. Now I knew I had been wrong. Even her face had taken on a new maturity. Then we were back at the edge of the mere and there was much to do. We unlaced our skates and trudged up to the house in silence.

3

I don't believe in Fate or Destiny and sometimes, shocking as it may be, I have even wondered if I really believe in God, but it did seem to me that some power, the Devil perhaps if he exists, and Nurse Starling used to terrify us with him often enough, was bent on twisting my life away from the plan I had made for it or else why should Bulwer have broken his leg so stupidly on that particular day and be forced to spend nearly two months with us at Ravensley.

He bore the setting of the bone with a stubborn courage. It was a straight break without complications, said Dr Thorney, but it would take at least three weeks for the bone to knit together when necessarily he must keep to his bed.

'Can you manage the nursing?' he asked when the splints had been adjusted and he had given his patient a strong sedative. 'Captain Rutland is no light weight. He will need to be lifted at first,' he paused delicately with a glance at Cherry and me.

'I will have Croft sent down. He is the boy's manservant, an excellent fellow, been with him for years,' said Joshua Rutland.

'And there's Ram Lall,' said Justin. 'He had plenty of experience of nursing in India and is far stronger than he looks.'

'We shall need extra help in the kitchen,' said Cherry, 'why don't we ask Mrs Starling to come up each day? She can always leave Jenny in charge.'

I looked at Justin and saw the tightening of his mouth but he only said, 'Very well, if you're sure there is no one else.'

'No one as capable, Uncle, and living so close.'

It sent me down to Thatchers the next day to ask Oliver if he could spare his housekeeper, only to find that he was not there.

'He was away to London early this morning, Miss,' said Mrs Starling drying her soapy hands on her apron as she came out of the steamy kitchen. 'He said there's little enough to be done now on the farms with the snow an' all so he would take the opportunity.'

I looked round the room. She kept it neat and clean, but it was bare and without comfort. Oliver had this absurd pride. He would accept nothing from his uncle or from me.

'When will he be back?'

'He didn't say, Miss. Seemed glad to be off, I thought. Needs a bit of a change, I shouldn't wonder, after all that nastiness of the trial. So I can come whenever you want me. There's only Ben and Seth at home now and Jenny can see to their food.'

I felt curiously bereft as I walked back to Ravensley. All these months Oliver had always been there when I wanted him, even if he sometimes frowned and was out of temper. When he had gone to London last year, he had been unhappy, I knew that, though he said so little about it, so why had he gone there again? A useless question to which I had no answer.

The shock and the cold took toll of even Bulwer's strength. For a couple of weeks he burned in a high fever so that Ram Lall and Croft had difficulty in keeping him quiet and avoiding damage to the fractured bone and Joshua Rutland stayed on in considerable anxiety. But then he began to mend. His father went back to London and Bulwer became bored and restless, chafing against the enforced idleness, insisting on hobbling around on crutches so that it was all Cherry and I could do to keep him amused.

It never seemed to strike Justin how he was throwing us together. He was building airy plans on what he intended to do at Ravensley with the help of Joshua Rutland's money. I didn't understand completely, but sometimes when he talked on and on about it, I thought Oliver was right. He knew nothing of the Fens or of the people who lived there. He had this vision of himself as a great landowner, rich, respected, powerful, and I thought he was possessed by a fury to prove himself, a kind of revenge against the father who had once disowned him, and it was I who would share his kingdom with him. It was a dream I had long cherished and that had suddenly become tarnished because of what had happened to me. Desire, craving, obsession, whatever it was I felt for Bulwer, had now, by some subtle alchemy, become part of something else. I did not want it, I fought against it, to fall in love was a weakness I could not afford.

I thought I knew Bulwer—brash, arrogant, ambitious, caring little for those he thrust aside to get what he wanted. He was all these things, just as I was, but no one is as simple as that. He had another side, one he kept hidden, one of which he was ashamed, and I only glimpsed it because now in sickness and pain he was vulnerable for the first time.

It came to me slowly like the day Croft told me something of himself. He was a stocky little man, a few years younger than his master. I went into the pantry one day and saw him polishing Bulwer's boots.

I said casually, 'How long have you been with Captain Rutland, Croft?'

'Seven years, Miss.' He held out the boot, looking at his work critically. 'Lovely, aren't they? Made by Hoby, you know, bootmaker to his late majesty. He used to boast that if the Duke of Wellington had used any other bootmaker, he would never have carried the day at Waterloo.'

I smiled as he went on rubbing vigorously. 'Were you in service before?'

'Lor' no, Miss.' He looked up at me with a cheeky grin on his pointed Cockney features. 'D'ye know why the Captain took me on? 'Cos I pinched his watch out of his pocket and he nabbed me.'

'Do you mean you were a thief?'

'Aye, I suppose you'd call me that. I were one of eleven, you see, and a poor old time we had of it, I can tell you, with me Dad gone off somewhere and me Mam working like six to keep the lot of us. So I cleared off when I were fifteen and got in with a gang like meself. One fine night, just off Piccadilly, I saw this toff strolling home, cigar in mouth, humming to himself, merry-like . . . you know what I mean, Miss . . . easy game, I sez to meself, so I tackled him. Lor' lumme, I never made more of a mistake. Before you could say up and at 'em, I were on me back in the gutter and he were standing over me. The others had vanished of course, quicker than greased lightning, catch them risking their skins for a pal! The Captain, he yanks me up. "I'll have you whipped, me boyo," he sez, "I'll have you packed off to Botany Bay . . ." Then, d'ye know what I did? What with the fright an' all and not a bite in me stomach all day, everything went sort o' black. Next thing I knew, I were sitting on the step of a fine house in Arlington

Street and he were looking down at me. "You skinny little scarecrow," he sez, "when did you eat last?" "Dunno," I mumbled. I was afraid of him, see, and he sez, "Come on, you damned rascal," and he opens the door, pushes me inside and sits me down to beef and bread and champagne and I dunno what else.'

'And after that he took you on as his servant?' I asked incredulously.

'Aye, he did, after I'd been cleaned up a bit. "Set a thief to catch a thief," he sez to me joking like. "You keep 'em off my back, Croft, and you'll not lose by it." '

It had been generous, not that Bulwer would ever have admitted such a thing. He was an exacting master and once when Croft was helping him down the stairs and jarred him badly at an awkward turn, he swore at him roundly, sending him off with a stinging box on the ear when they reached the bottom.

'You shouldn't do that,' I protested. 'Croft worships you.'

'So he damned well should,' he growled. 'He'd get a boot up his backside if he didn't. He'd have been hanged long since but for me.'

Bulwer was not a reading man. He would look at a book and toss it aside after a few minutes and the long hours confined to the sofa which the doctor commanded drove him frantic with boredom. Oliver had sent word that he was delayed in London so Justin was often out during the day and it was I who sat with Bulwer. Sometimes Cherry would be there and sometimes Hattie, working away on her endless embroidery, but it was to me he talked.

There was an afternoon when we were alone. The light was going so that I was thankful to put my needlework aside and sit staring into the leaping flame of the fire. Bulwer had been half asleep. Then quite suddenly he began to speak of his mother who had died when he was still a child. It was only after her death that his father, profiting from the war with France, had become rich.

'She had the worst of it,' he said. 'I was only eight but I remember it well and how hard she worked alongside my father. She never had any comfort and they buried her in the worn-out gown she wore at her wedding. Afterwards there were other women out for what they could get but none permanent. I suppose father loved her in his own way.'

'Were they kind to you?'

'I don't think they took much notice of rich Josh Rutland's brat. Then he packed me off to Harrow. I was the upstart, the parvenu, the boy whose old man shovelled tea over a counter among all those blue-blooded sons of Dukes and Earls,' he went on savagely. 'I bloodied their pretty noses for them. There weren't many who could stand up to Bull Rutland.'

I knew exactly how he had felt because in a different way it had been the same for me, a fight to prove myself as good as Cherry, the little heiress, and the other pampered spoiled girls during the hateful year we had spent at that high class academy. We had no bloodied noses, but I doubt if boys are any worse than girls when it comes to malicious spite.

'I swore I'd get even with them and I did,' he said. 'Money can buy your way into most things.'

'But not quite all.' I could scarcely see his face in the half light, but we seemed so close, I risked a question. 'Why did you want Clarissa?'

I expected an angry retort, but he was staring broodingly into the fire. 'Most women had fallen into my arms like ripe plums, but not Clarissa, she was so cool, so aloof, so damned . . . patrician. Her father was easy game, but not she . . . it made me angry . . .'

'So you tried to pull her down . . .'

'What do you know about that?'

'Only what I've heard.'

He stirred uncomfortably. 'I did it for a wager, to prove something to myself and the damned thing went wrong. I had to stop them laughing at me . . .' He turned to look at me. 'Do you despise me for it?' I shook my head and he stretched out a hand, closing it over mine. 'We're two of a kind, you and I, Alyne, do you know that?' There was something different about him. His eyes held mine and his touch awoke an immediate response in me. I waited for what I hardly knew. 'We know what we want and we go out to get it,' he went on. 'Justin is going to be a great man before he is done and you're going to queen it beside him, just as I'm going to show those fellows who take their seats in the House of Lords and can't pay their gambling debts at Crockfords that the son of Joshua Rutland, tea-broker and tradesman, is a better man than they are.'

It was so true what he said and yet I felt suddenly chilled as if a breath from the frosty world outside had entered the room. I was not sorry when Annie came in to light the lamps followed by Jethro with Cherry, both of them rosy-cheeked from a long walk and a battle in the snow.

Towards the end of February the doctor pronounced Bulwer's leg strong enough for him to ride, provided it was a quiet horse and he didn't tire himself by doing too much. There was now little need for him to stay on with us and he talked of returning to London, but still lingered.

One morning when I was dressing, Cherry came into my room. She looked me up and down in my dark green habit.

'Riding again? You always used to say you hated the horses and now you're out every day with Captain Rutland.'

'Someone has to go with him.'

'There is Croft.'

'He looks for more amusing company than his manservant and you know what Justin says—keep him happy. You can't imagine that I enjoy it, do you?'

'I wonder.' She came to stand beside me and I could see her face in the mirror and the little smile on her lips. 'And I keep on wondering. Are you in love with him, Alyne?'

I moved away abruptly. 'Of course not. What utter nonsense you do talk.'

'Is it nonsense?' Cherry fiddled with the toilet articles on my dressing table. She has grown up a lot lately. She no longer flies into childish tantrums. Then she turned to look at me. 'I should be careful if I were you. Ram Lall watches . . . you as well as me . . . and I don't trust him.'

I avoided her eyes. 'Why should he watch you? Have you been seeing Jake again?'

'No.'

'Well then, what is there for him to see?'

'You know that better than I do.' She turned back at the door looking over her shoulder at me. 'You'd better be extra careful today. They say the ice is beginning to melt. There could be flooding.'

It was one of those days that come suddenly in late February and make you realize that soon it will be spring. It was very early when the horses were brought round and we rode quietly through the fragrant morning, skirting Greatheart and crossing the stretch of the Fen to an ancient grassy track only faintly outlined in the turf and going on and on towards the north.

The air smelled sweetly of growing things. There were white violets hidden in the grass at the edge of the track, but there was still ice on the pools. It was thawing, but I thought Cherry exaggerated when she spoke of flooding. It is rare for it to come before March.

We trotted side by side. Bulwer had been silent for some time and I stared ahead. 'Do you know this bridleway is one of the oldest in the Fen country? It winds its way through fields and woods until it reaches the sea. They say it was here before even the Romans came.'

We were riding through a green gloom, the thick trees arching overhead though they were still leafless and it was as if suddenly I was one of those thousands who must have used this road, trudging northwards through sun and rain, the rich and the poor, the princess looking for a lover and the pilgrim searching for his God.

I was aware that Bulwer had turned to me. He said, 'Where did you learn all that?' and realized that I must have been speaking my thoughts aloud.

'I don't know. Old Lord Aylsham used to speak of it and Nurse too. I remember her telling us that Black Shuck haunted this road and he is the hound of Thor, the God of Thunder in old Norse legend, and the Aylshams have Viking blood. It used to fascinate Oliver.'

Bulwer's hand caught at my bridle and pulled me close to him. 'Was Oliver your lover?'

I was startled. 'I ought to be offended at such a question.'

'Are you?'

'Why do you ask?'

'You speak of him so often.'

'Why shouldn't I? I have known him for a long time.'

I had the queerest feeling that we were all bound up together, Oliver, Bulwer, Justin and I, and I shivered almost as if Black Shuck himself were breathing down my neck. Then I pulled away urging my horse to a canter, Bulwer caught up with me laughing and the moment passed.

Just before noon we came to a church. It was very small and isolated, its tiny tower overgrown with ivy and the crumbling tombstones surrounding it buried deep in the rank grass. I had a fancy to go into it, much to Bulwer's disgust. It was dark inside and smelled of damp and decay. There was only one notable feature close to the altar, a splendid tomb with an alabaster effigy of a knight in armour and his lady beside him in her long gown.

'This place reeks of the dead,' said Bulwer. 'Let's get out of it.'

'In a moment. I want to see first.'

I stared down at the high-cheekboned face under the wimple with an odd feeling of recognition and jumped when a dry voice said, 'Are you interested in the Lady Martha Leigh?'

The man who came through the vestry door must be the Vicar, I thought, as ancient and crumbling as his church. 'The Lady who?'

'Martha Leigh. She lived five hundred years ago and she is fortunate to be buried here. There were those who would have burned her for a witch.'

'Oh for God's sake,' muttered Bulwer.

I stayed him with a hand on his arm. 'Why did they want to burn her?'

'It's an old story. I found it once among the church records. It seems she had some sort of power over animals, over people too perhaps. She sheltered all kinds of wild beasts in her manor and there were many who called them the spawn of the devil.'

'How did she escape?'

'Who knows now? Maybe her husband was too powerful for them. He even put one of her animals on her tomb. You can see if you look closely. A very strange creature crawling up and laying its head under her hand. All nonsense of course, but they were very credulous in those days.'

Leigh . . . Martha Lee . . . was it possible? It seemed now that I knew that strong face cut in alabaster, that I had once seen its living likeness. I said, 'Do the family still live here?'

'There's only one of them left and she is abroad. The manor has been shut up for a long time. Her brother died twenty years or more ago, tragically so they say. I was not here then.'

'It's cold as a tomb and about as cheerful,' said Bulwer, 'and

I'm damned tired. Is there anywhere near here, sir, where we can rest and find food?'

'It's a poor enough place, only about fifty scattered houses and the manor, of course, but there's an inn a mile up the track. It's used by anglers but you'll not find many there yet. The Black Dog it is called. There's a widow who keeps it. It's a decent enough place. She'll cook you a meal.'

'And provide some brandy, I hope,' Bulwer shivered. 'Something to drive out this cursed chill if you'll pardon me, sir.' He took my arm.

I looked back at the Vicar. 'What is this place called?'

'Westley-by-water. Not many come here.'

'I don't blame them,' muttered Bulwer. 'Come on, Alyne.'

Out in the churchyard I pulled back teased by a memory. 'You go on and unhitch the horses. I want to look for something.'

'What now, for heaven's sake?'

I found it outside the stone wall, a gravestone overgrown with moss and yet not entirely neglected. There would be primroses later and daffodils. I pulled aside the tall grasses to read what was written, so faint that I had to trace it with my finger. Just the name, 'Alyne' and beneath it the one word 'drowned'. There was something else too. 'God pity her', nothing else, no other name, no date.

I stared down at it shivering. It was like seeing your own grave. I too had no name I could call my own.

'What is it? What have you found?' Bulwer had come back. His eyes followed my pointing finger.

'It's like meeting the ghost of yourself.' Suddenly I was shaking uncontrollably and he pulled me to my feet, holding me closely against him.

'Now that's just plain silly. Some village slut threw herself into the river and those unchristian dogs buried her outside the pale. What's that to do with you?'

'I don't know,' but I heard Martha Lee saying 'I only knew one who had the power and to her it brought death.'

'You're cold and you're hungry, my sweet, that's what is wrong with you and we can soon remedy that.'

I was behaving stupidly, I knew that. The early sunshine had vanished and there was a chill wind. I said, 'We've come a long way. I think we should turn back.'

'You forget. I'm an invalid. I need rest and food,' he was smiling as he led me back to the horses and helped me to mount. 'I have a mind to try the Black Dog.'

'If we don't stay too long.'

He hoisted himself into the saddle and we trotted down the track. The inn proved to be no further than half a mile from the church. The taproom was a poor enough place, but the landlady was a clean decent body obviously overawed by Bulwer's appearance and manner.

'There's my own parlour, sir, with a good fire burning. You and your lady will be comfortable there. There's not much in the house at this season, but I could cook you eggs and there's a prime cut of ham.'

'Splendid. Have you brandy? We need something to warm us.'

'Aye, I have that, sir. My late husband always kept a good cellar for the gentlemen when they come for the fishing.'

I still felt strange as if something or someone from that lonely grave had taken hold of me. I couldn't stop shivering and when the woman came back with a fat black bottle, Bulwer filled half a glass and brought it to me.

'Drink that down,' he said. 'There's nothing like brandy for getting rid of ghosts.'

The spirit burned the back of my throat, but it warmed me too. I began to shake off the feeling of oppression. When the food came, it was hot and appetizing and I suddenly discovered that I was hungry. Bulwer could be amusing when he wished. He talked of London and some of the mad antics he and his set indulged in. He poured some more brandy and I found it easy to laugh and forget my foolish thoughts. He leaned across the table, his hand on mine.

'That's better. That's more like my Alyne.'

Afterwards he poured himself another measure of the spirit and eased the boot from his injured leg.

'Is it painful?' I asked.

He grimaced. 'I think perhaps we have ridden too far. Give me an hour and I can face the journey home.'

It was when the landlady came in with candles that I realized how the day had darkened though it was only an hour after noon. She set them down on the table before she turned to us.

'Have you far to go, Ma'am? 'Tis raining hard and I fear the waters will rise with the tide.'

'We have to return to Ravensley. Surely we can still get through.'

'Ravensley?' she repeated doubtfully. 'That means you must cross part of Greatheart. There's one of the Fenmen outside in the bar. He'd know better than me. Shall I ask him to come in?'

I looked at Bulwer and he nodded. 'By all means. We'd better know the worst.'

She opened the door. 'Come in, Moggy. The lady wants to ask if she can ride back to Ravensley.'

The figure that came through the door seemed as broad as it was long with the old coat and the thick sacking over his shoulders. The water still dripped from his moleskin cap and ran in a cascade down his leather breeches and sodden boots.

'Nary a chance, Miss. There's a reg'lar blow coming in from the sea and one of them danged high tides. It's risen four feet down by Packman's Corner and druv me out o' my cottage.'

'But we're sixty miles and more from the coast,' protested Bulwer.

'Beggin' your pardon, sir, but that don't make no difference. The sea pushes hard and the water comes wellin' up. The snow's been meltin' all this week over the Fens and now the ice is breakin' away.'

'Damnation! How long are we likely to be marooned here?'

'Can't say zackly. Could be a day, could be longer.'

'Oh no,' I exclaimed. 'That can't be true.'

'Nay,' said Moggy grinning devilishly. 'Mebbe 'tiddn't quite as bad as that. But it'll be four or five hours till the tide turns. It'll likely leave the causeway clear enough, but you'll have a wet trip of it.'

'Fancy that now,' said the landlady, clucking with her tongue. 'Who'd have thought of such a thing after the lovely morning it was? Treacherous the Fens are, I used to tell my Jem that. I weren't born here, but he were, and I couldn't get him to leave the place nohow. Don't you fret now, Ma'am. You can stay here. I'll make a good fire and you'll be warm and snug.'

'But it'll be dark by then,' I said. 'We must get back.'

' 'Tiddn't possible, Miss,' put in Moggy. 'Not unless you wants to drown, you and the Cap'n with you. Tell you what . . . me and my mate outside will keep watch and let you know the minute 'tis safe to venture. How would that be?'

'We'd be more than grateful,' said Bulwer, putting his hand in his pocket and proffering a coin.

'Nay, sir, keep your money. We don't want nothin' for helpin' those in trouble.' He touched his cap and shuffled through the door.

'Dashed independent lot, I'll say that for 'em,' murmured Bulwer.

'The Fenmen are all like that. They'll poach your game and take what they can from the land, but they'll not accept what they call charity.'

'That's true enough,' said the landlady, bustling around remaking the fire. 'And it's a hard life they have, most of 'em. You'll be cosy enough now. Just give me a call if you want anything else. You don't need to worry. The Black Dog has never been flooded. The land rises, you see, like an island. Moggy'll be keeping good watch and there's nowt he don't know about the Fens.'

She closed the door firmly behind her and left us alone. Bulwer had kicked off his other boot and sat with long legs stretched out to the blaze, brandy glass in hand. He looked up at me and grinned so that I was afraid, not of him but of myself. All these weeks the feeling between us had grown, intensified rather than diminished by his accident and now in this tiny room isolated from all the familiar things of home, it rose to a burning pitch and there was no escape. I felt strange as if I didn't belong to my sane practical self, as if some other person had taken possession of my body. I knelt on the rag rug by the fire and held out my hands to its warmth.

'They'll be wondering where we are.'

'If the waters are rising here, they must be flooding at Ravensley.'

'Not necessarily, and I'm sure that Fenman knows who we are.'

'Does it matter?'

'It might if Justin comes back before we return.'

'Does he distrust you?'

'He has had no cause.'

I had a feeling that we were talking at random, as if words were no longer important. We sat for a little in silence. Bulwer put down his glass and leaned forward. He drew me back against his knees and pulled the pins from my hair so that it fell around my shoulders. He buried his face in it.

'It's like silk,' he murmured, 'and it smells of summer.'

'What do you know of such things?' I said teasingly. 'Are you turning poet?'

He turned me to face him. 'Who knows? You do strange things to me.'

'Nurse Starling used to call me witch-child when she was angry and that was often enough.'

'And ever since you have been weaving your spells.'

He began to kiss me slowly and thoroughly. His hand fumbled at the neck of my blouse, then moved down to my breast and I shuddered. At first I resisted but it was like fighting against the rising tide of the sea as it storms across the Fens. It had the same inevitability. The battle was lost from the start. It should have been sordid in this poor room on the rag rug in front of the smouldering peat, but it was not. He was surprisingly gentle and then fiercely passionate. We were devoured by a wild hunger that rose to a crescendo so that when it was all over, I was exhausted and yet wonderfully content.

We sat for a long time without speaking. Bulwer had pulled the long padded cushion from the settle behind him and leaned back, his arm around me and my head against his shoulder. I thought of neither the past nor the future but only of the mindless present and was happy until he shattered my peace.

He stretched up to the table, brought down the brandy and filled his glass. He held it to my lips and I sipped a little.

'Warmer now?' he said lightly. 'No more ghosts?'

I shook my head. 'None.'

He held the glass to the glow of the fire, his eyes on the golden spirit before he said, almost casually, 'When do you marry Justin?'

It broke my dream. It brought me back to harsh reality shaking me out of my content. Perhaps even unconsciously I had hoped for something else and now realized its impossibility. I drew away from him.

'He has been talking of June.'

He was still staring down at the brandy, swirling it a little before he drained it. Then he put the glass carefully back on the table. He said without looking at me, 'What would you say if I were to ask you to take your chance with me?'

'Do you want me to go away with you?'

'Yes.'

For the moment my head swam dizzily and then I knew with a cold certainty that it was not at all what I dreamed.

'As your mistress?'

He turned to me then, warmly, urgently. 'We could have fun together. We're alike, you and I. I'll give you anything you want, an apartment, clothes, jewels, a house of your own if you like, a pretty little villa out at St John's Wood . . .'

'Among all the other kept women.'

'Well, what's wrong with that?'

'With every door in society closed against me.'

'Not all, only the damned dull ones.'

'There is such a thing as marriage . . .'

He looked away, his voice cold. 'Marriage is another matter altogether.'

'Why? You were willing to rape Clarissa and then marry her.'

'Clarissa is different.'

'Oh yes, of course she is different,' I was suddenly possessed by anger, all the pent-up bitterness raging through me. I got to my feet. 'Clarissa's father is a beggar. He can give her nothing but a load of debts. You don't love her and she detests you, but her cousin is the Duke of Devonshire. She's part of that fashionable world, those blue-blooded aristocrats you affect to despise and yet would crawl to if only they would accept you. And I, I'm nothing, just a slut from the Fens, like that poor nameless creature in the churchyard, someone with whom you can amuse yourself and then cast aside as so much rubbish when you weary of her.' I knew I was shouting at him and couldn't stop myself.

He pushed himself up with one hand on the settle. 'Damn you, keep your voice down. Don't play the innocent with me. You wanted it as much as I did. You planned it, didn't you, right from the start and now you've succeeded, you want more . . .'

'No, no, it's not true . . .'

'Oh, yes it is. You can't fool me. Well, my pretty little witch, you've met your match. This time you are not having it all your own way. You can come with me if you wish, or you can play safe and marry Justin, and if he finds out what we've done together today, you can turn to Oliver whom you keep at your bidding like a pet dog on a string, poor devil, but whatever you do, you'll go on wanting me, my sweet, and I'll win. You'll come begging me for it in the end.'

'No, I won't, never, never. This once and never again,' I blazed at him.

'We'll see about that.'

He limped round the table and caught hold of me, crushing me against him, his mouth seeking mine again, savagely, brutally. I fought him, but he was strong and my senses betrayed me. I felt the hunger stir again. Oh God, dear God, I thought desperately, what have I done? What shall I do if he goes away and I never see him again?

The tempest of our kisses was interrupted by a knock at the door. Bulwer released me and I hastily turned my back, trying to adjust my dress.

'Who is it? What the hell do you want?' Bulwer sounded angry.

'Beggin' your pardon, Cap'n, it's me, Moggy. The tide's beginning to go down. With me and my mate as guides, you could maybe find your road back.'

'Thank you. Wait outside and we'll be ready in a few minutes.'

'Right, sir, but don't leave it too long.'

Bulwer sat down, pulling on his boots and shrugging himself into his jacket. He glanced at me as I tried to pin up my hair.

'I'll pay the reckoning and wait for you outside. I suppose that clod out there knows what he is doing. I've no wish to drown.'

'He's no clod and you needn't be afraid. If he says we can get through, then it will be so.'

'Please God you're right.'

He went out and I tried to pull myself together. I gave up the struggle with my hair and tied it back with a bit of ribbon. When I went outside, the wind tore at my cloak and the rain blew across in icy cold gusts. The woman of the inn urged us to stay and Bulwer hesitated, looking at me questioningly.

'We're damned fools to try it. It's black as ink.'

'You can stay if you wish,' I said. 'I'm going back.'

'Don't you worry, Miss,' said Moggy cheerfully. 'We knows the ways. We'll see you safe, won't we, Ned?'

'Aye,' grunted his companion who was no more than a squat black shape in the wet darkness.

Bulwer swore under his breath. Then he lifted me into the saddle and hoisted himself painfully on to his own horse. The Fenmen each took a bridle.

It was a nightmare journey, sometimes splashing through a foot of water, sometimes through a muddy sludge left behind by the retreating flood.

'Christ, what a hellish country!' muttered Bulwer when his horse stumbled jerking a groan of pain out of him. We were soaked to the skin before we had done half the distance and it was icily cold. The two Fenmen plodded on, head down, swinging their lanterns, never at a loss and leading us by devious routes of their own until at the end of what seemed to go on for ever, they halted and Moggy pointed ahead.

' 'Tiddn't far now. No more than a couple of mile and the road's clear.'

Bulwer put his hand in his pocket and brought out some coins. I saw the gleam of gold in the light of the lantern. 'Here,' he said and held it out. 'Buy yourself a drink for us and thank God we got through all in one piece.'

'Ah well, put like that,' said Moggy, 'it's mighty good of you, Cap'n. We'll drink your health and the lady's too, won't we, Ned?'

'Aye,' grunted his companion.

For an instant the light from the lantern fell on his face and it was startlingly like Oliver, a wild savage Oliver, who glared at me fiercely before he turned and plodded into the darkness with Moggy following him. It gave me an unpleasant jolt as if somewhere out on the Fens there lived a dark spirit that sought the destruction of the Aylshams, the same violence that had murdered Oliver's father and attacked Justin and now hated me too because I was linked with them. I had thought the tales the others had told were exaggerated but now I had seen it for myself.

Bulwer said impatiently, 'Let's get on, for God's sake. What are you staring at?'

'Nothing. It was just that I thought . . . oh never mind.' Wearily I turned my horse and together we set out on the track to Ravensley.

4

I could see men with torches as we trotted up the drive and at first
I thought it was something to do with the flooding. Then one of
them saw us. He shouted back to the others and I realized that
they had been preparing to come out in search of us. They came
crowding up asking what had happened. Bulwer answered briefly,
lifting me from my horse. Then Justin was there, pushing his way
through them. The torchlight lit his sallow face and I knew at
once he was in one of the rare rages that we had all learned to
fear. He seized me roughly by the arm.

'Where in God's name have you been? Do you know what time
it is, past ten o'clock.'

'We were trapped by the floods.'

'Floods? What floods? Where? What are you talking about?'

'It's true enough,' said Bulwer shortly coming to my side, 'and it
is I who am to blame. We rode further than we intended and
stopped to rest at . . . where was it, Alyne?'

'The Black Dog at Westley.'

There was a queer sick look on Justin's face and behind him I
caught sight of Ram Lall, black eyes gleaming in the torchlight.
Justin looked from me to Bulwer.

'What the devil took you there?'

'Why does one go anywhere?' said Bulwer with a shrug. 'It was
somewhere to ride.'

'You needn't be so damned casual about it. I had expected better from you, Rutland.'

'Are you trying to pick a quarrel with me?'

Bulwer sounded dangerous and I moved to intervene, but
Cherry was before me. She had come running from the house, a
shawl round her shoulders, her hair blowing in the wind. She put a
hand on Justin's arm.

'Alyne is safe, Uncle, surely that's all that matters. Just look at them. They're soaked and it is freezing out here. They must come in and get warm.'

Justin grunted and took my arm, pushing me towards the house. At the foot of the stairs, he gripped me by the shoulders staring into my face. 'If I thought . . .'

'Thought what?' I said. 'What is wrong with you? I am wet through and icy cold. Do you want me to die of a fever?'

'All right, all right. I'll come to you later.'

I pulled away from him and went straight to my room. Cherry came with me. There was a bright fire burning on the hearth and I was grateful for its warmth. I was shivering violently by now and she helped me to strip off the wet clothes and brought me towels, helping to rub life back into my frozen limbs.

When at last I was in my dressing gown, she said, 'Sit down and I'll finish drying your hair.' Presently she began to brush it with long soothing strokes. 'What really happened today?' she asked quietly.

'Exactly what I said. We went too far. Bulwer's leg was painful so we stopped to rest and eat something at the Black Dog and then the rain came down. One of the Fenmen warned us of the danger and it was he who guided us back.'

'And is that all?'

'What else should there be?'

'I don't know, but you looked different . . .'

'How different?'

'Happy somehow and guilty too.'

I sat up. 'Cherry, you do say the silliest things.'

'Perhaps. Uncle Justin was very angry when he came home and you had not returned.'

'I know that,' I said dryly and felt too weary to care. 'Is that my fault?'

'I did warn you, didn't I? Are you hungry? Shall I tell Lizzie to bring you supper?'

'A hot drink, that's all. Nothing to eat.'

'Very well.' At the door she paused and looked back. 'By the way, Oliver is home.'

'How do you know?'

'Mrs Starling told me. I thought you'd be pleased.'

She went before I could question her, but there had been an odd look of triumph on her face as if she was happy about something.

Lizzie brought me hot chocolate and I was sitting close to the fire, the cup in my hand when there was a knock at the door. For an instant I thought it might be Bulwer and caught my breath trying to steady myself before I called out, 'Who is it?'

'It is I, Justin. May I come in?'

He did not wait for my reply, but opened the door. I thought he had come to reproach me again and I could not endure any more.

I said, 'I'm tired. I was just going to bed.'

He crossed the room and stood looking down at me. 'I'm sorry if I was rough with you tonight. I didn't mean to be, only . . .'

'Only what?'

'Rutland is so much younger than I and you've spent so much time with him.'

'It was what you asked me to do . . . over and over again. Don't you remember?'

'I know, I know, but then I never dreamed . . . Damn it, it was something Ram Lall said.'

'If you believe his lies,' I said furiously, trying to forget the afternoon. What Bulwer and I had done together was over. It had not happened to me, but to that other Alyne who had taken possession of me for those few hours at the Black Dog.

'I don't believe him,' he said quietly, 'if I did, I don't know what I might do.' His hand moved gently over my hair. 'You are so beautiful, Alyne. I couldn't bear the thought of losing you.'

I steeled myself not to move away from his caress. 'That's foolish. Why should you lose me?' I had never seen him in this mood before. He was always so self-contained, so sure of himself. I pressed my advantage. 'Justin, will you promise me something?'

'What is it?'

'When we are married, will you send Ram Lall back to India?'

He drew away from me a little. 'What has poor Ram done that I should break his heart by dismissing him?' he said lightly.

'He doesn't like me. He spies on me . . . everywhere I go, everything I do, he seems to be there watching me . . . please, Justin, please send him away.'

'My dear, you are tired and overwrought. You don't know what you're asking. I couldn't do it.'

'Why couldn't you? He's only a servant.'

'He has been more than that, far more. When I first went to India, I nearly died. He nursed me through long months of sickness. I owe him my life and afterwards he became attached to me. Try and understand, Alyne. Like me then, he had no one else. For several years, trying to make a life out there, in that hell, he was my only companion.'

'Until you met Jethro's mother . . .'

'Yes.' He looked away from me and I felt a little shiver creep up my spine. I was not sure if I knew what he meant. The devil's shadow, that was what Nurse called him, and for some reason that I couldn't explain, I was suddenly afraid. Then before I could say anything, Justin had turned back to me, smiling, the firelight bringing colour and warmth to his face. 'He has been a loyal servant for close on twenty years. It would be rank ingratitude to send him away. He will do you no harm, I promise you, and I did not come here to talk about Ram Lall, but of you.'

'What is there to say about me?'

'That first evening I came here,' he said slowly, 'it was like an invisible cord drawing us together. I knew well enough that Oliver was in love with you, but I could only guess at your feeling for him . . .'

'Justin, must we talk of all this now?'

'There is something I have been wanting to tell you.'

'It's late and I am very weary.'

'It's not much to ask surely.' He moved to the rug in front of the fire leaning one hand on the mantel. 'You don't like Jethro, do you?'

'What has that to do with it?'

'It's natural, I suppose. You think he will be my heir, but it is not so.'

That did surprise me. 'You mean he is not your son.'

'He is mine right enough, but his mother . . .' he paused looking away from me. 'His mother was a woman I loved very much, but we were not married.'

'Why?'

'She already had a husband.'

'Did she leave him to go to you?'

'Yes.'

'Who was she?'

'Alyne, I don't want to talk about her. She is dead. It's in the past.'

'I want to know who she was. If I am to be your wife, I think I have a right to know.'

'No. One day perhaps, but not now. It has nothing to do with us, nothing at all. Listen to me, Alyne,' he came to kneel beside my low stool. 'This is what is important. This is what I want you to understand. You've been robbed of your heritage just as I was. I want you to know that your children will inherit Ravensley, not Oliver, not my brother's son.'

'Why do you hate Oliver so much?'

'Love, hate, what do the words mean? He is damnably like his father and Robert stole from me what I wanted more than anything in this world. Now I have won part of it back and I intend to keep it. It belongs to us, Alyne, to you and me.'

A few months ago and I would have been exulting in my power over him, but now I felt nothing but a dry emptiness. Justin put an arm round my waist, one hand pushing back the weight of my hair and caressing my neck. I endured his kiss and felt nothing but a faint distaste.

He said, 'You're worn out, my dear, and I don't wonder. To-morrow when you are rested, we'll begin to make plans for our wedding.'

He went soon afterwards and I lay in the bed, the sheets comforting from Lizzie's warming pan, the cheerful fire making shadows dance across the ceiling while the wildest thoughts tossed their way through my mind and would not let me rest. What would happen if I got out of bed and crept through the silent house to Bulwer's door? For an instant the leap of desire racing through my body made me giddy. Then I bit my lip, burying my face in the pillows shocked and ashamed. He would laugh and make love and then put me aside. An hour's diversion and nothing more. I slept fitfully and in my dreams it seemed it was he who came pleading with me and then mysteriously turned into Justin, an angry Justin with Ram Lall, threatening and menacing at his back. I woke still tired, my head aching, glad to dress and go downstairs. Cherry was in the breakfast room when I went in.

'How are you feeling this morning?' she asked.

'Well enough. Where is Captain Rutland?'

'Gone. He left very early before you were up and asked me to thank you for all the kindness you had shown him.'

Kindness, I thought ironically. He had got what he wanted and now he was off to new conquests without a single word for me. Bitterness was like a heavy lump in my throat. I swallowed coffee and could eat nothing.

The rain had gone and the morning had that peculiar watery brilliance that comes in early spring. In the hall I met Jethro wildly excited and tugging at a harassed Hattie.

'I'm going to see Oliver,' he announced.

I knew then that that was what I wanted too, more than anything. I longed to return even if only for a morning to the simplicity and safety of childhood. I wanted to forget the rage of passion for Bulwer, the burden of Justin's demands upon me. Above all I wanted Oliver's strength, his gentleness, his kindness, that lay so warm beneath the surface coldness and had never yet failed me.

I said, 'I'm going to Thatchers. You can come with me if you like.'

'Are you sure you don't mind, Alyne?' said Hattie ruefully. 'Sometimes I am forced to realize that I'm not so young as I was.'

For the first time in months I looked at her and saw how old she was and how tired. We had always taken her for granted. I said abruptly, 'Of course I don't mind.'

When I was dressed, we set out to walk to Thatchers. Justin's revelation had made me feel differently towards the boy. I thought he looked better than when he had first come and he skipped happily ahead of me, keeping up a running fire of questions to which I paid little heed.

At the old farmhouse there was tremendous bustle. A carrier's cart stood outside and crates were being lifted off. The door was open so I went into the hall and turned into the living room. The place was in a turmoil, furniture being unpacked, books scattered on the table, rolled-up rugs on the floor. I was staring around me in astonishment when Clarissa came through the door opposite calling something back over her shoulder. She stopped when she saw me.

'How are you, Alyne? I had not expected visitors so soon.'

'Where is Oliver?'

'He'll be here immediately. He has been up at Copthorne to see how my father stood the journey.'

'Your father?'

'Yes. He has been very ill, you know, he is coming to live with Aunt Jess.'

Something fell with a crash in the next room and Oliver exclaimed, 'Damnation! That was my fingers! At this rate we'll be sleeping on the floor tonight!'

He came through the door, laughing and rubbing his bruised hand. He was in shirtsleeves, his hair tousled, a smudge across one cheek.

'Well, look who's here,' he said cheerfully. 'Ben is in the kitchen, Jethro.' As the boy ran off, he moved towards Clarissa. 'You're almost the first to hear the news, Alyne. Clary and I were married a week ago.'

It was what I might have expected and yet I didn't. He went on talking and the words were meaningless until I heard him say, 'You must excuse me. There are a thousand things to be done.' He picked up his coat from the chair. 'I'll be up to see my uncle presently and I'll bring Jethro back.'

'Wait a minute.' Clarissa pulled him back, laughing up at him. 'You can't go like that. You look like the sweep.'

She wiped the smudge from his face with her handkerchief and he caught her hand kissing the fingers. 'Don't do too much, my dear. I'll be back soon.' He nodded to me carelessly, as he went through the door. 'I'll see you later, Alyne.'

I looked across at Clarissa. She was thinner than when she went away, but her fine-boned face had its own beauty and her eyes were clear and serene. For the first time in my life I envied her.

I said, 'So you captured him after all. It was very clever of you. Oliver could never bear to be in anyone's debt.'

'It was not like that at all, but you wouldn't understand.'

'Why wouldn't I?'

'You want things and you don't scruple how you get them. It was the same when we were children. But this time you mustn't be greedy, Alyne. You can't have Justin and Oliver. He has a right to a life of his own.'

She didn't know. She thought it was all so simple and it made me angry. I said, 'A life you have always been determined to share. Was it true after all what you said at the trial?'

She flushed. 'No, it was not. You should know Oliver well enough for that.'

'I'm beginning to think I don't know anyone.'

'I'm not a fool, Alyne. I know about you and him.'

'Did Oliver tell you?'

'No.' She looked away for a moment, then faced me boldly. 'He doesn't love me yet, not as he loved you, but he will.'

'Are you so sure?'

'You cannot be sure of anything in this life, but you can work for it and hope for it.'

I looked round at the bare room without luxury or elegance. 'How can you accept all this when you could have had Bulwer Rutland?'

'Money isn't everything.'

' "Better a dish of herbs where love is" . . . do you remember when we had to learn our Bible texts on Sunday?' I said scornfully. 'Only a romantic idiot would believe that one.' I was hitting out at her because of my own indecision, my own unhappiness.

'Don't let's quarrel,' said Clarissa calmly. 'We have always looked for different things in life, let us hope that if we get what we want, it proves to be all it seems.'

Justin and I were married in May, a full month earlier than had been planned. 'There is no reason to wait,' he said, 'and if we're taking a wedding trip to Italy, it is better to travel before the heat of high summer,' and suddenly it seemed to be what I wanted more than anything, to be my own mistress, to be free of Ravensley, free of the brooding silence of the Fens, free of the folly that had entangled me with Bulwer Rutland.

'It's unlucky,' mumbled Nurse Starling with gloomy prophecy, 'marry in May and court dismay.'

It was too much after the strain and fret, the flurry of preparation with so much still to be done. I laughed in her face and she reached up at me with her claw-like old hands, seizing me by both arms and shaking me as she had done when I was still a child.

'Laugh like that, my lady, and you'll have the devil on your back if you've not got him snapping at your tail already.'

'If you don't stop your nonsense, then you'll have to go,' I said angrily. 'It's high time Lord Aylsham pensioned you off anyway.'

'He'd not dare . . . he'd not dare . . . there'd be God's curse on him if he did.'

I saw the fear in her eyes and how the old face crumbled. Send her away from Ravensley and she would surely die.

'Oh for goodness' sake!' I said impatiently. 'Finish darning those sheets. With all the guests, we're going to need every scrap of linen in the house and more.'

My wedding gown had been ordered in London; ivory satin trimmed with ruchings of fine lace and I went up the aisle of Ely Cathedral on Oliver's arm, my head held high, certain that every eye was on me and I did not permit myself to dwell on the irony that it should be he giving me in marriage to his uncle.

There were none among the guests who crowded the nave and the townsfolk who swarmed on the steps outside who would dare to sneer at me now. Justin waited for me at the altar. He had a dark distinction that singled him out from other men. I was proud that he had chosen me, proud that I would be Lady Aylsham of Ravensley at last. I must cling to that, I told myself. It was what I had wanted for so long. It had been a hard fight and now it was mine. Let Clarissa play the farmer's wife and believe herself happy. The witch child from the Fens had wealth and a fine position in the county and it would be my son who would inherit Ravensley and not any boy of hers. When Justin put the ring on my finger and put back the veil to kiss my cheek, I raised my eyes for the first time, but it was not he, not the smile on the dark face that I saw, but Bulwer Rutland, half hidden in the shadow of the side aisle, leaning against a pillar, his arms folded.

I had not expected it and it shook me. Old Joshua had told us that trouble had flared up again in his leg, that he had been granted leave of absence from the regiment and on doctor's orders had gone abroad.

'I've been writing to Paris,' he said, 'but I've no idea where the boy is. He talked about going to Switzerland and then over the Alps to the Italian lakes.' He winked and looked sly. 'I think there was someone he hoped to meet there.'

Another woman, I thought, and shut my mind against it. But it was not true. He was there, standing very still, his eyes on me, burning into mine, and I felt the sweet agonizing stir in my flesh. For a frightening moment I thought I might faint.

'Are you all right?' whispered Cherry as she took the wedding posy from my hands.

'Why do you ask?'

'You look so pale.'

'It's only the heat.'

There was a weakness in my limbs that made me thankful to kneel, to bow my head to the altar and pray for strength.

The wedding party came back to Ravensley and since we were not to leave until the next morning, the festivity went on and on, the jests becoming more ribald as the champagne flowed and my headache grew worse. I did not look to see if Bulwer had come back with his father. I didn't want to know. Oliver and Clarissa left early taking Jethro with them. He was to stay at Thatchers for a few weeks while we were away. Cherry was dancing with Clarissa's brother who had come down to visit his father. Harry Fenton was a handsome boy . . . no money, not much of a match of course, but perhaps he might help to cure her infatuation with Jake Starling. I felt too weary to care.

I had taken off the wreath of flowers and the long lace veil. It was stiflingly hot in the drawing room and the windows had been opened. I had to escape if only for a few minutes. I went out to the terrace and stepped down on to the lawn. It was not yet quite dark and there was a fresh sweet scent from the grass that had been cut that morning.

Early roses had just come into bloom and I bent over them, touching the creamy petals faintly flushed with pink. I did not hear the footsteps behind me until the arms came round my waist turning me to him. His mouth devoured mine hungrily and I could not deny him. It was as if the intervening weeks had vanished and I lived again that first moment of ecstasy. Then he drew away from me.

He said angrily, 'I thought the wedding was to be in June.'

'Justin wanted it earlier.'

'And you?'

'I saw no point in waiting.'

He was staring at me. In the faint light I saw how pale he was, his eyes had a wild look, quite unlike the Bulwer I thought I knew. He said quietly, 'When I found father's letter waiting for me in Paris, I rode all night to the coast and met with every frustration, a foundered horse, the Folkestone packet springing a leak . . . every damned mile of the road here, my horse's hooves were hammering out "too late".'

'Too late for what?'

'What the hell does it matter now?'

But I had to know; I had to hear him say it as you press on the agony of a half-healed wound.

'What do you mean? Too late for what?'

He seized hold of me, pulling the pins from my hair, running his fingers through it, twisting it into a rope around my throat. 'You damned witch, what have you done to me? Everywhere I've been, your face haunted me . . . I tried the gaming tables, the race-courses, the Clubs, even the women . . . and it was no damned good . . . a pale-haired witch was there first, laughing at me, so I came back to Ravensley as fast as horse and boat could carry me, but you couldn't wait, could you? You had to grab at everything with your greedy hands in case you lost it.'

The injustice struck at me. 'What should I have waited for? For you to come back and claim me as your whore, your fancy woman? . . . Justin offered me marriage.'

'And I didn't. Why should I marry a penniless slut too free with her favours? Tell me that. Why, why?'

A fierce anger surged up in me and I hit him hard across the face, he laughed and grabbed hold of me, his hands round my throat.

'Why? Because I love her . . . d'you hear that? . . . I love her most damnably . . .'

Then we were in each other's arms again. I felt his cheek rough against my skin, the taste of his kisses, the thrust of his body against mine.

'Oh Christ, how I've ached for you,' he was murmuring, 'and then to come back to this!' He drew away from me a little, his eyes searching my face. 'We could go now quickly before anyone guesses.'

For an instant I was tempted and then knew sickeningly how impossible it was. There would be a few weeks of wild happiness, but it would not last, it could not. What would we be but two guilty people on the run? It would mean rupture with his father, all his ambitions blighted, and I knew my Bulwer. He was not the stuff of which martyrs are made or even great lovers.

'No,' I said and it was agony to deny him, 'no, I cannot.'

'Yes, yes, yes.' He caught me against him, urging me. 'Come with me. It will be so easy.' I shook my head and he kissed me again, his tongue forcing open my lips, driving me wild. I struggled against him before I lost all strength, all will to resist.

He said fiercely, 'I swear I'll never beg again.'

But I would not yield. I dare not. It was too much to lose. Already I'd been away from the house too long. Soon they would be looking for me and if Ram Lall were to see us together, it would mean the end of all I'd fought for . . . I tore myself away from him, not daring to look back, running across the grass and going in by a side door so that no one should see my dishevelled state.

Lizzie was in my bedroom tidying it, folding the covers on the bed. She stared at me in astonishment and I put my hand to my hair realizing how strange I must look. She grinned knowingly. 'I've put all your things in the master's room, Miss Alyne,' and then she giggled, 'Lady Aylsham, I should say.'

'Yes, I know. You can leave all this now, Lizzie. I'll just tidy my hair in here.'

'Very well, Miss . . . my lady.'

She went out of the room and I wondered what story she would carry back to the kitchen.

I was still shaken. I still couldn't believe it had happened. I raged against it. It was so unfair. It couldn't be true. Bulwer had only said what he did to torment me now that it was impossible . . . and yet there had been something different about him, something that convinced me of his sincerity. Oh God, why had I let Justin persuade me? Why hadn't I prevaricated, played for more time . . . why? I sat there on the little bed where I had slept since a child until it was quite dark and the rage had died down to a dull ache. Then I went down to the room that had once belonged to

Oliver's grandfather, to the bed that I must share with a man I
didn't love, a man of whom sometimes I was afraid, to the bed
where one day I would have to bear Justin's son. I stared at the
rich hangings, at the trunks in which Lizzie had already packed
the magnificent trousseau he had bought for me; around my neck
were the jewels that were his wedding gift and the wide gold band
of bondage was on my finger.

I wondered about that other Alyne who lay in the wet spongy
earth of the Fen churchyard and to whom the power had brought
only tragedy and death . . . I shivered and then through the open
door I heard them calling for me, Cherry first and then Justin.

'I'm coming,' I called back to them in case they should seek me
out. With a few swift movements I swept back my hair letting it
still stream down my back as I ran down the stairs. I laughed and
was the merriest of them all, jesting with them, flinging the flowers
from my wedding posy into their outstretched hands. I drank the
champagne, glass after glass until I was dizzy and it was time to go
upstairs with Cherry.

She helped me to undress, holding up the wedding gown against
her, smoothing the fine satin. 'It's so beautiful.'

'I shall never wear it again,' I said shortly. 'You can have it altered when you marry Harry Fenton.'

She looked startled. 'Why do you say that?'

'Why does anyone say anything? I thought you were enjoying
his company. I'm tired. Please go, Cherry.'

'All right.' She paused to look at me curiously. 'Are you happy?'

'Of course I'm happy. This is my wedding night, isn't it?'

'Yes, but I've thought sometimes . . .' She suddenly put her
arms round me, giving me a quick hug before she went out of the
room.

I looked after her in surprise. It is not like Cherry to show me
any open affection.

I stripped off my shift and stood for a moment looking down at
the smooth length of my body. Sometimes I have exulted in my
own beauty, but tonight I could take no pleasure in it. I pulled the
nightgown over my head and climbed into the high bed.

It was a little time before Justin came and I had shut my eyes to
ease the sharp pain in my head. The click of the door roused me.

He stood just inside in his long purple dressing gown, his face sallow in the light of the candles.

He said quietly, 'Did you know that Captain Rutland was here?'

All kinds of thoughts went through my mind before I decided on the simple truth. 'Yes.'

'Did you speak with him?'

'For a few minutes only.'

'Why did he leave so suddenly without a word to me or his father?'

Oh God, what had Ram Lall seen? What had he told Justin? 'He was not feeling well, he said. He had made the long journey simply to see us married and to offer congratulations.'

Justin was standing quite still, watching me, and I nerved myself to meet his eyes.

'Why are we speaking of Bulwer Rutland, now of all times?'

'Why indeed?'

Then suddenly he relaxed. He smiled and crossed to the bed. It was then that I saw the whip in his hand, the whip with which he had once punished Jethro and threatened Cherry. I waited trembling, but he tossed it carelessly on the chest, stripped off his dressing gown and pinched out the candles on the table.

'Alyne,' he was muttering thickly, 'Alyne,' and came to me through the darkness.

Part Four

OLIVER

1831–1832

Two loves I have of comfort and despair.

William Shakespeare

I

Clarissa and I quarrelled again this morning. It has happened far too frequently during the last six months, always sparked off by something quite trivial so that afterwards we regret it, make all kinds of good resolutions and then a few weeks later it happens all over again.

This time it was Colonel Fenton who was the bone of contention. I had been out on the farm very early as I often am nowadays and came back for a late breakfast.

Clarissa poured my coffee and said carefully, 'Aunt Jess tells me that you've been loaning money to Papa again.'

'What the devil has it got to do with her?' I said annoyed.

'Since she has the care of him, it matters very much. You know perfectly well what happens. He goes into Ely, loses every penny at that wretched gambling club, drinks more than is good for him and more often than not, has to be brought home.'

Tom Fenton may be an old rip, but he is bored to distraction by the tedium of life down here and sometimes I sympathize with him. I said placatingly, 'My dear girl, I have the greatest respect for Miss Cavendish, but if your father sometimes feels a need to escape from her, don't let us deny it to him for the sake of a few paltry guineas.'

'Do you feel a need to escape too?' she said with a sudden flare of temper. 'Is that what it is, Oliver? Do you find our life together unbearable and is that why you are so understanding towards him?'

And that, stupidly enough, irritated me beyond measure. I pushed away my plate and got to my feet. 'Once and for all, I have no liking for gambling, drinking or even spending a night with a whore, you ought to know that by now, but that doesn't mean that I would forbid it to others.'

'I know, really I do,' said Clarissa, staring down at the table, 'I shouldn't have said that, but we owe you so much already, Papa and I. I can't bear to think of the debt piling up and up and no means of ever repaying it.'

'You owe me nothing, you never have. Any debt between us was cancelled out long ago and anyway this has only happened twice in the nine months your father has been here. I don't know what all the fuss is about.' I moved away from the table. 'If anyone wants me, I'm going to have a word with Will Burton at the farm and afterwards I shall be riding over Greatheart.'

'I suppose that means you are going to meet Jake?'

'Perhaps.'

I went out before she could say anything more. I think that Clarissa would rather I abandoned Jake to his fate, not because she dislikes him, the childhood bond is still too strong for that, but because she is so afraid that if the authorities find out that I have been harbouring a criminal, I would suffer the maximum penalty.

Ben had brought Rowan into the courtyard. He has turned out to be quite a useful lad with the horses and I take pleasure in training him. I was already in the saddle when Clarissa came running from the kitchen with a basket and held it up to me.

'Take it. If you're going to be out on the Fen all day, you will need food.'

I knew what it contained, pies, ham, butter, fresh baked bread, enough provisions to last Jake for a week or more. I reached down to touch her cheek.

'He'll be very grateful.'

'Take care,' she whispered.

'I will. Don't worry.' For an instant we were close, then I urged Rowan away and trotted up the track.

I always enjoy talking with Will Burton. His experience of farming is so much wider and more practical than mine and his advice is invaluable. I am grimly determined to hold on to my small inheritance and to build on it. My uncle's contempt has acted like a challenge. I will make a success of it here on my own ground in the Fens even if only to prove to him that more can be achieved by fair means than by driving men to desperation through poverty and starvation. For the past five months, ever since the wedding in May and his going abroad, I have been master here and I must confess that I have found it pleasant. It is almost as if time had rolled back and my uncle's return was no more than a bad dream until something jerks me back to reality and I remember that he will be returning in another month, that Alyne is now his wife and that I am married to Clarissa, a woman I respect and am fond of, but do not love.

I refused Will Burton's invitation to share his wife's good dinner and it was long past noon when Rowan followed the winding path across the Fen. I was hungry but there was plenty of food in the basket and I could eat with Jake. It had been a long dry summer so that although it was October already, the dykes were still low and there was no flooding. The air was fresh and full of the sharp spicy scent of bog myrtle and water mint. I rode with a slack rein, letting Rowan pick her own way but still keeping a wary eye for strangers. Agitation has largely died down now after the savage sentences passed on the rebels of last winter, but I have a strong feeling that the calm is a fragile one and that at the least thing it could explode again into violence.

It is nearly a year since Jethro showed me that gold and cornelian seal and I knew instantly that it had been one of my mother's most treasured possessions. I remembered how when I was very young she would let me handle it and point out to me the finely carved coat of arms that had belonged to her own family. I had thought about it for a long time and did not like the conclusion to which I had come. She and my uncle had been lovers. She had not died in Rome as we had believed but had abandoned Cherry and me to go to him and destroyed my father's happiness for ever. I could not be certain, but the ugly thought was there, filling me with bitterness and an insane desire to seize my uncle by the throat and throttle him for what he had done to her. For years I had worshipped her memory and now he had tarnished it. I could scarcely endure even to be in the same room with him. It would have choked me to sit at his Christmas table and it drove me up to London, anywhere to be out of reach of his biting tongue, away from Alyne flaunting his rich gifts on the grave of my mother, away from that old ruffian Joshua Rutland and his upstart of a son whose very glance dishonoured any woman at whom he directed it.

I was in a wretched state of mind, ready to throw up the sponge and get out of the country. For one mad night I even contemplated putting a bullet through my head. I had no intention of calling on Clarissa. What she had done at the trial had shocked me even if it had saved my life, but I had tried to make amends and she had rejected me so I tried not to think of what I owed to her.

It was by pure chance that I heard what had happened to her father and it sent me hotfoot to Soho Square. The house looked shabby and ill-kept. I was appalled when a sluttish serving girl opened the door and gave me a saucy look when I asked for Miss Fenton.

'There aren't many as come askin' for Clarissa these days,' she said impudently. 'You'd better come in.'

There was a seedy-looking, down-at-heel fellow lolling at his ease in the hall, a mug of ale at his elbow, and I knew at once what that meant. They were dunning the Colonel for debt and he was there to make sure there was no moonlight flit. The servant girl showed me into the drawing room. It looked dusty and unused and curiously bare as if it had already been stripped of anything saleable.

When Clarissa came, she tried hard to brave it out. She greeted me calmly, asking after everyone at Ravensley and chatting about this and that until I asked her bluntly what that unpleasant wretch was doing in the hall.

'It's nothing,' she said, 'just a temporary embarrassment. We shall come round, we always do, only Papa is sick and this time I am a little worried about him.'

I stopped her by taking both her hands in mine and giving her a shake. 'Now don't go on pretending there's nothing wrong because I know different. Come and sit down and tell me the truth so that we can decide what is to be done.'

'It's Joshua Rutland,' she said hopelessly after a moment. 'Father owes him a great sum of money and now he wants it repaid.'

'I never thought of Josh Rutland as a money-lender.'

'He's not.' She moved away restlessly, staring out of the window so that I could not see her face. 'You don't understand. It was a kind of bribe . . . if I had married his son, nothing more would have been said about it . . .'

'And your father agreed to such an arrangement?' I said incredulously.

'Yes. I know it sounds horrible, but he was desperately

hard-pressed . . . oh please, I don't want to talk about it, but I couldn't marry Bulwer Rutland, I couldn't . . .'

All that past unpleasantness and the vile gossip about her suddenly became clear to me. It explained a great deal.

'I'm very glad you didn't,' I said. 'So now out of revenge his father is calling the money in, is that it?'

'I don't know,' she turned to me very close to tears. 'Oh Oliver, I keep on remembering that it is all my fault. All the time I was down at Ravensley, Papa has been struggling to pay it off and now they are going to sell us up, house, furniture, everything we own, and he's ill, really ill. The doctor says the shock and distress could kill him.'

'Now listen to me,' I said firmly. 'They like to threaten but they can't do it, not immediately and anyway I'll damned well make sure that they don't. I'll go and see Josh Rutland myself.'

'Why should you do all this for us?'

'Do you imagine I'm going to stand by and see you hounded by that old brute? Is it possible to have a word with your father? Is he well enough?'

'Yes, I suppose so,' she was still doubtful.

'Good, then let's do it at once. It's better not to delay too long in matters of this kind.'

I was shocked when I saw Colonel Fenton. I remembered him as a spry elegant man and he was handsome still but he looked pitifully thin, his eyes sunken, his cheeks flushed and a blue look around his mouth. He roused himself as we came in.

'What is it now, Clary? Someone else demanding their pound of flesh?'

'I've brought a friend to see you, Papa.'

His eyes brightened. He pushed himself up against his pillows. 'Well, this is a surprise. Young Aylsham, isn't it?' He extended a shaking hand. 'Delighted, my dear fellow. Very kind of you to find the time. We're rather short on visitors these days, isn't that so, Clary? How is your uncle?'

He spoke with a jaunty gaiety but it was easy to see that the last months had taken a grim toll.

Clarissa said, 'Oliver thinks he may be able to help us, Papa.'

'Very good of you, but our troubles are not your concern.'

'Indeed they are,' I said, 'very much so. I don't know if she told

you, sir, but a few weeks ago I asked Clarissa to marry me. She refused me, but I'm not prepared to accept that as final. I've come to
London for the express purpose of asking her again and this time
enlisting your help.'

To this day I don't know why I said it. I had not had any such
intention, but suddenly it seemed the right thing to do, the only
thing that would pull my life together, give it purpose and make it
worthwhile.

The Colonel looked from me to Clarissa, thin eyebrows raised.
'You have my goodwill, my boy, for what it is worth, but you may
not find it so easy to persuade her. I must warn you that Clary
won't marry except to please herself as I know to my cost.'

The sheer effrontery of it after he had not scrupled to sell his
daughter to Rutland's son amazed me and yet I could not entirely
despise him. There was something likeable about the devil-may-
care courage and when he had failed, he had not whined about it.
If he went down as he very well might, it would be with colours
flying.

'I shall do my level best,' I said with a quick glance at Clarissa's
stony face. 'Now you'd better tell me all about the loan.'

'Very well if I must.' He sighed and nodded to Clarissa. 'Better
make sure Betsy is not listening outside the door and then leave us
alone, there's a good girl.'

Clarissa went out without a word and I closed the door after
her.

'I've twice given that damned bitch Betsy notice to quit, but she
won't go,' growled the Colonel.

'Like that, is it?'

'You don't need to remind me,' he gave me a half-ashamed grin.
'I know it's my own fault, but it was so cursed lonely when
Clarissa walked out on me.'

'Leave it to me. I'll send her packing.'

He leaned back with a sigh of relief. 'Thank God for a man in
the house. Harry's too young. He hasn't the authority though he
tries, poor lad.' He eyed me for a moment. 'Clarissa has not been
herself since she came back from Ravensley. She won't talk about
it and pretends it is nothing, but I know better. Is that due to you?'

'Yes,' I said abruptly. 'But there is time to talk about that later.'

'You *do* care for her?'

'Very much.'

'Hm-m . . . can you support her? I seem to remember your uncle knocked all your hopes on the head.'

'Not lavishly,' I said shortly, 'but she won't starve and she won't end up in a debtor's prison.'

'Touché,' he grinned at me. 'Well, beggars can't be choosers, I suppose. Let's get down to business.'

Joshua Rutland proved easier to tackle than I had thought when I went to call on him at his house in Arlington Street. Maybe it was because he had just returned from Ravensley and was distracted with anxiety over his son's accident. He poured it all out to me and I listened politely.

'I am sorry to hear of it,' I said. 'I had no idea. I rode into Ely that same night and came up to London early the next morning.'

'The doctors hint that he could limp for the rest of his life,' he said a little pathetically, almost as if he was seeking reassurance.

That ought to bring Bull Rutland's conceit down a peg or two, I thought unsympathetically. Aloud I said, 'I'm sure they are being pessimistic. We have had broken limbs on the ice before now, they usually mend well enough. Mr Rutland, there is another matter on which I would like to speak with you.'

He shot me a keen glance. 'Oh and what is that?'

'It seems that Colonel Fenton is in your debt for a considerable sum of money and is now being pressed for repayment.'

'That's true enough. He had the money from me more than a year ago on a certain condition and he's spent it. Easy come, easy go, you know, with men of his stamp. Now he has to face the consequences.'

'To the extent of harassing him into the grave and inflicting considerable hardship on his daughter?'

He looked at me shrewdly. 'What is your interest in this affair?'

'I intend to marry Clarissa Fenton.'

'The devil you do!' Then unexpectedly he laughed. 'Damn me if I didn't have a strong notion of that when you were looking so hang dog at Christmas.'

'I'll see that you are repaid, but it cannot be done all at once. My means are limited. You will have to wait for it.'

'Shall I indeed? Now look here, young man, I'm not a damned blood-sucking usurer, nor am I the heartless brute you seem to think. But a debt is a debt and I have a man of business whose job it is to press hard when he thinks fit. Still, in this case . . .' he rubbed his chin thoughtfully. 'Tell you what . . . I'll call him off . . . I'll even wash out the whole debt as a wedding present . . . on one condition.'

'I'm not asking for any favours,' I said stiffly.

'Don't get on your high horse with me. I could ruin Colonel Fenton and you too, in a couple of shakes, if I were so minded.'

'I don't think we have any more to say to one another, Mr Rutland,' I said furiously. 'The money will be repaid.'

'For God's sake, young man, must you fly off the handle like that? At least listen before you throw it back in my face.' I waited reluctantly and his red monkey face split into a grin. 'That's better. Aylshams are not God Almighty, you know, though your uncle seems to think so. I've been intending for some time to buy a property in the country . . . oh, you can sneer if you like . . . the old tea broker trying to shove his way into county society . . . that's what you are thinking, isn't it? Well, why not? It's been done before.'

'What has all this to do with me?' I said impatiently.

'I like what I've seen of your Fens. There's a challenge there, a potential and that appeals to me. I've heard there's a house and land coming up for sale soon on the other side of that great Fen of yours . . . Westley-by-water or some such name. The owner is abroad so they tell me but when the time comes, I'd like you to look it over for me. Give an opinion. I'm not buying a pig in a poke.'

'You can employ surveyors more expert than I.'

'Probably, but maybe not so honest. Miss Clarissa told me once that you were to be trusted and she's a young lady of whom I have a high opinion. What do you say?'

I had an idea that there was some other motive behind it, but I was not sure where it lay. I said slowly, 'I'll do what I can.'

'Fair enough. I'll let you know when the occasion arises.'

'I'd still rather not be under any obligation.'

'You're a stiff-necked pair, aren't you, you and your young woman? Do what you like. I'll see you're not pressed.'

Clarissa was a much more difficult nut to crack. She refused me pointblank. 'I'll not be married out of pity. I'm grateful to you, tremendously grateful. I don't know what Papa and I would have done, but it's putting an unfair burden on you.'

'Now listen to me, Clarissa. I only persuaded the old man because he has a *tendresse* for you. I believe there's a sentimental streak hiding somewhere under that tough hide. I know I'm not offering you much. It's going to be hard work and not much fun and certainly nothing like the brilliant society you are accustomed to in London. You'll miss it.'

She smiled faintly. 'I don't think I shall.'

'Do you dislike me so much?'

'You know it's not that.' She stared down at her clasped hands and suddenly a kind of desperation seized me. This once it had to come right. I swung round to face her.

'The truth is I need a wife badly.'

She looked up at me. She has fine eyes, large and clear with long silky lashes. 'Why do you need her? To help with the hard work?'

'Damn it all, Clarissa. You went to a great deal of trouble to stop them hanging me, you can't abandon me now. What do you want me to do? Go down on my knees and beg prettily like Prickle does for a biscuit?'

She laughed at that. It is something we share, a sense of the ridiculous. We are amused by the same things. She still argued against it, but the battle was basically won. We were married by special licence and Harry gave his sister away because the Colonel was not well enough. He was protesting vigorously at being taken down to Copthorne at the mercy of his sister-in-law.

'Jess will talk me to death,' he groaned. 'I doubt if I shall survive her tongue a month.'

'Nonsense, Papa,' said Clarissa briskly. 'You've a great deal in common if you only knew it and anyway there's no choice. Oliver can't keep a house in London and in the country as well so that is all there is to it.'

The sale of the house in Soho Square and its contents, except for a few pieces we took down to Thatchers, just about paid his outstanding debts and set Harry up in rooms though how long that is going to last I don't know. We have Clarissa's tiny income added to my own so we manage, and she is wonderful. She never grumbles. She has transformed Thatchers. She cares for my comfort. She is a good companion and she interests herself in the estate and our own small part of it and yet sometimes it is as if there were a wall of glass between us. Alyne would have done none of these things, yet perversely I still ache for her. When I walked up Ely Cathedral and gave her to Justin, it was tearing out part of myself and Clarissa knows it. Perhaps that's part of the trouble, that and being grateful to each other. I owe her my life and she believes she owes me the rescue of her father and herself. I didn't tell her that I had shouldered the debt to Joshua Rutland and when she found out accidentally a few months ago, she was horrified. It's not a good basis for living together. It makes you too careful not to offend and the result is that somehow you do that very thing. I've taken to sleeping apart most of the time on the plea of getting up early because I would not make too many demands simply to assuage my desperate hunger for another woman. I don't know how Clarissa feels, only that she never gives herself to me freely and completely. There's always a barrier. Sometimes lately I have wondered what will happen when Alyne comes back with Justin and then I deliberately shut my mind against it.

Rowan snorted pulling at the rein and I realized that I'd reached the place where I usually tether her and go the last half mile on foot. It is the very centre of Greatheart, a network of islands where the land is mostly bog with the river winding through it, but not dangerous if you are familiar with the paths. I left Rowan contentedly munching the rich herbage, took the basket and walked on.

Jake lives in what is little more than a shack though he has rebuilt the walls and mended the reed-thatched roof. Last spring when the ice melted, the floor was flooded to the depth of a couple of feet and at my urging he reluctantly took refuge in one of the attics at Thatchers. Clarissa and I lived with nerves stretching to breaking point for weeks because the soldiers were still rounding up the rebels and with people in and out of the house there was always the risk of discovery. It was not a good beginning to our married life and though Clarissa stood up to it well, I don't wonder that she is not anxious for it to happen again. I had come today with a proposal to make to him and I was thinking about it as I plodded up the rough track.

The door was shut and it occurred to me that he might be out fishing or hunting. He shoots plover in season and wild duck and geese which Moggy or Nampy sell for him in the markets. He has always refused stubbornly to accept a penny from me. The Starlings in their way are as proud and independent as the Aylshams.

No one locks doors on Greatheart. The Fenmen do not steal from one another though they'll beat you down to the last farthing over a shrewd bargain so I pushed up the wooden latch intending to leave the basket for him if he were not there, and then stopped dead on the threshold.

Cherry was lying on the makeshift bed of bracken and straw while Jake knelt beside her, his arms round her waist, his head close to hers, both of them too engrossed with each other even to notice the door opening.

I had known all about her infatuation with Jake, but had thought it a childish folly forgotten already. All the year she had hardly mentioned his name and I could have sworn knew nothing of his hiding place. The hot flush of anger took me by surprise so that for an instant I was speechless and in that time Cherry saw me. She sat up with a little cry and Jake turned his head and then rose slowly to his feet.

How difficult it is to rid oneself of the prejudices of one's class. I had known Jake all my life. He has been close as a brother. I know his value, his integrity. He is worth a dozen of the young men I hunt and drink with and yet the sight of my sister in his arms filled me with a violent rage. I heard myself speaking as savagely as my uncle might have done.

'What the devil is this? What are you doing here, Cherry? Are you utterly shameless?'

She struggled to her feet with Jake's help. 'Don't speak like that, Oliver. It's not what you think . . .'

'What, in God's name, am I supposed to think?'

'Please listen . . .'

Jake put a hand on her arm. 'No, Cherry, leave this to me. Let me explain.'

I seized hold of her and pulled her away from him. 'What is there to explain? When am I to expect a bastard for a nephew?'

She flushed and slapped me hard across the face. 'How dare you say that to me? How dare you?'

I caught both her hands in mine and we stood there, glaring at one another. Then I looked across at Jake.

'It is you I blame. How could you do this to her? Don't you realize she is a headstrong child?'

'I don't think you know your own sister, Oliver.'

'I'm not a child.'

Cherry wrenched herself away from me and looking into her face, I realized suddenly that she was right. She had grown up and I had never noticed it, thinking of her still as the baby I had to protect, the little sister who tagged after her big brother admiringly.

She spoke calmly with a dignity that put me to shame. 'You are not to blame Jake. He has repeated to me a hundred times what you have just said, but I love him and he loves me. I'd marry him tomorrow if he would have me, but he won't . . .'

I glanced from her to Jake feeling the anger begin to drain away. 'It is unthinkable.'

'Do you imagine I don't realize that?' Jake had come and put one hand on Cherry's shoulder. 'I've told her over and over again. Even if I were a free man I know you would never consent though Aylsham and Starling blood has been mingled before now. I've told her that she shouldn't come here . . .'

'But I have come, haven't I?' She reached up to touch his cheek. 'And I don't intend to stop whatever you or Oliver says or Uncle Justin either. In two years I shall be twenty-one. Then I can do what I like. No one can prevent me.'

'Except Jake himself,' I said grimly. 'How long do you think he can stay here, a hunted man, a fugitive from the law? One of these days you will be followed and if they find you with him . . .'

'We'll go to prison together.'

'For God's sake, don't talk so childishly. You'd better go, Cherry. I'll speak to you at Ravensley tonight.'

'I'm not going to leave you alone with him.'

But Jake intervened. 'Please, Cherry, it would be best, really it would.'

'All right, but only because you ask me.' She stood on tiptoe to kiss him and I saw the pain on his face and the longing. Then he picked up her cloak and put it round her shoulders. 'Don't let him bully you, dearest,' she whispered.

'I won't. Go now, Cherry.'

'How did you come here?' I said.

'By boat. It's moored on the other side of the island.' She paused by the door to look up into my face. 'I'm not giving him up, Oliver, whatever you say.' Then she went quickly.

We were left staring at one another and for a moment I saw Jake as she saw him. He has looks and dignity, an air of pride even in the plain rough clothes of a working man, and he has done much to improve himself. Then the utter futility of it struck me.

I said harshly, 'This has got to stop.'

'I know that. I've said it to myself a hundred times, but it's not easy. You of all men should realize that.'

I knew he thought of Alyne and it was true, yet it made me angry. 'Maybe I do know, but there can be no future in this either for you or her.'

'I am aware of that too,' he said with extreme bitterness. 'Miss Aylsham of Ravensley and a man like me. It is out of the question, isn't it? Far better to marry her off to a weakling like Hugh Berkeley or a young waster like your brother-in-law Harry Fenton . . .'

'Insults won't get you anywhere,' I said coldly.

'God damn it, do you think I don't know all about that? She has no conception of what my life has been or is likely to be. What does she know of the agony of hunger or the despair of poverty? Madness, isn't it?' He passed a hand over his face. 'But, oh God, Oliver, it's such sweet madness!'

I said bluntly, 'Are you lovers?'

'No. Not that we couldn't have been . . . she was willing,' he said with an angry pride. He moved away from me to the bare hole of the window with its crude wooden shutter. 'She offers herself to me with the innocence of a child. How the hell could I take advantage of that?' There was silence for a moment. Then he turned round. 'What are you going to do about it?'

'I don't know yet.' Then I picked up the basket and put it on the table. 'Clarissa packed this for you and I'm hungry. We can at least eat.'

'If you say so.' He looked puzzled, then grinned a little reluctantly and we pulled up stools to the table. The tension between us eased a little. We had eaten together like this on a hundred hunting or fishing expeditions.

I cut into Clarissa's excellent chicken pie and we ate in silence. She had had the forethought to put in a bottle of wine. Jake found the mugs and I filled them before I spoke.

'I came here today to make a suggestion. It so happens that through my uncle I've had dealings with a man who runs a small coastal service carrying goods out of Yarmouth. I think for a consideration one of the Captains could be persuaded to take you on board when he sails round to Southampton. From there, it should not be too difficult to obtain a passage to Canada. Money's tight with me as you know, but Clarissa will agree with me about this. We could put together enough to give you a start and there are opportunities in that country, good ones for someone like yourself.'

'Paying me off . . . getting rid of me, is that it?'

'For heaven's sake, Jake, that was never in my mind. I knew nothing about Cherry until I came here today. But what future is there for you in England with the law as it is?'

'I know you're right. I've told myself that more than once. I must get out if I am to survive.' He got up and paced up and down the narrow hut and then swung round to face me. 'Believe me, Oliver, I'm grateful to you. You've been more than a friend, but you're hard pressed too. I'd not take more from you.'

'Don't think of that. We'll find it somehow.'

'No, listen, it's not just that. There's something I want to say, something I want you to understand about me.' He paused a moment as if groping for the right words and then went on slowly. 'When they hanged my father, it did something to me, not at once, but like planting a seed that grows inside you. I made up my mind that I would do what I could to help those like him, good people, hard-working people who have no rights, no voice in their lives, no justice from those in power over them. Not your father, Oliver, nor you, but men like your uncle, like Sir Peter Berkeley, like Lord Haversham . . . so many of them who ride roughshod over men like us. I read, I listened to what was said. In a small way I think I did do something. You see so many of us are helpless because we can't speak, we can't express what we feel and know to be right, we haven't the right words.' He hit his fist hard against the doorpost in angry reproach. 'You know how it all ended. I don't know what craziness sent me out poaching with Moggy and Nampy that night. I was driven by rage and frustration. Those weeks after the harvest, after your uncle's dismissal, had been hell. I didn't want to go and yet I wanted passionately to hit back, at your uncle, at anyone, I didn't care who it was, and I've regretted it ever since. The irony of it was that I did nothing, never fired a shot nor set a trap. Not one of those damned pheasants, not even a squirrel, suffered because of me.'

'Your sentence was rank injustice.'

'You did your best and risked a great deal to get me free of it. If it had not been for you, we'd have got nowhere in our fight for better conditions. We owe something to Captain Swing, eh?' He grinned, then was angry again. 'But what was the result? A shilling increase in wages and already in some places, they are cutting it off again, nothing but suppression and savage punishment so that now no one dares to raise his voice. The hunger of those you love is a powerful weapon to subdue even the most determined rebel.' He leaned forward emphasizing his words with a blow on the table. 'But it's not yet finished, Oliver, not here or anywhere throughout the country. I can sense it beneath the surface and I'd not leave England until I've seen something valuable arise out of it.'

I knew much of what he spoke, but not how deeply and passionately he felt. I said, 'And Cherry? What of her?'

'That has been my greatest folly,' he said wryly. 'You may not believe me, Oliver, but I didn't intend it, I swear I didn't. Love . . . the soft things were not for me. I had a purpose and that was to be enough. But it creeps up on you, it takes you unawares. I think I've loved her from the very first, even when we were children. Then when I knew how she felt . . . hell and damnation! I've known it was hopeless from the start, that's why I'm going away.'

'Going away? Where?'

'I don't know yet, but I've been thinking of it all summer. I want to move around the country, talk to others like myself, find out how they feel, try and draw them together in a closer bond. It should not be too difficult to go from place to place. There is always work for a man who is willing and able to turn his hand to most things.'

'When will you go?'

'Now perhaps it would be the sooner the better.' He looked around the bare room. 'I travel light. There's little to take.'

It was a solution and I was ashamed at the way I leaped at it. 'You'll need food and money.'

'No . . .'

'Yes. Don't be a fool and don't argue. Come to Thatchers tomorrow night. Clarissa will make up a packet for you and there'll be a few guineas, something to set you on your way.'

'It's generous of you, but it's not necessary.'

'I wish I could do more. You'll come back?'

He made a wide gesture that included all the Fens. 'Never to see this again would be like ripping the heart out of my body. I'll get a message to you somehow.'

'And Cherry?'

He hesitated. 'I've been trying to bring myself to tell her. Now perhaps it's better if I don't see her again. Explain to her, Oliver. Make her understand. Don't let her hate me for it.'

'I don't think I could,' I said dryly. 'You'll have to take care. The arm of the law is long.'

'That's a risk I must take.'

I poured more wine into the cups. 'We'll drink to your luck.'

He drained the mug and put it down. 'There's something else, Oliver, something I think you ought to know now that I'm going away.' He dropped on to the stool leaning across the table and whispering almost as if he feared he might be overheard which seemed absurd in this lonely place.

'There's a man hiding out here on the Fens who bears a grudge against the Aylshams and most particularly against your uncle.'

'The man who is said to resemble me?' I smiled. 'I've always believed that part of it to be pure fancy and there are always men who bear grudges, particularly in these times, and God knows, some of them have justice on their side after last winter.'

'No, there is more to it than that. He was there on the night your uncle was hurt but he kept himself close. Moggy knows who he is and he'll not give him away, but sometimes in his cups he talks, and there have been hints dropped. I believe it goes back, right back to when your uncle was first sent away.'

'But that's more than twenty years ago.'

'I know and I was only a youngster then as you were, but I do remember things. I used to hear my father and mother talk. It meant little then, but now . . . I have questioned Mam but she gets upset. She won't talk about it.'

I stared at him remembering how my uncle had been as a young man, remembering my mother, and I clenched my fists. 'Go on. What did you know?'

'Did you ever hear that my grandmother had a child before she was married, a son, whose father was Lord Aylsham?'

'My grandfather, do you mean?'

'Aye, the old Tiger himself. I don't know if he ever knew, maybe he did and gave money, but the baby was sent away and when he grew up, he lived and worked over Westley way.'

'Did you ever see him?'

'Once or twice when I was young. He had hair the colour of yours, Oliver, and then when I was five or six, something happened to him, something terrible. My father was away for several days and when he came back, he brought a boy with him, older than me, ten or eleven perhaps. "He's your cousin," he said.'

'Was he his son?'

'I always thought so. He was a queer sullen boy who treated us like enemies. The young 'uns were terrified of him. I was glad when after a year he ran away and we never saw him again.'

'What happened to him?'

'I don't know and if my father knew, he never said.'

'And you think this man could be he?'

'It is possible.'

It was absurd, too fantastic to be believed, and yet I still remembered vividly the face of the boy who had spat at me and been transported to the penal colony in Australia. Men have been known to serve their sentence and somehow save the money to return, but would the flame of hatred, the desire for revenge, burn for twenty years?

Jake went on. 'I've sometimes wondered if that is why your uncle had it in for us, the way he treated me and Mam. You see his name was Starling too.'

I could not meet his eyes. Surely my father must have known and yet he had said nothing. He was a good man, a kind man, and he had let them destroy a boy who could have been his own nephew. There was no certainty, and yet it made me feel ashamed.

'My grandfather didn't know what retribution he was pulling down on the heads of his descendants,' I said dryly. 'Thank you for the warning. I'll keep it in mind.'

'Don't laugh, Oliver. The Fens are strange places and Greatheart more than anywhere. It has known too much suffering and misery. It can breed queer thoughts. I know, believe me.'

'Maybe.' I thought of my father lying in the muddy pool with the chill of death on him and shivered. Then I got to my feet. 'I must go or it will be dark before I arrive home and Clarissa will be anxious. You will come tomorrow? I'll be expecting you?'

'I will come. Don't be hard on Cherry, will you?'

'What do you take me for? She is my sister and I'm fond of her. I don't want to see her hurt.'

'Will you take the basket?'

'Bring it with you tomorrow.'

I slapped him on the shoulder and went out quickly. The light was going already and a white mist was curling up from the water blowing hither and thither like smoke. In a second the hut had disappeared from view. If I had not been so familiar with the path, I could have been easily lost. I was walking waist high through a milky vapour in a hushed silence, no murmur of bird or animal which was why Rowan's whinney and the trampling of hooves sounded so startlingly loud. I ran the last few yards splashing through water and mud. The mist blew away temporarily and I saw a man unhitching the mare and trying to force her away.

'Stop!' I shouted. 'Let her be, you damned rascal!' and when he still urged her on, I launched myself at him. He let go the bridle and we grappled together. He was shorter than I, but thickset and powerful, and he fought back savagely. I don't know what might have happened if he hadn't slipped in the slimy mud and gone down backwards with me on top of him. I was furiously angry by then. The Fenmen are not thieves and I was known the length and breadth of Greatheart.

'Rob me of my horse, would you, you wretch!' I exclaimed breathlessly, my hands on his throat. He twisted under me. His hat had fallen off and in the brief light, with a shock of disbelief, I was staring down at my own face.

It had come so pat on Jake's warning that I had a curious feeling that he had been there all the time, dogging my steps all the day through, maybe even listening outside the hut.

'Who the devil are you?' My fingers tightened. 'Answer me, damn you!'

But he only glared up at me with eyes as blue as my own. Then his knee came up with a bruising suddenness. I lurched sideways and he was up and off into the marsh with a lightning speed. In an instant he was swallowed up by the mist and to pursue him over that treacherous ground would have been madness.

My coat and breeches were in a sorry state and it took me some time to recapture Rowan. When I reached Thatchers, Clarissa exclaimed at my filthy condition and I concocted a hasty story of Rowan stumbling and being thrown which I think she only half believed, but there was no point in alarming her unnecessarily. All the same, the knowledge that a potential murderer was hiding out on the Fens, whether his hatred was directed against me or against my uncle, was not pleasant and I wondered if I should warn Justin when he returned.

At supper Clarissa said, 'Cherry came in to see me for a few minutes late this afternoon. I thought she looked very upset, but she wouldn't tell me why.'

'I know why,' I said grimly. 'I surprised her and Jake together when I went there today.'

'Oh no . . .'

'It's a damnable business. It seems they have been meeting all this summer.' I looked at her with sudden suspicion. 'You are very close with her. Did you know about this?'

'No, of course not. But I did know she was much too fond of him and so did Aunt Jess. Last year when he was imprisoned, she went to see him in the gaol.'

'She went to the prison in Ely?' I repeated aghast. 'How do you know?'

'I went with her.'

'My God, why does everybody know more about this affair than I do? Why wasn't I told?'

'I did want to, but she wouldn't have it. She said you would only be angry and I was afraid your uncle might find out. I dreaded what he might do to her.'

I was extremely annoyed and I showed it. 'How could you allow her to do such a thing? If it had got out, you know what would have been said of her. Her good name ruined for ever, and probably mine too for permitting such a thing.'

Clarissa looked at me oddly. 'Perhaps she doesn't mind that.'

'Well, I do. She's my sister, isn't she? Are you reproaching me?'

'No. But sometimes I think you don't realize how hard it has been for her, living at Ravensley with Alyne and your uncle. What are you going to do?'

'It so happens that I need to do nothing. It is Jake himself. He is going away.'

'To Canada?'

'No.' In a few words I outlined Jake's plans and she listened in silence.

'Poor Cherry,' she said at last.

'For heaven's sake! What other solution is there? Isn't this the best thing that could happen?'

'Perhaps. But it's hard to realize you come second to a man's dreams.'

'Now you're talking nonsense.'

'Am I?'

'Clarissa, will you do something for me? Will you explain to her, make her understand it is not I who am driving Jake away, that it is his own decision?'

She smiled faintly. 'I did not think you such a coward, Oliver.'

'I am about things like this. Cherry likes you, admires you. She'll take it better from you than from me.'

'And you'd not be her executioner. That's the truth of it, isn't it?'

'It's not that . . .'

'All right. I don't relish it, but I will do it.'

'Bless you. Make it tomorrow and don't tell her he's coming here. To meet won't help him or her.'

We rode up to Ravensley together the next day and I left her with Cherry while I went up to the attic. I wanted to find out something for myself.

Hannah Starling was the eldest of the Starling family, a good ten years older than Isaac, so she was nearing seventy and growing more frail every day. It was quite a time since I'd been up there and she was pathetically glad to see me. I had to answer a lot of probing questions about myself and Clarissa before I could get down to what I had in mind and then hardly knew how to start.

'I was over at Westley the other day,' I said casually. 'Didn't you have a half-brother who lived there once.'

She gave me a sharp glance. 'Why are you asking?'

'Somebody said something. I was curious.'

'Curiosity killed the cat.' How often she had snapped that at me when I was a child. Then she looked up at me slyly. 'We don't never talk about him. Anyway I were only fourteen when I come to work here and I only saw him the once.' And then as sometimes happens with old people, she went on mumbling as much to herself as to me. 'He had the looks though, half Aylsham, see, though we never said nowt about that. 'Tweren't nothing to boast of. He worked for the Leighs of Westley. Fine cottage he had an' all, better than Isaac's . . .'

'What happened?'

She peered up at me. 'What d'ye want to know for?'

'No particular reason.'

Then she leaned forward whispering. 'He were murdered. It were hushed up. I never knew the rights of it, but Isaac did and your uncle. The honourable Justin Aylsham, as he was then, he knew something. He was over at Westley more than once. I mind your grandfather shouting and him laughing and throwing up his head proud-like. " 'Tisn't my fault," he sez, "if some fool gets himself killed." Alice, that were his wife, she took it hard. She were never right in the head after. 'Tweren't long afore she died.'

'And their son?'

'Nasty spiteful varmint he were. Isaac did everything for him and he threw it back in his face as if it were dirty slops. Ran off one day and never another word from him from that day to this. "Good riddance," I told Isaac. "You've enough mouths of your own to feed without takin' on a nephew as never sez even a thank you."'

But I could find it in my heart to be sorry for a boy who had lost both father and mother in such a cruel manner.

She leaned forward again, clutching at me with her thin old hand. 'When does your uncle come back?'

'Soon, within the month.'

'Too soon for you and for all of us. You mark my words, Mr

Oliver, I've said it before and I'll say it again, he's a black Aylsham and I remember what my old grandfather used to say of one of 'em. Your great uncle he'd have been and the living image of him as has come back from the dead. So wicked he were, his shadow withered up the young grass as he walked on it and the look of his eye had a curse in it.'

'Now look here, nurse, it is ridiculous to talk like that . . .'

'I saw your uncle grow up from a baby, black he were from the day he were born and a temper so you'd have thought a devil lived inside him . . .'

'That's enough. He's Lord Aylsham now and he is married . . .'

'Aye, to the witch's brat, and much good may it do him and her, settin' her up to queen it over us, puttin' her in your dear mother's place . . .'

'Listen to me,' I said sternly because I had to stop her. 'She is mistress here now and you'd better learn to curb your tongue for your own good.'

'Aye, I know that and I'll keep quiet but I can't stop the thoughts comin' and goin' in my head . . . you were well rid of her.'

She would have gone rambling on for hours if I had let her so I cut her short abruptly and went downstairs. I had learned little more except to confirm what Jake had told me, but it lay uneasily at the back of my mind.

Clarissa was in the schoolroom with Jethro and Miss Harriet. I looked at her questioningly and she gave me a little nod so that I knew she had spoken to Cherry and I felt guilty because I had left it to her and not done it myself.

Jethro said, 'Can Ben come up and play with me as usual this afternoon?'

'Not today, but tomorrow with Hattie's permission, you can come to Thatchers.'

That was another problem that would have to be faced. We had grown lax during the months Justin had been away and I'd not see the child punished for what had been my responsibility. The boy had been happy during the summer and I did not want it spoiled. Was he my half-brother? Sometimes I felt almost sure, but I had not faced up to questioning Justin. My mother's betrayal was still a wound that I found difficult to accept calmly. I wondered what had been in his mind. If Jethro was my mother's child, then Ravensley would be mine if Alyne did not bear him a son. I closed my mind against that possibility and took Clarissa's arm.

'It's time we went home.'

Outside waiting for the horses to be brought round, she said, 'What is wrong? Has something happened?'

'Why do you ask?'

'You've looked disturbed ever since you came down from seeing Nurse Starling.'

'It's nothing. You see too much.'

'Is it because Justin and Alyne are coming back soon?'

'For heaven's sake, must you go on and on?'

'Why do you always shut me out, Oliver? Your problems are mine.'

'Now you're talking rubbish. There are no problems.'

I helped her into the saddle and followed after her down the drive. We rode back to Thatchers in silence.

Jake did not come that night after all. In the morning I found the basket propped up against the back door but no other sign of him and I knew why. He had his own pride and he would not accept anything from me, especially now.

Clarissa took the empty basket out of my hands. 'I don't like what he is doing,' she said. 'It's dangerous. He could be recaptured and sent back to the prison. You should have persuaded him to follow your plan and go to Canada.'

'Jake has always had a way of falling on his feet,' I said abruptly because I too was unhappy about it. All the time I had spent with him, it had been Cherry who had been in my mind and not Jake. I did not know how bitterly I was to regret it.

2

Justin came back at the end of November and I knew at once that Alyne was not happy. It was not apparent in her looks. She was more beautiful than ever. She had learned style and elegance in Paris and Florence and Rome. There was a polish, a sophistication, that had not been there before and my uncle must have spent lavishly. Her clothes had an expensive simplicity and she wore them with poise and distinction. Watching her that first evening, it made me angry. I wanted to rush Clarissa to London and dress her in the finest creations that money could buy, only I did not have the means, and the very fact that she did not ask me for it nor expect it, seemed to make my frustration worse.

On the surface there was no rift. It was only natural that Justin's eyes should always be on his lovely young wife, showing her off proudly to his guests, but where Alyne was concerned, I had a sixth sense. There was a tension between them that occasionally showed itself in little barbed remarks that could have been jests and yet were not, darts that were spiteful and meant to hurt. Once when I went up to the house very early, they were still at breakfast and I saw how pale Alyne was, her eyes swollen with tears or sleeplessness, and yet when I asked her one day if anything was wrong, she was brusque with me.

'Wrong? Why should there be? We have had a wonderful trip and Justin gives me everything I could possibly want.'

'Perhaps that's not enough.'

'For heaven's sake, Oliver, it's not I you should be fretting about, but Cherry. When Justin gave her the presents we had brought for her, she took one look at them, then burst into tears and ran out of the room. He was very put out.'

'Maybe she is a little upset at seeing you look so fine,' I said lightly. 'This is her home after all as well as yours.'

'I'm not likely to forget it,' she said dryly. 'Has she been seeing Jake?'

'Why on earth should she?' I said too quickly.

She gave me a sharp look. 'Don't be silly, Oliver. I know she was meeting him last winter.'

So even Alyne had been aware of it. I felt quite unreasonably angry. 'He is not here now.'

'Thank goodness for that. If Justin were to hear of it . . .'

'You'd not tell him?'

'I might if I thought it was for her good. He'd not like his niece running after an escaped convict.'

'He's not that.'

'What else is he?'

'Don't be so damned provoking,' her knowing little smile irritated me beyond measure. I seized her by the shoulder. 'You know perfectly well there is nothing in it.'

She stood quite rigid in my hands. 'Don't do that. You're hurting me.' I muttered an apology and she took a step away from me. 'Because we all once played together as children doesn't bind us together for ever, Oliver. Now I have other things to do and so have you.'

Sometimes I was not sure whether Alyne was friend or enemy, but she still had so much power to disturb me that I kept my visits to Ravensley strictly to business except for Christmas when Justin entertained widely and Clarissa and I could lose ourselves among a crowd of guests.

The New Year's ball at the Assembly Rooms in Ely had always been attended by everyone of note in the county. I went there first with my father when I was eighteen, but I had not gone again since he died, and had no intention of doing so this winter if it had not been for Colonel Fenton.

Ever since our marriage, Miss Cavendish had turned over the running of her small farm to me. 'It'll go to Clarissa when I'm gone,' she remarked dryly, 'so you may as well have the management of it now. Tom doesn't know the first thing about the land and wouldn't know a turnip from a potato so it'll take a weight off my shoulders.' But she still liked to be consulted and when one morning after Christmas I called at Copthorne to have a word about the spring sowing, she asked me if I was going to the ball.

'No, I don't think so. I'm not much of a one for junketing, especially nowadays.'

'And why the devil not?' said the Colonel looking up from *The Times* newspaper. 'What's the virtue in being such a dull dog? How old are you for God's sake? Twenty-seven? If you want to turn yourself into a recluse, there's no need to treat your wife as a household drudge.'

'I'm not doing any such thing,' I said a little taken aback. 'Clarissa feels as I do.'

'She says she does because she knows it's what you want, but that doesn't mean she likes it. Damn it, she's not some kind of nun. All young women enjoy an opportunity to flirt with other men now and again. If I'd known what I do now, I'd have done my damnedest to prevent her marrying you and stuck it out in London, debtor's prison or no.'

'Now look here, sir . . .'

'No, you listen to me for once. You're an Aylsham, aren't you? Your father was a man of note in these parts, so go and show yourself, prove that you're not letting your uncle ride roughshod over you. Your wife has better blood than the whole lot of them put together, so be proud of her. She's worth a dozen of that prinked-up miss he has decided to make mistress of Ravensley. Are you ashamed of Clarissa?'

'No, of course not . . .'

'Then don't behave as if you were and don't talk to me about being short of the ready. I've heard enough about that this past year and I tell you here and now I could make a better show on quarter your income. Try and make Clarissa happy for a change.'

'Clarissa is perfectly happy,' I said stiffly.

'That's what she tells you,' he retorted, 'but I know different. Not that she says a word, she's too damned loyal. What about breeding a son or two, make her feel she has a husband who's got spunk in him, in bed and out of it . . .'

'Easy, Tom, easy,' interrupted Miss Cavendish.

'Don't stop me, Jess. I've had this bottled up for weeks and so have you so don't shake your head at me.'

'It's true, Oliver, though I'd not have put it quite like that. You ought to make more of yourself.'

'You've a damned fine wife even though I say it myself,' grumbled the Colonel, 'so why the devil are you hiding her away?'

I was furiously angry with him at first and made no bones about showing it, but afterwards, riding home, I was reluctantly forced to acknowledge that there was some truth in his attack. Dismounting in the courtyard I went in search of Clarissa and found her in the dairy superintending the separation of the milk from the cream. I seized hold of her and took her outside.

'What on earth's the matter?' she exclaimed. 'I'm busy. The cream was just beginning to thicken.'

'To hell with that! Now you listen to me. I've been accused of every crime under heaven this morning. Your father says I'm neglecting you, turning you into a household drudge.'

'You don't want to listen to Papa.'

'I couldn't help myself,' I said ruefully. 'Now, do you want to go to this damned ball in Ely or don't you?'

'Yes, I do, very much,' she answered simply.

'Then why the devil didn't you say so?'

'I thought you'd hate it.'

'I do, but that's neither here nor there. So look out all your finery and mine. We're going to make a show of it if it kills us.'

'But Oliver . . .'

'No "buts", we're going. And it's tomorrow so you'd better get Mrs Starling and Jenny to heat their smoothing irons if we're not to look like a couple of scarecrows.'

She flung her arms round my neck and kissed me warmly before she ran into the house and I stood there, dumbfounded at the whims of women, until feeling suddenly lighthearted, I found myself whistling as I took Rowan to the stable.

In the end it was decided that all four of us should go in the carriage together and what with one delay after another, we arrived a little late and so made something of an entrance. The Colonel, tall and lean, could still look spryly elegant despite the ravages of sickness and Aunt Jess on his arm in the splendour of a gown at least thirty years out of date made an imposing figure. They sailed into the ballroom in front of us and I looked down at Clarissa and grinned.

'Well, here we are, my dear, for better or worse.'

I was surprised at the warmth of the friendship extended to us. Perhaps subconsciously I had been allowing the memory of the trial and the consequent unpleasantness to overshadow me all this year. Now suddenly it was no longer important. It had even acquired a kind of glamour and Clarissa had become something of a heroine without a word being said. I had not expected to feel so proud of her success when she was wisked away from me by this man and that and returned flushed with excitement and pleasure.

Even Lord Haversham, resplendent in black velvet with diamonds in his cravat, ambled across to slap me on the shoulder.

'Glad to see you back among us, my boy, and to hear that you are making good at that little place of yours. Thought at first the county was going to lose you when your uncle came back. Wouldn't have liked to see that. Not altogether sure of him, you know, no bottom, not quite the thing . . .' He let his words trail away and raised his eyeglass. 'Damned fine figure your wife has. I've heard Devonshire speak of her of course and the Colonel had an excellent record in the late war. Pity he let himself go to pot.'

'He has been sick,' I said defensively, 'but Clarissa and Miss Cavendish are excellent nurses.'

'Good, good, you're a lucky fellow. Won't object if she gives an old man a whirl around the floor, eh?'

'Of course not, my lord. I'm sure Clarissa will be honoured.'

She came back to me afterwards, laughing gleefully. 'I've had a proposition. Lord Haversham hinted ever so delicately that if I ever wanted a change, he would be at my disposal.'

'Damn him for a lecherous old rake!' I exclaimed. 'He must be all of seventy.' But I suppose there isn't a man living who does not feel proud when his wife is desired by other men.

The rift in the evening was caused by Bulwer Rutland. I had not expected to see him there though Justin had said something about his father coming down shortly to look at the property he intended purchasing. I was taking a glass of punch with Sir Peter Berkeley when I saw him dancing with Alyne.

'By Zeus,' said Sir Peter, 'little Lady Aylsham blooms like a rose. Never seen anything like it. You lost out there, my boy. No wonder Justin is jealous.'

'Is he? I hadn't noticed it.'

'Look at him, my dear fellow, green as a spring lettuce. He's never taken his eyes off her and that chap Rutland has a taking way with him. Women can never resist the King's uniform.'

'I'm quite sure Alyne is only doing what her husband wishes,' I said coolly. 'My uncle hopes to transact business with Joshua Rutland.'

'Well, that's as may be. By the way, Oliver, is your sister here this evening?'

'No.' In point of fact Cherry had refused to come, but I lied gamely. 'She has a slight cold and we thought it better that she should not become overheated. It's so easy to take a chill at these affairs.'

'Quite so. Hugh will be disappointed.' He paused to take another glass of punch. 'What would you say to a match between them, eh? The boy has always been attached to her. I shall speak to Lord Aylsham first of course since he is her guardian, but I know she thinks a great deal of you.'

'It must depend on Cherry,' I said cautiously and felt a touch of anxiety. She could be headstrong and had never been more than mildly fond of Hugh. Then there was her unfortunate passion for Jake. I could foresee trouble ahead.

'Well, well, we shall have to see,' went on Sir Peter heartily. 'I can rely on you not putting her against it.'

'I shall do nothing to interfere with her happiness one way or the other.'

Later in the evening, coming back from the cardroom where the Colonel and Aunt Jess were safely ensconced, I saw a couple in front of me, hidden in the shadows of the dimly lighted corridor, and would have taken care to avoid them if I had not recognized the cream silk of Alyne's gown. Rutland had his arms around her and she appeared to be struggling with him.

'Let me go,' she was saying, 'please, please, you must let me go.'

He only clasped her closer, forcing his kisses on her, and I acted instinctively. I took him by the shoulders and threw him away from her. He came back at me furiously and my fist struck out, hitting him across the mouth. He stumbled back against the wall.

'Damn you, Aylsham, I'll have satisfaction for that,' he exclaimed.

Alyne was standing beside me, trembling, pale as her gown, and I said, 'Go, go quickly, back to the ballroom.'

'Is he hurt?'

'No, of course not. Go now,' but I was too late. Justin had put aside the velvet curtain that draped the doorway and came towards us.

'What has happened?'

'Nothing. Rutland and I had a difference of opinion and I am afraid I lost my temper. I apologize for causing a disturbance.'

He looked from me to the Captain. 'Is this true?'

'Yes,' muttered Rutland thickly, dabbing at the blood trickling from his split lip. 'It was between Aylsham and myself.'

Justin's eyes narrowed. 'Are you sure you were not quarrelling over my wife?'

'Great heavens, what are you talking about? Of course not,' I exclaimed. 'Alyne happened to be coming along the passage and saw us. She is a little upset. I think you had better take her away.'

'I see.' He stretched out a hand and drew her to him. 'Come along, my dear.'

She went quietly enough, but she looked back over her shoulder and I believed her grateful for my lie because even then I did not fully understand.

Rutland and I were left facing one another. He straightened himself. 'You're a damned impudent fellow, Aylsham. I've called men out for less.'

A public scandal was the last thing I wanted. 'I've no doubt you have,' I said, 'but if you think I'm going to fight you and have Lady Aylsham's name dragged through the mud, you can think again. Just keep away from her in future, that's all.'

'What is your interest?' he remarked unpleasantly. 'Isn't your wife enough for you?'

'Are you trying to provoke me? If so, come outside, and we'll get down to it in earnest.'

He glared at me and then thumped his fist against the wall. 'Hell and damnation! Why did I ever come to this cursed place?'

He turned on his heel and went down the passage. I wiped the blood from my bruised knuckles and strolled back to the ballroom.

I did not mention the incident to Clarissa and when we returned in the carriage, all four of us together, we talked of other things. The Colonel had experienced a run of luck at the card table and boasted of it gaily to Miss Cavendish.

'It won't last five minutes if I know you, Tom,' she said caustically. 'You have a perpetual hole in your pocket.'

'Great God, Jess, do you have to be such a sourpuss? Can't a man indulge in one small vice in his old age? There's not much I am allowed.'

'Now don't start being sorry for yourself,' she said tartly. 'If it were not for Clarissa and me, you'd be begging your bread at the street corner.'

These two regularly argued, wrangled and insulted one another, but enjoyed every minute of it and on the whole, rubbed along very well. A jolt in the road threw Clarissa against me and I slid an arm around her waist and we exchanged a smile. The carriage deposited us at Thatchers and went on to Copthorne. It was a cold night; no snow had fallen as yet, but the stars were brilliant in a frosty sky and a silvery rime sparkled on tree and bush. Jenny had lighted a fire in the bedroom and when I came in, Clarissa was sitting at the dressing table in her nightgown, fumbling with the clasp of her necklet. I lifted the silky brown hair, released the catch and then on impulse gently kissed the slim nape of her neck. I felt her tremble and put my arms around her, drawing her back against me.

'May I stay tonight?'

'You know you don't have to ask.' She put up her hand to take mine and her eyes fell on my grazed knuckles and the speck of blood on my cuff. 'Whatever have you done to your hand?'

I withdrew it quickly. 'It's nothing, I hit it accidentally.'

She turned to look up at me. 'Oliver, you've not been fighting?'

'Is it likely?'

'I don't know. Someone was talking about Captain Rutland and he did leave early. I never dreamed it could be you.'

'He annoyed me.'

'Was it because of me?'

'No.'

'Alyne then?'

I moved away. 'Why all these questions?'

'Was it Alyne?'

'If you really want to know, he was forcing his unwelcome attentions on her.'

'Are you so sure they are unwelcome?'

I rounded on her. 'What the devil do you mean by that? Are you implying that she was encouraging him?'

She shrugged her shoulders and picked up the hairbrush before she said, 'She enjoys playing up to the men who surround her. I think she does it deliberately.'

'That's a vile thing to say as if she were some common trull.'

'I said nothing of the kind.' She was brushing her hair with long, slow strokes. 'She still means a great deal to you, doesn't she, Oliver?'

'You seem to forget she is my uncle's wife.'

'And you are married to me, but it doesn't really make any difference, does it? You still love her.'

Why didn't I throw myself at her feet, put my arms round her and tell her it was not true? I wanted to and yet some innate honesty kept me back. Instead I said, 'You must be feeling very tired. It has been an exhausting evening one way and another. I'll leave you to sleep in peace.'

She made a little move towards me, but I would not see it. Outside the door I paused and nearly went back, but an absurd pride prevented me and so another opportunity to mend things between us was lost.

On an evening in late March I was riding home across the Fens. All day I had been fighting a strong wind, blowing over the marshes from the sea bringing the hungry screaming gulls with it, but now it had largely dropped. The great black sails of the windmills revolved sluggishly against an apple-green sky streaked with the sunset glow of crimson, orange and gold. A bittern boomed hollowly from the coverts, a sure sign of spring, and through the evening hush there came faintly the wraith-like songs of the reed warblers nesting in the wilderness of grasses and sedge along the dykes. It was a moment I knew by heart and yet one which never ceased to move me, a moment when I felt myself one with the wide-stretching sky and the wild creatures that lived in the marshes as much part of its freedoms as any Fen Tiger. And soon, too soon, it would be gone for ever. In a month the engineers would move in, tearing down the dark guardians that had stood sentinel for over a hundred years, destroying the wild loveliness and drowning the song of the birds with the incessant thump-thump of the steam engines.

With the help of Joshua Rutland's loan the first of the new pumps would be installed this summer and by next winter two more would be in use and then the invasion of Greatheart would begin, an invasion resisted bravely through the years ever since Hereward the Wake had defied William of Normandy. But it seemed that no resistance was powerful enough to stand in the way of my uncle's greed.

It was progress in its way, I supposed. It would end in more cattle being pastured, more crops grown, more gold rolling in to deck Alyne with jewels, but there were perils too, practical ones as well as those which are indefinable and yet are always present where the lives of the poor and the voiceless are concerned. The practical ones were obvious and I had done my best to put them clearly to Justin for his own sake as well as for those who lived out on the Fens, but he refused to listen.

'The value of the windmills has been proved now for more than a century and the dykes can carry the volume of the water raised safely enough,' I said, 'but the steam engines will raise the flow to a far greater extent and as yet no one can be sure how it will affect the land.'

'That's what we want, what we need. The wind is fickle as a woman, but the engines will work continuously by day and night.'

'And that surely is where the danger lies,' I argued. 'They recognized it even when Vermuyden first tried to drain the Fens two hundred years ago and he went ahead to his own danger and the loss of many lives. We've experienced it ourselves. The peat shrinks when it is drained and so you can't measure the fall of the ground. The river estuaries silt up. They have been doing so for years now and when the ice melts and the high tides come with the spring, the banks will burst.'

'You exaggerate. You're like the people here, Oliver, you can't see beyond what you've always known. The engineers assure me that the stronger flow of water will clear the silt. Besides think of the tremendous saving in labour. One engine will do the work of a great many windmills.'

'And what will happen to the millmen?'

But he had brushed that aside as of no importance and it was not only they who would suffer but all of those who lived and obtained their food from Greatheart. There were other arguments that I could not put strongly enough. He was trying to do too much too quickly and those who advised him thought only of a quick profit.

I had received one brief note from Jake and everywhere he had found small knots of men binding themselves together. 'One day they may even form a union,' he wrote, 'and think what that will mean. It is far harder to break a bundle of faggots than to snap a single twig.'

'Union?' repeated Clarissa frowning when I spoke to her about it. 'It doesn't seem right somehow to join together against an employer.'

'It would give the peasants strength and power to bargain,' I said thoughtfully, 'and yet I doubt if it will come to anything. Jake is too optimistic. Men being what they are would never agree. There would be endless argument.'

I was thinking of it when I crossed the corner by Spinney Mill and Jack Moysey waved a cheerful hand to me. The millmen are a race apart, sturdy, independent, great fishers and wild fowlers, living out their lonely lives as watchful and faithful as their gaunt charges. Many a time when we were boys out in the dawn fishing in the mere, Jake and I had shared Jack's breakfast, a fat tench, golden-sided and luscious, split open and fried in butter over a bucket with holes drilled in it and filled with glowing coals.

Beyond the mill the cattle moved slowly through a faint mist creeping out from the water and I thought of how ancient this scene was, going back a thousand years to when the Black Monks must have come here with their fishing rods and fowling nets, trudging home along this same track with a brace of wild duck slung on an osier wand or a string of slippery, silvery eels.

The light was fading now and the wind blew colder. I shivered and urged Rowan to a trot with a queer feeling that all those who had lived and worked and found refuge in this wild and lovely place were crowding together at the back of me, begging for my help, pleading with me to save them from being driven out into desolation. It was absurd and I tried to shake myself free from it, but the feeling remained and what happened a week later seemed in some odd way to be part of it.

It was very early one morning, the household only just astir and Clarissa not yet out of bed when there was a frantic knocking at the door. I heard Mrs Starling open it and the murmur of voices.

Clarissa said sleepily, 'What is it?'

'I don't know, but it sounds like trouble.' I ran down the stairs as I was in shirt and breeches. Cherry was in the sitting room, her cloak clutched around her, while Mrs Starling hovered anxiously in the hall. I went in quickly and shut the door.

'What is it? Is it Alyne?'

'No, why should it be Alyne?' she said breathlessly. 'It's Jethro. He has run away.'

'Run away? How do you mean? When?'

'He must have gone in the night or very early this morning.'

'Does Justin know?'

'Not yet.'

'But why? Surely he should have been the first to be told.'

She shook her head. 'No, you don't understand.'

She was trembling and upset so I went to her taking both her hands. 'Now, come along, Puss, it can't be as bad as that. Sit down and tell me quietly. It's probably no more than boyish mischief.'

'No, it's more than that.'

Then Clarissa came in, pulling her dressing gown around her. 'Cherry, at this time in the morning! What has happened? Is someone taken ill?'

'No. It was last night.' Cherry stared down at her clasped hands, trying to keep her voice steady. 'As you know, Uncle Justin has been away for a couple of days and we didn't really expect him back until today. But he returned during the evening and went up to Jethro's room. I think he had brought something for him.'

'Well, what of it?'

She looked up at me. 'I don't know how it happened, but Jethro must have smuggled Ben in somehow. He found the two of them in bed together.'

'My God,' I exclaimed. 'It's my fault. I've let them see too much of one another during last summer.'

'There was nothing wrong in it, I'm certain of that. Jethro is lonely and he plays all kinds of games with Ben and loves to share everything with him. I know that and so does Hattie though we kept it from Uncle Justin.' She paused and then went on quietly. 'When he saw them, I think he went mad. I heard him shouting from my own room. I don't know what he did to Ben, but the boy was so terrified that as he ran out, he fell headlong down the stairs. When I went to him, he picked himself up and fled out of the house, and then . . .'

'Go on, Cherry, and then what?' said Clarissa.

'Uncle Justin whipped Jethro, really whipped him.' She covered her face with her hands for a moment. 'It was horrible because the child did not cry out, not once. I begged him to stop and so did Alyne, but he wouldn't and when Hattie and I would have gone to Jethro afterwards, he forbade us to go into the room. He turned the key in the lock, but he didn't take it away.' She looked up at me, her lips trembling. 'I know I should have done more, but he frightens me. I waited until I was sure he was shut in his own room, then I crept back and turned the key. Jethro was lying very still so I thought he must have cried himself to sleep. I covered him with a blanket and left him. But I couldn't rest. I went back very early this morning and the room was empty.'

'Perhaps he had just run out into the garden or gone to the stables. You know how fond he is of the horses.'

'No, I looked everywhere. Besides he had taken things with him, the little things he loves. You know what I mean.'

And I did, all those small treasures dear to a boy's heart. I could see the child, shocked and desperately unhappy, gathering them into a bundle and running from the house, but where . . . that was the question. Then a thought suddenly struck me. I said, 'Wait a moment. What has happened to Ben? Perhaps Mrs Starling knows.'

I opened the door and she came at once, sensing that something was wrong.

'Is Ben here?'

'No, sir. He went up to the big house last night. I didn't want him to go because of Lord Aylsham, but he said he was away from home and Master Jethro had asked him to go most particularly. He hasn't done anything he shouldn't, has he, sir?'

'It seems the boys may have gone off somewhere together.'

'Ben wouldn't let him do anything foolish, sir, I'm sure of that. He's a careful lad and he's that fond of Master Jethro.'

'I know. Now don't worry. I'm sure they're all right.'

When she had gone back to the kitchen, Clarissa said, 'Where do you think they have gone?'

'I'm not sure, but I think it possible they may have taken the boat. Go back to the house, Cherry, warn Hattie and try to keep it from Justin if you can. Get Alyne to help you. I'll go out and look for the young idiots.' I tried to speak lightly but my anxiety was growing.

Clarissa said, 'I'll dress and come with you.'

'No, better not. Stay here in case Ben comes back. I'll get some of the Fenmen to help in the search. We'll find them.'

My guess about the boat was right because it had gone from its mooring and my anxiety deepened. Ben was handy enough with the paddles, but he was not over strong and Jethro was totally inexperienced. I had taken them for fishing expeditions last summer and sometimes Clarissa had organized picnics with Cherry and the boys, but they had never been allowed to take the boat out alone and they did not know the waterways and their hidden dangers. I tried to think of all the places we had visited where they might have gone in their flight and it was not until I had made fruitless searches in half a dozen likely spots that I decided to penetrate deeper into the Fens and enlist the help of Moggy and Nampy.

As I guided the boat in and out of the bends of the river, I don't know how many times I seemed to see two small bodies floating face upward in the muddy water or suffocated in the green slime of a peat bog so that it was all the more maddening as I glided up to the reed-thatched hut to hear gales of boyish laughter mingled with Moggy's gruff tones.

I reached the bank, tied the mooring rope and strode purposefully up the path. The two boys were seated one either side of the wooden box that served Moggy for a table while he doled out heaped spoonfuls from a steaming iron cauldron.

Jethro looked up at me with sparkling eyes. 'We're going to

have "sparrow pudden",' he said. 'Moggy says it's what every proper Fenman has for breakfast.'

The sight was too much after the worry of the last few hours. I could willingly have boxed their ears, both of them. I said with exasperation, 'I hope it chokes you! What do you mean by running off like that? A fine dance you've led us!'

'There en't nuthin' like my "sparrow pudden" for puttin' strength into growin' boys,' said Moggy placidly. 'Now you eat that up and don't leave none while I have a word with Mr Oliver.'

The boys gave me a quick look and then went to work with their horn spoons and I had to turn away to hide a smile. I'd eaten 'sparrow pudden' myself and the dish of little birds cooked with a bit of beef, a slice of bacon and a thick suet crust is a rare treat for a hungry lad.

Moggy took my arm and drew me out of earshot. 'I found 'em a mile or more away, up river, and in a poor old state,' he whispered. 'The little 'un there, he's got weals on his back thick as my finger. I've put goose grease on 'em, rubbed it well in and never a squeak out of 'im. 'Tiddn't right to treat a nipper like that, 'tiddn't decent.'

'No, Moggy, it isn't, but the boy was disobedient and his father is strict.'

'My old Dad used to take 'is belt to me when I sauced him, but 'tweren't vicious like that.'

'I've got to take them back.'

'Aye, that's what I thought. They arst me if I could tell 'em the way to the sea, talked about gettin' on a ship, poor little beggars, so I brought 'em back 'ere first with a mind to send Nampy to you.'

'It was good of you, Moggy.'

'That little lad, 'tiddn't 'is fault as 'is father is what 'e is. There's bad days comin', en't there, Mr Oliver? Jake said so afore he went away and I hear what's talked of when I go about. Old Lord Aylsham, your father that was, he wouldn't never have let us be driven out of our homes.'

'No, he wouldn't, but it's not my land any longer, Moggy. It belongs to my uncle.'

'Aye, I know that and I know about him too, more than he thinks for.' Moggy's face darkened but I didn't want to be drawn into deeper argument when I could offer no solution. I turned back to the boys.

'Come along now,' I said briskly. 'Eat up. We must go home. I've wasted enough time on you as it is.'

Jethro put down his spoon and stared straight in front of him. 'I'm not going home.'

'Now that's foolish,' I put my hand on his shoulder. 'Listen, Jethro, I know your Papa punished you and it hurt and you thought it unjust, but you did disobey him. He had forbidden you to bring Ben into the house but you did, and it made him angry.'

'It were my fault,' broke in Ben suddenly. 'Mam said I shouldn't go but I wanted to, and then I ran away because I was afraid.'

'I'm glad you did. He might have killed you,' said Jethro sombrely.

I noticed then how very pale he was, dark shadows under his eyes and there was a thin weal across Ben's cheek where the blood had dried, and yet what could I do? I said quietly, 'You mustn't say that.'

'Why not if it is true? I think he wants to kill me too. He hates me now because he has Alyne instead of Mama and he doesn't want to be reminded of her.'

The huge dark eyes that looked up at me were curiously adult. Then the slow tears formed and rolled silently down his face. I gripped his shoulder hard. 'It will be all right, Jethro. I shall go back with you.'

'You won't let him hurt Ben?'

'No. Ben shall go home to Thatchers.'

'There now,' said Moggy cheerfully. 'That's all settled. You go off with Mr Oliver and he shall bring you back another day and I'll take you to see my eel traps. Fine big fellers I catch, thick as your arm.'

Jethro got slowly to his feet. 'I'd like that. Thank you, Moggy, for the "sparrow pudden". It was lovely. Come on, Ben.'

The boys sat huddled together in the boat saying little as I rowed them back and I wondered how I should tackle Justin. I was still undecided when we reached Ravensley. I sent Ben to Thatchers with a scribbled message for Clarissa and walked up to the house with Jethro.

The boy looked white and exhausted and I was glad when Cherry came running down the stairs and met us in the hall.

'I've been watching for you,' she said. 'Thank goodness, you found them.' She put her arm round the little boy. 'We'll go and find Hattie, shall we? She has been so worried about you.'

I said, 'Where is Justin?'

'In the library and he knows,' she whispered. 'I don't envy you.'

I walked straight into the room without knocking and said abruptly, 'I've brought your son back to you.'

He looked up from his desk with his mocking smile. 'I suppose I ought to be grateful but there was really no need. He would have come back when he was hungry.'

'He could also have been drowned. Have you thought of that or don't you care?'

'Is there any necessity to be melodramatic?'

'There is every necessity when you thrash a child of eleven merely for your own pleasure.'

'What the devil do you mean by that? The boy was deliberately disobedient and insolent into the bargain so I punished him. What right have you to interfere? He is my son.'

'He is also my half-brother.'

For an instant I saw his face change, then he pulled himself together. 'Who told you that?'

'Does it matter? I'm right, aren't I? My mother didn't die in Rome. She left my father and went to you. Why? In God's name, why?'

He did not answer at once and when he did, he kept his eyes fixed on the papers in front of him. 'It was a long time ago. If you must know, we both wanted her, your father and I, but she chose Robert, quiet, sensible, trustworthy Robert . . .'

'Because she loved him.'

'No!' He brought his fist down violently on the desk. 'No! It was I she loved always . . . but she was afraid . . .'

'Why should she be afraid?'

'God knows! I was young. I'd not lived like a saint, what young man does? They lied to her about me and she was only eighteen.'

I had guessed already and yet still found it hard to accept. 'What did you do?'

He shrugged his shoulders. 'What does it matter now? I was

crazy for a while. There were times when I wanted to kill her and Robert too.'

'Were you lovers? Is that why grandfather sent you away?'

He smiled to himself. 'Perhaps.'

I remembered the whispers, the servants talking. It had meant little to the small boy I was then. There was so much I didn't know. 'Was she happy with you in India?'

His eyes shifted. 'What is happiness? She sickened in the heat. She was never well after Jethro was born. What point is there in talking of this now?'

So it had all been for nothing. It was my mother I was sorry for. I said slowly, 'She must have told you that grandfather was dead. Why didn't you come back then?'

'I could not have Ravensley . . . and her.'

'Did my father know?'

'Maybe. I found a way to write to her, but not at once. She never told him. Perhaps he guessed.'

His air of indifference enraged me. I was seized with a sudden vivid memory of my father, big and fair, behind his littered desk, the two spaniels sprawled on the rug beside him, and myself standing, awkward and shamefaced, while he tried to frown, reprimanding me for some boyish prank. And now in that same chair sat his brother, the man who had disinherited me, had robbed Cherry of the happy days she might have spent with her mother, taken Alyne from me and took a wilful pleasure in tormenting an unhappy innocent child. I leaned across the desk.

'You deliberately wrecked his life and hers and now you're punishing her son because he can never be your heir, because it maddens you to know that if Alyne doesn't bear you a child, then Ravensley will come back to me, to Robert's son. It's like a disease, isn't it, a corroding sickness because you still can't be sure I shall not be master here when you are dead!'

He said coldly, 'What can you know of me or my life?'

I don't know what possessed me that morning, but I couldn't stop. I went on hammering at him.

'I don't know what happened here, twenty years ago or why you persecute the Starlings with such venom, but one thing I do know, out on the Fens there is a man whose hatred burns in him like a fire.

What did you do to set such a flame alight? He has tried to kill you once and failed, but he could try again. I'm warning you.'

'How do you know?' he said through dry lips.

'That's not important, but I do know.'

'If it is true, then he should be found and taken up.'

'Try it. Send the soldiers hunting through the wilderness. Perhaps your engineers will drive him out with the birds and the wild creatures when they invade Greatheart, and then who knows what will happen. The Fens have a way of taking their own revenge.'

A tremor seemed to shake him and yet I knew he was no coward. It was something else, some inner torment that shook him, then he threw back his head and laughed, harshly, mirthlessly.

'My God, Oliver, you talk like that crazy old fool up in the attics. Do you think I care a damn for you or for your wild man hidden in the marshes? And you'll not have Ravensley. I'll make sure of that. Alyne is young and she is mine, d'you hear? Mine. There is time yet to breed half a dozen sons.'

We were glaring at one another, only the width of the desk between us, and it was he who lowered his eyes first. He leaned back in the chair with an impatient gesture.

'Enough of this foolery. You may care to know that I'm arranging for Jethro to be sent to school in the autumn.'

'Perhaps that's best. At least the boy will be away from you and have friends of his own.'

He tossed a paper across the desk, reverting dryly to the business of the day as if I were no more than his clerk. 'There's a petition sent in by the millmen. They want to know what will happen to them when the engines are installed. You'd better deal with it. Perhaps some of them could be trained to work the new machinery.'

It was the first concession he had ever made so perhaps I had won some sort of victory. I took up the paper silently and went out of the room.

Alyne came out of the dining room as I crossed the hall. In her pale green morning gown with her long hair tied back with a ribbon, she reminded me of the drift of daffodils coming into bloom under the trees of the orchard.

She said, 'Cherry tells me that you have brought Jethro back. We are very grateful.'

'I'm not sure Justin is.'

'He hates to admit to any kind of weakness.' She raised her eyes to mine. 'I did try to stop him, you know, but sometimes he . . . it's as if a fury possesses him.'

I took her hand drawing her towards me. 'Are you frightened of him?'

'Why do you ask?'

'It was something Cherry said.'

'About me?'

'No, about herself. Alyne, if he should . . . if anything should happen to frighten you, you would let me help, wouldn't you? You would come to me.'

She looked at me oddly as if it were not I she saw but some distant and unfathomable future. 'If ever I were to feel like that, then I don't think anyone could help me.'

I was still holding her hand when Justin came to the door of the library. I felt his eyes run over us and deliberately did not move away.

He said, 'I thought you'd gone already, Oliver. Come in, my dear, I want you.'

'I'm coming.'

She withdrew her hand quietly and went to him leaving me staring after her, aware of some deep trouble, and yet still miles away from the truth.

3

I was kept so busy during the spring of 1832 that I never once thought about Sir Peter Berkeley's proposal of a match between Cherry and his son so that when the question did arise, it was quite unexpected and in the event disastrous. There had been trouble when the engineers began work on the steam engine. I never really got to the bottom of who was responsible since I had spoken with the millmen, most of whom I had known since a boy, and they had been reasonably content with my pledge that their jobs would be secured to them. But I had my suspicions. That vengeful spirit that waited for any opportunity to harm Justin Aylsham would have found it easy to arouse opposition. There was a spirit of faction abroad as Jake had written to me, a restlessness, a dissatisfaction, especially among the younger and more thinking men. Up in London the government had at last been driven to bring in a bill of reform but it had been rejected twice already and each time a wave of futile anger seemed to surge through the whole country. Up in Norfolk ricks had been set on fire, the house of one of our acquaintances had been burned to the ground, and here on the Fens the foundations for installing the new machinery had no sooner been dug than the whole place had been wrecked, the timber stolen and the new engine smashed.

Justin was furious and in this instance rightly so. He stormed and threatened and would have had half the villagers arrested on suspicion alone if I had not pointed out that to do so would only bring more violence.

We were standing together looking down at the scene of devastation. 'I'll not be beaten by a bunch of vandals who can think only of destruction,' he said in a bitter rage. 'I shall go on with it if it takes the rest of my life and every penny I possess,' or all that Joshua Rutland will loan you, I thought cynically, wondering what that shrewd old man would have to say. Justin turned to me, the eyes in the sallow face hard as blue stones. 'Someone was responsible for this, someone organized these wretches . . . who, Oliver, who? Don't pretend you don't know, you who are so thick with these rascals.'

'It could be one of a dozen,' I replied levelly, remembering Moggy's stony face, Nampy's sullen silence. 'I've questioned them closely but the Fenmen are loyal, they cling together whatever they may privately think and they are united against the stranger.'

'Meaning me, I presume,' he said flatly. 'I was born and bred among them and yet I am still the foreigner. I don't believe you. You have had a free hand in the months I have been away.'

'Have you any fault to find? We have never been more prosperous.'

'I'll grant you that,' he said grudgingly, 'but there is another matter.' His eyes narrowed. 'What have you done with Jake Starling?'

His question took me by surprise and I replied unguardedly. 'He is no longer here.'

'So he *has* been hiding out on the Fens,' he said triumphantly. 'I knew it. You have protected him ever since his escape.'

'If you know so much,' I said quickly, 'then you will know also that he went away from here months ago.'

'Then where is he? There has been ugly rioting on the Suffolk border. When I was in Ely last week, I heard something of it. There are agitators moving from county to county stirring up dissension. Is he one of those?'

'Why ask me? The last knowledge I had of him was that he had left the country. By now he will be free of you and of the law.'

'I hope for his sake and yours that that is true,' he said dryly, 'because if he has been responsible for any part of this, I swear I'll have him by the ears and this time he'll hang for it.'

I was disturbed though I would not let him see it. Somehow I must get a warning to Jake, but I had no certainty of where he was. The one thing of which I was absolutely sure was that whoever had caused riot and disorder, it was not Jake. He had learned the futility of that last year as I had.

The disgruntled engineers started work again and it was during a mood of depression that Clarissa persuaded me to take time off and attend the spring races at Newmarket with her and Cherry.

It was a lovely April day, the sky like shot silk with scudding white clouds and the turf a vivid green under the brilliant sunshine. The sight of the horses, the jockeys in their brightly coloured silks, the cheerful greetings of friends, all combined to lighten my spirits. The Colonel was in his element. With Clarissa on one arm and Alyne on the other, he was strolling in the paddock, explaining the intricacies of form, placing their bets for them and enjoying himself hugely. I only hoped he would not plunge too deeply. The burden of the debt to Joshua Rutland hung over me heavily at times and I was only too glad that neither he nor his son were there.

Cherry was being escorted everywhere by Hugh Berkeley and appeared to be taking pleasure in his company. She looked happier than I had seen her for many weeks and I hoped that she had begun to put Jake out of her mind. After all she was still very young, I argued to myself, perhaps I had been worrying too much over nothing.

It was during our picnic lunch that I had a curious conversation with Colonel Fenton. I was leaning against the wheel of the carriage watching Alyne with the familiar dull ache, aware how much she had changed from the girl I had loved for so long. There was a brittle quality about her, a feverish gaiety that I had never noticed before. She was surrounded by a group of young men, swarming around her like wasps around a honey jar, and she moved from one to the other with a glancing look, a provoking smile, a touch here and there, so that I saw how they closed in on her and the desire that flamed in their eyes.

The Colonel brought a bottle of champagne and filled my glass and his own. He nodded casually towards Alyne. 'That young woman is riding for a fall,' he remarked. 'There'll be a sad reckoning before long if she is not careful.'

'Oh come, it's not Alyne's fault if men show how much they want her.'

'It is if she lets them see too plainly how much she enjoys it.' He sipped his wine thoughtfully. 'I doubt if that dried-up stick of a husband of hers is much good to any young woman.'

'What on earth has put that idea into your head?'

'I have my eyes, haven't I? There's something about her. She may not realize it but she's asking for a man.'

'Nonsense,' I said uncomfortably.

'There's a spice of the devil there. I wouldn't mind showing her a thing or two myself given half a chance.'

'You? Oh come now, Colonel . . .'

'You needn't look like that, my dear Oliver. I'm still capable of giving a woman pleasure,' he said dryly, 'only if I did, I should have Jess to deal with, to say nothing of you. Pity, but there it is. Take a look at Justin. If ever a man looked like murder, he does.'

It was the second time it had been pointed out to me and it affected me unpleasantly. I thought that he exaggerated, but there was something unpredictable about Justin, a hidden violence. I had always been aware of it, yet surely he was deeply fond of Alyne. Of her feelings, I had never been sure, and today there was something about her that disturbed me, a wantonness as if she flaunted her body deliberately simply to taunt him. It spoiled the enjoyment of the day. I turned away from it and went in search of my wife.

Clarissa and I had always shared a passion for horses even if just now we were unable to indulge it. It delighted me to see how happy she was.

I said, 'Hold out your hands.'

'Whatever for?'

'Don't argue. Do as you're told,' and into them I poured fifty golden guineas.

'Oliver, where did it come from?'

'I didn't pick a pocket. I made a bet and it won.'

'Do you know what I should like above everything?' she asked looking up at me and then putting the money carefully into her reticule.

'What would you like?' I said indulgently.

'I'd like to own a racehorse of my own.'

I laughed aloud. 'I'm afraid that won't buy you one,' I said teasingly. 'You know, Clary, there's quite a lot of your Papa in you. You're a born gambler.'

'Perhaps that's why I married you,' she said with a touch of spirit. 'Papa is enjoying himself so much. Thank you, Oliver, thank you for everything.'

'Silly! What is there to thank me for? Wait until I buy you that racehorse.' I bent my head to kiss her lightly on the lips.

'Not here. People will see.'

'To hell with them. It's a poor thing if a man can't kiss his own wife when he pleases.'

Then Cherry was there laughing at us. 'It's not at all the fashion, Oliver. You should be kissing someone else's wife,' and we were all three very merry together.

Maybe it was a good thing that we didn't realize it was going to be the last carefree day for a long time. It began that very evening though at the time I was not aware of it. Cherry came back to Thatchers to sup with us. Afterwards when we sat by the fire, she picked up Prickle, fondling her ears and not looking at us.

'Hugh Berkeley asked me to marry him today,' she said.

'The devil he did! What was your answer?'

'No, of course. How can I possibly marry him when I love Jake?'

Clarissa and I exchanged a glance and I said, 'He's a good man, Puss, a kind man.'

She moved impatiently. 'I know that, and he'll be rich when his father dies and he can give me a fine establishment and I'll be Lady Berkeley one day. Alyne keeps telling me that and I don't want any of it.'

Clarissa said, 'Has Sir Peter spoken to your uncle about it?'

She shrugged her shoulders. 'I suppose so. Hugh is so very proper. He'd never do anything of which his father didn't approve.'

I leaned forward and put my hand on hers. 'Don't be rash, Cherry. Give yourself time. Think about it. It could be an excellent thing for you.'

'How can you say that, you of all people?' She pulled her hand away, squeezing Prickle so hard that she squeaked in protest. 'I know Uncle Justin would be glad to be rid of me. He wants the house to himself and Alyne, but I'm not going to marry a man I don't love simply to please him.'

Even then I didn't understand fully the strength of her will nor how much the friction had grown between her and Justin.

The next few weeks were filled with all kinds of problems including a great deal of trouble with the delivery of materials for the new installation. Justin asked me to go north to Lincoln to contact the suppliers and I came back very late one night, exhausted by a long ride through the pouring rain. Clarissa met me with an anxious face.

'There has been trouble at Ravensley,' she said as she helped me off with my riding coat.

'Now what's happened?' I asked wearily.

'It's Cherry, Oliver. It seems that your uncle is insisting that she agrees to marry Hugh. Alyne told me. I think to do her justice she tried to persuade him to be gentle, but he went into one of his rages and he has locked Cherry into her room until she does as he commands.'

'But he can't behave like that. This is not the Middle Ages. What the devil does he think he is, some domestic tyrant? It's utterly ridiculous. I had better go up there, I suppose.'

'Oh not tonight. You're worn out and it's late already. Besides it may only make matters worse. Better to wait until the morning. He may have calmed down by then and Cherry too.'

I hesitated, but I ached with fatigue after a harassing day and the thought of food and a warm fire was very tempting.

'Very well. I suppose you're right. I'll go first thing tomorrow.' Nothing warned me that so simple and obvious a decision was the wrong one.

We were awakened soon after dawn by a thunderous knocking at the door and remembering that other time when Jethro had run away, I was out of bed instantly. Before I reached the bottom of the stairs, Justin had stormed into the house.

'Where the devil is she?' he was shouting. 'Where have you hidden her?'

I prevaricated. 'Who, for God's sake? What are you talking about?'

'As if you didn't know! Your sister walked out of the house last night. She took a horse from the stables and some of her clothes. Where has she gone? That's what I want to know. Where?'

'I don't know any more than you do and now I'm asking something in my turn. What have you done to a child like that to drive her out of her own home?'

'Child?' he repeated derisively. 'She's an obstinate, ungrateful, vicious young woman. All I've done has been for her own good and she has chosen to defy me.'

'I would remind you that you are speaking of my sister.'

'Sister or not, she shall suffer for this,' his face contorted into rage. 'If she has gone to that damned rogue, if it's Jake Starling who is at the bottom of this, then I'll have him up for abduction of a minor. I swear to God he'll not escape me a second time so you had better find her . . . and quickly too.'

He flung himself out of the house and I let him go, knowing that it was imperative I reach them before he did for I had little doubt that Cherry had gone to Jake, but where . . . where, in God's name?

Mrs Starling, half dressed, had come out of the kitchen and I gripped hold of her. 'You must tell me. Have you had any word from Jake in the last few weeks, a message of any kind?'

'Aye, sir, I have, a day or so ago, but you were away and he said not to tell . . .'

I shook her roughly. 'It could be a matter of his life, don't you understand? I must know.'

'He was going to some place t'other side of Ramsay . . . out on Bury Fen it is . . . a tinker Moggy knows, name of Jim Dale.'

'Would Miss Cherry be aware of this?'

She shook her head hopelessly. 'She asked me often enough, but I minded what you told me and never said a word, but Ben, he knows, he could have said something.'

Ben and Jethro, and I could guess how Cherry would worm it out of the boys. 'All right, Mrs Starling, thank you. That's a great help.'

I went upstairs to dress and Clarissa said, 'I heard what Justin was saying. Do you think that Cherry will have run to Jake?'

'How can I be sure and yet it is the kind of mad notion that would come into her head.'

'Does Mrs Starling know where he is?'

'She has told me something but God knows if he will still be there. I must go now as quickly as possible. I have to bring her back and warn Jake. Justin is like a madman when he is thwarted.'

'I wish I could come with you.'

'Much better not, my dear. It will be necessary to ride fast and go by a route they're not likely to follow. Please God let me get there in time.'

I avoided Ely taking a slightly longer detour across the open Fen and urging Rowan as fast as I dared. It had begun to rain again and the track was rough and slippery with mud. Now and again I wondered if I was on a wild goose chase. Perhaps Cherry had run out of the house on a crazy impulse, had realized her folly by now and had already returned . . . and yet, knowing her, I doubted it. I watched the road but met few travellers on such an abominable day. It was near noon when I reached Ramsay at last, Rowan sweating, and the water dripping from my sodden hat. It is a small town, the houses mostly grouped near the Abbey ruins. I passed the old portal and saw the words engraved in the stone by the Black Monks a thousand years ago . . . 'Take heed, watch and pray, for you know not when the time is.' The message struck me ominously and I urged the mare on. Outside the town I met a man driving a small flock of miserably wet sheep and I leaned from the saddle.

'Do you know a tinker, name of Jim Dale?'

He stared at me glumly. The Fenman can be dour towards a stranger. He nodded slowly. 'Aye, it's half a mile further but I don't reckon as it'll do you any good. If you've pots to mend, you're out o' luck. He en't there, leastways he weren't t'other morning.'

'Never mind. I'll go on. He may have returned.'

He turned to stare after me as I drove the tired mare forward, slithering over sticky mud and then down into a hollow where, through a thicket of tangled scrub, I could see the rude hut and a shed close by where doubtless he did his tinkering. It had no door and as I slid from the saddle, I noticed that a pony had been tethered out of the rain and guessed that Cherry must be somewhere near.

I led Rowan into the shelter, then went quickly towards the hut and lifted the latch. She was huddled on a low stool by a dully burning peat fire. She looked up as the door opened, then jumped to her feet backing away towards the wall.

'I'm not going back, Oliver, I'm not. I'm not going to be forced into marrying Hugh.'

There was a note of hysteria in her voice and I said soothingly,

'All right, Puss, all right. No one is going to force you to do anything.'

'How did you know I was here?'

'Never mind about that now. Where is Jake?'

She relaxed a little and came back towards the fire. 'He has gone into Ramsay.'

'Why?'

'I don't know. He said he had to go. It was important. There were men he had to see.'

'When is he coming back?'

'Soon. About noon. He promised. When he does, we are going away,' she said with a touch of defiance. Then wearily she put up a hand to push back her disordered hair. 'Is it noon yet? I seem to have been waiting for hours and hours.'

'Poor Pussie.'

I stretched out a hand and drew her towards me. She resisted at first, then leaned against me, shivering a little, and I could see the traces of tears on her cheeks. I knew so well how she had run to him in a fine flourish of defiance, expecting to be carried away, rescued from the ogre like the heroine of a romance, but life is never like that. It is full of hard, uncomfortable practicalities and Jake must have been at his wits' end to know what to do for the best. But first things first. Cherry must be persuaded to go back with me to Thatchers and with the money I had brought with me, Jake must be got away into safety, down south perhaps where he could escape out of the country.

I could not decide whether to go out and look for him or wait until he returned and while I hesitated, Cherry gave a sudden exclamation.

'What is it?'

'Oliver, look! There are men coming.'

She had gone to the window and pushed back the wooden shutter. I drew her away so that she should not be seen and peered out myself. Just topping the rise came four horsemen. Through a misty blur of rain I recognized my uncle leading them, then a short stocky man whom I knew by sight. Justin must have forced the Captain of the Militia to accompany him. Behind them came one of his soldiers, a shambling fellow carrying a gun loosely across his saddle bow and beside him rode Ram Lall.

'He's got Ben with him,' whispered Cherry. 'Ram is holding him in front of him. Oh God, what could they have done to him to make him tell them about Jake?'

It didn't bear thinking of, but there were other things more urgent. I said quickly, 'Was Jake on foot? Which way will he come?'

She shook her head. 'I don't know, but he wouldn't take the pony.'

I couldn't think what to do for the best. They were a little way off, but if I went out of the hut, they must see me and whether I took Rowan and made a dash for it or went on foot, they were bound to follow for there was little cover anywhere on this bare fenland. The most I could hope to do would be to draw them off the scent and give Jake a chance to get away when he came back.

I opened the door with this intention, then everything seemed to happen at once. Jake's tall figure appeared on the top of the ridge and he began to stride down into the hollow towards the hut. I called a warning. He looked up, saw me, then must have noticed the horsemen and grasped the situation. He began to run back across the moor. At the same time Ben screamed out to his brother. The Captain was shouting, 'Stop, stop, I tell you, stop in the King's name!' But Jake did not pause. The soldier raised his musket. Ben screamed again and struggled to free himself. The horses seemed to cannon into each other and the gun went off. It was a chance in a thousand. I doubt if the wretched militiaman really meant to shoot, but Jake seemed to stop in mid air. Then slowly, very slowly, he took a few staggering paces, spun round and fell forward.

Cherry pushed past me. She ran across the grass, stumbling and picking herself up again. She fell on her knees beside him. When I reached her, she was trying to lift him. He groaned and rolled over on to his back.

'Gently,' I said, 'gently.'

'He's not really hurt. He can't be,' she was saying frantically. 'He can't be. It's not possible.'

There was not much blood, only the ragged burn where the bullet had gone through the worn coat. I raised him a little, opening his shirt.

He muttered, 'Oliver . . . I'm glad . . . you're here . . .' A little froth of blood bubbled from his lips. I knew little of surgery, but I saw where the stain spread. If the ball had pierced the lung, no doctor, not even God Himself, could save him.

'Oh Jake, Jake dearest,' Cherry looked at me desperately. 'There must be something we can do, there must be . . .'

I had my arm under his head and held him against me. I said, 'Hold on, old fellow, you'll be all right. We'll get you inside . . .' Useless futile words, trying to sound confident while all the time something screamed inside me that a man couldn't die like that, so quickly, not a strong man like Jake, it was absurd, it couldn't happen.

His face had an ashen look. His lips were moving but I couldn't hear. I bent closer.

'I tried,' he muttered, 'I did try . . . but it was no good . . .'

Cherry had hold of his hand. She was pressing it against her mouth. His eyes opened wide and were fixed on her. He tried to smile and couldn't. His lips formed her name but there was no sound, only a long sigh, and his life went with it.

'Is the fellow dead?'

Justin stood looking down at us. Beside him the Captain wore a worried frown.

'We never intended it, my lord. Most unfortunate. We wanted to take him alive. It's what we needed, you know, to make an example of him . . .'

'Your trigger-happy friend has done our work too well for us,' said my uncle sardonically.

Ben burst through them and fell down beside Jake. 'They made me tell,' he sobbed. 'They said it would be better for you, that you wouldn't have to live in hiding any more, I thought, I thought . . .'

'Don't Ben,' I said gently, 'don't.'

Justin put a hand on Cherry's shoulder. 'Come along, my dear. I'll take you home.'

She sprang away from him as if she had been stung. 'Murderer! You wanted him dead and now you have killed him. I'll never go back with you, never. I'd rather die!'

I was on my feet now. I said, 'She's my sister. I think you had better leave her to me.'

We faced one another while the rain still fell on Jake's dead

face. Then Justin shrugged his shoulders. 'Very well, if that's what
you wish. Much good may it do you.'

He walked away and Cherry suddenly came to life. She was
screaming at him, her voice cracking. 'You think you're God, that
you can do what you like with people, but you can't. They despise
you for it, all of them, Alyne too, more than anyone. She loathes
you as much as I do . . .'

She sprang after him and to my horror I saw she must have
drawn the clasp knife from Jake's belt. I moved fast, but Justin
was quicker. He swung round, catching her wrist and bending it
back until the weapon dropped from her fingers.

He said with icy contempt, 'What do you think to do? Murder
me?'

The Captain and his fool of an assistant had turned to stare
with greedy curiosity. I said quickly, 'Let her be. Haven't you done
enough? Can't you see she is distressed?'

But Justin did not move. His fingers dug into her flesh and he
said with a deadly intensity, 'Never say such a thing about Alyne
again, d'you hear me?'

Cherry had gone very white, but she outfaced him, leaning forward and whispering. 'It's true, I swear it is true . . .'

'It's a damnable lie.' He released her, throwing her violently
away from him. Then he turned and walked back to where Ram
Lall held the horses, the others shambling after him sheepishly.

Cherry was trembling. 'I hate him, I hate him,' she sobbed. 'I
wish I had killed him.'

'A lot of use that would have been. Now pull yourself together
and help me.'

A touch of harshness seemed to be the best way of preventing a
breakdown and temporarily it succeeded. Jake was tall, but very
spare, and I was strong. With Cherry and Ben helping, I hoisted
him over my shoulder and carried him back to the hut out of the
drenching pitiless rain.

I did not want to leave her alone with only Ben for company
while I went into Ramsay, but I could not take him away and neither could I abandon him. Something had to be done. Then I was
saved from the necessity by Jim Dale's return. He must have
watched the whole incident from some hidden spot, anxious not to
be involved, and now he crept furtively across the grass and slid

quietly through the door. The tinker was a small man with a nut-brown face and a wiry angular body. He looked down at Jake with a sombre anger.

' 'Tiddn't right, Mister, 'tiddn't fair. He were a good man. He had them listenin' this morning like never was. They'd have followed him anywhere and there en't many like that these days.'

Cherry gave a stifled sob and he looked at her curiously before he turned to me. 'What's to do now, Mister?'

I was not going to leave Jake to the mercy of the parish. I would not let him be thrust into a pauper's grave. He should come back to Ravensley where Starlings had lain beside Aylshams for close on three hundred years.

The tinker's eyes brightened at the sight of the gold. He promised to see that the body was carried the twenty-odd miles to Ravensley on the following day.

'And there'll be a tidy number walking with it, Mister, to see him put away right. He was well thought on.'

It was poor consolation and yet I was glad of it.

The rain had stopped at last by the time we were ready to leave, but a wind had sprung up, the sky was still leaden and everywhere was dripping with moisture. It was one of those days when spring seems to have gone into hiding and the Fens look at their worst. I was worried about Cherry, but there was nothing I could do but get her back to Thatchers as quickly as possible on our wearied horses. She was quiet and apathetic as I lifted her into the saddle. Then I took Ben up in front of me and we rode back in silence.

It was evening when we reached home, the light beginning to fade. Clarissa must have been on the watch for she came hurrying out of the house and put her arms around Cherry as I helped her from the saddle.

'Oh you poor child! How wet you are and how chilled. Come in quickly.'

At the touch of sympathy, Cherry gave a little moaning cry and collapsed against her, weeping so bitterly that Clarissa looked at me questioningly above the bent head.

I could not bring myself to say it aloud. I shook my head and led the horses to the stables, unsaddling and rubbing them down myself as if the physical labour somehow prevented me from thinking and kept grief at bay.

Ben had run to his mother and I thanked God that I had been spared the wretched duty of breaking the news to her myself.

When I went into the house, the room was empty. Clarissa was still upstairs with Cherry. I had eaten nothing all that day but the thought of food nauseated me. I poured a glass of brandy and took it to the fire, watching the steam rise from my soaked breeches and caring nothing for it. The numbness was passing and the agony had begun, like the blood flowing back into a frozen limb. I swallowed the brandy and poured another. The spirit warmed my empty stomach but did nothing to deaden the sharpness of the pain. There was bitter regret too and a feeling of guilt from which I couldn't escape.

When Clarissa came back, I was sitting on the settle, watching the glowing embers and remembering, remembering far too much. She moved so quietly that I did not hear her until she was beside me, her hand on my shoulder.

'Your coat is wet through. You should take it off.'

'He's dead,' I said violently. 'Murdered by a stupid damned fool for nothing. It's so useless, so futile. What is God thinking about to allow such an idiotic damnable waste of life!'

'I know,' she said and slid round until she could kneel in front of me. 'I do know.'

But I could only think of myself and my overwhelming misery. 'No, you don't,' I said brutally. 'How could you? You never knew him as I did. In your secret heart you're glad. You always wanted me to be rid of him.'

I saw the startled pain in her eyes and didn't care as if in hurting her, I was somehow helping to assuage my own wretchedness.

'That's not true, Oliver, you know it is not true.'

I hated myself for what I was doing to her and yet could not bring myself to say so. I looked away from her. 'Is Cherry all right?'

'She is in bed. I've given her a hot drink and a soothing draught to help her sleep. She is terribly unhappy and saying all kinds of wild things, poor child.' She paused a moment. 'She is terrified of Justin and what he may do to her, but when I told her that she could stay here with us, she said, "Supposing I have a baby."'

'Oh God, not that too.'

'Don't be angry with her.'

'Angry? For heaven's sake, how can I be angry?'

'She's very afraid, but very proud too. I couldn't destroy it. I think the fact that they loved one another, just once, is all she has and she clings to it. We are going to keep her with us, aren't we, Oliver?'

'That's for you to say. There may be difficulties with Justin.'

'Then that's settled, she shall stay here.' She stood up. 'Take off your wet clothes and I'll bring you some food.'

'I don't want anything.'

'Oliver, please . . .'

'For Christ's sake, get out of here and leave me alone.'

'Very well, if that's what you want.'

She went quietly out of the room and I sat on alone until the fire had died to ashes. Grief was like an iron band round my chest that nothing would ease and at last, chilled and stiff, I got up and went upstairs. As I passed the door to Clarissa's room, she called to me softly.

I paused uncertainly and then went in. The candle was still burning. I crossed to the bed. 'What is it? Do you want me to fetch you something?'

She looked up at me and I saw the tears glistening on her lashes. 'I loved him too. Please don't shut me out, Oliver, please. Let me share it with you.'

I was so weary, I could scarcely stand. I sat heavily on the bed. 'I blame myself. I was thinking all along of Cherry and not of him. I should have forced him to go away, leave this cursed country. There was so much he wanted to do, so much he had it in him to accomplish, and now it has all gone.'

'Not gone, not entirely, not while you are still here.'

I stared at her. 'What can I do?'

'Don't think of that now. Come to bed.'

The hand that touched mine was warm, but I would not yield. 'I shouldn't . . . I'm not fit . . .'

But she went on, her face very gentle in the flickering flame of the candle. 'I've been lying here thinking of when we were children. Jake could be so strong and yet so kind. We didn't realize it then, but do you remember? It was always Jake who carried Cherry when she was tired and he once dived into the river to rescue her doll when she'd thrown it in out of temper . . .'

'Oh God!' I said, 'Oh God!' The iron band had shifted a little, something seemed to break inside me and I could not stop myself. At last I could let go. At last I could let grief have its way with me.

I woke very early. We had forgotten to draw the curtains and the brilliant light of a spring morning was pouring into the room. A solitary thrush sang its heart out in the hawthorn outside the window. The pain was still there and the coming day promised only further distress and yet I was comforted.

I looked down at Clarissa. Last night she had held me in her arms while I wept like a child and yet I was not ashamed. With one finger I traced the pure line of her cheek and then bent to kiss the half-opened mouth.

She stirred sleepily. 'Is it time to get up?'

'Not yet.'

I kissed her again and she turned to me with a little sigh. For the first time I felt the stir of a desire that was not lust, not the mere gratification of passion, but part of love, a love born out of companionship and living together and shared sorrow. I drew her towards me and she opened her eyes.

'What is it?'

'I love you.'

Her eyes widened and then she smiled. Her arms went round me and there was no barrier, no glass wall, only warmth and a giving and a fulfilment. I thought afterwards how strange it was that Jake's death marked the true beginning of our marriage.

Part Five

CLARISSA

1832–1833

How should I your true love know?
From another one?

> William Shakespeare

I

It was June when I knew with certainty that I was going to have a child and I hugged the knowledge to myself and told no one. Our happiness was too new, too fragile, too wonderful, to be threatened by anything, even this for which I'd hoped for so long. I was not at all sure whether Oliver would welcome the coming of a child. I wanted to hold it within me for a little longer, savouring the joy of it, a secret delight which presently I would share with him and find renewed pleasure in the sharing.

I liked to believe that I had conceived on that morning after Jake died, that morning when Oliver first said 'I love you', and out of grief and wretchedness we found our way to a new understanding, though afterwards I felt guilty about it in the face of Cherry's misery. But more than likely, I was being hopelessly romantic. My pregnancy could have come out of other nights, and days too, for these last few weeks it was as if we had suddenly been released from constraint and it might have been a long delayed honeymoon. There was an afternoon when he came in unexpectedly, still smelling faintly of leather and the stables, and found me in my shift. I was changing my gown because I had at last prevailed on Cherry to come visiting with me and he came and put an arm round my waist.

'Don't dress, my dear, not just yet. I like you like that.'

'Oh darling, not at this time in the day, it isn't decent.'

'Surely I can pleasure my wife any time I choose,' he said laughing, 'only not with my boots on,' and he sat on the bed and kicked them off before pulling me down beside him.

It was not really like Oliver, or like me for that matter, but I was marvellously happy and didn't care who knew it, any more than I did only a week ago when we rode out together one morning, exercising the horses. 'Getting ready for that racehorse of yours, Clary,' he said gaily. After eating a picnic lunch far out of sight of anyone but the birds, he pulled me into his arms and we made love with joy and abandon, lying on the grassy turf with the rich scent of the meadsweet all around us and I no longer wondered whether he had done the same with Alyne. It had no importance now.

Strangely enough it was Papa who first guessed about the baby. I was up at Copthorne one morning. He had not been too well and was out in the sunshine, lying back lazily in his chair with the two dogs at his feet and Prickle on his lap. He watched me energetically weeding the border. Aunt Jess's rheumatism had temporarily got the better of her.

He said suddenly, 'Tell me, child, are you breeding?'

I sat back on my heels. 'Really, Papa, do you have to be so coarse? I'm not a rabbit.'

'Don't be squeamish, girl. We're not in Mayfair now. Down here we call a spade a spade, or so Jess tells me. Are you?'

'Why do you think so?'

'It's a look you have. You're going about with the light of triumph in your eye, a complacency, I think I'd call it, a conscious superiority over us poor males. I remember seeing it in your mother when she was carrying you.'

'Oh Papa, you really are absurd. Why should I feel superior or triumphant?'

'God knows, but women do. So Oliver has done his duty by you and about time. Does he know?'

'Not yet, and don't tell him. I'll never forgive you if you do.'

'Wouldn't dream of it, my dear. When am I going to be a proud grandfather?'

'February, Dr Thorney thinks.'

'I hope I live to see it.'

'Of course you will. Don't talk like that.' But I looked at him anxiously. The last attack had been a severe one and he was thin and frail. I picked up my basket and he caught at my hand as I passed him. 'Are things better between you?'

'Yes.'

'And you're happy?'

'Very happy.' I bent to kiss him. 'And I'd be even happier if you would take care of yourself and not go racketing off to Ely.'

He grimaced. 'A man needs to break out sometimes. Take care, Clary, don't be too happy, don't tempt fate.'

'What utter nonsense. I don't know what you mean.'

But I knew he was thinking of my mother and that laughing challenge that had caused her death. To be wildly happy invites misfortune. That is what these country folk say and they have a hundred superstitions to avert the malignity of gods far older than the Christian one. I would have done well to heed them, to touch wood or make sure of throwing salt over my left shoulder when I spilled it, but I went on being gloriously content and never realized how easily and how quickly it could be shattered.

At first Oliver had wanted to cut himself off from his uncle, throw the stewardship back in his face. 'He can go to the devil any way he chooses,' he said violently after the day when Jake was buried and the sorrow and the weeping were over. It was I who persuaded him not to make the break.

'Too many depend on you. You are a mediator between them and Justin. You can't just turn your back. Jake didn't. In the end he sacrificed himself to what he believed in.'

I saw the pain in his eyes and knew I was right. I went on quickly, 'There's Cherry too. He owes a duty to her and you must see that he pays it. This can't last for ever. She's so young. One day she will want to marry.'

There were difficulties with Sir Peter Berkeley, but Oliver went to see him and smoothed it over. 'Let it wait for a little,' he said to him. 'You know how wayward young girls can be. Tell Hugh to be patient.'

I don't know what he and Justin said to one another, but he came back from Ravensley taut and tight-lipped so I did not question him and we went on as before only we no longer visited the big house in the evening. Jethro came sometimes with Hattie, but I scarcely saw Alyne and didn't mind at all except that I was worried about Cherry. She was not pregnant and I was thankful for her sake as well as ours. It would have created too many problems, but I think in a way she was disappointed. In the mood she was in, she wanted to flaunt her love in a fine spirit of bravado, but now there was nothing, only the ordinary round of everyday living and the grief of loss. She was listless and apathetic and I could interest her in nothing. Then something occurred that promised a solution.

One afternoon when I was taking tea at Copthorne, Aunt Jess said apropos of nothing, 'Your father has not been looking at all the thing this past month, Clarissa. I'm thinking of taking him to Bath.'

'I wish you would not talk about me as if I weren't here,' remarked my father tartly. 'I'm not a parcel to be taken anywhere and I detest Bath . . . a society of dreary dullards for ever groaning about their gout or their belly-aches.'

I hid a smile. 'I think it is an excellent idea, but why not make it Lyme Regis? You will have sea breezes there.'

'Ugh!' shuddered Papa. 'And what, pray, am I expected to do all day in that confounded dead-nor-alive hole? Climb up and down to that pernicious Cobb? I would much prefer Brighton if we have to go anywhere.'

'Very well, Brighton it shall be,' said Aunt Jess unexpectedly. 'Now I come to think of it, I've not been there since his late Majesty completed that monstrosity he called the Pavilion. Thank goodness, our present King has more sense than to indulge in such foolery.'

'William is too damned stupid to think of it,' muttered Papa disparagingly. 'I'll only go on one condition.'

'Oh, and what's that?' demanded Aunt Jess frowning at him.

'That we take Cherry with us. A pretty young girl is just what I need and she's been looking peaky lately. It will do both of us good. I can show her around.'

I was not at all sure how much Papa had guessed, but I think he had a pretty shrewd idea of what had happened.

Oliver was dubious when I told him about it. 'It'll cost a pretty penny and I'll bet you a guinea to a shilling that she won't go.'

'Done!' I said triumphantly since I had already thought of a way to persuade her. She had always had a friendly teasing relationship with my father and I pointed out to her that since I could not go myself, she would be doing me and Aunt Jess a favour by bearing him company and keeping a watchful eye on him. Cherry is one of those young women who want to feel of use, particularly just now.

I took her up to London to do some shopping, taking Hattie

with us. We enjoyed the change in a quiet way and Harry called on us at our lodging. I had not seen him for nearly a year and though he put on a show of being very cheerful and lighthearted, I thought I detected a note of uneasiness under the gay banter.

'Well, how's life treating you down on the Fens, Sis? With all due respect to Oliver, who no doubt is a fine fellow, it must be damned dull at times.'

'It's not dull at all,' said Cherry with sudden spirit. 'It's no more dull than a dreary round of balls, receptions and routs, with a great deal too much drinking, too much gambling, too many women and . . .'

'Here, hold on, that's not fair,' protested Harry, quite taken aback. 'I'm not guilty of all those vices at one and the same time. What have I done to deserve such a scolding?'

'Oh I hear about you,' said Cherry with a toss of the head. 'You're like Captain Rutland, all showy uniform and fine manners, and hollow as a straw man inside. Why don't you do something useful with your life, something to help others, make this country a better place to live in . . . ?' She suddenly flushed scarlet, bit her lip and hurried out of the room.

'Well, I'll be damned!' exclaimed Harry staring after her. 'What the devil has bitten Cherry? She's like one of those earnest young women who are forever preaching at you. I used to flatter myself that she rather favoured me.'

'She's not been well and she easily gets upset,' I said hastily. 'That's why Aunt Jess is taking her to Brighton with Papa.'

'Hm-m. I might run down there and see the old man while they are there. I'll get the Bull to loan me his dog cart. Might be able to take them about a little.'

I smiled to myself. 'I wish you would. Harry, do you see much of Captain Rutland?'

'On and off. He's changed, you know, Clary. Don't go about like he did. Quite the sobersides these days. Talks about getting out of the regiment and settling down.'

'Is he going to be married?'

'Not that I know of.' Harry grinned at me affectionately. 'Why? Are you sorry now that you gave him the go-by?'

'No, I'm not.'

I knew about Joshua Rutland's intention to buy Westley Manor, only held up because the owner was still abroad, and the thought of Bulwer Rutland living so near to us gave me an indefinable sense of uneasiness that no common sense was quite able to dispel.

We were away for a week and when I came back, I was hectically busy for a few days helping them pack and get ready to leave. Copthorne was to be left in Prue's charge and Aunt Jess had a list of instructions for her a yard long, ranging from giving the store cupboards a good turn-out to making sure the dogs didn't eat too much and scaring off the birds which were attacking the soft fruit.

It was a morning in July when at last the luggage was all strapped down and I saw them off in the carriage; and it was not until past five o'clock after a long session with Prue and Patty that I walked back to Thatchers.

It was one of those close heavy days when though there is no sun, the heat seems to bear down on you like a thick blanket. For the first time I was feeling my pregnancy. My head ached and I could feel the sweat running down my back under my light summer gown.

When I reached the house I walked round to the back. The Ravensley gig was standing in the courtyard and I was reminded of that other day two years ago when I had first come to Thatchers and seen Oliver with Justin. He had not come here since the business with Cherry and I was mildly surprised and curious. I looked through the window as I had done then and what I saw held me rooted to the spot, shocked and unbelievably wretched.

Alyne was standing in the middle of the room with Oliver behind her. I could not hear what they were saying, but while I watched, I saw him unhook the high neck of her muslin dress, gently touch her naked back and then bend his head to kiss it. I saw how she turned and looked up at him with a desperate appeal and how he drew her against him, his arms round her. Then I could not watch any longer. Perhaps if I had not been so weary, if I had been feeling more myself, I might have acted differently. I might have burst in on them, angry, indignant, demanding explanation. But I had come back looking forward to the joy of a quiet evening. Now, I had thought, now was the time to tell Oliver that we were to have a child, and it was like being hit in the face, all my happiness wiped out. I didn't stop to think. I just knew I had to get away for a little, anywhere so I wouldn't have to see his loving tenderness towards another woman.

I ran blindly down the track, taking no heed of where I was going and presently found myself by the river where a boat is always moored during the summer. I stepped into it with a feeling that to let myself drift for a while into the loneliness, the emptiness of the Fens would help me to come to terms with what had happened.

I paddled slowly. It was still oppressively hot and near to the banks or where the water flowed under a canopy of foliage, there were clouds of stinging gnats and irritating little flies.

I don't know how long I let myself drift, perhaps an hour or more, and it was not until I realized that I could not go on for ever, I must go back however reluctantly, that I first noticed the rising of the mist. This was a phenomenon particularly belonging to the Fens more in summer than in winter when there was any sudden change of temperature. It was curling up like white steam clinging to the reeds and sedge and rolling across the water.

I was not frightened at first. I had been on these waters so often with Oliver and with the children, but the mist had a way of blowing apart for a second so that I thought I saw my way ahead and then closing in again so that I was never sure whether after all I had taken the right channel. What in daylight was perfectly easy and straightforward became hidden and mysterious in the thick stifling fog. In this vast emptiness there were no landmarks. Once I was sure I saw Spinney Mill in the distance and steered towards it, only to find it had vanished when next the mist parted.

I don't know how long I paddled backwards and forwards for I had no watch with me, but with a growing panic I realized that I was covering the same ground without recognizing it. The mist had begun to close in bringing a grey twilight and the heat had given way to a dank heavy chill. I shivered in my thin dress. The evening hush had gone. The Fens had come to life and the shadows were filled with haunting sounds, the wailing cry of some great bird flying unseen overhead, rustlings in the reeds, the hoot of a nighthunting owl, a distant shriek that might have been a polecat or a marauding hungry dog.

I had never thought of myself as particularly nervous, but there was something eerie about this enormous wilderness when night shut it in and it came to me with something like real terror that I was hopelessly lost. Oliver would come to look for me, I knew that, but not at once. It would never occur to him that I had been so foolish as to venture on the Fens in the evening with a mist coming up, and even if he did, how could he hope to find me in this fog that deadened all sound? I could cry out and he be only a few yards away and we could still miss one another.

I tried to reason with myself. If I moored the boat, I stood a chance of finding one of the shelters built here and there for beasts or lost travellers, crude rough places but better than spending the whole night on the black water hung with wet, clinging vapour.

I drew in to the bank. Beyond the tall rustling reeds I could see the shadowy outlines of buckthorn which seemed the most likely place to find shelter so I tied up the boat and stepped out on to the bank. The last month had been dry so the ground was not too muddy, but groping my way through the mist was a frightening experience. Branches clawed at my dress or brushed across my face. Once I was tangled in the hanging strands of bindweed that seemed to twine itself around me so that I tore frantically at hair and neck. Then I was free of it and in a sort of clearing and I stood still, unable to decide whether to go forward or back. All around me the mist closed in like a prison cell. Then suddenly I stiffened. Something was thrusting its way through the undergrowth, something that snuffled and panted. I tried to tell myself it was a strayed sheep or a frightened cow, but all I could think of was Black Shuck paddling across the Fens with flaming eyes and slavering jaws, Thor's demon hound whom to look on brought death, and for an instant I was paralysed with terror. Then out of the scrub burst a huge shaggy black form and I turned and ran in the opposite direction, stumbling, falling, fighting my way through thorns and brambles until suddenly my feet gave way beneath me. I was sinking. I struggled wildly and only made it worse. I had fallen into one of the green morasses, the cold wet slime was already halfway up my legs sucking me down. Something seemed to leap at me, a hot breath was on my neck, I screamed again and again, and then plunged down a giddy slope into blackness.

When I opened my eyes, it was so dark that for several seconds I could distinguish nothing. I appeared to be lying on a bed of straw or bracken with some kind of rough sour-smelling sheepskin over me and gradually I realized that the wall beside me was of split saplings and that I was not alone. A yard or so away there was a dimly burning lantern with a hunched figure squatting beside it.

My head swam as I tried to sit up and the hunched figure straightened itself and came over to me, carrying the lantern. His face was in shadow but I saw that he was a solidly built, stocky man. With him came a big black dog which thrust a cold nose against my hand licking me with a rough not unfriendly tongue. So much for Black Shuck! I felt ashamed of my panic.

'You're quite safe now.' My rescuer had a dry rusty voice and I had the impression that he spoke seldom and then unwillingly.

'Where am I?'

He ignored my question. 'In the morning when the mist clears, I'll take you back.'

'Do you know who I am?'

'Aye, I do that.'

He shifted the lantern slightly, the light fell on his face and it was Oliver, a rough, unkempt, unshaven Oliver, with a tousled mop of red-gold hair. I was shut into a hut with a would-be mur- derer, a savage, who had tried to kill Justin and bore a flaming hatred for all Aylshams. Involuntarily I shrank away from him and he must have noticed it at once because he said dryly, 'Don't be afeared. It en't you I want, nor him you're married to.'

'What do you mean?' I was still shaking a little.

He grinned wolfishly with a flash of white teeth. 'It's the black one I'm waiting for and one of these days if there's any justice left in this damned old world, then God will give him to me.'

He's mad, I thought, I'm shut up with a madman, miles away from help with only the mist and the hungry bogs of the Fen out- side if I did make a rush for the door . . . and yet he must have pulled me out of the marsh. I could feel the mud drying on my legs and the hem of my gown was thick with it.

'Who are you?' I asked feebly.

He shook his head and moved away coming back with a cup. 'Drink it,' he said, 'it's milk. 'Tisn't much but better than nowt.'

I was not hungry, but I suddenly realized that I was unbearably thirsty and I swallowed it gratefully. He went back to the bundle of straw on which he had been sitting leaving the lantern beside me and the great dog stretched on the floor between us.

It was a weird feeling to be lying in this tumbledown shack in the middle of nowhere with this strange half-wild man who had been kind to me in his rough way. I lay there for a long time without saying anything and he never moved, only the dog snored and whimpered now and then in his sleep. I dozed for a little and when I opened my eyes again, he was still sitting in the same place and I don't know what impelled me but I found myself speaking my thoughts aloud.

'Why did you try to kill Lord Aylsham?' My question seemed to rattle round in a black emptiness and he took so long to answer I thought he must have fallen asleep.

At last he said gruffly, 'It's a debt, a debt I owe to my Dad.'

'What kind of debt?'

Then slowly and at long intervals he told me his grim story and I had a feeling it was not I to whom he spoke at all but as if it was being forced out of him; a justification that, in the darkness of that bare place, would fall on the empty air and be forgotten. He needed no question once he started, no prompting, as if some force inside him was driving him on to speak in his own defence.

'I were only a youngster, nine or ten,' he began in that rusty, dry voice. 'My father worked for the Leighs at Westley. He were good at growing things and he had the care of the fruit and the vegetables and we lived in a cottage on their land. Sometimes Sir Henry came there and talked to him. Once or twice he gave me a sixpence. He were a tall fine-looking man but shy, never went anywhere and lived a quiet life with his two sisters up at the great house. They didn't have many visitors but one day a dark man came riding up the drive, young he were, no more than four or five and twenty and proud on his black horse. My Mam watched him go by with a queer look on her face. "That's the honourable Justin Aylsham, Ned," she said to me, "half-brother to your Dad." I stared at her 'cos I didn't understand. It didn't make no sense to me then. For a year or more he came often and sometimes I saw him walking in the gardens with the young ladies.

'Then one day my Dad went down to the Black Dog in the evening for his pint of ale and I went with him. I were sitting outside when there were high voices raised in the parlour where the gentlemen sat over their wine when they came for the fishin' an' that. Presently Sir Henry rushes out with Justin Aylsham after him, their faces black with anger. There were furious words between them and then they left, Sir Henry going back to the manor and Mr. Aylsham riding away on his black horse.

'I heard my Mam and my Dad talkin' and talkin' that night when I was supposed to be asleep up in the attic, but I didn't know what it was about except that I saw my Dad go out in the morning soon after dawn and I crept out after him but hidden like, because he was a stern man and didn't care for me taggin' at his heels unless he said so.

'He went across the fields till he came to a quiet grassy place on the edge of the Fen and when he got there I saw that he stood within the shelter of the trees and I hid behind some bushes. We waited for a little and then I saw the two horses comin' from opposite directions and it was Sir Henry and Mr Aylsham. I've heard about men fightin' duels since but I never knew one that was fought like this without seconds or surgeon or witness. Sir Henry had always been a quiet, peaceable man who never quarrelled with no one. I thought my father would step out and stop them but he didn't. Maybe it were more than he dared do. Mr Aylsham brought the pistols and they each chose one. Then they tossed a coin. Three shots they fired and at the third Sir Henry fell to his knees. I was too terrified to move but I saw Justin Aylsham go up and look down at the man he had murdered.

' "You asked for it, you damned fool," he said scornful like, "and now you've got it."

'Sir Henry tried to struggle up but he fell back. Then I saw the blood and my father ran out to kneel beside him holding him in his arms.

'Mr Aylsham said, "What the devil are you doing here?" and I thought he looked afraid.

'My father stood up. "He's dead and it's you who've murdered him."

' "No, my man. It was a fair fight. If he'd been a better shot he might well have killed me. If you know what's good for you, you'll keep your mouth shut," and he threw a purse of money on the ground and walked away.

'I mind how my father picked it up and weighed it in his hand. Then he went after Mr Aylsham and grabbed him by the arm.

"That for your blood money!" he shouted and hurled it into the river. "I'll see you pay for this!"

' "And just how do you propose to do that?" says Mr Aylsham and I heard his devil's laugh as I ran to them across the grass.

' "You bastard!" yells my father. "You'll laugh t'other side of your face by the time I've done!"

' "Bastard from you, that's rich from my father's by-blow!" says Mr Aylsham sneering and then my father was at his throat and they were fighting like madmen there on the green grass by the river.

'My father had won many a bout on the fairground, but Mr Aylsham was tough and wiry, slippery as a serpent. Once he were forced to his knees. "Lord Aylsham shall hear of it," panted my father, staring down at him. "Not if I can help it," he answers savagely. Then he were up and they were at one another again. I don't know how it happened but he threw my father so that he hit his head against one of them old tree stumps and rolled sideways and down into the river. Mr Aylsham looked down at him, then he brushed himself down and walked to his horse. I ran after him. I begged him to pull my father from the water, but he laughed in my face, thrust me to the ground and rode away. I tried and tried, but my father were a heavy man and stunned as he was, he couldn't help himself. I ran back home and my Mam came with one of our neighbours. They dragged him out of the river but he weren't breathing no more. They pumped the water out of him and my Mam knelt by him, her mouth on his, trying to breathe the life back into him, but he lay dead as any stone.'

His voice which had grown rougher and more intense died into silence and I lay there, seeing the whole scene vividly in my mind's eye, the riverbank in the cold light of dawn, the two men lying dead, the weeping woman and the frantic child.

'What happened then?' I breathed.

He did not answer at once and when he did, it was with a savage bitterness that made me shiver.

'It were hushed up. Sir Henry must have been attacked and shot by poachers, they said, my father died in defending him, and none to listen to a boy who cried out over and over again that it were murder. The Aylshams were powerful and the old Tiger feared all through the Fens. Better to say nothing than risk losing what little they had.'

Justin Aylsham, twice murderer, and now rich, respected and married to Alyne at Ravensley that should in all justice have belonged to Oliver. It was fantastic, wildly melodramatic but it had the ring of truth. I sat up, leaning forward, and the dog rolled over, thumping his tail on the floor.

'What did you do?'

'My Mam were never the same after,' he went on still in that same dry, toneless voice. 'She used to sit staring into the fire, hardly speaking. One day not long after, I were sitting outside when a carriage stopped and a big man got out, bigger than I had ever seen, and he went straight in to my Mam. He came out again after a little, never looking at me, brushing past with a black storm on his face and, frightened, I ran to my Mam. There were a pile of money on the table and her staring at it. "What did he do to you?" I cried out to her but she never moved, just went on staring. "That were your grandfather," she sez at last. "To the likes of him gold can pay for anything even a man's life, his own son's life." Then she grabbed hold of me, shaking me like a madwoman. "Remember that, Ned, remember that always!"

'She went out that night and never came back. One of the Fenmen found her on the bank where my father drowned, just lying there, wet through. She took a chill and died of it.'

He spoke little of what had happened after that and I guessed at most of it. The double loss had bitten deep into him like a canker, a black corroding hatred so that he rejected his Uncle Isaac's kindness, running away to join up with a gang as wild and lawless as himself, a savagery that erupted into the riots when Isaac Starling was hanged and had won him seven years' transportation to the penal colony.

'You can't know, Missus,' he muttered, staring into the darkness, 'but hate's better than love. It keeps you going, it burns in you like a fire, it don't let you rest. They told me Justin Aylsham were dead, but I knew better. I worked and I saved, hour by hour, day by day, and I were lucky. I got a passage home where others stayed on in slavery. I had a purpose, see. It were that kept me living when things were at their worst.'

I remembered what Oliver had told me about his father and I said, 'Was it you who attacked Robert Aylsham?'

He gave me a quick sly look. 'Nay, it weren't though I saw him riding home across the marsh and I sez to myself, "I could do it quick and no one any the wiser and one Aylsham the less." He must have been riding careless for his horse stumbled and threw him. I saw him lying there stunned, half in the water, and it reminded me of my Dad and I all but left him there to drown. But something held me back. He were the only one to speak up for me that time I come up for trial so I pulled him out on to the bank. 'Tweren't my fault he died from it.' He thumped his fist on his knee and in the dim light I saw the grim set of his face. 'Then that other came back as I'd known he would. The Devil looks after his own.'

The mist had begun to creep into the shack, curling in corners and I shivered, partly from the chill and partly from the macabre story and the man who waited with cold determination to avenge an old wrong.

I tried to pull myself together. I must do something. I sat up. 'It's terrible and I know how cruelly you must have suffered, but it's twenty years ago and what good will it do now? Why not give it up? Go away from here, make a new life in a different place. I'm sure my husband would help you if I were to ask him.'

He turned to look at me with that fleeting resemblance to Oliver which came and went like a shadow and he said nothing. I knew then that my question was too ridiculous even to be answered. Then he got to his feet. The dog would have gone with him, but he spoke harshly to it and it slunk back again. Then he went out into the night.

The hours crept slowly by and without the company of the dog, I think I might have been terrified. It came to lie beside me and somehow I was comforted. I must have dozed on and off but, whether sleeping or waking, I was disturbed by uneasy dreams. Then suddenly I was wide awake and it was broad daylight. The door was open and he was standing there, filling the opening.

'Come,' he said. 'It's time to go.'

I struggled up from my rough couch, stiff and aching all over. Outside shreds of mist still hung in long wisps but a fresh breeze blew them apart and the sun was already breaking through.

He plunged ahead and I followed after him. He led me back to where the boat was moored. He got in after me and took the paddles while the dog sat upright in the stern. He took me in and out of the channels with scarcely a glance and I realized how hopelessly I had gone astray the night before. Then he drew in to the bank and I saw the reed-thatched hump of a cottage and Moggy bending over a pile of nets. He looked up and came bounding down to the water's edge.

'Great jumping rabbits, if it isn't Missus Aylsham? Mr Oliver were here not half an hour gone, nearly out of his wits. He found the boat gone and were thinking you lost, drowned, and I dunno what else.'

I managed a smile. 'I very nearly was. If it hadn't been for . . .' but when I turned round, my rescuer had gone, vanished into the thickets. Moggy nodded his head.

'That's Ned all over.'

'I wanted to thank him.'

'He's a queer one. He won't take nowt.'

'Do you know him, Moggy?'

'Not know zackly, Missus, but I see him off and on. You look fair done. You come along o' me.'

Suddenly I was so desperately weary, I longed only for home. So it was Moggy who rowed me back to the landing stage and would have come up to the house with me if I had not refused.

'There's no need. I'm all right,' I said. 'If you see Mr Oliver anywhere, will you tell him?'

'Aye, I will that. You take care now.'

I regretted my independence as I began to trudge up the track. My legs felt like lead and every now and then a sick giddiness swept over me so that I had to stand still until it passed and I could struggle on. When I reached Thatchers, I had to cling to the doorpost for a moment. The sun was up by now and the door was wide open. I was filthy, my hair hanging in ratstails round my face, my dress torn and bespattered with mud and slime. I pulled myself up the steps and went through the hall. Oliver was in the sitting room, the coffee pot in his hand, and opposite him stood Alyne, fresh and lovely in her white muslin gown. I stood and watched them, all my strength draining away from me.

'Oliver,' I mumbled, 'Oliver . . .'

He turned and the coffee pot crashed down on the table. 'Clarissa! My God, what has happened to you?'

'Nothing. I got lost, that's all,' then the floor seemed to come up to meet me. I swayed forward and for the second time in my life I fainted.

I don't remember much about the rest of the day. I know they stripped my filthy clothes from me and washed away the mud, but the chill and the long wearying night had brought on a light fever. I felt faint and sick and though I knew Oliver was there some part of the time, he did not question me. Then Dr Thorney came at midday and gave me something cool and bitter to drink and I must have slept. When I woke, it was evening, and I felt much better, refreshed and clear-headed. The curtains had been drawn and the candles lit. The doctor must have come back because he was talking to Oliver at the other end of the room.

Out of the murmur of voices I heard Oliver say, 'You are sure it is not serious?'

'No, I don't think so. At first I thought we might lose the child, but now I believe there is little danger of it if we are careful. Rest and quiet, Mr Aylsham, that's what she needs. Two or three days with nothing at all to worry about and your wife should be right as rain.'

'Thank God.'

They went quietly from the room together, leaving me with my bitter thoughts. I remembered everything now, Oliver and Alyne together as I had seen them last night and again when I came back this morning. For the last few weeks I had been living in a fantasy world of my own making. It was Alyne he loved still. I had not believed it possible but jealousy, like hate, could burn in you like a fire.

Oliver came back within a few minutes. I was tempted to close my eyes and pretend to be still sleeping, but when he came up to the bed and put his hand on my forehead, I couldn't. I looked up into the beloved face with a foolish desire to weep.

'Are you really feeling better?' he said. 'I've been worried sick about you.'

'I'm quite all right now.'

He sat on the side of the bed and took my hand. 'Darling, why didn't you tell me?'

'About what?'

'About the baby of course. Dr Thorney expected me to know and I didn't. I must have sounded a complete ass.'

'I was going to tell you last night.'

'Well, why didn't you? Why did you go off like that? Really, dearest, wasn't it very foolish to do such a thing especially now and after such a tiring day? What on earth made you take the boat? When the mist came up, I died a thousand deaths wondering what might have happened to you.'

'Are you sure? Did you even remember me when you were with Alyne?'

'What has Alyne to do with it? She was worried about you too. She came down here early this morning to ask if you had been found.'

'Or did she spend the night here? It was so easy, wasn't it, when I did not come back. I wish I hadn't come back. I wish I had been drowned out there on the Fens.' I felt the sobs gather in my throat and tried hard to swallow them down.

Oliver was staring down at me. 'You must still be sick to talk like that. What in God's name are you accusing me of?'

Then it all burst out. I couldn't keep it in any longer. 'I saw you when I came back from Copthorne, you and Alyne together downstairs.'

'What of it? She did come here. She was terribly upset about . . . about something that had happened . . .'

'So upset that you had to take her in your arms, caress her, kiss her, make love to her . . .'

'No,' he protested, 'no, it wasn't like that at all. Justin had asked her to bring me some papers and then . . . well, it was something I found out quite by accident . . .'

'Found out what?'

He hesitated and I could not read his face. It seemed a long time before he said, 'I don't think I can tell you. It wouldn't be fair to her.'

'Not fair to Alyne? What about me?'

He got up, took a pace or two away and then came back. 'Listen Clarissa. I'm still fond of Alyne . . .'

'Fond!' I exclaimed. 'Is that what you call fond?'

'Is it so difficult to believe? It has gone on too long to be forgotten all at once. But she doesn't love me, she never has. I've known that for a long time. But she is in trouble, deep trouble, and who else can she go to? I must do what I can to help her as I would anyone . . . Cherry, Jethro, even a dog . . . you do understand, don't you?'

And I did unwillingly because that was Oliver. He had come to my rescue and Papa's, he had protected Jake . . . and yet stubbornly I would not accept it. I said, 'I'd understand better if you'd tell me what the trouble is.'

'I can't, Clarissa, not yet at any rate. It is between her and Justin and I'd never have known if I hadn't pressed her.' Then he came back to sit on the bed, taking my hands in his, warm, loving, tender. 'It has nothing whatsoever to do with us, I promise you it hasn't. I have been happier these last few weeks than I have ever been in spite of Jake and now even more with the promise of a child. Don't spoil it, dearest. Trust me and love me.'

How could I help it when I wanted to believe, when I wanted his love above everything, so I let him take me in his arms and I returned his kisses and we were very close, but I still couldn't quite forget. He asked me what had happened and I made light of my panic and told him something of the man who had rescued me.

'His name is Ned. Moggy knows him.'

'Yes, I am aware of that,' he said slowly. 'His father was Ned too, Ned Starling. I wormed it out of old Nurse. It seems we shared the same grandfather. I didn't tell you but I met him once. He tried to steal Rowan or at least I believe he did. I know too that he has cause to hate my uncle but I'm a long way from the real truth.'

It was on the tip of my tongue to tell him everything I had learned during that strange night and yet I didn't. Maybe it was childish but if he could have secrets, then so could I. I said nothing and the moment passed.

'I mustn't tire you too much,' he said and stood up. 'The doctor was very insistent about that. I shall send Jenny up with your supper and then you must sleep.'

'You will come up again?'

'Yes, of course. Now you be a good girl and do everything you're told. I don't want anything to happen to my son.'

When he had gone downstairs, I lay quietly, trying to come to terms with what he had said. I knew now the real reason why I had deliberately withheld the truth from him. I was afraid of what he might do. Shocked and horrified, he might well outface his uncle, take Alyne from him, and then what? He loved me, I must believe that, and I ran my hands over my body where his unborn child slept, but I knew Alyne's power. I had always known it. In desperate straits and in dire need she would only have to cry to him for help and he would go to her.

Afterwards when it was all over, I wondered if it would have made any difference if I had spoken out that night. Perhaps and then again perhaps not. Life has a way of reaching its destined end whatever road we choose to take.

2

The first of the steam engines was installed on Spinney Fen by the end of July and Oliver took me one morning to see it. The tall brick chimney stack had none of the grandeur of the old windmill with its graceful sails, but of its capacity for draining the Fens, there seemed no doubt. The sixty horse-power engine could suck up the water from seven thousand acres, boasted the engineers. Jack Moysey, who had very nearly broken down and wept at the thought of abandoning his beloved mill, had suffered a change of heart and was now bursting with pride at his new skill. He showed me the great scoop wheel and demonstrated the power of the steam with an unexpected enthusiasm.

'Many a time I've watched them old sails with me heart in me boots,' he said, 'the wind's as wayward as a maid in love, but it'll be different now.'

'Let us hope so,' said Oliver shortly.

The smell of the oil in the new machinery, the frightening feeling of a power over which man had so little control once it was set in motion, was too overwhelming for comfort and I was glad to come out into the fresh air again.

We were just about to leave when Justin came riding down the track. I had not seen him since Jake's death and we were stiff and formal with one another.

He said politely, 'I hope I see you in good health, Clarissa.'

'I am very well, thank you. And Alyne?'

'She is away for a few days visiting an old school friend in London.'

I was surprised, but didn't say so. Cherry had always maintained that Alyne hated school and had never kept up old friendships. With the new knowledge I had of him still so fresh in my mind, I watched Justin curiously as he turned to Oliver. I thought he looked thinner, his face more sallow, the lines on it more deeply marked, and there was a darkness about his eyes as if he suffered from too many sleepless nights. Was it possible that any man could kill so callously and never feel pangs of remorse?

'By next year,' he was saying, 'I think I shall be able to boast that I've made two blades of grass grow where before there was only one and we shall see fields of wheat and barley instead of a wilderness of sedge and bulrushes.'

'Possibly, but at what cost? There is winter to come and we've yet to see it in action,' said Oliver quietly.

'By God, do you always have to be so pessimistic? I hope you'll remember to hold your tongue when Josh Rutland comes down. He has a stake in this business and next year, with his help, I'll have another sixty horse-power engine installed, this time on Greatheart. They will begin cutting the dyke through the Fen in the autumn.'

'That land has remained untouched for centuries. What is to happen to those who live there?'

'Most of them are people of little account,' he said indifferently. 'But they'll be warned. They'll receive eviction notices by the winter. Then it will be up to them. It has never been my obligation to provide shelter for wastrels and rootless men.'

He was hitting at Jake and I saw Oliver's mouth tighten, but he said nothing and after an instant Justin nodded to me, turned his horse's head and trotted away. Oliver was frowning. I knew how he felt and I knew too the need to make light of it. I leaned across and touched him on the arm.

'You know, darling, if it was anyone but Justin doing this, you'd admit that you are proud to be one of the first to see steam installed this side of Ely.'

He came out of his abstraction and smiled. 'Maybe I would. It wasn't that I was thinking of. Now, come along, my dear, that's enough for one morning. You are looking tired. We had better go home.'

'You are molly-coddling me,' I protested, but he was insistent. It was three weeks since the night on the Fens, three weeks of an exceptional heat wave, and it was true that for most of the time I had been not precisely ill, but never quite well and I knew that too often I had been irritable and on edge.

A day or so later a letter came from Cherry saying that Aunt

Jess and Papa had benefited so greatly from the sea air that they had decided to stay on a few weeks longer until the end of August.

'It's the very thing for you,' exclaimed Oliver when I mentioned it. 'You must go down and join them. It will do you all the good in the world.'

'I'm perfectly well.'

'No, you're not and don't argue,' he smiled and put a hand on mine. 'I've only to open my mouth and you snap my head off. I'll take you down myself and stay for a few days. How about that? Your father will probably be only too happy to escape from petticoat company for a little.'

'So that's it, you want an excuse to go gambling and racing with him,' I said tartly.

'Why not?' he went on teasingly. 'You and Cherry and Aunt Jess can talk fashion and baby linen to your hearts' content. So start packing and we'll travel by postchaise in comfort.'

We stayed overnight in London and drove down to Brighton the next day arriving late in the afternoon. The sun shone and the air smelled strongly of the sea as we came up the parade. The very first person we saw was Harry bowling along the highway in a smart dog cart with tall yellow wheels and with Cherry perched up beside him. He pulled up just as we alighted from the carriage and Cherry was down and throwing her arms round me in an instant.

'How lovely to see you, and Oliver too. Why didn't you let us know you were coming?'

'We only made up our minds at the last moment.'

Harry was shaking Oliver's hand. Then the box was lifted down and we all went inside. They had taken an apartment in one of the tall narrow houses overlooking the sea and while Oliver negotiated with the proprietor for an extra room, I had time to look curiously at my brother. He had always been something of a dandy, but his fine coat was covered in dust, his neckcloth remarkably untidy, he wore no hat and his hair, usually so stylishly cut, was blown all over the place.

I smiled at him. 'What on earth have you been doing with yourself?'

He grinned sheepishly. 'Cherry involved me in a Sunday school outing. I've been spending the afternoon organizing games for a number of extremely unpleasant children.'

'They were nothing of the kind,' said Cherry indignantly.

It was so unlike Harry that I couldn't help laughing and Oliver, who had joined us, said, 'Better you than me, my dear fellow. How the devil did you persuade such an elegant member of the smart set, Puss?'

'I told him it was that or nothing,' said Cherry frankly, 'and if he wanted to come with me, then he would have to make himself useful.'

Harry shrugged his shoulders helplessly and I smiled to myself because it was good to see Cherry come to life again with the light of battle in her eyes.

They knew nothing about the baby and so after we had eaten and the men went off together on some pursuit of their own, we had a long cosy chat and I was glad to be away from Ravensley even for a little, to forget all about Alyne and that lonely man who waited so grimly out on the Fens, and to talk over the absorbing topic dear to any woman's heart.

We had not left Thatchers for more than a day since we had been married and I was surprised at how much I enjoyed indulging in the social delights of Brighton though they were mild enough. Oliver had worked so hard to turn himself into a working farmer and make a success of it that it gave me pleasure to see how distinctive he looked among the fashionable young men we met on the racecourse or at the concerts in the Assembly Rooms. Papa took him off on mysterious excursions of his own and it delighted me to see how they wrangled, agreed to differ and yet thoroughly enjoyed one another's company.

Harry went back to London and Oliver was already talking of returning, leaving me to come back with the rest of the party, when one morning we decided to make a trip along the lovely valley of the Adur to the little village of Bramber. It is a pretty place, a few charming cottages grouped around the Norman castle whose ruins are scattered up the side of a steep hill. We ate a cold luncheon at the small inn and afterwards, when Cherry and Aunt Jess were gathering up bonnets and shawls to walk up to the castle, I said, 'You all go. I think I will stay here.'

There was a chorus of concern. 'Is anything wrong?' asked Cherry solicitously.

'I'll stay with you,' said Oliver.

'No, I will,' put in Aunt Jess.

'Now you've made me feel a thorough wet blanket,' I protested. 'I don't want anyone to stay with me. You go and I'll just sit here in the garden quietly till you come back.'

After a great deal of argument they set off at last and I sat sleepily in the shade of a huge apple tree and later, feeling relaxed and refreshed, decided to take a quiet stroll around the village and look at the ancient church. There was nothing in the least remarkable about it, but it was pleasantly cool and dark inside out of the glare of the sun. I was standing at the far end, amusing myself by reading the inscriptions extolling the virtues of people long dead, when I heard the door creak open. A man and a woman had come in and in the dazzle of light from outside I stared and stared scarcely able to believe my eyes for it was unmistakably Alyne, her bonnet fallen back so that I saw her face clearly under the pale hair.

Instinctively I had drawn back into the shadows of the chapel. She had come in quickly almost as if she were trying to escape and the man who followed her stood for an instant, a black figure in the shaft of sunshine, and though he was not in uniform I guessed it was Bulwer Rutland. He let the door clang shut behind him before he spoke, quietly enough, but with a sharp note of irony.

'What are you trying to do this time, my dear? Run for sanctuary?'

'You talk like a fool,' she said breathlessly.

'It is not I who am the fool.'

She was clinging to the end of one of the tall pews and he came behind her, putting his hands on her shoulders. They did not embrace and I could no longer hear what they said, but I was conscious of a tension, a suppressed anger in the low voices, and I was trapped, unwilling to reveal myself.

Then Alyne spoke and the words were sharp, full of pain. 'No, no, no! It is impossible. I cannot!' and she pulled herself away from him, running across the church and out of the door. He stood for a moment as if irresolute and then went after her.

I could not help myself. I hurried down the aisle and looked through the door. Outside beyond the steep slope of the church-yard was the handsome carriage with the elegant matched pair of horses. I saw Bulwer help Alyne into the high seat and then leap up himself, taking the reins. They went down the road at a fast trot.

I was shocked but not altogether surprised and quite appalled at the risks she was taking. How long had she been deceiving Justin and how long would it be before he found out? He had always watched her so jealously. I could not sort out my feelings as I walked slowly back to the inn. They had all returned from the castle, found I was not there and were just about to come out in search of me.

Oliver said, 'What was the use of staying behind if you were to go roaming around in this heat?'

'Don't be silly,' I answered, 'I only went as far as the church,' and could not make up my mind whether or not to tell him what I had seen. I could not imagine what his reaction might be and the thought crossed my mind that maybe this was the deep trouble which she had confided to him and he had refused to tell me. Yet somehow I was sure it could not be so. In some strange way, in spite of everything, Oliver still had a kind of ideal vision of the girl he loved. A liaison with Rutland, a man he disliked and despised, would have distressed him beyond measure.

I don't know what I might have done if it had not been for what happened the next day. We had spent the morning watching Cherry take her daily dip in the sea from one of the bathing machines. Nothing would have induced me to put a foot into the icy water at any time, but she splashed about in great style to the amusement of Oliver and Papa and afterwards we drank hot chocolate in the grand new Albion Hotel. We had just come in and were taking off our bonnets and shawls when the maid-servant came in all of a fluster and said a gentleman was asking most particular if he could speak to Mr Aylsham.

'What name did he give?' asked Oliver, but before she could answer, she was thrust aside and Justin came into the room. His eyes swept over us before he spoke.

'Is Alyne here with you?' he said abruptly.

'Alyne?' repeated Aunt Jess. 'Is there any reason why she should be?'

Oliver was alert at once. 'Why do you ask?'

'I expected her to be in London with her friends in Park Street, but when I went there, I was told she had left already saying she was going on to Brighton.'

'Was she expecting you?' asked Aunt Jess.

'No,' he admitted. 'I thought I would surprise her.'

Perhaps he suspected something already and had meant to surprise her in more ways than one. For a moment I was horribly tempted. It would have been easy to say casually, 'I saw your wife yesterday afternoon, driving on the Sussex Downs with Captain Rutland.' Then I knew it was impossible. For one thing Oliver would never have forgiven me and for another I would have despised myself. I said instead, 'Was she alone?'

'She had taken Lizzie with her, but the girl had not been well so she left her behind saying she would call for her on her way back through London.'

Cherry was looking at him with a queer look on her face. 'A girl friend of ours called Kitty Fisher married a man who lived in Sussex. Perhaps she has gone there,' and I knew by her heightened colour that she lied.

Justin turned to her at once. 'Do you have the address?'

'No, I'm afraid not. It would be at home somewhere but it's some time since we heard from her.'

Justin made an impatient sound. 'What the devil does she think she is doing?' he burst out suddenly. 'I'll not be treated in this manner.'

'Your wife is not a child. You can't keep her in leading strings,' said Oliver dryly. 'She has some right to a life of her own. Don't you trust her?'

Justin took a step towards him. 'Why do you say that? What has she been saying to you about me? What has she been telling you?'

'Is there so much to tell?'

Justin glared at him and there was a tiny strained silence before Aunt Jess broke it.

'Would you care to stay and eat with us, my lord? We keep country hours here and take our dinner at three o'clock.'

'Thank you, no. I shall return to London and go back to Ravensley tomorrow.' He looked at Oliver. 'I presume you will be returning soon.'

'When I am ready,' said Oliver calmly. 'As soon as I think Clarissa is fit to travel.'

Justin gave a quick hunted look around, then mumbled something and left.

'What in God's name is the man thinking about,' remarked Papa acidly as the door closed behind him, 'treating you like an errand boy and running after his wife like a scalded cat.'

'I'm surprised he did not put Ram Lall on to watching her every step,' said Cherry.

'Oh come now, my dear,' protested Aunt Jess. 'You're exaggerating.'

'I'm not, it is true. The devil's shadow, that's what Nurse calls him. I used to feel those horrid black eyes of his on me everywhere and on Alyne too, even before they were married. He padded about the house like a great big cat. Perhaps it is the kind of thing they do in India. I wonder if Uncle Justin was the same when he was married to Jethro's mother.'

'He was not married to her. Jethro's mother was also our mother,' said Oliver suddenly.

If someone had fired a shot through the window, there could not have been a more shocked reaction. Papa and Aunt Jess turned to stare at him and it was a moment before Cherry could find words.

'You mean that Mama did not die in Rome, that she left Papa and ran away to Uncle Justin?'

'Yes. I did not mean you ever to know, Puss, but now perhaps I think you should.'

'I can't believe it, I can't . . .'

'It is true.'

'How long have you known?'

'Nearly two years now.'

'And you said nothing. Did you know, Clarissa?'

'Yes. Oliver told me that time when Jethro ran away.'

'It must have come as a great shock to you, Oliver,' said Aunt Jess quietly.

'It did. At first I could not even speak of it. I could not accept that the mother I had worshipped should have abandoned us so callously and gone to him. Now I think I feel differently.'

'Have you told the boy?'

'Not yet. Perhaps when he is older. He is to go to school in September. To know that he is illegitimate is not a good start for a lad like him. I think he will feel it more than most.'

'This makes a great difference to you, Oliver,' said Papa thoughtfully. 'Justin has no son.'

Oliver smiled faintly. 'Don't bank on seeing us installed at Ravensley. As Justin pointed out to me, there is still plenty of time.'

Cherry had been standing quite silent, now she turned to her brother. 'I don't hate Mama,' she said vehemently. 'I feel sorry for her. I can't imagine anything worse than falling in love with a man like Uncle Justin and she must have loved him very much to do what she did. I hope Alyne is enjoying herself wherever she is and that she makes him suffer when she does go back.'

Later that night when we went to bed, I asked Oliver what had made him speak out like he did.

'I hardly know,' he said. 'I suddenly felt I wanted everything to be open, free of lies and deceit.'

Free of deceit . . . I felt the burden of what I had seen the previous afternoon and what I knew about Justin and again almost brought myself to tell him. I said slowly, 'Where do you think Alyne has gone?'

'How should I know? Why does he torment her like he does? Why can't he leave her alone? Isn't it bad enough to be married to a man like that?'

'No one forced her to marry him.'

'Do you need to remind me of that?' He pulled back the curtain with a violent gesture. 'It's hot tonight. Shall I open the window a trifle?'

'If you wish. I don't mind.'

He pushed back the casement, pinched out the candles and then came into the bed. After a moment he said quietly, 'I'm sorry, Clarissa, I'm all at odds tonight. You must forgive me.'

I slid my hand into his and he returned the pressure. I felt his light kiss on my cheek, but for the first time for several days a distance widened between us and it held me silent. I lay quietly close to him and told him nothing. The next day he went home.

I came back from Brighton at the end of August, greatly refreshed by my holiday. Oliver had had the bedroom repainted and Mrs Starling had stitched at new curtains and covers so that Thatchers seemed particularly welcoming. Aunt Jess had already suggested that when the baby arrived, Patty should leave Copthorne and come to us as nursemaid. She was a sensible girl and well trained so I was grateful, though I wasn't sure that Prue would be very enthusiastic.

The weeks rolled by and I lived in a fragile cocoon of contentment. It was as if my pregnancy shielded me from disturbance, an instinctive rejection of anything that might harm the child growing within me. Alyne had already returned and what happened between her and Justin I could only guess at, but Cherry, who occasionally went up to the big house to visit Hattie and her old nurse, reported stormy scenes and I shut my ears against it. Alyne had always been able to look after herself. She must work out her own salvation.

Jethro went off to school at the end of September, a little tearful when he came to say goodbye to Ben. He had brought a handful of treasures for him which he was reluctant to leave behind at Ravensley.

'You'll like it when you are there,' I said trying to cheer him up. 'There'll be a great deal to do and you will soon make friends.'

'Shall I?' he sounded doubtful.

'Of course you will,' said Oliver. 'Would you like me to take you instead of travelling alone in the coach?'

'Oh yes please.' Then the boy's face clouded over. 'You don't mind, do you? Papa says it is babyish and I ought to stand on my own feet, but it's all going to be so new and strange.'

'Well, I have to make a trip down south so we'll go together.'

That was Oliver's strong sense of responsibility towards his half-brother and it made me impatient.

'It's his father's place to take him,' I said when Jethro had gone off, looking a little happier.

'I sometimes think Justin doesn't know the meaning of the word,' said Oliver dryly. 'The boy hates him to come anywhere near him. At least he won't feel quite so alone. I remember how my father rode in with me and pushed a guinea into my hand when we said goodbye. It certainly helped me over the first home-sickness.'

Work began on Greatheart that autumn. They started to clear the ground and deepen the channels and already there had been serious trouble. The hired men came from some distance away and were eyed with suspicion and dislike. There were scuffles and slanging matches and at least one pitched battle was fought with some of the Fenmen whose fathers and grandfathers had regarded the wild stretch as their own property where they could fish and hunt and shoot at will. Few of them could read and printed notices had no more effect than the mighty winter wind they called a 'Fen blow'; they simply ignored both.

Oliver was busy from morning to night and he was out as usual when one day in November I had a very unexpected visitor. Winter had set in early and frost lay thick on grass and bare trees when Mrs Starling came bustling in and said a Mr Rutland was asking if he could speak with me. For an instant I thought it might be Bulwer, but it was his father who came stumping in, his face red from the cold, rubbing his hands and looking as broad as he was tall in his bulky fur-lined coat.

'I have a favour to ask of you, Miss Clarissa,' he said in his forthright way, 'that is if you feel up to it of course,' and I saw his eyes run over my swollen figure before he looked delicately away, 'and your husband won't shoot me for daring even to suggest such a thing.'

I smiled. I had never been able to dislike Josh Rutland. I had no doubt at all that in his business dealings he probably had very few scruples, but all the same there was something honest and decent about him and he had shown me some kindness.

'What is the favour, Mr Rutland? If it is within my power, I'd be glad to help you in any way I can.'

'It's Westley Manor,' he said. 'I can't tell you the problems that have come up one way and another, but I think now the end is in sight. My agent has suggested I take a look over the house. Now I'm not just thinking of myself, ye know. I'll never see sixty again and there can't be all that many years left, but there's the boy, see.

He'll be bringing home a wife one of these days. Would you come with me? I'd be grateful for your opinion.'

Bulwer was a year or two older than Oliver but still a boy to his father. Something prompted me to say, 'Why don't you ask Alyne?'

He didn't answer directly. 'Does that mean you're going to refuse me?'

I made up my mind instantly. 'Not at all. If it would help, I would like to come very much.'

I left word with Mrs Starling in case Oliver should come in and I set off with him in his handsome carriage, muffled in the rugs and shawls which he insisted on wrapping solicitously around me in case I should take cold.

It is not more than ten or twelve miles and though it was November there was no mist and the sun shone fitfully. As we skirted Greatheart I could see the deep trenches, the thick gluelike clay, the sluggish muddy waters, and turned away my head. Mr Rutland waved a disparaging hand.

'A mint of my money going out on that and nothing but delay, no headway at all. What is your husband doing about it, Miss Clarissa?'

'He is working extremely hard,' I flashed at him, 'but it's not just a question of battling with rain and frost and mud. It is lives and people, starving children and homeless women. To him that is more important and he feels strongly about it. He would not see blood spilled and it may come to that, Mr Rutland, before it is finished.'

He grunted but said nothing and as the carriage jolted over one of the many ruts in the rough track, he steadied me with his arm.

'Mustn't let anything happen to the little one, eh?' he said with a grin on his homely face so that it was impossible to take offence.

It was noon when we trotted past the Black Dog and my mind flew back to that night on the Fen and the two men whose quarrel had brought such fatal results, then we had turned up the long winding moss-grown drive. Westley Manor was a square stone building perhaps a hundred years old with fine long windows, all closely shuttered and hung with long strands of overgrown creeper, giving it a forlorn deserted appearance.

Mr Grimble, the agent, was waiting to meet us, a small baldheaded man so eager to make sure of a sale that he never stopped talking until Josh Rutland cut him short. Mrs Birch the house-keeper showed us round the house. The ceilings were high and delicately moulded, the panelling finely carved and when she opened the shutters I could see that some of the furniture, though old, was of good quality, but I have never known such a feeling of utter desolation. It was a house that had been empty for so long, it had become filled with ghosts, old loves, old passions, old despairs, smelling of damp and mould like the vast drawing room with its threadbare curtains and muffled chandeliers; like the great bed where the tapestry cover was in ribbons and mice dirts were scattered over the once-white pillows. I ran my finger along the top of the dressing table and it was black with dust. Mrs Birch bristled.

'I've only been here a year,' she said defensively, 'and when I came, it had been empty for twenty. I've only one pair of hands.'

Mr Rutland was tireless, insisting on seeing everything from attics to kitchens, but when he decided to visit the cellars I hesitated for the first time.

'I think perhaps I've had enough stairs. Would you mind very much if I wait here till you come back?'

'Whatever you say, my dear.' When Mrs Birch had gone off to fetch candles, Mr Rutland leaned across to me whispering. 'What do you think? Look there.' He pointed to the wall. 'Damp coming through all around the lower floors. It'll need a fortune to set it right.'

'It could be beautiful,' I said slowly. 'I think it has been once. It's like a woman who has been lovely in youth and has grown old and ugly through neglect and lack of love.'

He stared at me. 'Well, that's a rare flight of fancy and no mistake.' Then Mrs Birch came back and he patted my shoulder. 'Now you sit there, my dear, and take care you don't see no ghosts.'

One shutter had been pushed back, but the room was full of shadows. I walked across to the window and looked out on a garden that once might have been beautiful but was now hopelessly overgrown. The roses were a tangle of bare twisted branches and the stone figure on the edge of the pool was green with moss and cracked. This was the garden where the young Justin Aylsham had walked with the two sisters before he had killed their brother. I found myself speculating about them. How did they look? Were they flattered by his gallantries? I pushed the shutter further open and turned back into the room. A few pictures hung on the walls of what was once the dining room, none of them of much merit. One was obviously a portrait of Sir Henry Leigh, a tall good-looking man, charming but ineffectual, I thought, and beside it hung a small oval frame with a crayon drawing so faint that I could scarcely make it out.

Greatly daring I lifted it from the wall and carried it to the window. It was drawn in red chalk, the work of an amateur, Sir Henry perhaps, or one of his sisters. Then I started because the name faintly printed at the bottom was 'Alyne aged 15,' a frail haunting face surrounded by a mass of curly hair and as I moved nearer to the light, the fancy possessed me that I looked at Alyne's face, the Alyne I had known as a child, not the beautiful assured woman of today. As I turned it in a quiver of wintry sun, the eyes became suddenly alive, staring directly into mine, gently smiling as if they possessed a secret shared with no one. Then the light faded, the resemblance to Alyne vanished and it was no more than a rather poor crayon drawing. I heard footsteps and hurried to put it again in its place on the wall.

Mrs Birch offered us coffee but Mr Rutland refused. He took my arm. 'Thank 'ee but I think not. Mrs Aylsham is tired and I'll be taking her home. Mr Grimble will be in touch. I'd hoped to have a word with the lady who owns the house before I make a final decision.'

'Lady Leigh lives in Italy,' said the housekeeper primly. 'She has not been in England these ten years and more. I am told that she may be visiting her property once more in the New Year.'

'I am sure I hope so. Thank 'ee again.' He put some money in her hand and guided me out of the house.

'Well, I don't know,' he said as he helped me into the carriage and climbed in after me. 'Funny sort of place, ain't it? Cellars dry and sound as a bell, not a smell of dry rot anywhere and that's something to be thankful for. Floors of chestnut, panelling too, and worm'll never touch that.' He went on talking and I scarcely listened, thinking of that strange likeness, not sure if it had really been there and yet haunted by it.

As we came up to the Black Dog I saw the carriage standing

outside with its pair of finely bred greys and I recognized it at
once. Instinctively I tried to distract Mr Rutland's attention, but I
was too late.

'Damn my eyes, but that's the boy's turn-out!' he exclaimed and
called out to the man holding the horses. 'Is your master here,
Croft?'

I thought the groom looked startled. 'Aye, sir, he's inside.'

'Tell him I'd like a word with him.'

He called one of the stable lads to take the horses and went inside. A few minutes later Bulwer himself came out, looking slightly
flushed.

'What the devil are you doing here?' said Mr Rutland jovially. 'I
thought you still out of town.'

'I got back earlier than I expected and Croft told me you were
down here,' he said almost too glibly. He bowed to me. 'Good
morning, Mrs Aylsham. How kind of you to accompany father.
Well, sir, what do you think?'

'It has its points. Filthy dirty of course and needing a lot of
work done on it, but I like it. It's a gentleman's house. You'd
agree there, wouldn't you, Miss Clarissa?'

'Certainly,' I said.

'Plenty of room, my boy, enough for a family of grandchildren,'
he winked and poked his son in the chest. 'Go up there. Take a
look for yourself.'

'No, I don't think so. You're a better judge than I.'

It was then that I saw the bonnet and mantle left carelessly on
the high seat of the carriage and recognized them instantly.

Mr Rutland turned to me. 'What do you say, my dear? Would
you care to go in, take a little refreshment? It looks a decent
enough place. I daresay they can offer something fit for a lady.'

I met Bulwer's eyes and read in them the half reluctant appeal. I
shook my head. 'It has taken rather longer than I expected. I
would be glad to go home now if you are sure you don't mind.'

'Of course not. We will go on at once. What am I thinking
about? Take care of yourself, boy. Don't drive too fast.'

The carriage jolted forward and I sat back in my seat. How
could Alyne be so foolish as to risk meeting her lover so near to
Ravensley? A kind of exultation filled me. This was the second
time I had her in my power. I had never been so tempted in my

whole life. With a word to Justin I could destroy her and Bulwer too. Quite suddenly I found myself shaking.

Mr Rutland looked at me anxiously. 'Is anything wrong?'

'No, nothing. I'm a little cold, that's all.'

He wrapped the fur rug more closely around me. I gripped my hands tightly together but I still trembled because I had to face it, there was no escape. If I destroyed Alyne, if I rid myself of her once and for all, then I would undoubtedly lose Oliver too.

3

Christmas came and work stopped temporarily on Greatheart due to heavy falls of snow. Justin entertained a large house party at Ravensley, but I had no great wish to go into society just then and we spent the time quietly. Harry came down from London to spend the holiday with us and he and Oliver joined the hunting party on the day after Christmas. Cherry and I watched them ride past from the dog cart. Alyne looked more beautiful than I had ever seen her in a new riding habit of sapphire velvet. She waved to me as they went by and I thought it was the same as it had always been. The men's eyes followed her and she gloried in it. Harry was one side of her and Oliver on the other. I felt clumsy and awkward. The weeks had begun to drag unbearably and I longed for it to be all over and the baby safely born.

That evening we supped at Copthorne with Papa and Aunt Jess and Harry astonished us by suddenly declaring his intention of resigning his commission in the regiment.

'And what pray do you intend to do with yourself?' enquired Papa a little ironically.

'Lord knows, sir, but there must be something a man can take up. The army is no fun at all when there isn't a war on.'

'I shouldn't have thought a war was fun at any time,' said Cherry tartly.

'It can have its points, my dear,' murmured Papa. 'Is this a serious decision, Harry?'

'Well, I have been giving it some thought . . .'

'What did I tell you, Tom?' interrupted Aunt Jess. 'You should have put him to something useful years ago. Think of all the time wasted.'

'Oh I wouldn't say that, Aunt Jess,' said Harry loyally. 'I've enjoyed it most of the time but a fellow gets older you know. You have to think of the future, particularly when money's tight. Perhaps I can come and work one of Oliver's steam engines.'

We all laughed at that, but I did wonder. It did not seem at all like my gay young brother and it was not until the next day that I guessed at his reasons. He and Cherry went riding together and when they came in, I saw by the look in her eyes and the colour in her cheeks that something had happened. I asked no questions, but later on, she came into my bedroom when I was changing for the evening, chatting about nothing at all and fiddling with the articles on my dressing table until exasperated, I took the scent bottle out of her hand.

'You'll drop it in a minute and it was a present from Oliver. Heaven knows when he will be able to afford another. What are you trying to tell me?'

'Harry asked me to marry him when we were out this morning.'

'Oh . . . and what did you reply?'

'No, of course.'

'There is no of course about it. I know he is my brother and I suppose I am a little partial, but I did rather think that you liked him.'

'I do . . . in a way . . . but in any case I couldn't possibly marry a soldier.'

'So that's why he talked about leaving the regiment yesterday.'

'Perhaps . . . I did tell him how I disliked soldiers when we were at Brighton. You know what they did to the poor men here. It's a cruel brutal profession . . .'

'But that's not the only reason, is it?'

'No.' She moved away to the window. 'How can I marry anyone after Jake?'

She was so young. My heart ached for her. 'You can't go on mourning him for ever, my dear. He wouldn't have wanted it. Did you tell Harry?'

'No, I couldn't. It was dishonest, I know, but I was a coward. I thought . . . I thought if I told him everything, he might despise me for it.'

I was almost sure I could detect a note of regret. I got up and went to her. 'Harry won't give up, not if I know him. Leave it for a while. In any case he has nothing whatsoever at present on which to support a wife.'

I was not sure what Harry's reaction would be so I said nothing to him nor to Oliver, but Cherry had always been impetuous. That evening we were alone, Oliver sitting by the fire reading while I was busy embroidering some caps for the baby. Cherry and Harry were enjoying some noisy card game and presently after a wrangle over who had won what, she folded the games table and came to sit beside me, picking up my work and examining it.

'You're so clever with your needle, Clarissa. I haven't the patience.' Then she looked across at her brother. 'Oliver, have I any money of my own or has Uncle Justin taken it all?'

'Not quite. There is a couple of thousand in trust, not to be given to you until you're twenty-four or when you marry. Why?' he said without looking up from his book.

'I've been thinking. I have lived on you and Clarissa long enough. I would like to take a post somewhere and keep myself in future.'

'And what sort of post were you thinking of?' asked Oliver, humouring her. 'A governess? An old lady's companion taking the fat pug out? Aren't you being a little absurd, Pussie?'

'It's not absurd at all and don't talk to me as though I were a baby. I have thought about it very carefully. I met a woman down in Brighton, a Mrs More. She is connected with a society in London who are trying to establish schools for poor children and orphans. They need teachers badly and they do pay them, not much but something. If you could advance a little of what is really mine, I could work for them and keep myself.'

Oliver put down his book. 'I never heard of anything so preposterous in my life. Do you imagine for one minute that I'd allow my sister to go and work in places like that? They may be very worthy people but they work under terrible conditions and among the worst of the London slums . . .'

'All the more reason to help them.'

'This is crazy. You wouldn't last a week, Cherry.'

She was on her feet now, facing her brother. 'Why should you say that? I saw some of the children in Brighton. Everyone said I managed them very well.'

'They were the cleaned-up ones. I hope you're not responsible for putting this ridiculous idea into her head, Harry.'

'I? Good God, no. If there is anyone I can't stand, it is the preaching kind, the do-gooders.' Harry paused for a moment before he went on. 'I suppose I should really have spoken to you first, Oliver, but in actual fact I did ask Cherry to marry me this morning.'

'Did you indeed?'

'And I refused him,' put in Cherry. 'You're quite wrong about Mrs More and it is not ridiculous at all. I think they are wonderful people and I want to make something of myself. It's what I have always wanted and Jake knew. We talked about it often and often. He would have understood.'

'Jake?' repeated Harry. 'What on earth has he to do with it? I thought he died, poor fellow . . .'

'You might as well know now, Harry,' said Cherry, her face flushed, her eyes very bright, 'I meant to tell you anyway. I loved Jake and he loved me . . . oh I know what you're going to say. He was only Papa's gardener, a poor man, a labourer, not one of your smart set, but I don't care, he was the finest person I ever knew . . .'

Oliver stood up. 'Don't, Puss, there's no need, no need at all.'

'There is every need. I want Harry to know. I'm not ashamed of it . . . why should I be? He was your friend too, wasn't he? I would have married him if Uncle Justin had not murdered him . . . but it was not before we . . . we were lovers.' She flung the words into Harry's face, then choked, looking wildly round for a moment, and ran quickly from the room.

'Jake?' said my brother, shocked and bewildered. 'What the devil is she talking about? Jake? But I thought . . . is any of this true?'

'Yes, I am afraid it is, but not quite as you are thinking,' I said.

'The bastard!' he exclaimed. 'I can't believe it . . . she's so young, so lovely . . . how could you have let such a thing happen? How could he have taken advantage of her like that?'

'Jake did nothing of the kind,' said Oliver quietly.

'Oh I know he was a pet of yours,' said Harry savagely, 'it was always you and Jake even when we were children, but your own sister . . . it is vile, despicable . . .'

I saw the anger on Oliver's face and I came between them. Above all I didn't want them to quarrel and yet it seemed to me that Cherry's brother could explain the circumstances, man to man, better than I could.

'You don't understand any of it,' I said to Harry. 'Promise me you'll listen quietly to what Oliver has to tell you. It was not our fault nor was it hers. It was one of those things that happen and if anyone was to blame, it was Justin Aylsham.'

'I don't know how you can say that, Clary,' muttered Harry.

'You will, believe me you will. Think kindly of her, Harry, she has been so unhappy.'

'I love her,' he mumbled.

'Yes, I know.' I patted his arm. 'And now I'm going up to her.'

I left them alone together and went upstairs. Cherry was lying face downwards on the bed and I sat beside her.

'Why did you have to come out with it like that? Wasn't it foolish? Is that what you're going to do with everyone?'

'I'm not ashamed of anything I did and I want to be honest. I'm not going to lie and deceive like Alyne does.'

'Let's leave Alyne out of this. All you've done is to hurt Oliver and Harry quite unnecessarily.'

'I didn't mean to . . .' She sat up. 'Do you think he will go away now?'

'How can I tell what he will do? He is very upset. Don't you care for him at all?'

'I don't know. Sometimes I like him very much and then, when I remember Jake, nothing seems to matter any more . . . Oh Clarissa, how I envy you! You were so brave when Oliver was accused of murder. I admired you so much speaking out like you did . . . and now you're married and the baby coming . . . you're so lucky.'

Lucky? Yes, perhaps I was and I should thank God for it, but there are shadows in all our lives and though I tried to banish it, the thought of Alyne still lay unspoken between us.

Harry was so quiet for the rest of his stay that I knew he was distressed and he went back to London earlier than he had intended mumbling some urgent excuse.

'It's not going to be easy, is it?' said Oliver dryly, coming back into the house after seeing him ride off. 'God knows what is going to happen if she comes out with this to every young man who offers for her.'

'It's too soon. It's still fresh in her mind. Give her time. I'm not at all sure that Harry is the best choice for her anyway.'

He looked at me quizzically. 'That's a nice thing to say about your own brother! Harry's a good lad even if he is a trifle scatter-brained, and just now I'd be grateful for anything that distracted her from this crazy notion of teaching in one of the ragged schools.'

'Don't be too harsh with her. Opposition turns her into a rebel.'

'Don't I know it! And I've got enough trouble with rebels on my hands as it is.'

'Why? Has there been something new?'

'Not yet. But I cannot make Justin understand that burning the roofs over the Fenmen's heads may get them off the land but could lead to something far worse.'

'Surely he wouldn't do that . . .'

'He talks of it.'

'Will it be like it was before . . . during the Swing riots?'

'It could be worse. There's a different spirit abroad now, more vengeful, more vicious, especially among those who have little to lose.'

'You've not said anything about it before.'

'I didn't want to alarm you unnecessarily. Now I feel you should be prepared. I don't think it will affect us but you never know. Men maddened by despair don't always stop to think whose house they are burning down. Anyone with more than they have is the enemy. I have been seriously thinking of sending Cherry and you away from here and your father agrees with me.'

'So you've spoken to him before speaking to me. I won't go,' I said quickly. 'I'm not leaving you. Besides I don't think it will really happen. The people here are not savages. They would not harm you, not after all you have done for them.'

'Well, we shall see. Maybe you're right and I am wrong. I hope to God I am.'

And for a little it seemed that it was so. The frost continued crisping the snow, the mere froze over and there were a few days in the New Year when the skating contests were held and the Fenmen made holiday. The air resounded with jests and laughter, bets were made and money exchanged hands. We were lulled into a false security that continued quite happily until the day I went up to Ravensley.

It was at the end of January and a morning like any other, nothing particular about it. Hattie had been ailing on and off since Christmas and she had so few visitors, I felt it would be a kindness to sit with her for a little. Cherry would have come with me, but she had developed a slight sore throat so I went alone. Oliver drove me there in the dog cart and left me at the house before going off on business of his own. Hattie was pathetically glad to see me and I stayed for an hour or so chatting about anything that I thought would interest her until she looked tired. I tucked her up promising to come again soon and went downstairs.

I passed the open door to Alyne's little sitting room and saw her standing by the window. I hesitated for a moment uncertain whether to go in and she turned and saw me.

'Annie told me you were here. Come and talk to me, Clarissa, I'm bored, bored and restless, shut in by all this snow. I'd like to fly away from here, anywhere, free as those birds out there.' She turned back to the window and I crossed the room to her. Outside the seagulls, driven inland by hunger and the bitter winds, circled up with their piercing cry.

I glanced at her and thought she looked sick. She was pale as the extravagant cream velvet morning dress trimmed with swansdown. Her shining hair was tied loosely back with a ribbon but there were blue shadows under her eyes.

'I don't know,' I said lightly. 'Birds must have their troubles too. You know what they say in these parts . . . the seagulls are the souls of the drowned mariners. Perhaps freedom is only an illusion.'

'Perhaps.'

She was standing very still, her face close against the pane, and I saw that Justin had come out to his waiting horse. He swung himself into the saddle and went down the drive at a fast trot, two of the stablemen following after him.

'Do you know what he is going to do? He's going to watch them set fire to the cottages on the edge of Greatheart. It will teach them a lesson, he says. After that the others will know the meaning of the word eviction.'

So it had come at last. I felt a quiver of apprehension. 'Does Oliver know?'

She shrugged her shoulders. 'Probably.'

'I wish I could have warned him.'

'What good would that do? Justin always gets his own way.'

She was still standing staring out of the window, her hands pressed against the glass. Her lips moved though I could not understand what she said and the look on her face alarmed me.

I said, 'Alyne, is anything wrong?'

'Wrong? Not if I can help it. I hate him, Clarissa,' she said slowly. 'I hate him. I wish with all my heart that he were dead.'

There was such an intensity in her voice that it made me shiver. 'You shouldn't say such a thing even in jest.'

'Jest!' she repeated. 'Jest!' and laughed. It was not a pleasant sound. 'I'm not jesting. Would you jest about a man who did that to you?'

With a swift movement she slid one shoulder out of the loose folds of her gown and I saw the weals across the nape of her neck and going down her back.

Horrified I whispered, 'But why? Why should he do such a dreadful thing?'

'Because he enjoys it, because for him it is a substitute, a recompense for other things . . . things he cannot do . . .'

'What things?'

But she did not answer directly. Instead she dropped on her knees putting her hands on my lap, looking up into my face. 'Shall I tell you a secret, Clarissa, shall I?'

'What secret?'

'I am going to have a child.'

It was unexpected but in a way a relief. Women have strange fancies at such a time. 'But that's wonderful. Justin will be so pleased. It is what he wants more than anything.'

'It is not his.'

Suddenly I felt cold. I said through stiff lips, 'Then who?'

She smiled maddeningly, playing with one of the rings on her fingers, not looking at me. 'You are afraid it might be Oliver, aren't you? Well, it could have been.' She was lying in order to torment me, she must be lying. She sat back on her heels, watching me with those bright inhuman hazel eyes. 'Oh Clarissa, sometimes you are so innocent, so naïve. You would believe anything. Oliver is not a saint, you know. He's a man like other men. He has his needs. After all I ought to know.'

And for weeks now I had been ugly and shapeless with his child. I would not argue or plead, I couldn't. The wound was too deep. It was all I could do to hide the pain. I said urgently, 'The baby, Alyne? Who is the father?'

'Who can tell? If Justin knew, he would suspect half a dozen.'

But I didn't believe that. Whatever she was, she was not promiscuous. 'Is it Bulwer Rutland?'

She shot me a swift glance. 'Why do you say that?'

'I saw you together last summer. We had driven out from Brighton. It was in Bramber Church.'

'Why didn't you tell Justin? I know he went to you. He told me so.'

'I don't know,' I said frankly. 'It was on the tip of my tongue and then I couldn't say it.'

'Does Oliver know?'

I shook my head. 'No. Did you go to Captain Rutland from London?'

She did not speak for a moment. She was crouched on the floor, quite still, staring down at the hands in her lap. 'Yes, but only for a couple of days, and we've been together at other places . . .'

'Like the Black Dog at Westley?'

'Yes, there too, that was the first time . . . and since . . .'

Incredulously I said, 'But it is so close. You must be mad . . .'

'Perhaps I am, but then I love him. You won't believe it, Clarissa, I know what you think of me, but I do love him,' and, at that moment at any rate, whatever else she might have done, I knew she was sincere. She spoke the simple truth.

'How long has it been going on?'

'A long time . . . since before I was married . . .'

'Then why . . . ?'

'He didn't want a wife,' she said bitterly, 'he wanted a mistress . . . I didn't intend to go on with it afterwards, Clarissa, I swear I didn't. He begged me to go away with him, but I meant to play fair by Justin. It was his fault, not mine. Everything that has happened has been because of Justin.'

'Does he go to other women?'

'I wish he did. That would be easy. I should know how to fight that.'

'What then?'

She got to her feet and began to walk up and down the room, a hectic flush replacing the pallor of her cheeks.

'I've never spoken of it to anyone. I couldn't, it was too horrible, too humiliating.'

'Not even to Oliver?'

'Not even to him.' Then she paused in front of me. 'Why did you say that?'

'You told him something. I saw you that day in the summer . . .'

'The day you ran off into the Fens . . . so that was why. I often wondered.' Then she walked away from me again. 'It was accidental. He gripped my shoulder and I cried out at the pain. Then he made me tell him something of it and I begged him to say nothing. Oliver can be kind. I feel safe with him, but he does not know all.'

How kind had he been? I didn't know whether I felt hate or pity. 'What else is there to know?'

She hesitated and then came to sit beside me on the daybed. 'I'm so afraid, Clarissa, so terribly afraid in case Justin finds out.'

'You could tell him it is his child.'

'He would know I lied. You see . . . you see . . . he cannot give me a baby. He has never, never once . . . it is what torments him.' She stared in front of her, looking into the hell of her marriage. 'You can't know what it has been like,' she whispered. 'Sometimes for weeks and weeks he never comes near me and then it is night after night until he is driven mad with frustration and that is when he uses the whip. He wants the satisfaction of seeing me abject, humiliated, pleading with him, and I won't give it to him, I won't . . .' She paused and I said nothing. I did not know what comfort to give. When she went on, her voice was low, without hope. 'That is what drove me to Bulwer. I had to . . . you must see that . . . I had to have someone who was sane and normal, someone who could love as a woman needs to be loved otherwise I think I might have gone out of my mind.'

'Is it a sickness?'

'I don't know. It was there from the very first, all those months in Italy, and the jealousy, the ravening jealousy if I so much as smile at another man. There's Ram Lall too . . . everywhere I go, every step I take, I feel his eyes on me,' she began to cry silently. 'If Justin ever knows I carry another man's child, he will kill me.'

'What are you going to do?'

'What can I do? Get rid of it perhaps . . . there are ways. Don't look like that, Clarissa. It's easy for you. You're safe. You have a father for your child.'

'Have you told Captain Rutland?'

'Not yet. It will mean nothing to him. Why should it? He is not a man who cares to have ties forced on him.'

I had never liked Alyne. I had feared her power and was jealous of what she had meant to Oliver and yet now her despair touched me. I would have helped if I could but knew no way. Presently she got wearily to her feet.

'I must dress. Will you stay, Clarissa, just for today? I feel so alone. It isn't much to ask.'

'Yes, of course I will.'

It was only when she had gone and I sat on in the prettily furnished room that I remembered what she had said about Oliver. I did not know whether I believed her or not, but I could not stifle the dull ache in my heart, try as I might.

The short winter's day closed in very early. By four o'clock it was already dark and a light snow had begun to fall. Neither Justin nor Oliver had returned. Lizzie came in with candles and would have drawn the curtains but Alyne prevented her.

'Leave them. I prefer them open,' she said.

We had been sitting in the dining room which leads off the hall and looks out on to the courtyard. I stood up, folding the piece of needlework I had brought with me.

'It's growing very late. I really think I should be going.'

'No, don't please.' Alyne had been restless all the afternoon, wandering round the room, picking up her needle and putting it down again without adding a stitch to her embroidery frame. 'It would be far better to wait,' she went on. 'Oliver is bound to come back for you.'

'He may not if he is late. I am quite used to driving the dog cart myself and Cherry will wonder where I am.'

But I did stay after all. She had infected me with her nervous tension. I could no longer sit quietly and I joined her at the window. We strained our eyes, but could see nothing through the veil of snow until she clutched my arm suddenly.

'Look, Clarissa. Isn't that fire?'

Beyond the gardens, out on the Fens, there were points of light flickering, disappearing, constantly changing position. 'Not fire,' I said slowly. 'It looks more like torches.'

'They must be coming here.' There was a suppressed excitement in her voice, almost as if she willed it, as if the clash of violence was the only way to assuage her own unhappiness. But I could only think of the last time, the useless bloody battle, the brutality that had led to nothing but misery.

'I pray to God that you're wrong,' I said fervently.

Then suddenly there was commotion outside. Someone came riding furiously up to the house followed by two or three others. It was so dark we could not immediately distinguish faces and Alyne pushed the casement wide open and brought the candles to the window, the flames flaring wildly in the rush of cold air.

'Is that you, Justin?'

Now I could see him clearly. He was covered with mud; a dark streak down one cheek could have been dirt or blood.

He shouted, 'Get back inside and shut that window.'

'What happened to you?'

'I had a fall. It's nothing.'

'Are you hurt?'

'No.'

I could have sworn there was disappointment instead of relief on her face. Then he shouted up to us again.

'Get back inside.'

'Why? What is it?'

'Those damned Fenmen never know when they are beaten, but don't be alarmed. The militia will be here shortly.'

So it was going to happen all over again. I felt sick. I pushed Alyne aside.

'Where is Oliver?'

'God knows. I left him arguing with them. He thinks they will listen to him, but there's only one answer to wretches like that and that is a gun.'

Alyne slammed the window shut but she did not move away. She was trembling, her eyes blazing, and I thought she is standing there watching and it might be a play, a melodrama. If they killed Justin, she would laugh and applaud. She was not tormented by thinking of the man she loved alone among men whose blind anger could no longer distinguish friend from enemy.

The distant points of light had turned into a snake of fire winding its way across the Fen. A sudden towering blaze of light showed that someone whether by accident or design had fired a rick. It had stopped snowing and the night was dark, but now torches and lanterns had appeared in the courtyard with more men. Justin must have recruited all those working on the estate. Some of them were armed and they formed themselves into rough order. They were obviously only waiting for the militia to march out and head off the attackers who still came resolutely on.

Justin had come into the hall. He shouted for Alyne and she shrugged her shoulders.

'I shall have to see what he wants.'

She went out of the room and I stood for a few minutes longer, still watching, and then made up my mind. I don't think I had any very clear idea of what I was going to do. I did not think of my condition, only that if I could persuade someone to harness the dog cart I would go and find Oliver. I had no fear for myself. The Fenmen are not vicious. They would not harm a woman. It was Justin against whom their bitterness was directed.

I went out into the hall. No one was there and I fetched my cloak. I went down the steps, walking carefully for the ice had frozen hard under the thin coat of fresh snow. Some of the men had already moved off, others waited at the far side. I picked my way towards the stables and then stopped.

Through the shifting light I could see a man furtively making his way along the box hedge that skirted one side of the courtyard. He paused and looked round him, flattening himself against the shrubbery, and I saw for an instant before it vanished that fleeting resemblance to Oliver. He carried one of the long fowling guns used by the Fenmen and as I watched, he raised it carefully to his shoulder. At the same moment Justin came out of the house with Ram Lall close behind him. Both of them carried pistols and he stopped to say something to the Indian, a perfect target in the light of the lamp that burned beside the door. I stood as if paralysed. The man slowly levelled his gun and suddenly I found my voice. I screamed a warning. He fired but the shot went wide. Justin must have seen him; he and Ram Lall raised their pistols simultaneously and fired. The dark figure took a step forward, then collapsed to his knees. Ram Lall ran across to him and Justin followed more slowly. His words came quite clearly through the silence.

'Is he dead?' Contemptuously he turned the body over with his foot. 'So you lost out after all, my friend, like the rest of your breed. I've waited a long time for this.'

And so had his victim, waited more than twenty years. I thought of all that suffering, the years of patient work, the dogged determination, only to end like this, and the man who had caused so much tragedy stood there, smiling and triumphant. I wished passionately I had not cried out the warning. If I had kept silent, it would have been the end of Justin, it would have given back to Oliver the inheritance that should have been his, it would have saved Alyne, and yet I couldn't do it. I couldn't watch him being murdered in cold blood and so had left him free to kill. The injustice turned me sick.

I did not think that Justin had even noticed me and after a moment he called out something to the men watching fearfully from the far side and strode after them, Ram Lall with him. I crossed to look down at the silent figure. He lay face upwards, the blood spreading on his breast, and the frightening thought crossed my mind that somewhere out on the Fens, Oliver too might be lying staring up at the dark sky with the same sightless eyes. I shivered and could not bear to touch him. There seemed nothing I could do and now I wanted only to get home, away from the house, away from Justin and Alyne and the evil that seemed to cling around them.

I could not harness the cart myself so I must walk. It was not so far and I knew the path intimately, but I had not reckoned on quite so much snow or such intense cold. Soon I was unbearably weary. I had gone about half the distance when I skidded on the frozen track and slid into a drift. I had not fallen very heavily and I was not hurt, but the breath was knocked out of me and it was there, as I rested for a few minutes, that the first pain stabbed at me making me gasp. I tried to ignore it. It was nothing, I told myself, just weariness after an exhausting day. I forced myself to my feet, brushed myself down and struggled on, but now it had become increasingly difficult. Each step was a labour and my skirts, soaked and heavy with snow, seemed to drag me back. The pain came again and I knew with desperation that I must not pause even to take breath or I might not be able to go on.

I don't remember much about the last hundred yards. I could hear distant shouting and tried to hurry, stumbling through the darkness and the drifting snowflakes. I could see Thatchers and knew it was a haven I must reach. When I fell against the door, sobbing with relief, it seemed to open instantly and strong arms were lifting me up. There was light and warmth and Mrs Starling saying comfortingly, 'There, there, don't 'ee fret, my lovey. You're safe now, you and the little 'un.'

It was a long night and through the pain I was obsessed by that dead face with its haunting look of Oliver. Once before the curtains were drawn I saw the flame of fire. The others had gone downstairs when I heard the shouting outside. I had been so sure that no one would harm Oliver and yet they had come; they were there, maddened enough to burn down his house, and his wife and unborn child with it. I dragged myself off the bed and groped my way to the window. I saw torches flaring and a confusion of brutish faces. They were pressing forward. Someone saw me and screamed an obscenity. Then a dark figure seemed to leap up in front of them.

'Bastards!' he was yelling. 'Bliddy cowards, the lot o' you! There are nowt but women in there and one of 'em bearing a child to the man who has been your friend!'

A stone was thrown and a window pane shattered downstairs. Burning with a wild rage I tried to open the casement but it was too stiff for me and sobbing I sank to my knees. The shouting went on and I pressed my hands over my ears to shut it out. It seemed a long time before it began to die away. Then Cherry was beside me, putting her arms around me.

'It's all right, Clarissa, it's all right.'

'Those men out there . . . what are they doing? What do they want?'

'They're going away now. It was Moggy who stopped them. Did you hear him? He was splendid.' She helped me back to the bed. 'You must lie down. Ben has gone for Dr Thorney. He will be here soon.'

'Is Oliver here?'

'Not yet, but he will come. I'm sure he will.'

I didn't believe her. Later that night I heard myself calling for him with an agonized certainty that I would never see him again, and at another time I lay bathed in sweat, but quite clear in my mind, and over and over again heard Alyne say in her light mocking voice, 'Oliver? Why not? You're such an innocent, Clarissa!'

At some time I must even have slept a little because I dreamed I saw him unhooking her dress, kissing the red marks left by Justin's whip, and then the two of them lying together, his strong thrust and her little moan of pleasure. Then I was awake again, writhing with the agony of bearing his child.

I knew that Dr Thorney came and wondered dully how he had come through fire and snow and it was early morning when, after a searing pain that seemed nearly to split me apart, I lay utterly spent while they moved around me and was quite sure that the baby was dead. I shut my eyes against it and when I opened them again, Cherry was standing there, very pale with her dark hair tumbling about her face.

'Listen,' she whispered, 'listen, Clarissa.'

Incredulously I heard the thin wail of my son and wanted to cry but laughed instead because Mrs Starling was holding him up for me to see, a bright red face, a button nose wrinkled in disgust at his first contact with his new world, and a crop of red-gold hair.

I felt his kiss on my forehead. I had slept and woken again and he was there, his coat ripped, his face blackened by the smoke, smelling of the fire that had been part of my muddled dreams.

Oliver said, 'I had no idea, none at all, until I met Dr Thorney on the road . . . oh my darling!' I put up my arms and pulled him down to me, so glad to know that he was still alive that I could think of nothing else. 'Hey,' he said, 'hold on, pet, I'm filthy.'

I was laughing and crying at the same time. Then he straightened himself. 'Where is my son?'

He turned to the cradle turning back the coverlet. 'My God, I can't believe it! We've produced a Red Indian between us!' He smiled, one grimy finger gently touching the tiny cheek.

'Are you glad it is a boy?'

'What do you think?' He kissed me. 'You'll be as black as I am in a minute. I must go and wash.'

'Oliver,' I caught at his hand. 'I want to know what happened last night.'

'Later my love. You've had a bad time. They tell me you should rest.'

'I shall rest all the better if I know . . . please . . .'

He sat beside me on the bed, his face very serious. 'I tried to stop them. We came to blows once. Our Red Indian there nearly lost his father.'

So my fears had been justified. I gripped his hand tightly. 'Don't make fun of it.'

'It was like trying to turn back the tide. They set fire to part of the barn and they broke into the house. The militia had arrived by then and drove them out, but in that mood they were capable of anything so I took Alyne away. Justin would not leave. I looked for you but she said you had gone home and I never dreamed of this.' He looked towards the sleeping baby. 'What a night to choose!'

'Where did you take Alyne?'

'To Peter Berkeley at Barkham. That's why I took so long to get back. She looked ill and I wanted to get a doctor to her, but she would have none of it so I left her with Berkeley's housekeeper.'

It was Alyne he thought of, always Alyne. I pushed the thought away.

'They came here. It was Moggy who stopped them.'

'I know,' he said grimly. 'My God, if anything had happened to you . . . !'

'Oliver, there is something else.'

'No more now, my dear.' He stood up.

'But there is. That man from the Fens. He was there at Ravensley.'

He frowned. 'You must be mistaken.'

'No, I'm not. I saw him. He would have killed Justin but I cried out and then they both fired . . .'

'Who did?'

'Justin and Ram Lall.'

He stared at me. 'Are you sure? The courtyard was empty when we came back.'

'He *was* there, quite dead. I saw him.'

'It was very dark. You could be mistaken. Perhaps he was only wounded and was able to get away.'

So it was not finished after all and I was glad. I shouldn't have been, I suppose, but I was. There was a God in Heaven, a God who had sent Oliver back to me and would see justice done.

'What is going to happen now?'

'I am not sure, but Justin has had a bad fright. He will have to see reason in future, learn to compromise.' Oliver moved away from me to the window. 'It's going to be a hard fight, but this time I think I may win.'

4

Robert Oliver Aylsham was christened in Ravensley's dark little church where all his ancestors down the years had sworn solemnly to renounce the devil and all his works. I had asked Cherry to be godmother and there was a particular tenderness in her face as she looked down on him in her arms, bawling lustily as the water was poured over his forehead. Our son was obviously not going to accept anything meekly. I saw Harry watching her over the edge of his prayerbook and wondered how he really felt about her. At the moment, thank goodness, she was entirely absorbed in the baby and the question of leaving us to earn her own living had been temporarily forgotten.

It was only a small party. It had taken me some time to recover from that exhausting night and Oliver said very firmly, 'I'm not going to have you worn out preparing for a host of people to whom we owe nothing.' So it was only the family and those few who were closest to us.

I had not expected Justin to come at all. Relations had been very strained between him and Oliver since that stormy night and I knew there had been long arguments up at Ravensley as to what was to happen to those who had caused the riot. No real harm had been done and the damage was already repaired, but Justin had wanted to bring charges and Oliver was resisting him strongly so nothing had yet been decided. Whether it was Alyne who had persuaded him, I don't know, but the carriage drew up just as the service commenced and he came through the door with his wife on his arm. She looked particularly lovely in a dark green velvet mantle trimmed with silver fox. It was almost impossible to believe that the heartburnings of that morning when she had told me of her pregnancy and the disaster of her marriage had ever really taken place. I saw Oliver's eyes dwell on her for an instant before he turned back to his son.

We came out of the church into brilliant March sunshine. We had been enjoying a few days of warm spring-like weather which so often comes in England, breaking the stranglehold of winter, and is so welcome even if we have to return to the frosts and snow.

Robert lay quiet now in my arms, worn out by all that strenuous resistance to being turned into a Christian, and when I paused on the steps, Harry peered down at the small crumpled red face.

'Odd to think we all looked like that once,' he said teasingly. 'Rum little beggar, isn't he, Sis?'

'He's nothing of the sort. He's beautiful,' said Cherry indignantly.

He grinned at her. 'If you say so, then of course he must be, but he's had quite enough of your attention. Now it's my turn. You come with me. I'm going to drive you back,' and when she protested, he took her arm and firmly led her down the path.

'That's just what she needs. Someone who won't take no for an answer. Oliver is too soft with her,' said Aunt Jess. 'Now you give Robert to me, Clarissa. I'll take him back for you. All these people crowding around and staring at him will only set him off again, poor mite.'

I let her take him, smiling at Papa's resigned shrug of the shoulders as he followed after her. His air of utter indifference to all the fuss being made of his grandson did not deceive me in the slightest.

I was surprised at the number of men and women from the village and the estate who had pushed into the back of the church and who now came, curtseying or touching their caps to me. The men were pressing forward to shake Oliver by the hand. Even Moggy and Nampy were there, looking vastly out of place and quite unlike themselves in coats that must have been handed down from their grandfathers, hat in hand, their hair unnaturally slicked down with water.

'I've brought summat for the little 'un,' whispered Moggy, producing a brace of wild duck like a conjuror from where he had hidden them behind a tombstone. 'Shot 'em this morning down by Spinney.'

'Many thanks,' said Oliver grinning. 'He's a trifle young yet, but we'll be happy to eat them for him. Leave them at Thatchers, will you, there's a good fellow.'

'Aye, sir, that I will.'

He dragged a gaping Nampy away as Justin came out of the church and paused beside me. Alyne reached up to Oliver and kissed his cheek.

'I'm so glad for you. He's a fine boy.'

He took her hand and they walked down the path together, leaving Justin standing beside me on the step.

A woman appeared in the doorway. He moved aside to let her pass and then stood staring, both of them frozen into stillness. The drooping ostrich plumes on her hat hid her face from me, but I saw a queer flush creep into Justin's sallow cheek. Then he turned and walked quickly down the path, thrusting his way through so that people parted in front of him and stared after him in surprise.

The stranger's gloved hand clutched at the folds of her dark red riding dress and the face she turned to me was the colour of ivory.

'Who is he?' she whispered. 'For God's sake, who is that man?'

'He is Lord Aylsham, my husband's uncle.'

'Justin Aylsham is dead,' she said tonelessly. 'He died more than twenty years ago.'

'That was what we all thought, but it was not true. He came back from India shortly after his brother's death.'

A little shiver ran through her, then she smiled faintly. 'Forgive me. It has been something of a shock. I've been abroad for a great many years.' Her eyes still followed Justin as he took Alyne's hand to help her into the carriage. 'The girl with him . . . I've been watching her in the church . . . a strange lovely face . . .'

'She is Lady Aylsham.'

'His wife?'

'Yes. I know it must seem unusual. She is so much younger. Alyne is my husband's adopted sister.'

'Adopted?' she repeated. 'When was this?'

I don't know why I was impelled to go into so much explanation except that there was something compelling about the directness of her gaze.

'It was a long time ago. She was only a few days old, I believe, when they found her, like Moses in the bulrushes, my husband used to say. My father-in-law brought her up with his own family.'

'And he was Robert Aylsham?'

'Yes.'

She had recovered her composure. The thin distinctive face turned to me was calm except for the smouldering eyes. 'Thank you for telling me so much. It is not vulgar curiosity, I assure you. I have been away so long, it is difficult to pick up the threads. I am Martha Leigh.'

I started. 'Martha Leigh of Westley?'

'Yes.'

'But this is extraordinary. I visited there with Mr Rutland. As you must know, he thinks of purchasing it from you.'

'So you are the Mrs Aylsham who accompanied him. My house-keeper mentioned it to me. Perhaps we shall meet again.'

She held out her hand and I felt the warm, firm pressure, then she went down the path and I saw the waiting groom help her into the saddle, then mount his own horse and follow her along the road.

I was still standing there when Oliver came back to me and took my arm.

'We ought to go, my dear. It is beginning to blow cold and you must not take a chill.'

'Oliver, did you ever know someone called Martha Leigh?'

'The Leighs lived at Westley, but they went away after their brother died when I was still very young. The house has been shut up ever since as you know.'

'That was Martha Leigh. She has come back for the sale of the estate.'

'Has she, by Jove? Josh Rutland will be pleased.'

'She was asking about Justin.'

'It must seem strange returning after such a long absence. Now come along, my pet, they will be waiting for us.'

Thatchers was crowded. A great many more people came in than had been invited and needed to be greeted and entertained. There was no time to speculate about Martha Leigh. It amused me to see Cherry playing Hugh Berkeley off against Harry and both of the young men vying with each other for her attention. When I went upstairs to Robert, she came with me.

'Don't desert your admirers,' I said smiling at her. 'It wouldn't surprise me if they came to blows.'

'Oh nonsense,' she blushed a little. 'I don't care a paper of pins for either of them.'

'I'm glad to hear it. Now go back and take my place for a few minutes while I am up here. Don't leave Oliver to cope alone.'

'I'd rather stay with you and the baby.'

'No, you wouldn't. Off you go.'

When she had gone, I dismissed Patty to the kitchen and took Robert from his cradle. I had decided to feed him myself against everyone's advice except Aunt Jess.

'I don't believe in wet nurses,' I said flatly. 'You know what they say up here, a baby takes in the vices and virtues of his nurse with his milk.'

'What utter rubbish!' declared Papa who had somehow been drawn into the argument. 'You'll spoil your figure, Clary.'

'No, I won't, and I want my son to be all mine.'

I sat there for a little, enjoying the peace and quiet, until presently Oliver came into the bedroom.

'I guessed this is where you would be,' he said and took Robert from me. 'He's had enough. Do you want him to burst?' He laid the baby in the cradle and turned back to me. 'I think you are a great deal more fond of him than you are of your husband.' He bent over me, gently kissing my breast before I could hook the neck of my dress.

'If you believe that, then you'll believe anything,' I told him laughing and we went down very happily together to see the last of our guests.

Once or twice during the day I had thought of Martha Leigh. There had been something in her manner, something in the way she looked at Justin that disturbed me. But there was no opportunity to speak of it until later that night. After Cherry had gone to bed, Oliver took a look around outside, then came in, shutting and bolting the door.

'If this mild spell continues,' he said, 'we could be in for a sudden thaw.'

'Will that matter?'

'It might if it coincides with the spring tides. There could be flooding. It happened once some years ago.'

'Is there any real danger?'

'I hope not, but the banks could burst. I don't think that the dykes are sufficiently strengthened yet and I have already warned Justin that not even the engines could control that weight of water, but he won't listen. However I've got men on the watch at check points. We should have ample warning.' He yawned and stretched himself lazily. 'I don't know about you, my dear, but I'm tired out. I've drunk a great deal too many healths to our lovely boy. Bed, I think, is what is called for.'

'Not yet. I want to tell you something.'

'Oh Lord, must I hear it now?'

'Yes, it is important. I should have told you before but the time never seemed right. You remember that night when I was lost on the Fens?'

'Yes,' he said resignedly, sitting down again. 'What about it?'

So then I told him everything that Ned Starling had related to me in his dry rusty voice in that dark hut and he listened in silence until I came to the end.

'I suspected some part of it,' he said at last, 'but I didn't know about Henry Leigh or how Ned Starling's father died. Strange to think that poor devil who has brooded on his wrongs all these years is a cousin of mine, an Aylsham, one of us.'

'Justin is a double murderer.'

'In one sense, but what can be proved against him now? Men have fought duels before. Wellington drew a pistol on Lord Winchilsea not so long ago.'

'His victim did not die.'

'He might have done.'

'No, there is a difference, you know there is, and what about that poor man he left callously to drown.'

'He may not have realized that he could not save himself.'

'How can you speak like that?' I said indignantly. 'Are you on his side?'

'No, by God, no. Do you think I have forgotten Jake? He may not have fired the gun himself, but it was his responsibility. I can never forgive him for that. But this other business happened so long ago. There is no case against him in the eyes of the law.'

'Your grandfather must have believed him guilty. Isn't that why he disinherited him?'

'Yes, that is true,' said Oliver slowly, 'and it must have been Isaac Starling who told him. It explains a great deal, doesn't it? But even then grandfather would never have a word said against him. It broke the old man up when he believed him dead.'

'It's so unfair. Why should a man like that have everything and you nothing?'

'It's useless to talk like that, my dear. I've accepted it long ago. It's over and done with.'

'I wonder,' I said slowly.

'What do you mean by that?'

'Why did Sir Henry Leigh challenge him to fight in the first place? What was the real reason?'

'Does it matter now?'

'I don't know, but when I went to the Manor with Joshua Rutland, I saw a portrait . . . a crayon drawing of Martha Leigh's younger sister, Alyne . . .'

He looked up. 'What is there in that? A name's a name. I remember seeing it once on some medieval tomb . . .'

'It was not the name. It was the likeness.'

'Likeness? To whom?'

'To Alyne.'

'What!' He stared at me. 'You must have imagined it. The name, the half dark room . . . young girls can look very much alike . . .'

'That's what I told myself at the time. It was not obvious, yet it *was* there, but so much else has happened, I never thought of it again until today when Martha Leigh asked me so many questions.'

'It's quite natural. She has been away so long, everything must seem strange to her.'

He was arguing against it and so was I, but I knew the same thought was in both our minds and yet we could not put it into words. It was too horrible even to contemplate.

Oliver had risen. He stood leaning one arm against the mantel, looking down into the dying fire, his face in shadow.

'It's Alyne I am sorry for. It must be hell to be tied to such a man.'

'I think she consoles herself.' I had not intended to say any such thing and it brought an instant reaction. Oliver turned round.

'What the devil do you mean by that?'

Suddenly I was angry. 'What I say. She has plenty of men at her beck and call, even you. She has never really let you go. She has only to crook her little finger and you run to her. Even on the night Robert was born, it was Alyne who was your first concern, not me, not your wife or your child.'

'That's a damnable lie. I didn't know . . . how could I know?'

'Wasn't I in just as much danger as she was? How many times have you consoled her since the night she came here, crying to you, telling you how Justin made love with a whip?'

'Do you really believe that about me?'

'Isn't it true?' I said recklessly. 'Deny it if you can but Alyne boasts of it . . . and there are other men.'

'What other men?' he grabbed me by the shoulder. 'Answer me. What others?'

But I could not tell him. I wanted to, but I could not bring myself to shout into his face that Bulwer Rutland had been sleeping with her, had given her a child . . . if it was he . . . how could I believe anything she told me? I said, 'Find out for yourself.'

'Why do you hate her so much?'

'I don't, you know I don't, but she doesn't need my pity or yours. She never has.'

'Are you so sure of that?' Then he released me. He stood for a moment looking down at me. 'This is ridiculous. We're both tired and saying things we shall be sorry for tomorrow.'

'I wish I thought that was true,' I said and could not keep my voice steady.

'It is true. Isn't it time we stopped this wrangling over Alyne?' He smiled faintly. 'We've been through a good deal together one way and another since that day you perjured yourself for me. Doesn't all that count?'

'Yes, I suppose so.'

'You know it does. It is not Justin and Alyne who are important, it is us and what we do together. Don't you believe that?'

'Yes.'

'Well then, let's try and believe the best of each other, not the worst.' He leaned forward and touched my cheek. 'Go to bed now. Let them work out their lives as they must.'

'Will you come?'

'Later.'

But he didn't. I slept alone for the first time for many weeks and was utterly wretched. The knowledge that it was I who had caused the rift between us brought me no comfort.

I would have been only too pleased to keep Justin and Alyne out of our lives, but it was impossible. We were tangled together in spite of ourselves. All that week I went about the ordinary tasks of everyday with a feeling that some calamity hung over us and not even the ever present joy of my son could dispel the uneasiness.

The mild weather had turned to rain, a cold drenching downpour, day and night, and I knew that Oliver was worried. Every winter the fields flooded and the floors of some of the low-lying cottages were awash, but the Fenmen thought nothing of it. They waded about in their heavy boots, removed everything valuable to the upper floor and then cheerfully swept out the mud and slush. But some years it was different and this had been a particularly hard winter. The snow had piled in drifts for weeks before Christmas and the waterways had frozen to a solid block. As it began to melt, the river rose above the banks. Many were already homeless or living in the ruins of the hovels from which Justin had stripped the roofs.

Oliver had opened our barns and women, children and animals had sought shelter there. I gave them what food I could and they shivered over pitiful little fires. The rain stopped for a day so that we all took heart and thanked God. Then it began again, not so heavy but continuous.

One morning at the end of that week Oliver said, 'I still hope we may escape the worst, but I should feel a great deal happier if we were prepared. Ravensley has always been safe. I've got to make Justin understand that he must throw open the outbuildings, supply hay and straw, blankets, food, anything we can. If the waters go on rising, where else can the poor devils find refuge? Will you come with me up to the house, Clarissa? Alyne is going to need help.'

'How can I? There is Robert to be thought of.'

'You need not remain all day, only this morning. I don't think there is no immediate danger and in any case Thatchers has usually been safe enough. Justin will listen more readily to you than he does to me. Please come, Clary.'

I knew how deeply he was concerned so I went with him in the dog cart, leaving strict instructions with Cherry and Mrs Starling. We passed Dr Thorney on the road and he called out to us.

'Thank the good Lord, it is not raining so hard.'

'Don't be too sure,' shouted Oliver after him. 'There's still danger.'

He flourished his whip gaily and trotted on down the track.

'What the devil has taken him up to Ravensley?' said Oliver whipping up the pony.

'Perhaps one of the servants is sick,' but I felt a stab of anxiety.

When we reached the courtyard, one of the men came to meet us. 'Keep the horse standing for me,' said Oliver. 'I won't be long.'

Annie met us in the hall looking worried. 'Lord Aylsham is in the library, sir,' she said to Oliver. 'The mistress is not down yet.'

'Is she ill, Annie?'

'Not ill, Miss Clarissa, not exactly ill, but she's been ailing for a day or two.' She waited until Oliver had disappeared before putting a hand on my arm. 'I guessed what was wrong a good few weeks back,' she whispered, 'but I wouldn't let on. 'Tisn't my business and Miss Alyne has always been one to keep things to herself. She didn't want no doctor this morning. It were the master who insisted.'

'Perhaps I had better go up to her.'

I knocked at Alyne's door and then went in. I don't know what I had expected, perhaps to find her lying on the bed, distracted and in tears, but she was sitting in front of her mirror, fully dressed, brushing her long hair and twisting it into a loose shining knot.

'Have you come to be in at the kill, Clarissa?' she said calmly.

'Alyne, how can you talk like that?'

She smiled at my reflection in the glass. 'It's so stupid really. It had to come, I suppose, but I had rather it had not been just now. We had a mighty quarrel last night and I made a fool of myself by fainting.'

'What did you quarrel about?'

'Nothing to do with this,' and she laid a hand against her waist. 'It doesn't show yet but it has happened rather frequently lately, fainting, I mean, and sickness. It's not like me. That's why he sent for Dr Thorney.'

'And he will have told him?'

'Probably.'

'And Justin has said nothing?'

'Not yet, but in any case I'm going down now to tell him myself.'

I could not make her out. She didn't seem frightened or distressed or ashamed. If anything she had a look of triumph. She got up smoothing down her gown. The deep purple trimmed with silver braid set off the creamy pallor of her face and the pale shining hair. She gave one last look in the mirror and then turned to the door.

'Coming, Clarissa? It should be amusing.'

I followed her down the stairs, wishing that I was not there, and yet knowing that I had to see it through to the end. She went into the library with her head held high. Justin was seated behind his desk.

She smiled at Oliver. 'Good morning. Has Justin given you the good news? Dr Thorney has just told me that we are to have a child at last.'

I saw by Oliver's face that he knew nothing. Justin must have remained silent, swallowing the bitter truth, but Alyne flaunting it so defiantly was too much for his self control. He rose slowly to his feet leaning across the desk.

'You bitch,' he said, 'you bloody bitch!'

Oliver started forward but Alyne waved him back. 'Why? What is wrong?' she said in the same high bright voice. 'I thought you would be pleased. It is what you've wanted ever since we were married.'

The cruelty in her light voice almost took my breath away. Justin came round the desk to face her. We might not have been there for all the notice he took of us.

'Who is it?' he demanded and when she did not answer, he suddenly thundered the question, 'WHO IS IT?'

'Who should it be but you, my dear Justin?' she said lightly mocking. 'And don't shout. Do you want the servants to think that you can't even father a child?'

With a swift movement he seized her arm and bent it behind her back, towering over her. 'Damn you, tell me who it is.'

'Or you'll break my arm or flog me as you flogged poor Jethro . . .'

'Who?' He tightened his grip and she let out a little moan of pain.

Oliver said hoarsely, 'Let her be. You are hurting her.'

Justin turned on him, his face contorted into a snarling mask. 'Is it you? If it is, by Christ, you shall pay for it.'

'It's not Oliver,' said Alyne quickly. 'You ought to know him by now. He has principles. He respects a woman which is more than you have ever done.'

'Who is it then? Who?' He cried out and I think I almost pitied him at that moment, but Alyne was merciless.

'Who?' she mimicked, 'Who? Does it matter? Supposing I said I didn't know. It could be one of half a dozen.'

He let her go, staring at her, the colour fading, leaving his face grey. 'So Ram Lall was right all along.'

'Ram Lall!' she spat at him with a searing contempt. 'Your black dog, your filthy spy, the devil's shadow . . .'

'A whore,' he muttered, 'and I would not believe him, a bloody whore foisting a nameless bastard on me . . .'

'Is that any worse than you?' Suddenly she was screaming at him. 'Night after night until I sickened at your touch . . . is it any wonder that I wanted a man, a real man whom I could love and who would love me . . .'

He hit her so hard across the mouth that she staggered and fell to her knees and before I could stop him, Oliver had leaped at his uncle. They struggled together for a moment and then the force of his fist sent Justin reeling back against the desk.

I had knelt by Alyne but she pushed me away and got to her feet. 'Let him be, Oliver,' she said tonelessly. 'I'm not worth fighting over.'

He stood panting, a shocked pity on his face. 'I didn't know . . . I never guessed . . .'

'What will you do?' I whispered to her.

'Do?' She looked at me strangely and then across at Justin. 'He'll get over it. His pride will see to that.' She put a handkerchief to her bleeding mouth and with the same air of bravado, she walked unsteadily from the room.

Oliver said, 'Go after her,' but I still hesitated, looking at Justin who was supporting himself against the desk with his back to us.

'Go,' he said thickly, 'get out of here, both of you.'

Oliver did not stir. 'I'm not leaving until I'm sure you will not harm her.'

'She is my wife. What I do to her is my concern.'

'It is also mine. She is my sister . . .'

Justin swung round. 'Sister be damned! Do you think I don't know how you've wanted her . . . had her too, more than likely, married or not.' Then his voice broke for a moment. 'God help me, I love her! How can I endure it?'

'You'll not touch her . . .'

'I'll do as I please,' he snarled. 'Leave me alone, damn you!'

There was little we could do. Oliver took my arm, pushing me from the room. Outside in the hall, he said, 'I'm not leaving her here. Go up to her, tell her she can come back with us.'

Not that, please God not that . . . but I dare not say what was in my mind. 'Is that wise?'

'God Almighty, you know what he is as well as I do. Do you want to see murder done?'

I ran up the stairs, but Alyne's door was shut and locked. I shook the handle, I begged her to open it, but all she would say was 'Go away, Clarissa. I don't need you or Oliver.'

When I went down again, Oliver said impatiently, 'Where is she?'

'She won't come.'

'She must.'

'I tell you she will not.'

He paused. 'Very well. I'll take you home and then I'll come back. She may have changed her mind.'

The scene we had just been through had had the effect of temporarily blotting out the purpose of our visit. It was only when we went out to the courtyard that we realized what had happened even during the last couple of hours.

One of the stablemen came hurrying to meet us. ' 'Tiddn't no use taking the trap, Mr Oliver. You'll never get through.'

'What the devil do you mean?'

'It's true, sir. Jack Moysey was here only a few minutes ago. He told me to warn the master and to tell you. Nothing won't hold it, not even the steam pumps. 'Tis like a great wall of water, he sez, coming in over the Fens and it's taking everything with it.'

'But I must go back to Thatchers,' I said frantically, 'I must. There is the baby and Cherry . . .'

'All right, all right, my dear.' Oliver thought for a moment. 'I'll get there. I'll bring them back here.' He turned to the man. 'Saddle me a horse quickly.'

'I'll go with you.'

'No, that would be worse than useless. I can get myself through somehow, but not both of us. Now be sensible. You will be safe here.'

'What if the water reaches Thatchers?'

'If it does and I don't think it will, they can go to the upper floors. Cherry does not panic easily and Mrs Starling has seen flooding before now.'

'Oh God, suppose . . . oh Oliver, I'm so frightened . . .'

'Now listen to me.' He took both my hands, holding them tightly. 'It's going to be all right. I know it is. I'll go there first. I swear I'll see them safe. Now you help them to get everything ready here. There is going to be a great many homeless people by nightfall. They will need food and warmth and somewhere to sleep. Go ahead. Don't wait for Justin or Alyne. Get the servants working on it. They will do as you ask. They are Fen people. They know only too well what can happen. I promise I'll be back when I can.'

I knew he was right but the next few hours were the worst I had ever known. All the time I tried to organize some sort of shelter, had blankets brought down from the attics, examined the food supplies, instructed the cook to start preparing gallons of hot soup, I thought of Cherry and the baby. Thank goodness, Aunt Jess and Papa were safe enough. Copthorne was built on rising ground whereas Thatchers was tucked into a hollow, protecting it from cruel winds, but making it vulnerable to flood. Water has a dreadful inevitability. You cannot turn it back. It rolls on and on devouring all that lies in its path. In all the turmoil and anxiety, fantastic as it may seem, all thought of Alyne and Justin went out of my mind.

Late in the afternoon Lizzie brought me a tray of tea and I drank it scalding hot, feeling the warmth steal through me and grateful for it. A freezing wind had sprung up. No one who has ever experienced a real 'Fen Blow' can ever forget it. It comes tearing across the marshes with a whistling scream straight from the North Sea and the snow-covered fiords as sharp and keen as the knives of the Viking invaders who came in their longboats a thousand years ago.

I went out of the house again, wrapped in my cloak, the rain lashing into my face, and it seemed to my straining eyes that the water had crept nearer. Beyond the formal gardens there was one vast, grey, heaving sea. Suppose it came higher and higher, suppose it engulfed us all, even Ravensley . . . I shivered with fear as much as cold and I was just turning back when I saw a bedraggled little group trailing across the lawns. One of them broke away and ran towards me, crying out my name. It was Cherry, half weeping, half laughing, carrying a dripping wet Prickle and behind came Moggy, a huge bundle slug over one shoulder and in his arms, wrapped in a motley collection of rugs and shawls, a small screaming outraged baby.

'There, me hearty,' he said, dumping Robert into my arms, 'there you be, young master. Lively as a grasshopper he be and fair yelling his head off!'

If I could have fallen on my knees and thanked God, I would have done so. I did the next best thing and kissed Moggy's rough weather-beaten cheek.

'Lord bless me, Missus, that were a treat and no mistake!' he mumbled blushing to the eyes.

'I'm so grateful to you, Moggy. Where is Mr Oliver?'

'Gone with Nampy in the boat. There's a good many of them poor souls as'll be driven up to the roofs more than likely. I must go back meself.' One stubby finger touched the baby's cheek. 'You shut your noise now, young 'un. Safe with your Mam you be now.'

'Won't you stay for something to eat?'

'Nay, time for that later,' and he grinned before he stumped away across the soaked grass.

I hurried Cherry back into the house. A fire had been lit in Alyne's little sitting room. It was warm and cosy there. Cherry knelt in front of it, rubbing her hair with a towel and then drying Prickle while I fed the hungry baby.

'It was exciting at first,' she said, 'the water came rolling down the road like a brown carpet. But when it rose over the step and we could not stop it, I began to be frightened. We carried everything we could upstairs, but I'm afraid your carpets will be ruined, Clarissa.'

'What are carpets so long as you're safe!'

'Even when Oliver came, we had quite a problem getting into the boat. He climbed in the window and took Robert from me and then I jumped. He knew we'd be safe with Moggy.'

'What about Mrs. Starling and Ben and the girls?'

'They have gone up to the church. The Vicar has thrown it open and some of the villagers are already taking shelter there.'

It was not until the baby was sleeping in an improvised cradle and Cherry had stripped off her wet clothes that I thought of Alyne again.

'I'll ask her to lend you something to wear,' I said. 'You're much of a size.'

I went quickly along the corridor. The door to Alyne's room was wide open which surprised me and the room was empty. I selected a plain woollen dress from her crowded wardrobe and took it back to Cherry.

'She's not there. Put it on and look after the baby while I go downstairs.'

She was not in the dining room or the kitchens or anywhere in the house. I asked Annie and Lizzie but neither of them had seen her.

'There's a lady come while you were upstairs with Miss Cherry,' Annie went on. 'She brought a big box of foodstuffs with her and a heap of blankets and rugs that'll help with that lot out there. We're going to need every stitch we can lay our hands on before the day is done.'

'Who was she, Annie?'

'Never set eyes on her before. She came from t'other road in a fine carriage, mud to the roof it were, and the coachman swearing something terrible. She asked to speak with the master so I showed her into the library.'

'Is Lord Aylsham still there?'

'Never stirred, not even with all this going on.' Annie's face showed strong disapproval. 'That Indian of his took in a tray and came out looking as if something had bitten him.'

'When did this lady come?'

'Only a few minutes gone. I went in with her to take away his tray. He'd not touched a mouthful.'

I hesitated outside the library door, uncertain whether to go in or not. Justin must have remained there all the morning shut up in his misery, oblivious of what was happening outside his own front door. Anger welled up in me that Oliver should be risking his life and his uncle sat there, doing nothing, not facing up to his responsibilities.

I opened the door quickly and then paused because they were standing there, just as they had stood in the porch of the church, silently facing one another.

Then Martha Leigh said quietly as if she were finishing something already begun. 'You're a destroyer, Justin, like your Indian God over there, Siva, the destroyer. You killed the love between my sister and me, you murdered my brother . . .' he raised his head as if in protest and she silenced him with a gesture. 'I know what you will say. It was a duel and it was he who provoked it, but it was murder all the same. Harry was no shot and you knew it. I would have screamed your guilt to the whole world, but my sister stopped me because, God forgive her, she loved you still . . .'

He said with a tinge of impatience, 'Why talk of this now? I swear I never meant . . .'

'To break a young girl's heart,' she said derisively. 'Oh no, you only amused yourself, played with loves and dreams and lives as if you alone had the right, as if you were God and the rest of us your toys.'

'For heaven's sake, Martha, it is all over and done with.'

'Nothing is ever completely done with. It leaves scars. Did you never wonder what you had left behind you?'

'What do you mean?'

'There was a child . . .'

'I don't believe you.'

'It is true.'

'Where is this child?'

Martha Leigh moved for the first time, putting up a hand to her face wearily. 'I wish I could be certain.'

'You talk in riddles.'

She walked away from him to the window. The light had almost gone. The grey twilight from outside outlined the austere features. She spoke so low and quickly that I could scarcely hear.

'We went away from Westley. What else could we do, my sister and I? I found it hard to forgive her for Henry's death, for those nights she ran to you at the Black Dog. You know how she was, full of whims and fancies, your Fen witch you used to call her . . . she was wild with misery when you went away without a word. Once she tried to kill herself, slashing her wrists . . .'

'Oh God, no,' he muttered hoarsely.

'It is true,' she went on relentlessly. 'We thought she would feel differently when the child came, but a week after it was born, the baby disappeared from the cradle and she with it. Days later they took her drowned body out of the river, but they never recovered her child.'

'I am sorry,' he had turned away so that I could not see his face. 'I knew nothing of it . . . how could I know?'

'Did you ever give one thought to what you had done to us?' He did not answer and she went on quickly. 'The shock made me ill for a long time. When I recovered, I wanted only to go away as far as I could, out of this country. So it never came to my knowledge that a baby had been taken from the marshes, a baby with no name, no parents . . . a baby who could be your wife.'

I still could not see his face but I heard the great cry that was torn out of him. 'I will never believe it. This is your revenge, a mean cowardly revenge for a boy's folly . . .'

'No boy, Justin, but a man who took what he wanted careless of others. For years I dreamed of the child who had been lost . . . and now I dare not even hope because if it is so, then you have destroyed her too.'

He moved restlessly as if uncertain which way to turn and I could not remain hidden any longer. With a quick movement I opened and shut the door again and walked into the room.

He stared at me before he said hoarsely, 'Where is Alyne? Fetch her, Clarissa.'

'Alyne is not in her room. I came to ask if she was with you.'

'She must be there.'

'She is not in the house. We have searched everywhere.'

'Then search again,' he said violently. 'Ask the servants, ask everyone.'

We went through the house from top to bottom. We searched the barns, stables, the outbuildings. We questioned everyone, but no one had seen her. I don't think Justin had realized what had been happening in the last few hours. He had thought Oliver exaggerated that morning and had no experience of how swiftly the waters can rise. He stared at the huddled groups of shivering people, disturbed because he saw the dislike in their faces and the way they drew away from him. Ravensley was like an island in a desolation of waters.

It was when he returned to the house that one of the boys who worked in the yard came running up saying that a horse had been taken from the stables.

'My lady's horse,' he said fearfully, 'the one she always rides.'

'When was it taken?'

The boy looked bewildered. 'Some time ago, my lord. I weren't watching, see, with so much coming and going.'

'But what could she have been thinking of? Where could she have gone? To ride out into this would be madness.'

'She may not have realized how serious the flooding was. It has come so suddenly.'

'When did you see her last, Clarissa?'

'Not since this morning.'

'My God, what have I done?' He buried his face in his hands for a moment. When he took them away, he was deathly pale.

I knew what was in his mind. Had she gone out of the house with the intention of destroying herself as that other girl had done so long ago and yet somehow I didn't believe it. Alyne had not been in despair that morning. She had held some secret within her that had given her strength.

Martha Leigh looked from one to the other of us. 'What happened to drive her from her home at such a time?'

Justin did not heed her. He seized me by the arm, looking into my face. 'She must have had some purpose, there must be some clue. What is it, Clarissa? What do you know? Is there anywhere, anywhere at all where she might have gone?'

I said slowly, 'I did see her once at the Black Dog . . .'

'The Black Dog at Westley?'

I saw the look that passed between them. It was gone almost at once but I thought how strange it was that it should be there that Alyne Leigh had run to meet her lover just as her daughter had gone to Bulwer.

Justin said, 'She could never have got through.'

'She could. I reached here,' said Martha Leigh. 'The road was flooding but not impassable. The causeway there is far higher than the marsh.'

'I'll go there now.'

'But you can't,' I exclaimed. 'That was hours ago. By now it will be hopeless. There are men out searching all over the Fens. Oliver is with them. If she is there, they will find her.'

But he would not listen to us. He was like a madman in his determination. I believe to do him justice that he had been shocked into a sense of responsibility, that the grim sight of the men and women crowded into his barns had made him realize what he owed not only to Alyne but to those who depended on him for their very life.

We watched him go, taking Ram Lall with him and one of the stablemen. It was almost dark. They were carrying lanterns as they crossed the soaking fields to where the boats were moored.

Martha Leigh said quietly, 'Will you permit me to stay with you? I'd like to help if I can.'

'I should be grateful. There is only Cherry and she is very young.'

We went back to the house together and in the hall she paused. 'How much did you hear when you came into the library?'

I looked at her. 'Do you really believe that Alyne is your sister's child?'

'How can I be sure of anything? When I saw her in the church there was something about her, something in her face that drew me . . . and then when I knew where she had come from . . . I did not mean to speak of it, but he angered me . . .' She turned to me. 'Who is it who plays so wantonly with our lives? Is it God or the Devil?'

She was a strange woman, but she had a compelling power and a strength for which I was grateful during that long evening.

Many of the cattle and sheep had been already moved to higher land. The Fenmen have an instinctive knowledge of when floods will come, but no one had expected that this year they would be so devastating. Every available space was crowded with pitiful people clutching children by the hand and carrying bundles of precious possessions hastily snatched up at the last moment. There were dogs, a cat in a basket, children carrying kittens, a pet hen, a linnet in a cage, a goat, even a donkey, and we did our best to give them food, shelter and comfort. Cherry took over the children, raiding the old cupboards in the attics for toys to keep them amused, organizing games for the older ones. Martha Leigh had a way with animals that was little short of miraculous. She soothed snarling fights, calmed hysterical children whose pet had gone astray and sometime during the course of the evening we found a few minutes to talk quietly together and I told her a little of what Alyne had spoken to me.

She was kneeling beside a dog whose paw had been injured in its wild scramble to safety. Her skilful fingers adjusted the splint and bound it tightly with a strip of linen. She sat back, one hand gently caressing the whimpering dog.

'I have always believed that there are forces in us that we do not understand,' she said slowly, 'forces that lie beneath the conscious self. Perhaps deep down Justin was drawn to Alyne and never realized that it was not the bond between man and woman, but something instinctive, something quite different, and the conflict brought only fear and doubt that he tried to conquer in the only way he knew.'

I did not really understand her, but there was something about Martha Leigh that distinguished her from all others and I wondered how much truth might lie in what she said.

When I went up to Robert, the quiet room was like a haven of refuge. He lay there, so rosy and warm, not caring at all about his makeshift cradle, and it was at these times that I thought of Oliver and was overwhelmed with anxiety. Once, quite unashamedly, I went down on my knees and prayed to God to send him back to me before going downstairs again to the myriad tasks that still waited to be done.

It was very late that night when, exhausted and starving, Cherry, Martha and I sat down at last to a meal. Annie had just brought in the tureen of hot soup and we had scarcely swallowed a mouthful before Lizzie came flying into the room.

'He's found her! Mr Oliver has found Miss Alyne! He's bringing her in now.'

We forgot how hungry we were. I ran out into the hall with Martha behind me. Oliver was coming through the door carrying her in his arms. She lay, limp and lifeless, streaming with water, her face dead white, the long fair hair falling almost to the floor.

'She's breathing, but only just,' he said.

'Take her upstairs quickly. Lizzie, fetch the warming pan, bring blankets, hot bricks . . .'

He carried her up and laid her on the bed. We stripped the wet clothes off her. She was so deeply unconscious and so deathly cold that I was afraid.

I said to Lizzie, 'Is Dr Thorney still here?'

'Aye. He were out in the barn with Jim Gibson's broken arm.'

'Fetch him quickly and send someone to light a fire in here.'

I left Martha and Cherry to wrap her in warm blankets and put the hot bricks to her feet and went down to find Oliver. He was still in the hall with Moggy and Nampy. He turned to me as I came down the stairs.

'How is she?'

'Alive, but that's all. Thank goodness the doctor is here. Lizzie is bringing him. Where did you find her?"

'At the Black Dog. She must have got there somehow, but everyone had fled from the place already. The inn was empty and the water had already reached the first floor. It was only by chance that I saw her. She must have crawled as far as the window and was clinging to it. When I climbed in to get her, she collapsed. Where is Justin?'

'He went out in search of her as soon as we found that she had left the house.'

'When was that?"

'She must have gone this morning almost immediately after you left.'

'Why, Clarissa, why should she go to the Black Dog?'

'How do I know?'

'Is it true about the child?'

'Yes. We didn't miss her until this afternoon about four o'clock.'

'And now it's nearly midnight. I must go out again. I must try and find Justin and tell him she is safe.'

'You can't,' I exclaimed. 'You will never find anyone in the dark. You must rest and eat first.'

'You have no idea what it is like, Clarissa. The wind tearing down the trees, ripping up bushes, stripping off roofs and everywhere the water like a black torrent sweeping everything in front of it. Nothing could stand in its way. We thought once that the boat must go under and us with it.'

He was swaying with exhaustion and I prevailed on him at last to sit down and eat. I sent Moggy and Nampy to the kitchen.

'There's hot food there and something to drink.'

Moggy grinned and touched his cap. 'Thank 'ee kindly, Missus.'

I poured a glass of brandy for Oliver and filled a bowl with the hot soup. Cherry came in just as he started on it.

'Martha told me to tell you that the doctor is with Alyne now.'

'What is Martha Leigh doing here?' asked Oliver.

'She brought food and blankets and then stayed to help. She has been wonderful. I don't know what we would have done without her.'

He was too weary to question further and I was grateful.

He swallowed the last of the soup and stood up. 'I had better go. Justin doesn't know the Fens as we do.'

'Why should you risk your life for him?' said Cherry fiercely. 'I've been talking to those poor people out there who have lost everything and it is all because of him.'

'Not quite, Puss,' Oliver smiled faintly. 'Justin doesn't control wind and water.'

'It wouldn't have happened if he hadn't installed those beastly engines. That's what everyone is saying. Nothing like this would have happened if he'd never come back. It would all have belonged to you.'

'I'm not God either, Pussie, and now I mustn't waste any more time.'

It was Moggy who persuaded him that it was sheer lunacy to go out again in the pitch darkness where they could neither see nor be seen.

'There's nowt any of us can do now till first light. Then we'll find him if he's still alive.'

He still protested but it was not only his own life he would be putting in danger but the lives of the loyal men who had striven so hard all through the day. He let me help him off with his coat and I pushed him towards the sofa.

'Lie there,' I said, 'and I'll fetch a rug.'

When I came back, he'd already fallen asleep hardly stirring even when I pulled off his boots. I covered him with the rug and bent to kiss him. He mumbled something but whether it was Alyne's name or mine I couldn't be sure.

5

At first we thought we had lost her. Try as he would, Dr Thorney could not stop the bleeding. It went on and on and her life seemed to ebb with it. I think Alyne would have surely died if it had not been for Martha Leigh. She had a strength, a quiet determination as if she willed her to live.

At first light, though we were still anxious, there seemed hope at last and I went downstairs. Oliver was already awake and drinking a scalding cup of coffee.

'Moggy is waiting outside. I'm going now. God knows when we will be back.'

'I wish I could come with you.'

He put his arm round me and held me close. 'May I see Robert for a moment?'

When we went upstairs, the baby was still sleeping. Oliver knelt down beside the cradle and kissed the rosy cheek. 'This is what is important. If I can think of that, if I can keep you and him in my mind, then I shall be all right.'

'What do you mean?'

'I don't know. It's nothing really. Justin and I have been at odds for so long, it's got to end sometime and I have a feeling it will be now.' He rubbed a hand across his face and smiled a little. 'It's what old Nurse would call a black shadow falling across my grave. How is she by the way?'

'Prophesying gloom and disaster and enjoying every minute of it.'

'She would.'

'Dearest, must you go?'

'Yes, I must.' He got to his feet. 'I don't know what we would have done without you, Clarissa. I hope Justin is properly grateful.'

'It wasn't for him, it was for you.'

'Oh Lord, I almost forgot. How is Alyne this morning?'

Perhaps it was selfish of me, but I was filled with joy because for the first time it had come as an afterthought.

'It seemed as if she might lose the baby . . .'

'Perhaps it would be better for her if she did.'

'Don't say that. The doctor thinks now that she will pull through if we take care.'

'At least we can do that.'

I wrapped myself in my thick cloak and walked with him to where Moggy waited with Nampy in the boat. The devastation was beyond all description. A grey sea of water still lapped greedily at the edge of the land, an occasional bare tree scarcely visible in the waste. Branches, household goods, dead chickens, a sheep, a pig, even a horse, bloated and hideous, floated sickeningly on the surface and beyond there must have been other more terrible sights.

I hugged Oliver. 'Take care of yourself, darling.'

'I will. Never fear.'

I could not bear to watch them row away, it was too frightening, too final. Instead I turned my back and walked briskly up to the house where I could occupy myself with the thousand things that still remained to be done.

It was Moggy who told me what happened, briefly, graphically, so that it was as if I saw it with my own eyes.

'It were full light when we come up to Spinney. You know the mill, Missus. There's a catwalk round it higher than most and Lord Aylsham were up there, clinging to the rail. He must have climbed it some time in the night. The wind were enough to blow the hair clean off your head and at any minute I thought to see him whipped off by the gale. Mr Oliver shouts to him to come down the iron rungs and we'd be there to take hold of him, but he wouldn't budge and when I brought the boat round t'other side, I saw why. Ned Starling were at the top of the ladder, just sittin' there, not movin'. 'Twere like the spider and the fly, see. He had him trapped. Mr Oliver calls to his uncle to jump, but he were scared like enough. So then he sez to me, "It's no good, Moggy, I'll have to go up there meself." I tried to tell him it weren't no use. I knows Ned, see. He en't a bad man, but about that one thing he en't quite right in his head.'

'What happened then?'

'Mr Oliver, he goes up the rungs and I couldn't hear what he sez 'cos of the wind's howl, but I know he's arguing with Ned. They were standing close together and I reckoned he had Ned pinned against the wall for he shouted to his uncle to come quick, but he didn't move, not at once, and suddenly Ned must have hit out hard because Mr Oliver come backwards over the rail and his head struck against the roof of the scoop wheel as he fell. Lord Aylsham gave a sort of scream, but I didn't see properly what he did 'cos I was pulling Mr Oliver out of the water and him with blood all running down his face and dead to the world. The next thing I hears is a mighty splash and they were both of 'em, Lord Aylsham and Ned, off the mill and into the water. Nampy tried to row towards them. We could see them struggling together, but I were desperate worried about Mr Oliver. I got him comfortable as I could with me coat under his head and when I looked again, they were gone, vanished, no sign of 'em anywhere, so I sez to Nampy, "We've got to get him home quick."'

'Thank God you did,' I said fervently.

Never, never until my dying day shall I forget seeing the two Fenmen carrying Oliver between them across the grass and into the house. Every fear seemed suddenly to have become the dreaded reality. I couldn't move. I stood there paralysed, staring down at the blood, the matted hair, the white face without a trace of life.

It was Martha Leigh who took charge, who said, 'Bring him in carefully. Don't jar him.'

They laid him on the sofa where he had slept the night before and she bent over him. It seemed a long time before she said, 'He's not dead, it's concussion, I think. We'll fetch the doctor and see what is to be done before we move him.'

He was unconscious for the rest of the day and part of the night and except when I had to attend to the baby, I hardly moved from his side. Towards dawn, he stirred, groaning a little with the pain of his head, and asking what had happened. I made him drink the sedative the doctor had left and presently he slept.

In the morning Annie came in, looking shocked and upset, to tell us that Justin had been found.

Oliver struggled up in the bed. 'Is he dead?'

'Aye, sir, he is that. Stone cold dead.'

'Where is he?'

'Outside . . . in the courtyard.'

'I'll come down.'

'You shouldn't,' I protested. 'The doctor said you must lie still after that injury to your head.'

But he insisted so I helped him into a dressing gown and he groped his way uncertainly down the stairs.

The men moved aside as we came through the door. Justin and the man who had waited so long and so patiently for his revenge lay together, their arms tightly around one another. They might have been bound together in love rather than hate.

Oliver stared down at them silently until Moggy ventured to break the silence.

'What do you want us to do with them, sir?'

'Carry Lord Aylsham to his own room and take . . . take the other to one of the barns. Treat him decently. He was driven to do what he did.'

Moggy nodded. 'Aye, sir, we'll do that.'

They bent over the bodies, but Oliver still did not move. He looked so white and sick, I thought he might faint. I reached for his hand and felt his fingers grip mine tightly. He straightened himself as the men moved slowly away. I saw him shiver in the raw wind.

I said, 'We had better go in.'

He turned to me then with a faint smile. 'Don't worry, Clarissa. I'm all right except for a damnable headache.'

We went into the house together and after I had persuaded him to go back to bed, I nerved myself to go out to the barn where Ned Starling lay decently shrouded under a white sheet. A black mongrel dog, soaked and shivering, lay beside him. He must have crawled from the floods to find the master he loved. Ben was on his knees, coaxing him to eat from a bowl of meat scraps.

'He's starving,' he said glancing up at me defiantly so that I guessed he had plundered the kitchen when cook's back was turned.

'All right, Ben, you can look after him for me,' I said quietly and left them together.

On that terrible day I never gave a thought to Ram Lall and it was not until that evening that he crept back to the house. He had never spoken much but now he crouched in the kitchen, a silent shivering bundle staring vacantly in front of him and so stricken at the loss of his master that even the servants took pity on him and let him stay there by the fire. Devil's shadow and Black Shuck, I thought ironically, they had both loved in their own way.

For more than a week we were completely isolated and then very slowly the water began to recede leaving an indescribable wreckage behind it. As soon as he could, Oliver was out directing the rescue operations. With his uncle's death everything fell on his shoulders. When the road to Westley was cleared sufficiently to get through on horseback, Martha Leigh left us though we urged her to stay. She was not a woman to betray her feelings and I had no clue as to what she intended to do.

'I shall see you again before I return to Italy,' was all she said when I thanked her for everything she had done.

There had been so much destruction, so many lives lost, that Justin's funeral was necessarily a quiet one. He was buried beside his brother and his father in the family vault and when we came back from the church, I went up to see Alyne.

She had taken his death very calmly, scarcely saying anything, and with so much to attend to, I had left a great deal of the nursing to Cherry and Annie Pearce. She had made a slow but steady recovery though Dr Thorney had not yet allowed her out of bed.

When I went in to her, she was sitting up against the pillows, a lacy white shawl around her shoulders. She looked fragile and very lovely.

'Is it all over, Clarissa?' she asked.

'Yes. Peter Berkeley and a few others have come back. Oliver is with them now.'

'He hasn't come up to see me.'

'There has been so much to do. He has been out every day in the week and he is still in great pain from the fall.'

'How like Oliver to try and rescue Justin and nearly get himself killed. Why didn't he leave him there? No one would have known.'

'Do you really need to ask that?' I said dryly. 'How are you feeling today? Are you strong enough to talk for a little?'

'If you wish it.' I drew a chair up beside the bed and she looked across at me. 'What do you want to talk about, Clarissa?'

'There is the future to be thought of.'

'Yours or mine?'

'Both.' I paused for a moment, not sure where to begin. 'I've not asked you before but why did you go to the Black Dog that day?'

'I thought you might have guessed.' She raised her head. 'It doesn't matter now so you might as well know. Bulwer was to have met me there. We were going away together.'

So that was why she had flung that last defiance at Justin. 'What happened?'

'He was not there. When I reached the inn, there was no one. It was empty. At first I thought I would wait and then suddenly when I went inside, I heard that dreadful booming sound and I knew that the banks had burst. I started to run down the road but the flood came so quickly. It nearly took me with it. I don't know how I got back to the house. I remember climbing the stairs to escape the water. I was terrified.' She trembled a little and put up a hand to her face.

'It must have been dreadful. Thank God, Oliver reached you in time.'

'I remember seeing the boat and trying to call out to them, then nothing more until I found myself here. Those first few days I wanted to die . . . I think I might have done but for Martha Leigh.' She turned to me, her eyes wide. 'Do you know, Clarissa, I saw her when I was a child without knowing who she was and in some queer way I felt I was a child again and it was she who was holding me back, refusing to let me go.'

So Martha Leigh had told her nothing. Did she truly believe Alyne was her sister's child? Did I for that matter? We were silent for a moment, then Alyne stirred a little in the bed.

'It was silly of course. Life has to be lived whatever has happened to you. Today for the first time I've begun to realize something, Clarissa. I am Lord Aylsham's widow and the child, if it is a boy, will be his heir.'

I stared at her. The thought had never crossed my mind. It had seemed so natural, so right that Oliver should be master of Ravensley now that his uncle was dead.

I said slowly, 'But it is not Justin's child.'

'Who is to say it is not?'

'I know and Oliver knows.'

'It would be your word against mine and do you really believe that Oliver will publish it abroad that his uncle's widow is about to bear a bastard?'

I knew she was right. Oliver would remain silent whatever it cost him and it made me furiously angry, not for myself, but for him, that he should be cheated a second time, forced to play second fiddle to another man's son.

I said, 'What about Captain Rutland?'

'What about him? He didn't come when he promised, did he?' Her face was stony, but behind it I sensed a bitterness, a cruel disillusionment. 'Perhaps he never even meant to come.' Then she turned to me with her tiny mocking smile. 'Don't look so distressed, Clarissa. Perhaps it will be a girl. Then you will be Lady Aylsham of Ravensley after all.'

I didn't know if she was deliberately tormenting me or if she was determined to play her trump card, but I had a weapon too, and the desire to use it, to wound irrevocably, so burned inside me that I could not remain still. I got up and walked away from her, staring out of the window, hating myself for what I was going to do.

I said, 'Alyne, how much did Martha Leigh tell you of herself?'

'Very little,' she said surprised. 'But I liked her. She has asked me to visit her before she goes back to Italy.'

'Did she tell you that twenty-three years ago, her sister had a child?'

'No. Why should she?'

'And that the sister, deserted by her lover and in great distress, drowned herself?'

'Drowned?' she repeated and there was an odd shaken note in her voice. 'What has all this to do with me?'

'Because she did not drown her child. The baby was found abandoned in the Fens.'

'So that was why she died . . .'

I turned to look at her and saw that she had gone very pale. 'Why do you say that?'

She was staring in front of her. 'I saw her grave once in Westley churchyard. She had the same name as me and I knew it then. It was as if she stretched out a hand to me. That's what you mean, isn't it? She was my mother.' She put her hands up to her face and there was wonder in her voice. 'Alyne Leigh of Westley Manor was my mother. And my father? Who was my father? Do you know that too, Clarissa?'

I had to move away before I could say it. I could not watch the joy die out of her eyes. 'Alyne Leigh's lover was Justin Aylsham.'

There was a long pause before she said faintly, 'I don't believe you.'

'I think you do,' and I went on quickly before my courage should fail me. 'And if you intend to put Bulwer Rutland's son in the place that should belong to Oliver, then I shall tell what I know, I shall tell everyone that your husband was also your father.'

'I can't believe it, I won't believe it. It's a lie, it must be a lie.'

Her hands were convulsively clutching at the coverlet and I was suddenly horrified at what I had done. I was not even sure that it was the truth. No one could be. Martha Leigh had kept silent and I had betrayed her.

'Oliver would never let you do such a thing,' she whispered. 'Never . . . I know it. He loves me still.'

And that hardened me against her. 'Are you so sure? You can't go back, Alyne. Things have changed. Oliver has a son now.'

Our eyes met and I knew there would be a fight between us with no quarter given, then I was out of the room, leaning back against the closed door, breathing hard as if I'd run a great distance. It was some minutes before I could pull myself together and go downstairs to join our guests.

The concussion had left Oliver with exhausting headaches. That evening after everyone had left and we had supped together, he lay back on the sofa with his eyes closed and I sat on a footstool close beside him.

After a little I said, 'Oliver, what are you going to do about Alyne?'

'Why? Is she worse?'

'No, she is making an excellent recovery but the baby will be born in the late summer.'

He opened his eyes and sat up. 'I have never asked. Perhaps, in a way, I haven't wanted to know. Who is the father of her child?'

'Bulwer Rutland.'

His mouth twisted in disgust. 'That infernal bastard! And he left her to face it alone.'

'No, he didn't, it seems. Alyne was to have met him at the Black Dog, but he never came.'

'Cried off more than likely. Where is he now for God's sake?'

'Does it matter?'

'If I wasn't tied here, I'd go up to London. Hunt the fellow out and take a horsewhip to him.'

'How would that help?' I said dryly. 'There is something more important to us. Do you realize that so far as anyone outside of us knows, her child is Justin's heir?'

I saw by the tightening of his jaw that he had already thought of it and faced it. He said wearily, 'That's something we will have to cope with when the time comes just as I have to face breaking the news to Jethro. Alyne is Justin's widow and I shall make proper provision for her.'

Oh God, I thought, is it to go on for ever? Must I endure her still living in this house with Bulwer Rutland's son growing up as an Aylsham, inheriting the title, taking precedence over my Robert? There must be some other way out, there must be.

I said, 'Oliver, Martha Leigh's sister did have a child, a baby she abandoned on the Fens when she drowned herself.'

He looked up at me frowning. 'How do you know?'

'From Martha Leigh herself.'

'And Justin was her lover, that is what you mean, isn't it? Did he know about the child?'

'She told him before he went out to look for Alyne that night.'

'My God, what a hell he must have gone through. Perhaps that's why he did what he did. He no longer cared to live.' He got up and walked restlessly away from me. 'I don't believe it. Why should Alyne be this child? There is more than one baby abandoned on the Fens.'

But I persisted. 'Do you think your mother spoke of Alyne when she went to him in India?'

He turned round on me. 'Would you turn him into a monster? He knew nothing of her that first day he came here. I remember his surprise and how he looked at her even then.'

And suddenly I knew he was right, knew it by my own reaction. If Oliver's mother had ever suspected that the baby her husband took into his home was her lover's child, she would have kept it jealously hidden in her heart and never given him the satisfaction of knowing it.

Oliver said, 'You've not spoken of this to anyone, Clarissa?'

'No . . .'

'Then put it out of your mind once and for all. I want no part in it, do you understand?'

'Very well,' and I prayed that he would never have to know how mercilessly I had used my knowledge that very afternoon.

For several days nothing more was said and the subject was not mentioned again between Alyne and me though sometimes when I looked at her, I found it hard to choke down the bitter words.

The floods had been so severe and so widespread that we were still very largely isolated out at Ravensley. The mail coaches had been unable to get through so we were cut off from news and our first visitor from London was Harry who arrived unexpectedly one evening on a jaded horse, both of them splashed with mire to the eyes.

'Thank God, you're all safe,' he exclaimed bursting into the drawing room in his wet coat and muddied breeches. 'I went to Thatchers first and my heart was in my boots when I saw the fearful state it was in so I rode on to Copthorne. Aunt Jess told me you were here.'

'How on earth did you get through?'

'My horse fell twice and threw me overboard, but we managed it. Oh Clary, I'm glad to see you!'

I had never thought Harry cared so much and I was between laughing and crying as he hugged me. He wrung Oliver's hand and beamed at Cherry, giving her a quick impulsive kiss on the cheek before she could protest. Then he turned awkwardly to Alyne.

'Father told me of Lord Aylsham's death. It must have caused you great distress.'

'You needn't upset yourself, Harry,' she said composedly. 'I am growing accustomed to being a widow.'

He looked disconcerted so I said hurriedly, 'Are you hungry? Have you eaten?'

'No, by Jove, I haven't, now I come to think of it. Not a bite all day. I didn't want to waste the time. I was too anxious to get here.'

'Come and take off those wet clothes and Annie shall bring you some supper.'

Later in the evening when we were all sitting quietly together talking over what had happened, Harry said, 'I don't envy you the clearing up. It's going to take a long time before the land is fit for anything at all.'

'Six months at least,' said Oliver, 'and I'm faced with something of a problem. I've tried to send a message through to Mr Gwilliam. He is the Aylsham solicitor and holds my uncle's will as well as all the particulars of his dealings with Joshua Rutland but I doubt if it has reached him yet. As soon as it is possible to leave here, I shall have to ride up to London myself.'

'I don't imagine Josh Rutland will be worrying very much about business matters just at present,' said Harry sombrely.

'Why?' I asked. 'Has he been taken ill?'

He looked around at us. 'Of course you won't have heard. I keep forgetting how cut off you've been. We only had final confirmation just before I left London. It's about the Bull.'

'What about Captain Rutland?'

'He is dead.'

The shock momentarily silenced us. Then Alyne stood up. She looked very frail in her black dress. 'How did he die?' she said. 'How? I must know.'

'He was drowned.'

'Drowned?' repeated Oliver. 'In God's name, how did that happen?'

'I don't know what was biting him,' said Harry a little diffidently, 'but I do know he left London in a great hurry. He was on his way down here and he always drove as if the devil were after him. He must have hit these damnable floods. The carriage overturned and was smashed to pieces. He hadn't a ghost of a chance.'

'Poor devil!'

Alyne was standing quite rigid, her hands clasped in front of her. 'Oh God,' she whispered, 'I didn't know. I thought . . . I thought he didn't care . . .'

I went to her quickly and put a hand on her arm. 'Are you all right?'

'Yes, quite all right.' She let herself drop on the sofa again. 'Go on, Harry, please.'

He was looking at her curiously. 'I didn't mean to distress you. I forgot how well you must have known him. I mean he stayed quite a while at Ravensley that time he broke his leg, didn't he? It was such a ghastly thing to happen and to the Bull of all people!'

'Did Captain Rutland say why he was coming down here?' asked Cherry, ignoring my warning glance.

'No, he didn't. He had been talking in the mess about giving up his commission and going to live abroad but he never let on why and was damned shirty when we ribbed him about it,' said Harry blundering on. 'We all thought there was someone he was sweet on —you know what I mean—and she'd given him the old "Come hither" . . . not good form of course but the Bull never cared much about that where a woman was concerned . . .'

'Isn't it bad enough that he is dead? Must you go on and on about him?' exclaimed Alyne suddenly so that Harry looked startled and abashed. Then she got to her feet. 'I'm sorry . . . please forgive me. I think after all that I am a little tired . . . will you excuse me?'

She went quickly from the room but not before we had all seen the silent tears running down her face. Harry closed the door after her.

'Oh Lord, there I go again, talking out of school. I should have had more sense especially so soon after Lord Aylsham's death.'

'It's not just that,' I said. 'She had a pretty bad experience herself. She was caught in the flood and she could have been drowned if Oliver had not reached her in time. She is not fully recovered from it yet.'

'Oh heaven, that makes it worse. What an idiot I am! Why didn't you stop me?'

'You weren't to know,' said Oliver and abruptly changed the subject. 'I think we've talked quite enough about our troubles. Tell us, Harry, have you given any further thought to your own future?'

'On and off,' he said with a glance at Cherry. 'As a matter of fact I'd be glad of your advice while I am here.'

All that evening we talked resolutely of other things. I had an idea that Harry suspected the truth but I did not confide in him. It was not that I did not trust my young brother, but he could be indiscreet and Oliver would not have cared for the Aylsham name to be bandied about among his comrades in the mess. But all the same it had brought the problem of Alyne into the forefront of our minds, sharply emphasized by something that happened a few days after Harry went back to London.

It was a bright morning and we were so grateful for the sun after so much grey sky and rain that we went walking in the garden. If Alyne wept for her lover, she did not reveal her grief to us. She kept to her room for a day after Harry broke the news, but now she was down again, pale but quite composed.

The air was keen but we were well wrapped up and there was a smell of spring at last. Daffodils were breaking through their green sheaths and under the hedge, primroses were coming into bloom. Oliver was waiting for his horse to be brought round and he pointed across the Fen to where the retreating water had left a thick muddy sludge.

'God knows when we shall be able to start the spring sowing. Will Burton is in a fearful fret about it.'

Then the head stableman came hurrying across the grass. 'Jack Moysey is here, my lord, asking to speak with you most particular.'

'That will be something to do with the steam pump. They have been trying to get it working again. Forgive me, my dear, I had better go.'

'He says the engineers are in a right old fix, my lord, what with the mud an' all clogging them machines. They would like you down there soon as possible,' the man went on as they walked away together.

I saw the frown on Alyne's face but she said nothing. I had been very aware that all this time everyone employed on the estate had instinctively turned to Oliver. It was almost as if his uncle's time here had been only an interlude and they had thankfully turned back to the man they trusted. It was the same at the house. The servants came to me or Oliver for instructions though once Alyne was up and about, I had been at pains always to defer to her. The fact that we had to remain at Ravensley since Thatchers was still uninhabitable made it worse. I had occasion to speak quite severely to Annie Pearce but she had only pursed her lips and shrugged her shoulders.

'I've never thought of Miss Alyne as my lady and never will,' she said obstinately.

For days I had been expecting an explosion and that night it came. Cherry had gone to spend the evening with Papa and Aunt Jess. Oliver had been working in the library and came into the drawing room rather late with a letter in his hand.

'I've heard from Gwilliam at last. Berkeley had the mail collected from Cambridge and sent it on to me. He writes that he hopes to be with us in a few days' time. It will be a relief to know where we stand.'

'Aren't you taking rather too much on yourself?' said Alyne quietly. 'You are not Lord Aylsham yet, you know.'

I was certain that Oliver had scarcely thought about it. The weight of responsibility had been too heavy and there had been too much to be done. Now he turned to look at her.

'I am sorry if it has seemed so. I hoped I was merely lifting the burden from your shoulders while you were sick.'

'I know that and I'm grateful, but I am quite well now and I am Justin's widow after all and this is my house.'

That touched me on the raw. I said quickly, 'Do you wish us to leave?'

'I am afraid that would scarcely be possible, would it,' she said sweetly, 'with Thatchers as it is. But I think Oliver might remember and impress on the servants that at present no one has any claim to Ravensley or to the title.'

'If the men have been speaking out of turn, I regret it. It seemed unimportant in the circumstances, but if it offends you, I will mention it to them.'

'Perhaps you have forgotten that if my child should be a son, then it is he who will be Lord Aylsham of Ravensley, and not you.'

Oliver had stooped to put another log on the dying fire and he straightened himself before he answered. I waited breathless because suddenly the issue had leaped into life between them and I felt there was nothing I could say.

'I think it is you who have forgotten something,' he said at last. 'According to your own statement the father of your child could be one of half a dozen.'

She flushed a little but her voice was quite steady. 'When I said that, I was distracted, almost out of my mind, you must have been aware of that.'

'Not entirely. I knew you meant to hurt Justin, and I believed you, so did he, so did Clarissa.'

I think his attitude had taken her by surprise. 'Whatever you believed then, you cannot prove it.'

'Perhaps not, but there is another consideration. Would Captain Rutland have wished his son to grow up a liar and a cheat parading a title and a name that did not belong to him?'

'Bulwer is dead,' she said, 'I want the best for my baby and I intend to have it.'

'I shall not permit it, Alyne. I tell you now quite frankly, I will not allow Rutland's child to take the place that belongs to my son.'

'How will you prevent it?' she answered with a maddening note of triumph. 'It's a dirty business raking into the past or will you carry out Clarissa's threat, will you spread the tale that my husband was also my mother's lover and drag the name of Aylsham through the mud to become the scandal of the century?'

Oliver's eyes flickered to me and then went back to Alyne. 'If my wife did say that, then she was fighting for Robert as I shall fight.'

'I wonder. You won't like it, Oliver. There will be a great deal of dirt-slinging because I'll not accept it easily and I shall win, you know, a helpless widow at the mercy of her husband's greedy nephew.' Then she shrugged her shoulders. 'Maybe it will never come to that. Maybe the baby will be a girl. You won't object to a Miss Aylsham of Ravensley, I suppose. It's a gambler's chance.

Your Papa would appreciate that, Clarissa. I should advise you to think it over very carefully, both of you.'

She left us then with her little secret smile and within a few minutes Oliver and I were bitterly at odds with one another which was absurd when for the first time he had outfaced her saying all the things I had hoped he would say. Perhaps it was because we were tired and on edge that our tempers frayed so easily.

It began quietly enough. I simply said, 'If it would help, Oliver, we could stay with Aunt Jess and Papa. I know it would be a little crowded with Patty and Jenny and the baby and I don't know what Cherry will want to do . . .'

'I shall do nothing of the kind,' he said abruptly. 'Ravensley is large enough, heaven knows, and I have as much right here as Alyne. Besides everyone knows where to find me and it is a great deal more convenient than living at Copthorne.'

'But if Alyne doesn't want us here?'

'Damn Alyne and her whims! In this instance she must put up with it.'

'Very well, if you say so, but it is I who have to be with her all the day through and from now on, it looks like becoming a great deal more difficult.'

'I don't see why. Surely the house more or less runs itself and there is something else.' He turned to look at me frowning. 'Why, in God's name, did you have to threaten her with that tale about Justin and the Leighs? I thought we had agreed not to mention it. Martha Leigh has had the decency to remain silent. Couldn't you do the same? Once the servants get to hear of it, you know what will happen as well as I do. There will be a crop of wild rumours spreading everywhere. Things are bad enough without a stain of that kind on the family name.'

'She made me angry,' I said defensively. 'She boasted of what she could do to us.'

'Do you think I would use such a vile story if I were ten times more certain of its truth?'

'I was only thinking of you.'

'By God, you should know me better than that! I'd rather live in penury the rest of my days than dirty my hands with digging up such a detestable scandal! Whatever Justin did and the Lord knows I hold no brief for him, he is dead now and so is the girl he dishonoured. It is in the past and in any case it is not Alyne's fault. No blame can possibly be attached to her.'

That was what stung me. 'It is always the same with you. It is Alyne you're thinking of, always Alyne. She mustn't be hurt; she must be shielded from everything, even her own folly. She chose her own bed, let her lie on it. She drove Justin nearly insane with jealousy; she took Bulwer Rutland as her lover, now she is carrying his child and it matters more to you than your own son. Papa was right. He said I was a fool to marry a man to whom I'd always be second best.'

'Damn your father! If it had not been for me, he would have died in a debtor's prison and if Joshua Rutland chooses to call in his loan, and heaven only knows what he will do now that his son is dead, I could very well end up there myself.'

'Do you imagine I'm not conscious of what I owe you every day of my life?'

'Oh to hell with it!' he exclaimed violently. 'I've never regretted it and never will. Let's put an end to this once and for all.'

But I couldn't stop myself. It had gone on too long. So we went on flinging angry hurting things at one another until I couldn't endure it any longer. I said, 'If you feel like that, then I shall take Robert and Patty and go to Copthorne myself. That will leave you free to settle matters with Alyne just as you please.'

I went quickly out of the room before he could stop me and ran upstairs to the nursery. It was quiet there. A shaded lamp was burning and Patty was dozing by the fire. She looked up as I came in.

'Is anything wrong?'

'No, it's all right,' I said. 'Don't disturb yourself. I just want to look at the baby.'

'He is sleeping, my lady.'

'I'm not my lady, Patty. I do wish you would remember.'

'I'm sorry, Ma'm. It just slips out natural like.'

I looked down at Robert. He lay there so contented, his arms flung above his head, tiny fists clenched. He had such a strong look of Oliver that I wanted to weep, but I had made up my mind. I tucked the blanket round him and bent to kiss him before I said, 'You can start packing early tomorrow, Patty. We are going to Copthorne.'

She looked startled. 'Will the master be coming with us?'

'No, he has too much to do here. I want to be gone by midday.'

'Shouldn't we wait until we have sent word to Miss Cavendish, Ma'am? Prue will be very put out.'

'For heaven's sake,' I exclaimed. 'Will you do as I say and stop arguing?'

'I'm sorry, Ma'am, I only thought . . .'

'It's all right, Patty,' interrupted Oliver. 'You needn't concern yourself. We're not going to Copthorne, any of us.'

He must have come in quietly behind me and I turned on him, feeling my temper rise. 'I don't care what you do but I intend leaving here tomorrow.'

'You're doing no such thing. Now come along, my dear, it's very late. Patty needs her bed and so do I.'

He had me firmly by the arm and I couldn't stand and argue with him in front of the nursemaid. Already she was staring at us curiously. I went with him but in our own room I broke away.

'I am leaving you, Oliver. You can't stop me.'

'Yes, I can.' He closed the door quietly behind him.

'How? Do you intend to lock me up?'

'Not at all. I shall first of all appeal to your good sense . . .'

'I am tired of being sensible and patient and long suffering,' I said passionately, 'it has got me nowhere,' and I walked away from him, turning my back so that he should not see the miserable tears that in spite of myself I could not control.

'Secondly,' he went on calmly, 'you are my wife and you'll stay because I need you and don't want you to be away from me even the short distance to Copthorne.'

'That's no reason at all,' I said in a muffled voice and he came up behind me putting his arms round my waist.

'I would have thought it's the best there is. I am sorry for all those things I said to you downstairs, but I find all this business just as painful and harassing as you do. Clarissa, when are you going to forget this foolish jealousy of Alyne?'

'I wish I could,' I whispered, 'but she is so beautiful and you were so very much in love . . .'

'That was a long time ago and I have changed and so has she. As for the rest,' he drew me round to face him, 'though you try so hard not to believe it, you are beautiful too.'

'Not like her . . .'

'God help me, I don't want another like her! I want you. I know I have been like a bear with a sore head since Justin died,' he grinned, 'a very sore head in fact . . . you must be patient with me, my love. I need to be soothed and cherished.'

'Oh Oliver . . .'

'That's better, that's more like my girl.' He began to unhook my dress and bent his head to kiss the hollow of my breast. 'You see I do love you very much . . .'

'Truly?'

'Truly. You and none other. Do you believe me this time?'

'I suppose I must.'

'Good.'

He pulled me closer to him. We had not loved since Robert was born, firstly because of my weakness and then because of the stress and strain of the floods so that our need was urgent and it was all the sweeter because it had been so long. I think I knew that night that he was mine, completely mine as he had never been before, and whatever was going to happen to us, we could face it together.

Mr Gwilliam arrived two days later. For some reason I had pictured him as a thin dry stick of a man, but he turned out to be plump and rosy, almost completely bald and with shrewd grey eyes behind his thick spectacles. He knew Oliver well of course and bowed low over Alyne's hand.

'Such an unforeseen tragedy,' he said. 'I was deeply grieved to hear of it. Whatever induced Lord Aylsham to take such a terrible risk?'

'We were all at risk,' said Oliver shortly.

'My husband nearly lost his own life in trying to save his uncle,' I put in quickly.

'So I gather. It must have been a shocking experience. I saw some of the damage during my journey. I greatly fear recovery will be slow.' He looked questioningly at Oliver. 'I wonder if I could have a few words with you, Mr Aylsham, before we get down to business.'

'I don't see why,' interrupted Alyne. 'Surely it is I whom Lord Aylsham's will concerns most closely.'

'And Mr Aylsham also,' remarked the lawyer dryly. 'He is after all the heir to the title.'

'Not unless . . .'

But Oliver intervened before Alyne could say more. 'Perhaps it would be best to proceed at once, Mr Gwilliam, that is if you are not too fatigued after your drive. Will you take a little refreshment first?'

'Thank you. A glass of sherry wine would be most welcome.'

There was something portentous about his manner that kept us on tenterhooks, but he took his time, sipping his sherry and assembling papers from his leather bag with paralysing slowness. Then he looked around at us over his spectacles.

'There are one or two bequests to servants. Strictly speaking they should be present.' He consulted his papers. 'In particular a Mistress Annie Pearce and Ram Lall, Lord Aylsham's Indian body servant. Then there is Jethro Aylsham, natural son to the deceased.'

'Jethro is at school and I thought it best not to bring him home.'

'So I understand, Mr Aylsham, and he is of course a minor.'

'Can't we get this over and done with?' said Alyne impatiently.

The servants were summoned headed by Annie and Ram Lall. They sat down together close by the door. It was amusing in a way to see how after Justin's death she had taken the unhappy Indian under her wing. Mr Gwilliam adjusted his spectacles and took up the parchment. There was nothing remarkable about the first part of the will. The title and estate would go to the next male kin who would be Oliver unless . . . here Mr Gwilliam's glance rested on Alyne for a moment and I wondered if he had guessed. Even now her pregnancy was not obvious to those who did not know her well. I waited for her to interrupt but she said nothing and he went on smoothly in his formal lawyer's voice. There was provision for Jethro's education, a small bequest to Annie Pearce, a larger one to Ram Lall and a jointure for his wife. It was less than I had expected and I saw the colour spring into Alyne's face.

'Lord Aylsham had sunk a great deal of his private fortune into the estate,' murmured Mr Gwilliam almost apologetically, 'and it is, I fear, much encumbered, but no doubt he felt sure that his nephew would see that his widow was housed and provided for.'

He paused and Oliver said, 'Is that all?'

'No, not entirely. Lord Aylsham visited me early this year and added a codicil.'

Alyne looked up and Oliver said, 'Just one moment, Mr Gwilliam. I don't think we need the servants any longer.' He dismissed them with a wave of his hand. 'Thank you. You may go now. Annie, will you see that a room is prepared for Mr Gwilliam? He will be staying with us tonight.'

'Thank you, my lord. It is very kind of you.'

When the door was closed, Alyne stood up. 'Before we go any further, Mr Gwilliam, I think you should know that I am with child.'

'Is that so?' The lawyer kept his eyes fixed on his papers. 'I was not aware of it and certainly Lord Aylsham said nothing of it.'

'He did not know, but it does make a difference, does it not?'

'It could in certain circumstances.' Mr Gwilliam took out a silk handkerchief and began to polish his glasses.

Alyne sat down again and Oliver said, 'I think perhaps you had better tell us the rest.'

Mr Gwilliam gave him an appealing look. 'Believe me, my lord, I did try to persuade him. It is most unusual, but he was quite determined.'

'For heaven's sake,' exclaimed Alyne exasperated. 'How much longer have we to wait? What is this codicil?'

The solicitor replaced his glasses and took up his parchment. In dry-as-dust legal words Justin declared to the world at large that he disowned any child born of the body of his wife, Alyne, Lady Aylsham, since for reasons that need not be stated, their marriage had remained unconsummated.

There was a viciousness about it that could only have sprung from a most bitter and painful jealousy and for a moment it kept us silent. Then Alyne got to her feet.

'How dare he make such a statement? How dare he? He has dishonoured me. He has put me to shame.'

'Believe me, my dear lady, I did not undertake this willingly.'

'He must have been out of his mind.'

'No, that is not so. I am afraid that he was not in the least deranged.'

'When did he do this?'

'Not so long before these unhappy floods. During the latter part of February.'

I looked at Alyne. It was more than a month after she had told me that she was pregnant so perhaps he had guessed and had made provision against it even though hoping against hope that he was mistaken. How contrary are our emotions. I thought I hated Alyne but at that moment, though it demolished every vestige of her claim against Oliver, I felt desperately sorry for her. She stood for a moment, quite still, then head up and with dignity she went out of the room.

'Most regrettable,' murmured Mr Gwilliam, 'and even worse than I had imagined. That is why I wanted a word with you beforehand, my lord. We might have found some way to soften it.'

'She would still have had to know. I should be obliged if you would keep this to yourself.'

'Most assuredly,' replied Mr Gwilliam in a shocked tone. 'Family feuds and disagreements are best kept secret.'

'I shall see that she is well cared for,' went on Oliver.

'Naturally. I am quite sure of it.'

Cherry had sat quite silent throughout the proceedings, but as soon as Mr Gwilliam had retired to his room to rest before we sat down to dine, she jumped to her feet.

'I'm so glad. Uncle Justin must have known her for what she is.'

Oliver was sharp with her. 'Don't hit her when she is down, Cherry. But for the grace of God, you might have been in like case yourself.'

'I would have been proud to bear Jake's child,' retorted his sister, 'I would never have cheated as she was intending to cheat you. Oh I know all about it though you and Clarissa thought you were keeping it from me. And I know quite well what would have happened. You would have given in to her, you old softie,' and she put her arms round Oliver's neck, hugging him, 'and now you can't. For once, without knowing it, Uncle Justin has proved your friend.'

'You'll say nothing about this, Cherry.'

'Of course not, silly, but it does make a difference, doesn't it?'

'Oh go on with you, Puss. You'll please to remember that I am your guardian now and in future you will do as I say.'

'Does that mean I can't start a school in the village if I want to?'

'My God, where did that idea spring from?'

'I've been thinking about it for quite a time. I even talked it over with Harry when he was here and he considers it a splendid notion.'

'Oh he does, does he? Well, I don't. I never heard such nonsense.'

'Only I had to wait until I was quite sure that you would be Lord Aylsham because then you wouldn't want Thatchers and could let me have it.'

'So that is what you've been hatching up between you. Did you know about this, Clarissa?'

'Not a word.'

'Well, will you?'

'Will I what?'

'Let me have Thatchers for a school?'

'I don't know . . .'

'Perhaps Harry could come and live here as well when he gives up being a soldier . . .'

'Now will you stop!' He laughed and slapped her on the bottom. 'I've a very long way to go before I can make any decisions like that.'

For a moment Cherry's irrepressible enthusiasm had lightened the oppression we felt, but it was not a very comfortable evening. Alyne didn't come down again and Oliver took Mr Gwilliam into the library to discuss business directly we had eaten. Cherry bubbled away happily with all kinds of plans as we sat over our needlework while I faced the unwelcome thought that, though in a sense we had achieved what I had always wanted for Oliver, the question of Alyne's future still remained unsolved.

It was astonishing how the rumours spread. Though none of us breathed a word about Justin and Alyne, the servants had somehow got wind of it and hints of a most unpleasant scandal crept back to us in garbled fashion. Even Sir Peter Berkeley touched on it delicately when he came one day to discuss the flood conditions.

'It's the very devil,' Oliver said to me afterwards. 'I hardly knew what to say to him. We've got to put a stop to it.'

'I don't see how. To reprimand the servants and forbid them to talk will only give it added importance.'

Then when we went to church on Sunday, it came startlingly into the open. It was only a bunch of village lads, young hooligans giggling and calling obscenities after Alyne when she walked down the path to the carriage. They took to their heels when Oliver turned on them angrily while a great many of the older folk looked ashamed and hurried away.

Alyne faced us tight-lipped when we returned home. 'They think to drive me out of Ravensley but they'll not succeed.'

'Don't make too much of it. They will forget it in a few weeks,' I said uncomfortably.

She looked directly at Oliver. 'The kick of the devil always comes when you least expect it. You said that to me once. I should have married you, shouldn't I, then I would not need to stand here like a beggar . . .'

'Don't talk like that, Alyne. You know it is not true.'

'Isn't it? Clarissa might not agree with you. Ravensley is her home now, not mine. We're back to the old days, aren't we? The mighty Aylshams and the brat from the Fens. May I have the carriage, my lord?' she went on ironically. 'I want to go to London.'

'You know you can have it any time you please, but do you think you should venture just now? The roads are still in pretty poor shape.'

'If I lose my bastard, it won't matter to anyone but me.'

'Alyne please!' I exclaimed.

'Don't worry, Clarissa. I don't intend to drown myself as my mother did.'

Oliver said evenly, 'If you care to wait a couple of days, I will escort you to London myself. I have to go there very soon.'

I did not then guess at her intention and it was not until the following day that I realized what a fool I was to be so concerned for her. Alyne had always known exactly what she wanted and gone all out for it.

Papa and Aunt Jess had come up to spend the afternoon with us and we were all in the drawing room. Oliver and my father were studying a plan of the estate. Aunt Jess was bent over Robert's cradle watching Cherry trying to attract his attention by rattling the silver bell on his coral.

'He's smiling at me,' she declared triumphantly.

'Nonsense, he's far too young,' I said laughing at her and picking up Prickle who watched jealously from the corner of the rug.
Annie knocked and came in.

'Mr Rutland is asking if he may speak with you, my lord.'

Oliver looked up in surprise. 'The very man I want to see. Show
him in, Annie.'

When Joshua Rutland came through the door, I could scarcely
believe my eyes. He looked ten years older, his sturdy figure
shrunken, his jaunty self-confidence all vanished. I went to greet
him.

'Mr Rutland, this is indeed a pleasure.'

'I would have come before.' His eyes ran over us and rested for
an instant on the baby. 'This has been a bad business in more
ways than one.'

'Indeed it has,' said Oliver warmly, coming to take his hand.
'And we have a great deal to discuss. I think you know Miss
Cavendish and Colonel Fenton. Won't you sit down, sir?'

But he did not move. 'It has been bad for all of us and the
money is the least part of it,' he said heavily. 'You know, I expect,
that I have lost my boy.'

'Yes,' I said gently, 'my brother told us. You have our deepest
sympathy.'

'Drowned in these damnable waters,' his voice broke pitifully. 'I
wish to God I'd never come here, never set foot in these cursed
Fens.'

It was difficult to find adequate words and in the silence Alyne
appeared in the doorway. I never knew whether she had been told
of his arrival or if it was pure chance, but she looked unbelievably
lovely. She was one of the few people whose beauty is enhanced by
mourning. Her skin was creamy white against the black velvet and
the widow's cap did not hide the pale shining hair. She took a step
towards him.

'I too have wept for him, Mr Rutland,' she said huskily. 'When
Harry Fenton told us what had happened, I did not know how I
could go on living.'

He was staring at her. 'You dare to say that to me, you his murderess, standing there, bold as brass, and my boy driving himself
through hell and high water to reach you . . .' His voice was ris-

ing. I moved towards him and put a hand on his arm, but he shook me off and went on. 'What did you do to him? How did you bewitch him so that he threw up everything that mattered, his father, his career, his very life . . . ?'

Alyne said in a whisper, 'How did you know?'

'I'm not a fool, Miss, I knew something was going on, but not this. In Christ's name, what was it that brought him down here like a madman? He always drove too fast. I told him over and over that he should take more care.' The old man was trembling. 'I'd have known nothing if Croft hadn't told me where he had gone . . . and all for you . . . all my plans for him thrown overboard for an adulterous bitch . . .' He had seized her by the shoulders and was shaking her in a frenzy so that she cried out.

'It is not true. I loved him.'

'Love . . . what can you know of love?'

Then Oliver had gone to him. 'Let her be, Mr Rutland.'

He let his arms fall, all the anger gone out of him. 'I'm sorry,' he mumbled, 'sometimes these days I hardly know what I'm doing.' Oliver guided him to a chair and he dropped into it muttering. 'One thing I'm sure of, I'll never come here again, never set foot in this damned place . . .'

Papa had poured some brandy into a glass and brought it to him but the old man pushed it away, staring broodingly in front of him.

Alyne had recovered herself. She pushed back her disordered hair. 'Mr Rutland, did Bulwer tell you why we were intending to go away together?'

He shook his head. 'He weren't one to say much of himself.'

She walked unsteadily across the room and fell on her knees beside him. 'Didn't you know that you were to have a grandchild?'

He watched her face and then looked away. 'How can I believe it?'

She put a hand on his. 'Look at me, Mr Rutland. Would any woman confess to such a thing if it were not true?'

He touched her hair with one stubby finger. 'Maybe not . . . if only I could be sure . . .'

'You can be, I swear it. Clarissa knew and Justin too before he died.'

'Eh lass, you told him to his face, but that were a brave thing to do.' He was wavering already and she pressed home her advantage, defying Oliver, defying all of us to contradict her. 'If the child I carry is a son, he could have been Lord Aylsham, but I'd not cheat, I'd not want Bulwer's child, your grandchild, to bear a false name.' The tears were rolling unheeded down her cheeks and Mr Rutland leaned forward, cupping her face between his two hands. She had given him hope and he clung to it pitifully.

'Did you love him so much?'

'With all my heart.'

He stared at her for a long moment before he stirred and pulled himself to his feet. 'I had intended to have a word with Lord Aylsham and then go on to Westley. What should I be doing with a great house like that? It was for the boy I wanted it.'

Alyne had risen with him. 'Let me go with you. Martha Leigh was here helping us through these terrible days. I would be glad to see her again.'

'Are you sure you should go so far?' he said tenderly.

'Of course. I am quite well and it would make me so happy.'

He looked round at us. 'I will take good care of her.'

'Naturally,' said Oliver, 'and when you return, my wife and I would be pleased if you would stay with us.'

'Thank you. I am most grateful.'

When Alyne's bonnet and cloak had been fetched and she had gone off with Mr Rutland in his carriage, Aunt Jess looked round at us.

'Well, I don't know,' she said severely to Oliver. 'I guessed there was something afoot but nothing like this. You and Clarissa have known all along, I presume.'

'It was after all a family matter,' said Oliver placatingly.

'By Jove,' exclaimed Papa suddenly. 'That was the prettiest piece of play-acting I've seen outside the theatre. There is a young woman who knows just what she is about! She chose exactly the right moment to tell that heartbroken old man that his beloved son had left a child behind him.'

'It must have cost her a great deal,' murmured Oliver.

'My dear fellow, you must be jesting! Joshua Rutland is a great deal richer than you are. He could buy up Ravensley and hardly notice it. If he adopts her child as his heir . . . and it is quite obvious to me that he will be eating out of her hand in no time at all . . . she will be living in clover for the rest of her life.'

'Papa, how can you be so cynical?' I said warmly. 'Alyne loved Captain Rutland.'

Cherry said fiercely, 'She never loved anyone but herself and I think it is disgusting. She will persuade him to buy Westley from Martha Leigh and she'll go on living there.'

'What if she does?' said Oliver. 'We still have Ravensley.' He walked across to the windows. 'It's going to be a hell of a struggle but I daresay we shall survive.'

'Of course you will,' said Papa heartily. 'I've been thinking, Oliver. With your views you should take your seat in the Lords. The country needs young blood there, by God it does.'

'Perhaps.' He smiled wryly. 'I could wish that Jake were still with us, that's all.'

He was quiet after that, not saying very much and now and again I stole a glance at him, a little uneasy, a little disturbed.

It was not quite dusk when Papa and Aunt Jess drove off in the dog cart and Oliver turned to me on the step.

'Fetch a wrap, Clarissa, I want to show you something.'

When I came back, he was waiting for me carrying a lantern. 'Where are we going?'

'You'll see.'

We walked across the courtyard and round to the back of the stables. I could see that one of the stalls had been cleaned out and freshly painted.

'What is all this?' I asked.

He pushed open the half door and held up the lantern. The foal was quite splendid, coal black with one white blaze.

'Do you like him? He has a pedigree as long as my arm.'

I was breathless. 'Oh Oliver, is he really mine?'

'All yours. We'll race him under your colours and I've asked your Papa to supervise his training.'

'Oh darling,' I exclaimed suddenly stricken. 'Can we afford it?'

'Probably not. I've been puzzling all the afternoon where I can lay hands on some ready cash.'

'So that was it and I thought . . .'

'What did you think?'

'It doesn't matter.'

'You thought it was because of Alyne.'

'I didn't know, I wasn't sure . . .' The foal butted me skittishly with his nose.

'Careful now.' Oliver drew me back a little. 'I guessed as much. Somehow I had to prove you wrong. I've been thinking of it ever since Robert was born and I asked Berkeley to look around for me. When this came up a few days ago, I knew it was just the right thing.'

'You didn't have to prove anything.'

'I think I did.'

'Oh love . . .' It was foolishly extravagant and yet it seemed to me such a wonderful thing. It was nearly a year since I'd mentioned that impossible dream but he had remembered.

'Pleased?'

'Oh yes . . .'

'Good.'

He closed the stable door and we stood for a moment with the wind from the Fens stirring our hair and all around us that indescribable smell of water and grass and the coming spring. Then, arm in arm, we went back to Ravensley.